FORGED FOR PROPHECY

By Andrew Knighton

FORGED FOR DESTINY

Forged for Destiny
Forged for Prophecy

FORGED FOR PROPHECY

FORGED FOR DESTINY:
BOOK 2

ANDREW KNIGHTON

orbitbooks.net

orbitworks.net

Copyright © 2025 by Andrew Knighton

Cover design by Alexia E. Pereira
Cover images by Shutterstock
Cover copyright © 2025 by Hachette Book Group, Inc.
Author photograph by Richard Wilson

Orbit
Hachette Book Group
1290 Avenue of the Americas
New York, NY 10104
orbitbooks.net
orbitworks.net

First Edition: August 2025

Orbit is an imprint of Hachette Book Group.
The Orbit name and logo are registered trademarks of Little, Brown Book Group Limited.

Library of Congress Cataloging-in-Publication Data
Names: Knighton, Andrew, author.
Title: Forged for prophecy / Andrew Knighton.
Description: First edition. | New York, NY : Orbit, 2025. | Series: Forged for destiny ; book 2
Identifiers: LCCN 2025009011 | ISBN 9780316588294 (trade paperback) | ISBN 9780316581769 (ebook)
Subjects: LCGFT: Fantasy fiction. | Novels.
Classification: LCC PR6111.N63 F68 2025 | DDC 823/.92—dc23/eng/20250227
LC record available at https://lccn.loc.gov/2025009011

ISBNs: 9780316581769 (ebook), 9780316588294 (print on demand)

To the old Treasure Trap crew, my companions
in ludicrous, mud-stained quests on
Saturday afternoons.

Chapter One
Casualties

Raul ran out of the tree line, sword and shield swinging, his band of rebels following him into the battering rain. A storm was sweeping from the mountains into the foothills, with the sort of wind that sent even goats running for shelter, that blew down fences and chimney stacks, ruined wild nests and farmyard roosts. The storm was at Raul's back, pushing him faster down the slippery meadow. Its power filled him, sped him on, filled his lungs with laughter that was snatched away on the howling gale.

To his right, a man lost his footing, slipped, slid down the slope, cursing as his sword flew from his hand and his wooden shield slapped against the ground. A passing warrior shouted to the fallen man, but he waved her on, his expression more embarrassed than pained.

The rain hammered like the hard words of an angry lord, but it only made Raul more determined. This weather reminded him of winters in the Winding Vales, of the shutters banging on the old inn while familiar faces huddled by the fire, fields abandoned in favour of warmth and company. That was what he fought for. That made all the loss and pain worthwhile.

To his left, a wolf bounded across the open ground, straight toward the head of a seven-wagon convoy stretched out along a dirt road. A streak of grey fur and bared teeth, larger than any of the other wolves that lived in these woods, the archetypal nightmare of a wild beast. Something to cause alarm and confusion, to distract the convoy's guards, to give Raul and the rest a few more moments before they were seen. Yasmi was truly giving one of her finest performances.

A horn blew from the lead wagon. From under the other canvas, drivers and guards poked their heads out, all looking toward that sound, toward the wolf, toward the front of the column, away from Raul. The whinnying of the horses and creaking of wheels was barely audible through the storm, but he could see the drivers hauling at the reins, wagons slowing, hooves and wheels slipping in the mud.

Almost there. Raul pushed himself to an extra burst of speed, waving his sword high, urging his companions on.

An archer stood on the board of the front wagon. Raul knew that he didn't need to worry—it was nearly impossible to make a good shot in this rain, and Yasmi had planned her path to offer the worst possible target. Still, his chest tightened.

Then the flaps at the back of one of the wagons parted and a Dunholmi officer appeared, her blue tabard bearing the king's white crown heraldry, a silver dagger hanging at her hip. She looked straight at Raul and snatched up a horn.

He hurled himself forward. Her cheeks bulged and a note blasted from the horn, a rich and piercing sound, more confident and compelling than the one blown before.

Too late to stop that, but too late for it to matter. Even as a pair of infantry came tumbling out of the rear wagon, Raul reached them. He let his momentum carry him straight into the nearest one, catching the man between his shield and the corner of the wagon. There was a crunch and a groan, then a crack as Raul's pommel hit the side of the warrior's head. As Raul moved on, the blue-clad body slumped into the current of muddy water running down the road.

"For Estis!" Raul bellowed, waving his sword high. Yasmi had been teaching him to project, and his voice carried through the wind and the clang of blades.

"A new moon rises!" some of the rebels yelled in response, but others were too caught up in the fighting, a ragtag band facing the Dunholmi fighting line.

The Dunholmi troops had abandoned the last three wagons and formed up near the middle of the convoy, spears raised like a thorn hedge. The officer was in the middle, sabre in one hand and shield in the other. Raul's rebels stepped over the bodies of the isolated rear guards, blood running a red streak through the muddy stream of the road, and advanced toward that line. Caught up in the rush of battle, it took Raul a moment to realise that they were waiting for his command.

"Closer together!" he shouted. "I mean, form a shield wall!"

A rebel went down, run through as she advanced. The others drew together, trying to line up their shields, simple wooden boards with Raul's dagger-pierced moon painted in a startling red. They hesitated as some of the Dunholmi spears rattled against their shields while others lunged high or low, aiming for legs and faces.

Raul stepped up to the line and placed his hand on the shoulder of Helvus, a devoted fighter who a month before had been a farmer and a weaver. The Dunholmi were professional soldiers, warriors paid to guard and to fight, to hold other people down hard and keep a grip on their land; women and men trained for war, who had been taught to form ranks and to stand their ground. Raul's rebels weren't soldiers—they had the bare minimum of training and the most basic sorts of weapons, desperation and determination the only things that had pushed them this far. Now that the momentum had faltered, they risked becoming lost.

That was why they needed a leader, a saviour, a chosen one. It was why they needed signs and prophecies. It was why they needed Raul.

He just wished he knew how to lead.

"We can do this." Raul stepped in next to Helvus, who straightened, holding his shield higher. Other rebels looked at him uncertainly, waiting to see what came next.

Down the road there was howling, horses whinnying in fear, the twang of a bowstring through a brief lull in the wind. The Dunholmi soldiers advanced slightly, thrusting their spears at all angles. Raul channelled the tension from his chest into a sharp swing of his blade, a manoeuvre his father had taught him, to sweep a spear aside. Another spear slammed into his shield as he stepped forward, left a long pale scar as it slid across the wood. Then he was in among the Dunholmi, knocking one down, swinging his sword not to kill but to force an opponent back, opening a gap, making a moment of chaos that the rebels could use.

With a cry, they attacked. The two lines tumbled into each other, their neat imitation of a battlefield descending into something closer to a taproom brawl. Raul pushed his way to the centre of the crowd, batting away spears like they were nothing, focusing on getting to the officer. She was a pale woman with pale hair, muscular beneath her tabard and chainmail, her expression grim. When she saw him coming she raised her sabre, unfazed by his furious stare.

"You're him, aren't you?" she said, and Raul's chest swelled with satisfaction. "The one they've been talking about."

"My name is Raul Warborn," he said. "Son of Princess Aemiria, heir to the throne of Estis."

The lies barely caught in his throat anymore. The cause mattered more than the truth. He would make up for his deception once his homeland was free.

"Warborn?" The officer's laughter was sharp as the blade that twitched toward Raul, probing for a way past his sword and shield. "You've got to be kidding."

Raul blocked her sabre with his shield, then lunged toward her chest, forcing her back. She slid across the wet ground but kept both her balance and her poise. With her off hand, she drew a silver dagger, and raindrops shattered as they hit its charmed edge.

Raul advanced carefully, trying not to let the dagger distract him. He needed to be careful, that thing could cut through his pine shield like a butcher's blade through fat. But if he paid it too much attention, he might give her an opening with her sabre or a chance to find a better position and then—

A spear lunged from his right, tearing through the canvas cover of a wagon. Raul lurched away from its steel tip, lost his footing, sank to one knee just out of the spear's reach. Instinctively, he brought his shield up, catching the officer's sabre as she charged, the momentum of her attack jarring his arm all the way up to the shoulder. She pivoted, her dagger a shining sliver of light against the grey day, arcing toward his neck. But Raul's blade was moving too, and it was longer; he didn't have as far to reach. The officer's eyes went wide as her body's momentum met the thrust of his blade. There was a popping, grating sound as Drusil's simple, well-forged steel pierced chainmail, interlinked rings torn open and apart, followed by the wet sound of flesh. The officer gasped, the dagger fell from her hand, and the weight of her body slumped across Raul.

"Fuuuuck," she groaned as blood streamed down his arm, a hot damp to counter the cold of the rain. Then she tipped sideways and fell into the mud with a splat, taking Raul's sword with her. There was no dignity in death, but there could be revenge.

The spearman behind him, apparently one of the wagon drivers, leapt through the hole he'd torn in his canvas, lunging at Raul. Raul dodged the first blow, deflected the next one with his shield, and grabbed at the handle of his sword. But the blade was jammed between the officer's ribs and the remains of her armour, the rain-slicked leather grip slipping through his fingers.

With a wordless cry, the driver drew his spear back, ready

to run Raul through. A snarling shape bounded around the wagon and into him, bowling him over. Man and wolf rolled away from Raul, brown and red staining grey fur as Yasmi tore at the driver with her claws. The fresh, clear smell of the rain was fouled by the salt tang of blood and the stink of emptying bowels. Funny how Valens had never mentioned that detail in the stories he told Raul growing up. But then, the ugly truth wouldn't have served his cause.

Raul grabbed the dead officer's sabre. Half the soldiers were down and the rest were backing away along the road, abandoning their wagons.

"Helvus!" Raul shouted. "Get up into the middle wagon! Find that pay chest."

"Yes, Raul," the farmer shouted back, stowing his axe with a look of relief.

Raul took two careful steps toward Yasmi, who turned to face him with her long face tilted on one side. It was so much like facing a real dog that he reached out a hand as if to pat her, but she pulled her head back with a derisive snort. Raul would have blushed if his cheeks hadn't been so cold.

"Remember the plan," he said. "We need a different version of you now. I know you don't like changing in front of people, but..."

One of Yasmi's forepaws rose, brushing against the fur behind her ear. The paw kept moving forward, her face came with it, and her whole body twisted as she shifted into human form. In place of the wolf, a young woman crouched with a mask in her hand, strawberry-blond hair bound loosely back, the grey garb of a theatrical shifter plastered to her body with mud and rain.

"You take me to all the nicest places," she said with a smile that might have become playful if the blood on her hands hadn't grabbed her attention. She hooked the wolf's face onto her belt along with her other masks, then brushed her fingers across the cloth at her hips with a look of disgust.

"We still need the ogre," Raul said.

"Oh, do we?" She arched an eyebrow.

"Please?"

"Since you asked so nicely." She picked out a warty green mask. "But don't start thinking that you can give me orders just because everyone else expects it."

"Is this the time to worry about manners?" Raul prodded one of the bodies with his toe, then immediately felt guilty. Bad enough that people were dying without him treating their remains like debris.

"'There is no soul so wretched that vexed etiquette cannot make them worse,'" Yasmi recited. "Harnacht, act three of *The Prince's Lament*. Though I'm not sure my own manners will survive what's coming next."

She pressed the ogre mask to her face and started to transform. Lithe limbs bulged and stretched. Her skin turned green, littered with warts and patches hard as scabs. Her hair became a dark, greasy mop framing a square face with teeth the shape and colour of granite tombstones. Within moments, Yasmi towered over Raul.

"Where?" she slurred in a voice like sludge.

Raul pointed to the middle wagon, where Helvus had slashed through a stretch of canvas and was rolling its remnants back from the wooden frame. Yasmi the ogre stomped over, her gnarled feet throwing up gouts of mud, and ripped away the wood. Her movements were slow and clumsy but had a power that reduced wrist-thick beams to splinters as easily as Raul would pick up a pen.

"I think it's this one," Helvus said, tapping a chest with his knife. The chest was oak planks bound in iron, with a padlock the size of a fist. Thick chains were wrapped around it in every direction and to the wagon's base. If it had belonged to someone from Estis, a charm would have been carved into the wood around the lock, a mountain for endurance perhaps, or a maze on the lock to emphasise its complexity. But while plenty of ordinary Dunholmi used charms, and Raul had found them on some of the soldiers he'd fought, those in charge took a dim view of magic.

As thunder rumbled through the storm, Yasmi grabbed one of the chains in both warty hands and heaved. The links strained against each other, but they held. She clambered onto the wagon and took a firmer hold, one foot braced against the chest.

The rumbling grew louder. Raul jerked his head around to face the noise, and his hand tightened around the sabre as he saw what was coming.

"Cavalry!"

A dozen Dunholmi warriors wearing the white tree on bold blue of Count Alder were riding toward them. Their horses, leaner than a working farm horse but bulging with power, charged over a ridge and along the road, mud spraying from their hooves. The riders leaned forward, long spears couched under their arms, points extended. They galloped without reservation straight toward the convoy, spreading out as they went to become a deadly line of speed and shining steel.

Raul's heart beat wildly—this wasn't what was meant to happen. There hadn't been anything in the omens he'd read this morning. Had he cast them wrong? Had he missed it? Were the signs too weak?

For just a moment, Raul wanted to stand his ground. That was what the heroes did in stories, stood and fought against the odds, and that was how they won. But this wasn't a story; there were real lives at stake, brave people who had followed him on the promise that he knew what he was doing.

"We've got to go!" he shouted.

Most of them didn't hesitate. Whether out of fear or loyalty, they ran from the wagons, up the slope toward the trees, toward cover that could break up a charge and stop the cavalry crushing them beneath their weight and momentum. But some of them stood their ground, axes raised, shield toward the onrushing enemy. A woman named Katia looked at Raul with disappointment.

"What happened to standing up against the Dunholmi?" she asked. "What happened to needing this gold?"

"None of that does any good if we die here," Raul said, remembering the fight of another day, bodies sprawled across the flagstones of the palace in Pavuno, faces of friends stilled forever. "We can't win now, but if we live, then maybe we can win next time."

Katia glared at him, but her axe started to sag. Others looked doubtfully at the onrushing attack.

"I thought you were meant to be a hero," she muttered.

Raul raised his voice. "Back to the woods! Everyone, *now!*"

There was a crack. Yasmi tossed away a broken chain, but the chest, a month's pay for the occupying troops, was still chained to the wagon. With a roar of frustration, she grabbed it with both hands and heaved, but it wouldn't come loose.

"Leave it!" Raul shouted. "Come on!"

Yasmi roared again and bared her teeth.

"I said leave it! This isn't worth dying for."

Despite those words, Yasmi still didn't run. He couldn't leave her, not until he was sure that she had listened and was coming with him, that her own natural obstinacy hadn't mixed too badly with the stubborn solidity of the ogre.

The cavalry was almost to the convoy already. Half of them split off, trying to intercept Katia and other rebels on the way to the woods, while the rest galloped along the road, straight toward Raul.

With one last disgruntled rumbled, Yasmi's ogre leapt down from the wagon, which shook at the sudden movement. One warty hand ran up behind her ear, the ogre's face fell away, and the real Yasmi returned, her other hand already reaching for the wolf mask. Helvus jumped down beside her, eyes wide as he stared at the oncoming riders.

"Come on!" Raul shoved Helvus with his shield and started to run.

The slippery slope was harder going up than down, but they had a cobbler in the camp now, and the studs he'd put on Raul's boots kept him from going face down in the grass. Helvus ran alongside him, arms swinging, legs rushing in frantic movement, already gasping for breath. After a moment, Yasmi streaked past, grey-furred limbs stretching as she bounded up the slope.

Some of the riders on the road headed for the wagons but three followed the fleeing rebels. Raul and his small group were caught between the riders ahead, who had missed the other rebels heading into the woods, and those behind. The riders at the tree line turned, spear tips gleaming, and a horse whinnied as it pawed the turf.

Yasmi howled. Horses bucked and twisted away as they saw her fearsome form. Some of the riders, more experienced or luckier in their steeds, held them in place, but others were carried in a panicked rush across the meadow.

Raul's fear was rising as he heard hooves coming from behind, but he wouldn't let that fear show. Not in front of Helvus and certainly not in front of the enemy. He raised his sword and shield, readying himself for one last desperate fight.

Two riders ahead of them still. Yasmi leapt at them. One rider tried to stab her with his spear, but his horse reared in fear at the wolf, flinging him from the saddle; he landed head-first, neck at an angle no one could survive. As that horse raced away, Yasmi flung herself at the other, claws raking its side. The rider stabbed, Yasmi swerved, the horse whinnied and slipped across the slope, one leg giving way. Yasmi leapt again, roaring for effect, and the horse's panicked lurch sent it rolling onto its back, across its rider, with a sickening crunch.

Raul's heart was hammering and there was an ache in his side. His foot slipped and he twisted as his other foot came down, trying to keep upright, to keep moving. The hooves behind them kept thundering. The trees were close, but the enemy were closer.

He turned, raising his shield. A spear was hurtling toward him, too much power to be stopped, but that wasn't the only option. He turned the shield to an angle and the spear glanced off it. A swing of his sword made the approaching horse swerve around him.

Then came a sound like a hog being butchered, the wet thud and a squeal of pain. The rider who turned might have missed Raul, but he left his spear behind, right through Helvus's chest. Blood spurted along the shaft and dribbled from Helvus's pale lips as he toppled over.

Raul felt the weight of his armour tightening around his chest, armour that Helvus hadn't had, that wouldn't have protected him even if he'd worn it. He felt the raindrops on his face, heard the silence where Helvus's scream had been, and knew that one of them would never feel the rain again.

"Raul, come on!" Yasmi stood beneath the trees, wolf mask in hand, waving him on. More riders were coming, more cautious than these first two but no less deadly. He forced himself to look away from Helvus, to turn and run again up those last few strides, ducking to keep the branches out of his face. He got a dozen strides in, then turned and looked back.

The riders stopped at the edge of the trees. They were better armed than the rebels, better armoured, probably better trained. But they were used to fighting from horseback and there was no riding into woods like these. Some of them argued among themselves. One without a spear stared at Raul, who stared right back at her—her dark eyes bored into him with a stunning hatred. And beyond, Helvus's life flowed back into the land from which he'd been born.

"Come on." Yasmi spoke softly as she tugged at Raul's arm. "The others are waiting for their leader. Unless you want them to wait until more Dunholmi arrive, you need to make your exit."

"If I'd thought this through better, he'd still be alive," Raul said. "If I'd paid attention to the sounds sooner. If I'd thought to warn him when—"

"If you keep doing that, you're going to drive yourself insane." She laid a hand on his shoulder. There was blood on her fingers, but at least it wasn't their people's blood. "You can't control everything. Helvus knew the risks."

"I thought *I* knew the risks! I looked for the signs! I thought we'd only have to deal with the wagon guards. But I must have cast the entrails wrong, and now it's all on me."

"That's the problem, Raul. You're taking this all on yourself, and you're expecting too much. You're going to make mistakes, what matters is that you keep making the world better."

"Try telling that to Helvus."

The worst of it was that there *was* a way he could have done better. With the right tutor, an experienced diviner to teach him and help him, he wouldn't have missed this. But that meant working with Prisca and he…he just couldn't. Had he got a man killed by being as stubborn as she was? That thought left him feeling even more sick.

The Dunholmi had finished their discussion. One of them turned to gallop away, flinging up clods of dirt from the waterlogged ground. The others started dismounting.

"I know you don't feel much like a hero right now," Yasmi said. "But that's exactly who the others need to see. So unless you're planning to give up on this whole mad endeavour…" She paused for a heartbeat, and in that moment her words felt almost like a request, a plea for a different life. Then her expression hardened. "Then you need to get back into character and give them the show they're after. Remember, today you're not Raul of High Cross. You're Raul Warborn, saviour of Estis, King Balbianus reborn, and that man does not have doubts."

Raul nodded, took a deep breath, rolled his shoulders back into the confident posture she'd taught him.

"One last touch of drama." Yasmi flicked her fingers, leaving a spatter of blood across his cheek. "Now go lead us home."

With a stride that left no room for halt or hesitation, Raul headed deeper into the woods. As he approached, some of the rebels watched him warily, while others cheered half-heartedly. They'd lost friends today and they hadn't got what they'd come for. He was going to have to do a lot better if he wanted to stop this rebellion from falling apart.

Chapter Two
A Pit in Your Guts

Yasmi stalked back and forth across the sunlit clearing, fingers tapping against the masks on her belt. Acting came so naturally to her, she found it difficult to put the technique into words or explain how it worked to someone else. Usually, Tenebrial provided the words for her performances, every last syllable clear and evocative. She could declaim any of a thousand speeches from a hundred plays by heart, but explaining how she gave them was another matter.

"Imagine there's a pit," she said, "deep down in your guts. You're going to draw air down until that pit bulges like a brewer's belly, and then you're going to fill every last word with that breath. Understand?"

Raul shifted from one foot to the other, dead oak leaves crunching under his muddy boots. How could someone so tall, his tunic straining at the muscles inside, manage to seem so small?

"I think so," he said.

"Then try it."

She settled on a fallen tree trunk, one leg crossed over the other, brass bangles chiming as she laid her hands in her lap and watched him expectantly.

"It's not easy with you watching," he said, running a hand through his hair. He managed to look good while looking like he'd come straight from hay baling. The boy was infuriating.

"People are watching you all the time. That's what this is all about—helping you create a better impression."

Gods knew he needed it. While she might find him delightful, other people were less easily impressed by an unknown young man claiming the right to run the kingdom. He'd done well enough when Prisca's plans gave him a structure to work within, but now they were cut loose, relying on Raul's skills as a leader and orator, and stumbling rural charm wasn't enough to motivate a full-blown rebellion.

"It's just…" He looked at the trampled grass around his feet, one hand pressed against the back of his neck. "Performing for you is different."

Gods preserve her, was he blushing? And was that a treacherous heat creeping up her own cheeks?

Since when had she started acting like a little girl? If she wanted, she could go over to him, make an excuse of tidying that hair, let her hand linger on his cheek on the way down, lean in a little closer. They'd come close before, why not now? Didn't they deserve some entertainment better than weak beer and peasant songs around a campfire?

But before he'd just been Raul, the innkeeper's son, a country lad whose biggest responsibility was shovelling shit out of the stables. Now he was *Raul*, warrior, prophet, the last great hope of a kingdom. More importantly, he was the leading man in the most difficult and most important production she'd ever been a part of. Her mother had told her, before Yasmi was old enough for the lesson, that she should never screw anyone she would share a stage with because it could ruin their chemistry. And right now, the whole kingdom was their stage.

Still, that hair…

She jumped to her feet and clapped her hands together, frightening off a nearby pair of crows.

"Imagine that your audience are squirrels," she said, waving her arm. "Those ones in the pine over there. Without moving from where you are, you need to give that speech loud enough to move them."

"The squirrels?" He smiled. She did her best to ignore it. Her fingers found the wolf mask on her belt, and that gave her strength. The wolf would never be flustered, never pause, never back down. She would be as clear and certain as the wolf.

"That's right, the squirrels. I've performed for nobility." She tapped her chest. "But you…" She prodded him, then took a step back, arms folded. "You need an audience to match your talents. So, squirrels."

"All right."

He turned his attention away from her and planted his feet in a steady stance. His chest swelled, his mouth opened wide, and he spoke.

"'A dagger in the moonlight,'" he proclaimed. One of

the squirrels looked around, but the other was busy with an acorn. "'Not how a king should slide from this world.'" He seemed to swell and his voice grew louder, calling out Balbianus's final speech from *The True and Tragic History*. Now both squirrels were looking, tails twitching in agitation. "'But if my people's fate hangs on one last slip of my wrist, then let me buy their lives with mine.'"

He punctuated the last words with a fist slammed against his chest. The squirrels leapt off their branch and away, disappearing up the tree.

"I did it!" He turned to her, beaming wide, not the proud monarch anymore but not the hunched and nervous youth either. "See, I can be an actor!"

He swept her up in his arms and swung her around, the two of them laughing. Maybe she wasn't such a bad teacher, though he'd need a few more lessons to give that speech real punch.

"Not an actor," she said as he set her down. "An orator, and a prince."

"Hm." His expression grew serious, but at least he held her gaze. "You're right. I need to be more careful what I say."

She took a step away from him, her back straightening. This was why things were how they were; too much at stake for either of them to let down their defences, or to take time for themselves. And much as she missed the carefree parts of her old life, she'd chosen this. She was doing something that mattered, something real, and she was going to do it well.

"What you did just now, try it next time you're addressing the troops."

"Yes, Yasmi."

"And practice it when you get a chance."

"Yes, Yasmi."

"And don't you keep placating me with 'yes, Yasmi,' I'm not your mother."

The words tasted like dirt before they were even out of her mouth. It had been an instinctive retort, but she of all people should have known better than to use it on him. Nothing could be worse than her loss, but Prisca's betrayal of her adopted son came close.

"I'm sorry." She hung her head.

"Don't be." He touched her on the chin, and when she looked up there was only sadness in his eyes. "You're not the one who hurt me."

"Have you heard from her?"

He shook his head. "If I did, I'd tell you."

"You don't have to."

"Of course I do! You're my best friend and closest lieutenant."

"Lieutenant?" She headed for the path back down the valley, and he fell into step beside her, their footsteps and their words falling into a familiar, easy rhythm.

"Would you prefer deputy?" he asked in a playful tone. "Assistant, perhaps?"

"Definitely not assistant. That makes me sound like I clear up after you, and you can deal with your own sweaty shirts."

"Aide-de-camp?"

"Too fancy."

"Trusty right hand?"

"You've been watching too many plays."

"Whose fault is that?"

They walked on in comfortable quiet for a while. They always took their rehearsals well away from the rebel camp. While some of Raul's followers must understand that there was art behind what he did, it wouldn't be helpful for any of them to see how the stage was set.

Despite their reputation for desolation, life teemed in the foothills of the Winter Ridge Mountains. Doves cooed in the treetops. Mice and voles scurried between the roots. Elk watched the passersby from between the trees. Through a gap in the canopy, a kite was framed against a sky clear as ice.

"I wish I hadn't lost my temper," Raul said, subdued.

It took Yasmi a moment to realise what he meant.

"It wasn't your fault," she said, laying a hand on his arm. "After what she did, Prisca deserved every word."

"She's my mother."

"And she raised you in a lie."

"So did Da."

"He has the good grace to regret it. Prisca wouldn't understand another person's feelings if you screamed them into her face."

"I suppose." He kicked a stick into the undergrowth and a startled fox scurried away.

"Don't waste your guilt on her; all she'd do is turn it into a lever against you."

"It's not just that. She has contacts all over the country. We need people, weapons, armour, food. She could have helped."

"And would you have trusted her to use those contacts?"

Yasmi tensed as she thought about what Prisca had done to Raul, raising him into a tool of her political schemes. It was like something out of Tenebrial's plays. No one deserved to be treated like that, and no one should get away with it. When she spoke again, it was through clenched teeth. "Could you have trusted her?"

Raul's face crumpled. There was a hardness in his eyes that she didn't like to see, but that she needed him to have in moments like this.

"No." He jerked his head from side to side. "Never again."

"There you go, then. You're better off without her. We all are." She touched his arm again. "And I know what you're going to say, but a real mother doesn't act like that."

"Thank you." He looked up and around. "Is that an eagle?"

She followed his gaze. A shape was moving across the sky, but at this distance it was just another dark spot to her.

"How can you tell?"

"The wings, and the way it moves. It's like…" He hesitated. "I don't know how to explain, it's just one of those things. If you grow up around farmers, you learn to tell one bird from another. Which ones might eat the grain, which ones might kill the chickens, which ones you can catch and eat."

"Even I know you can't eat an eagle."

"We'll make a farmer out of you yet."

"Urgh, I'd rather be an aide-de-camp."

Trails of grey trickled up through the trees ahead of them, smoke from cooking fires and Drusil's new smithy, its scent at odds with the clear smells of a woodland on the cusp of winter. Voices reached them too, the indistinct ripple of conversation mingling with birdsong and rustling trees. One of those voices rose above the rest, a rich, strong tone punching through the surrounding sounds.

"Sounds like my father's also practising his projection," Yasmi said.

"That's no speech," Raul said. "He's calling for us."

Sure enough, their names rang out, Efron Dellest's voice sharpened with urgency.

Hairs rose on the back of Yasmi's neck. Was someone hurt? Had the Dunholmi found them?

She took off at a sprint, straight through the branches and brambles that fell across the path. Raul ran beside her, and then ahead, his longer legs giving him an edge. She reached for the wolf mask, but they were so close that stopping to shift would only slow her down.

The two of them dashed out of the woods, past the stumps of recently felled trees, onto the open ground beside a river where the rebels had made their temporary home. With its huts of uneven timbers and tree houses on the steeper slopes, it formed an idyllic image of a peaceful woodland village. There was a carpenter, a smithy, a few children at play, even a temple to Yorl and a small cairn for the local gods by the riverbank. If she'd wanted to paint a backdrop for a fairy town, she could have drawn on this scene, but even its calm beauty couldn't halt her current dread.

Despite her fears, there were no blue-clad warriors galloping up the trail, no clang of steel. The closest thing to combat was a group of actors and assorted volunteers in the small meadow on the far bank, practising manoeuvres with wooden swords and broom handle spears.

Yasmi's father rushed up the dirt trail toward them, his house robes loose around him, moustache flapping as he called out.

"There you are!" He flung his arms wide. "I've been looking for you everywhere."

Those robes were faded and threadbare, their ancient embroidery unravelling—that was why they'd been demoted from the costume box to casual clothes. But they looked even more sorry now, a wet stain down one side, a loose hem trailing in the mud.

"What's the matter, Efron?" Raul asked. "Has something happened to one of the patrols?"

Patrols. He really did sound like a general.

"It's your father, my boy," Efron said, seizing Raul's hands with a look of dramatic intensity. "He's lost his mind."

"Lost his mind?"

"To drink!"

Yasmi took a deep breath. She was going to have words with her father about this need to squeeze drama from every moment.

"Not again." Raul clenched his jaw.

"'Again and again, like the swine that returns to his ditch, once more to—'"

"Now's not the time for your Prince Patetchy," Yasmi said. "Is he at your house?"

"In the common shelter," Efron said with a pout, then kept on muttering. "My Patetchy was renowned all the way to the Golden Ocean."

With a great effort of will, she ignored him and hurried after Raul.

The common shelter was the simplest construction in their whole improvised settlement, and the most important. Made from overlapping sheets of canvas stretched on ropes between the trees, it provided a heart for a community trying to find its way of living. There, people gathered to cook and eat shared meals, to plan raids against the occupiers, to share drinks at the end of a long, hard day. Without even walls to keep the wind out, it didn't hold back the elements as well as their homes, but the fire in the centre provided one sort of warmth while constant company provided another.

As they approached, a murmur of voices came from the shelter. Some people were moving away, frowning as they went, while other lurked at its edges, watching. They quickly parted when they saw Raul coming.

"Get off me!" a voice boomed from under the shelter. "I can do this."

There were rows of benches under the canvas and tables between them. At one of the tables near the fire, people sat stiffly across from each other, some of them looking at the big man who stood at the head of the table, the others at the table between them. With one arm, he was waving a ladle, spattering people halfway across the tent. His other arm was grappling with a large iron pot, stew spilling over its lip as it tilted at an awkward angle. He tried to grip it between that arm and his body, a task made more difficult by the leather-wrapped stump where his right hand would have been.

"What are you doing, Da?" Raul asked, approaching the table like a farmer might approach a frightened lamb. There was something touching yet faintly ridiculous about seeing him approach Valens in this way, treating the vast, scarred veteran, a man built for fighting, like he might turn and run.

"'M helping," Valens said, louder than he needed to. "I can do that."

"That's good." Raul moved slowly around the table while Yasmi held back. There were things Raul could get away with that no one else could, especially where his father was concerned.

"I can," Valens insisted. "Can't I?"

The people at the table didn't meet his gaze. Most of them were looking at their empty bowls and the food spilled between them.

Pressing the iron pot between his arm and his belly, Valens stepped back from that table and staggered toward the next one. After three steps, the pot, greased with stew down the side, slipped from his grip and hit the ground with a clang, its contents pouring into the dirt. A woman in an apron glared pointedly from behind the pots bubbling over the fire.

"I'll get another," Valens said, waving his ladle at the people waiting to eat. "You sit there. I'm here to help."

He wheeled unsteadily around, but by now Raul was between him and the cook. Valens paused, staring at his son. Muscles like mountains slumped, his stew-stained shirt sliding down.

"Raul," he mumbled. "I can help, I promise. Gimme a chance."

"Of course you can, Da," Raul said. "But there are other people to help here. You need to come with me and Yasmi and help us with something else."

"Yeah." Valens tossed the ladle down on a table. "Yeah, I'll do that." He looked around, drunkenly trying to catch the eye of any of the rebels. "See, my son needs me."

He turned and stumbled. Raul darted in under one arm as Yasmi grabbed the other, wrapping it around her shoulders. Smells of stale sweat and bad booze made her gag. Valens's bulk staggered her, but she gritted her teeth and kept her feet.

"Fucking thing!" Valens kicked the fallen pot with an almighty clang. Despite its weight, it went flying across the tent, scattering observers. Valens's arm tightened around Yasmi, but he didn't even gasp at the pain that must have caused in his foot.

Together, Yasmi and Raul steered Valens out of the shelter and past the small temple. It was nothing like the ornate stone edifice to Yorl in Pavuno, but it wasn't like the small roadside shrines either, stacks of rocks or simple carvings where offerings were left for local gods. This was a place for people who didn't have much but who needed to believe that someone was on their side.

"Idiot," Valens mumbled as they staggered past an image of Yorl, his arm heavy across Yasmi's shoulder. "How you gonna watch over anyone with one eye, huh?"

He tried to kick one of the offerings on the steps, but Raul steered him away and down a dirt track between the trees.

"You can't talk like that, Da."

"Why not? You think Yorl was watching when the Dunholmi came? You think Avgar guided us to this hole in the dirt?" Valens snorted. "At least Loftus is still having a laugh."

Yasmi couldn't help smiling at that, despite Raul's frown. Any travelling player made small offerings to local gods, in the same way that they respected the lords of lands where they played and spoke highly of innkeepers however dreadful their ale. But travelling meant you didn't get attached to the gods of any country, town, or track. The names of the divine were as much for taking in vain as they were for praising on festival days.

Efron scurried ahead to the hut he and Valens shared. He pushed its door open and stood with a brittle smile as they manoeuvred Valens up to the door.

"'M fine," Valens muttered, stopping to lean against the doorway. "Just tired."

"My dear, you are drunk as a duke," Efron declared. "And not for the first time this week."

"You always said I should indulge more."

"I . . . Yes, you're right, I said that you should enjoy life. But is this enjoyment, eating until you groan and then drinking until you collapse?"

Valens flopped onto the edge of a bed and the wooden frame creaked under him. He stared at the floor, his shaved head hanging, fingers running across the leather that protected his stump. Sadness swelled in Yasmi. Valens had never been the life of the party, but he'd been solid as stone, a presence with the weight to anchor the world. The change she'd hoped for was that he could relax at last after a long life of hardships, so that he and her father could make each other happy. No one would wish for this.

"Don't deserve to enjoy myself." Valens waved his stump at Raul. "Failed you. Failed Fabia. Failed everyone."

"You didn't fail me, Da." Raul crouched in front of him, looking up to try to catch his father's eye.

"I did worse! I lied to you, all for . . . for . . . for . . ." Valens pressed his hand against his eyes. "Fabia died for the plan, and I fucked it up."

"It was a fucked-up plan." Yasmi was surprised by her own vehemence, and so were the others, judging by the way they turned to her, but at least it got Valens to raise his head and meet her gaze. She tempered her tone, forced herself to treat it as one more performance. "But you did it for good reasons, and you're trying to do better now. That counts for a lot."

"Failing to do better." Valens waved his stump. "'M not even a whole man."

"'Course you are," Raul said softly. "Would you say I was less of a man if I lost a hand or a foot?" He tapped Valens's chest. "It's what's in here that counts."

"'S even worse. Eighteen rotten years. Fake life. Fake sword. Fake prophecy. I did that."

Raul's eyes narrowed. If this had been different, if Efron had been the one who'd lied to Yasmi her whole life, then she wouldn't have stood for any of this self-pity. She would have let him know exactly how rotten he was, and sometime after, when the heat of fury and shame subsided, they would have found a way back to each other. But what Raul and Valens had was more fragile than that, so he took a deep breath and squeezed his father's remaining hand.

"That's in the past," Raul said.

"'S not." Valens shook his head, the movements loose and slow as his slurred words. "She's out there, scheming." He looked up at Raul. "You'll see, she'll find a way to ruin everything."

Looking at Valens's stew-stained shirt, the mess he'd left around his home, the sadness on Efron's face, it seemed like

Valens was ruining things perfectly well himself. Still, he was right. The more their rebellion grew, the more the prospect of Prisca's return loomed over them, a shadow that threatened to blot out the light of Raul's achievements. Prisca might be on their side in theory, another rebel against the occupiers, but she'd brought danger down upon the acting troupe and their fine theatre, wrecked Raul's joyful spirit, and nearly got half the people there killed. The person who'd kept rebellion alive was the one most likely to poison it.

"We'll deal with her when we see her," Raul said. "Right now, you need to dunk yourself in the river, put on some clean clothes, and rest for the day.

"I want to be useful." Valens sounded plaintive as a child.

"And you will be." Raul spoke firmly as he rose. "Tomorrow, once you've slept this off."

He walked out of the hut and Yasmi went with him, leaving Efron to deal with the next steps. Sunlight shone on them through bare branches of ancient oaks as they headed slowly back toward the river.

Raul stopped at the edge of the woods and ran a hand across his face.

"Can I help?" Yasmi asked, and inside she was begging him to say yes. The boy needed something—a friend to talk to, a shoulder to cry on, a drinking buddy, a quick fumble in the back of the theatre wagon, anything to ease the tension. Seeing him like this hurt her, just like seeing Valens hurt him.

And just like Valens, he didn't know how to let go.

"I should..." He hesitated, not quite looking at her but not stepping away.

"Yes?" She reached out a hand and his trembling fingers inched toward hers.

In the distance, someone was shouting his name. She kept her eyes on him, trying to hold him in the moment, but it was gone.

"I should go see what they're yelling about."

———————•———————

Even before he reached the storehouse, Raul could hear trouble coming. Voices ragged with anger and rising louder with each moment. A small crowd of rebels had gathered around two figures standing in the doorway, glaring and shouting over one another. Biallo, one of the star actors of Efron's troupe, and Katia, a former weaver who'd been on the failed treasure raid. Vegetables lay scatted across the ground, and they were both tugging at a torn burlap sack.

"What's the matter?" Raul asked as he stepped up between them.

"She's stealing supplies!" Biallo yelled, to indignant calls from the crowd.

"It's not stealing," Katia snapped. "I helped gather them, and that makes them as much mine as anyone else's."

As many people cheered for Katia's words as sounded support for Biallo. Around the edges, some of them started shoving one another.

"Stop that!" Raul pulled two of them apart, then looked back over his shoulder at Katia. "Why do you need the food at all? Ellena's cooking tonight."

"We won't be here tonight. We're leaving, and we're taking our share of food for the road."

"We?" Raul's heart sank. "Who's we?"

The crowd shuffled and split. A dozen rebels stood behind Katia, and as they looked at Raul their expressions ranged from embarrassment to hostility. Some of them were people he'd personally recruited to fight against the Dunholmi. All of them had seemed committed to the cause.

"But why?" he asked, shoulders drooping.

"Why do you think?" Katia asked. "This whole rebellion's a disaster. All we've done is burn a few isolated outposts, and now half the armies of Dunholm are chasing us around the hills."

"It takes time to change things."

"We've been here for *months* and the only thing that's changed is we've got hungrier."

"We can fix that."

"What, by robbing another wagon? Ask Helvus how well that worked out."

Raul hung his head. She was right, he'd put so much hope on that attack and it had been a failure, nothing to show for it but wounds and empty spaces around the campfire.

"We'll get better at this," he said. "With practice and... and..."

When princes were motivating their people in the plays, they always had at least three things, three reasons for hope or courage or determination. He'd got stuck at one, and now the trailing end of a failed thought hung in the air, a failure of its own.

"Practice?" Katia snorted. "Fat lot of good that'll do. We're not warriors. We weren't raised to fight like the riders of Dunholm."

"You're learning. You're getting better, all of you."

"Us? What about you? You're the one who planned that fuck-up the other day." Katia yanked the sack out of Biallo's hands and knelt down, picking up fallen vegetables and flinging them in. "This isn't worth throwing away lives for."

Raul gritted his teeth. How could she not understand? She had once, he was sure, or she wouldn't have been here, none of them would, but the enthusiasm they'd brought at the start was fading away and he didn't know how to fix it.

"We have to fight," he said. "Otherwise we'll spend our lives in fear of the Dunholmi, not free to run our country for ourselves."

"Easy for you to say, *Prince* Raul." Katia straightened to face him. "We win, you get a kingdom out of this, but what do we get? A different ruler and hoping that you're better than the governor was? I'm not risking my life for that anymore."

Raul looked down at his hands. He couldn't argue with this. If he saw the world the way she did, he would have left himself.

Katia slung the sack over her shoulder and stomped away. Most of the people who had stood behind her followed, though a few lingered uncertainly, and one even went to stand by Biallo.

"It's not that we don't want this," one of the waverers said, and his voice was a plea begging for something that Raul couldn't provide. "It's just..."

"I understand." Raul took a deep breath, tried to release

the disappointment in himself. "Yorl watch over you on your journey."

The man hung his head, purposefully not looking Raul in the eye.

"And you."

Then they were gone.

Chapter Three
The Worst Person

Valens groaned and rolled over, trying to bury his face in the blankets and the musty straw underneath, away from the bright light cutting through the cracks in the shutters. He used to drink any other warrior under the table and still fight at dawn. Now he'd be lucky if he could stand up straight before lunch. Dawn dragged him up despite that fact, habit like an officer booting him awake.

With a groan, he rolled over and brought his hand to the splitting pain in his head. Instead of rough fingers, smooth leather pressed his furrowed brow. He opened sticky eyes and stared at the place where a jet mourning ring should have been, smooth and black and solid against the softness of flesh. By the time he wore that ring, his hard-drinking nights had been behind him, but its coolness still brought comfort if he caught a fever or woke sweating with memories of Pavuno's fall. He'd promised Fabia's memory that he'd wear that ring until his dying day, and in return he'd got a small degree of comfort when he viewed it upon his finger.

But there was no comfort anymore.

He pushed aside the blankets and stood shivering in the gloom of the hut. The ashes in the hearth were cold and grey. After years on the road, getting up and out each morning, Efron never thought to bank the fire, and Valens didn't remember coming in the previous night. He sniffed his shirt, smelling stale stew and bile. Broken memories tumbled through his mind, gouging his heart with their sharp corners.

More apologies to make. More people he'd disappointed, over and over.

He fumbled his way out of the shirt and tossed it into a corner. Goosebumps prickled his skin as the crisp winter morning chased away the remaining fuzz of sleep, leaving behind the stabbing pain in his head, the empty ache in his belly, the thickness in his throat. From the bed, Efron mumbled something without really waking and pulled the blankets closer around him. That made Valens smile, for a moment at least.

There were clean clothes in the trunk at the bottom of the bed, but a deep breath told Valens that he needed to clean his body first. As quietly as he could, not wanting to disturb Efron or to have to face him yet, he bundled up trousers, shirt, tunic, boots, and belt, then eased the door open and crept out.

It was even colder outside the hut, his breath frosting white like the tips of the grass. He forced his shoulders down, ordered his body not to shiver, and strode naked through the trees, twigs cracking and fallen leaves crunching beneath bare feet. Some others were up already. They nodded to Valens as he passed, but no one tried to talk to him. Somehow, their paths always carried them away, whatever direction they'd been heading in before. He didn't blame them; he would have avoided himself if he could.

The scent of fresh-baked bread wafted from the ovens someone had built out of riverbank clay. Valens's mouth watered, though his stomach growled uncertainly and bile rose in his throat. Empty as he was, eating didn't seem a good idea yet, especially not if it meant facing people. The pain stabbed sharp through his head, and he wanted to rub at the spot where it came, but his hand was busy carrying clothes and he couldn't bear the thought of the leather-covered stump's touch. Instead, he marched faster through the village, out to the riverbank, flung his clothes down, yanked the leather cap off his wrist, and hurled himself into the current.

The shock of cold chased away all other sensations—pain, hunger, even shame. He burst from the surface gasping like a newborn baby, then sank back down. No need to scrub when the fierce current of the waterlogged hills and the shivering of his body would shake the grime away. He swam part-way up the river and back down again. He'd never been a strong swimmer, and his missing hand made his movements lopsided, but those movements were getting better. At least, Efron told him they were, but Efron was a professional liar with an interest in keeping Valens happy.

Even a warrior who'd spent whole winters on the march could only take so much cold. When his teeth grew so gritted he thought they might seize in place, Valens climbed onto the bank, wiped off what water he could, and reached for his trousers. Ellena, one of the camp's cooks, walked past. He'd noticed her enjoying the sight of him before, but today she strode past with pinched lips and he looked away quickly, shoulders hunched, fumbling with his clothes.

Gods be damned, every little thing was a trial now. Even pulling on his tunic or fastening his belt, movements he'd taken for granted his whole life, became a battle between him and the stump. He cursed and fumed, glaring at anyone who came close, until he was at least into his clothes. Tying laces was a thing of the past, and he'd be damned if he asked Efron to do them for him, so he stuffed their ends inside the boots instead. That would never do for a long march, but who was going to send a drunken, crippled has-been on one of those?

The pain had receded a bit, and the ache in his stomach was hunger now. Going to the shared shelter would be hard, but it wouldn't be the first time he'd mumbled apologies over breakfast. It was the quickest way to knock off the dirty scab and let the wound bleed itself clean. He took a deep breath and headed for the large canvas awning, but something stopped him in his place.

A familiar figure was approaching the rebel village, striding confidently up the riverside trail. She wore a simple tunic and trousers, a tinker's pack on her back, and carried a walking staff with a jagged lump of flint bound into the top.

"No," Valens hissed, and stomped down the track toward her. "No you fucking don't."

Some others had noticed who was coming, and Prisca's name rattled around the village like bare branches in the wind. Biallo, one of the actors, ducked out from the central shelter and ran off down a track, probably to fetch Raul. If Valens had his way, his son wouldn't be needed.

"Don't you come a step closer," he said, planting his feet wide across the path. He didn't have a weapon to rest his hand on, so let his arms hang loose, fist clenching and unclenching, as clear as he could be.

Prisca Servita stopped and raised an eyebrow, an extra angle in her sharp face.

"Good morning, Valens. You look like shit."

"And you are a shit. Now fuck off."

"You used to show some respect for ministers of the crown."

"You used to deserve it. Or that's what I thought."

"Well, that doesn't matter." She shrugged. "You'll doubtless be staggered to hear that I haven't come to exchange pleasantries with the face of stubborn defiance. I've come to talk with Raul."

"Our son doesn't need you."

"Don't you think that's for him to decide?"

"What I think..." Valens walked slowly toward her. His fist wasn't unclenching now. "...is that you got Fabia killed, then kidnapped and maimed a baby, and lied to the whole world to get what you want."

"You were part of it." She looked up at him, and her lack of fear only made his fury worse. "Just because you've become too weak to see this through doesn't mean that...that..." Her voice trailed off and she looked away for a moment, her gaze following the reeds swaying by the river. Then she blinked and looked back at him. "Your change of heart does nothing to absolve you of your part. If anything, it makes it worse. I still think our actions will contribute to a greater good. You just did what you were told because you didn't know any better."

Valens raised his fist. Inside, he was trembling, but his fingers were steady as steel, inching a knife's width at a time toward her throat.

"I could kill you right now."

"Go on, then."

She tugged down the neck of her tunic and stared straight into his eyes. He should do it—make the world a safer place, save Raul from whatever poison she was going to drip in his ear. But they'd lived together for eighteen years, an imitation of family that ended up feeling real. While he might hate her, she really was a minister of the crown, or had been, and obedience was the drumbeat of Valens's heart.

"How's the other hand?" she asked coldly.

Now his fingers trembled, so close he almost touched her throat. For the first time, her eyes darted down, uncertain. Then they met his again, two shards of flint.

"What happened to the ring, do you think?" she asked. "Part of Count Alder's collection, a souvenir of our defeat? I can't see anyone else claiming it."

He took a deep breath. He could do this. A simple blow straight to her throat, crush fragile old bone and let her choke on her final words. Or knock her down and grab a rock, beat out those brains she was so proud of. One breath, one blow, that was all it would take.

"At least you get your actor now." She looked away. "What's his name again?"

"You know," he growled. Then he noticed the way her gaze had softened, drifting off toward the trees. "Or do you?"

"Hm?" She looked back, eyes narrowing. "I do what?"

He laughed bitterly and took a step back.

"I don't need to kill you. The magic's already doing it."

"I don't know what you mean."

"Did you forget you told me, or do you think I'm too stupid to see the signs?"

She kept her face straight, but now that he was paying attention, he noticed the whiteness of her fingers around her staff, gripping tight like it was the only way to stop them from trembling. He hadn't sunk so far that her sickness made him happy, but there was satisfaction to it.

He turned his back on her, his one hand bunched into a fist. "Follow me. Raul can kick you out himself."

The pain in his head hadn't gone, but there wasn't such a weight of misery pressing down. At least with Prisca around, he wouldn't be the worst person in camp.

———————————— • ————————————

Count Brennett Alder crouched by the side of a backcountry track, a dagger in his hand. There were no proper roads out here, something he should fix when he had the time, and the early winter rains had turned the trail into thick mud that would put both horse and rider at risk as hooves slipped through at a gallop. Between that, the nearby forest, and the distance from the nearest outpost, it had been a smart place for the rebels to attack.

"My lord, do we need to linger?" Ketley Tur's voice was even more whiny than usual. He clutched his cloak tight around himself with a look of abject misery. "Surely there's little to be learned from mud."

"I'm not interested in the mud," Alder said.

He'd finally found the thing that had caught his eye as they rode in and hooked it out of the ooze with the point of his dagger. A medallion in the shape of a bear gleamed as it caught the light while mud dripped from its broken leather cord. He held it up and one of his chosen stepped forward, holding out his hand to let Alder drop the object in the palm of a leather riding glove.

"A charm," Tur said in a tone of disgust.

"Obviously," Alder said. "And equally obviously it was lost in the attack on our pay wagon, probably by one of these North March rebels. Something for strength?"

"Perhaps, my lord," Tur said in the uncertain tone that was a close as the chamberlain came to challenging his superiors. He waved a stick-thin finger at the overgrown slopes around them. "Though out here, it might be about summoning endurance and the ability to survive in the wild. This is part of their deceitful ways, slippery signs that have one meaning in a moment and a different one in the next, a way of hiding their intentions."

"Sounds like you've been studying magic, Tur."

"My lord, I swear, it's just to understand the enemy." Tur took a step back, hand clutched to his chest. "I would never—"

He slipped on the grass at the edge of the track, wobbled, waved his arms wildly, would have fallen if one of Alder's warriors hadn't grabbed him and wrenched him upright.

Alder strode up the slope toward the trees, accompanied by two more of his company, their footsteps heavy with purpose, heads turning to watch for danger. He had no real worries about Tur turning native—the man feared magic even more than he feared failing his superiors—but keeping him on edge brought out an extra effort.

The meadow's sward was broken near the tree line, stretches of grass churned where a horse fell. Smaller gouges showed where hooves had hammered the hardest, and there were trampled traces of what might have been footprints, though there was no certainty with signs like that in this weather, especially not days after the attack.

Still…

"Captain Brook!" he shouted.

Behind him, reins jingled as someone dismounted. The patrols up here muffled the metal of their chainmail and harness, to avoid being heard, but that wasn't how a count and his guard should travel.

Alder peered into the woods. The trees were mostly pines or something like them, though a few oaks and maples stood bare-branched, as exposed as the woods would be back home. The undergrowth looked thinner further in and broken by what might have been an animal trail, but might equally have marked the rebels' passage.

Footsteps came to a stop beside him.

"My lord?"

Captain Brook was the most ordinary-looking woman Alder had ever met. Average height, average build, muscled well enough for fighting but not enough to become freakish, like that rebel from the raid on the palace. Like many of his chosen, her skin was the soft brown of the eastern plains and deltas, and her hair was cut short for soldiering. But Alder wouldn't have emerged from the shadow of his father's setbacks if he couldn't tell the character beneath the clothes.

"You've spent time in the highland garrisons," he said. "What do you think of their escape route?"

Brook's eyes were still as she stared into the woods. Water dripped from branches and a horse snorted as it pawed the ground down by the trail. Overhead, an eagle shrieked and then dropped into a hunter's dive.

"Unless they doubled back, there are two or three ways they could go," Brook said, pointing. "North to skirt around that peak, or west, which might take them to the Alesia River. We can check the maps of the North March at Fort Ironhold and see where the mostly likely routes are from there."

Alder didn't bother asking about tracking their prey; Brook's silence confirmed his own suspicion that it was too late.

He whirled around and strode back down the slope, Captain Brook and Alder's personal guards following. Eight more Dunholmi riders waited by the road, all with lances, bows, shields, and sabres, wearing the white tree on Dunholm blue that was the livery of House Alder. No crowns in the heraldry up here. Accepting royal help would have meant admitting that he couldn't solve the problems of Estis for himself, which would amount to admitting that the attack on the palace, the escape from the cells, the broken monument, the growing rebel attacks were all his fault. Alder's hand clenched the pommel of his sabre. Weakness had been his father's undoing—it would not be his.

"Saddle up," he commanded. "We're heading back to Ironhold."

"Very good, my lord." Tur laid a twitching hand on the saddle of the placid pony they'd found for him. "Then back to Pavuno, I assume. The first of the suitors your uncle arranged arrives within the week, and the staff will want your opinion on accommodation, preparations for the banquet, parting gifts, any—"

"I trust you to set it in order, Tur," Alder said, swinging easily into the saddle. Fellstride, black as night and elegant as an empress, snorted and swished his tail as the count's weight settled on his back.

"Really, my lord?" Tur tried to mount but his foot slipped from the stirrup. Brook stepped up silently to help him.

"Really." It was easy to trust Tur with things that weren't urgent, where he could fuss over the details to his heart's content. "I'll be gathering the local garrisons and the strike force we left at Silver Vale, then heading further into the hills."

"My lord…" Tur hesitated, caught between his habitual obsequiousness and his inevitable worries about failing those higher up the feudal tree. "His Majesty's correspondence on this matter has been consistent. He expects you to find a wife, sire heirs, and ensure the stability of the Alder estates."

"Let's not pretend that this is about putting me out to stud. King Lorrin wants me hitched so that I can't use the offer of engagement to build my own power bloc at court. Once I'm married, he'll know who I'm bound to, and he can counterbalance that with alliances elsewhere."

He wouldn't have said these things out loud back home, but here the only prying ears were squirrels and peasants. Every woman and man in his company was loyal to him or beholden to his family, and either way they wouldn't be telling tales.

"My lord, you do a disservice to both yourself and the king." Even Alder's small words of dissent had put Tur on edge, hands clasped and head twitching from side to side.

"Of course, yes, I'm forgetting my real value—as a reward His Majesty can give to some other noble house. Unless he's more focused on foreign policy. I hear that the king of Saditch has an eligible sister, maybe Lorrin wants the power of my loins to calm that stormy sea."

Brook snorted her laughter while Tur kept up his nervous grin. Perhaps he was right to be uncomfortable. Plenty of houses back home envied the influence of the Alders. Alliances could be forming against him right now, and marriage was the easiest way to shore up his own position. But marriage had its risks as well as its rewards. His uncle the king could lumber him with someone unbearable, embarrassing, or inconsequential. He needed to go into these negotiations from a position of power, which meant proving his worth.

"The rebels need dealing with," he said. "Right now, I can crush them with the small army I have up here. If I wait and let the infection grow, who knows how hard we'll have to crack the whip."

"Indeed, my lord, but couldn't one of your captains do this?"

Brook gave Tur one final shove and he slid into the saddle with all the dignity of a windblown scarecrow.

"This is my priority, Tur." Alder patted the sword hanging from his saddle, the long, elaborately engraved one with the ruby in its pommel. "Unless you think that the rebels don't matter?"

Tur wore the same expression he'd had cowering behind the throne as this sword and its wielder charged in, set on overthrowing Alder. Even an imagined threat left the chamberlain hunched and cowering. He really was a wretch, and that made him pleasingly predictable.

"Very good, my lord." Tur grabbed the reins and clenched his legs to his pony's sides, accidentally setting it into motion. "Uh, my lord…"

"Stop fretting, Tur, we're not leaving you behind."

Alder set his heels to Fellstride's flanks. With his chamberlain and his troops riding along, he set off at a smart trot down the trail, back to maps and manpower and a chance to settle this mess.

Chapter Four
A Deeper Strength

The hammer was a satisfying weight swinging in Raul's hand, raising a clang and a shower of sparks from the red-hot alloy of the half-made lantern. This might not be as important as his other work—bringing people together, leading them into action, keeping them motivated—but it was far more satisfying, a straightforward task he could work out how to do. He swung the hammer again, watched the sparks kiss his leather apron, and smiled.

"You can do better," Drusil said, tapping a hammer against her hand as if it were no heavier than a twig. "Give it some heft."

Raul raised the hammer high, sweat running from his arm down his side, and swung with all his might. The blow clanged through the forge like a temple bell summoning the people to prayer.

"Better." Drusil, her muscles bulging, reached out with a long pair of tongs and turned something in the fire. Glowing coals shifted and a fresh wave of heat hit Raul, one more advantage to being here instead of out in the creeping cold of winter.

Two more blows, then he laid the lantern's rounded plate down on the anvil and looked around. Drusil was already holding out the stamp that they'd designed together, the one with an icon of a cloud gathering across the sun, a single beam of sunlight shining through. Illumination but also concealment, things they needed for nighttime raids, even more so as the nights grew longer and darker. If he'd worked out the symbols right, then this wouldn't just give them magical light like Drusil's previous lanterns had done. It would give them a slender beam, enough to illuminate a specific path without drawing attention, and the eyes of casual observers would pass over without even noticing the light they saw.

If he'd adapted the symbols he'd found in books correctly.

If he'd followed Drusil's instruction for the alloy right.

If this charm worked the way he hoped.

If they got lucky.

A slender thread to hang anything on, but wasn't that his whole life now? Everything hung on the threads of stories and symbols, of hope and heroism, a few brave souls bound together by a noble cause. At least if this thing worked, they'd have a better chance of success, and maybe more of the rebels would look at him with hope instead of uncertainty.

He took the stamp and placed it against the lantern housing, but Drusil snorted. He looked up.

"You know better," she said.

"I need to reheat it." He set the stamp down and picked up a pair of tongs, ready to thrust the lantern back in the fire.

"You do." Drusil looked past him and her eyes narrowed. "But you might need to deal with this first."

Raul turned to look out through the open south side of the forge. He expected to see some of his followers coming in search of guidance or to settle a dispute. Instead, for the first time in months, he saw his mother walking toward him, with his father leading the way.

The tongs suddenly felt heavier in his hand. He set them down, pulled off one of his thick leather gloves, and pressed two fingers against his crumpled brow. When he looked up, Prisca was still there, for better or for worse.

She stopped at the entrance to the forge, examining the signs cut into one of its posts. There was an eye crossed through for concealment and a bull's head for endurance, same as at the doorways of all the buildings they'd raised. The houses had carvings of hearth fires too, for warmth and welcome. Small charms to help the world along.

"Good choices," Prisca said, then looked past the post. "And it's good to see you, Raul."

Her smile was thin, cold. Looking back, perhaps it had always lacked warmth, the love and welcome he'd read into it nothing more than childish hope.

"What are you doing back here, Prisca?" Was this the right place for that conversation, the right way to start it? He shifted his weight from one foot to the other and pulled off his remaining glove.

"I'm glad you've finally stopped calling me Ma. You needed to grow up."

"I have work to do." He gestured at the forge, its heat rising as Drusil worked the bellows, taking herself away from the awkward family reunion. In theory, this was the sort of work that Raul should set aside when anything else came along. After all, a leader had to focus on leading. But right now, he felt a powerful urge to lift the hammer and beat the metal again.

"More magic lanterns?"

Prisca stepped inside the forge, peering at his work. Raul glanced past her at his da, half expecting him to step up and throw her out, but Valens was leaning slumped against the post, pressing his hand to his head. While Raul grappled with how to respond to her presence, Prisca picked up the stamp and examined it.

"An interesting adaptation," she said. "And you've taken up smithing. You always were a fast learner."

In spite of himself, Raul smiled. He shouldn't care what she thought, and this was probably just manipulation. Still, part of him responded to praise that he'd always had to work so hard to hear.

"I have a good teacher," he said, waving his gloves at Drusil.

"If a job's worth doing, it's worth doing well," the blacksmith answered. "Especially when it comes to teaching someone else."

"I like to think that at least one other teacher played a part," Prisca said, setting down the stamp.

Raul took a deep breath. Loath as he was to offer her anything like a compliment, she was right.

"I couldn't have done it without your lessons," he said. "Or the books you left behind."

"There, was that so hard?"

"Don't push your fucking luck, scribe," Valens rumbled.

Prisca stiffened but didn't respond. Raul looked past her at his da. Were those words slurred from yesterday's drinking, or had that just been his lowest, most menacing tone?

"I presume you've come back for a reason," Raul said.

"Absolutely. I've brought information that could help us win this fight."

He took a deep breath. Not long ago, he'd viewed his mother as a smart woman rightly proud of her work. Now he saw arrogance and disdain for others, a scheming politician who couldn't understand why anyone would ignore her. She would never stop being his mother, never stop mattering to him, but that didn't mean he could ignore everything else she was.

"Why would I trust anything you tell me?" he asked.

"Because we both want the same thing—to free Estis from its occupiers."

Raul looked to Valens, who was staring blankly at the ground again, and Drusil, who simply shrugged, an artisan who could judge the quality of iron but not of people. With Yasmi out on a raid, this was going to be on Raul.

With deliberate slowness, he put away his tools, took off his apron, and hung it from a peg on the wall. Then he pulled on his tunic, leaving the toggles on the front unfastened.

"Thank you, I'll be back tomorrow," he said to Drusil, then turned to Prisca. "Come."

Even as he strode past, he caught her moment of hesitation, an unwillingness to come to heel at her son's command. But Prisca had been a minister to the king and queen of Estis, had worked with lords, generals, and the royal coven. She understood the need to respond to hierarchy.

Her footsteps were swift and sharp as she followed him toward the central shelter, Valens lumbering along behind. Everyone eating breakfast in the shelter looked around as Raul approached, and some of them did a double take when they saw who was with him. A few touched their fingers to the edges of their knives for luck, while others hurriedly emptied their plates to get away.

"Biallo," Raul said, singling out the actor turned rebel. "Please can you find some people to guard the trail, and a couple of scouts to snoop around downriver. If anyone followed Prisca here, I want to know."

"Of course, Raul."

"I know what I'm doing," Prisca snapped.

"That's what I'm afraid of."

There were bread platters holding chunks of roasted fowl by the fire. Raul picked up two of them, handed one to Prisca, then walked back out from under the shelter toward the riverbank. He would have liked to stay in the warmth by that fire, to have people around in case he needed them, but Prisca was good at using people and he couldn't give her the chance.

He sat in the sunlight by the river. It was harder to hide anything in the bright light of day. Experience had taught him that, as had the books of folk wisdom and magical theory.

Prisca sat cross-legged facing him and nibbled on her meat without any sign of pleasure. Was she even thinner than she had been? He shouldn't worry about a thing like that, and yet...

"Get on with it," he said before more doubts could get in the way.

Prisca considered him for a moment, then set her food aside and leaned forward, trailing a finger in the dirt.

"You're weak," she said. "I can give you strength."

He stared at her in disbelief. "If you've come here to insult me—"

"Not you as an individual. Your movement. It's a fine thing, but it's weak compared with the dangers you face, a few hundred civilians facing thousands of warriors."

Raul tapped a finger against the crust of his platter. She might not have said it out loud, but he was half the problem here. In the stories, the heroes knew how to lead, how to plan a campaign, lead a battle, fill warriors with courage. But in the stories, the prophecies about the heroes were real and they were destined for victory. All he had was what he could make for himself.

"You think you can change things?" he asked.

Of course she did. Prisca always thought she understood the world better than anyone else.

"Remember King Balbianus?" she asked.

"How could I forget. Your play about him sent me down this path."

"Efron's play, or Tenebrial's, if you'd rather credit the writer than the actor and director."

"*Your* play. Your version of history. Your scheme to whip up rebellion."

"That last part's true, but what you call my version of history is grounded in the facts of our nation's founding, and I've been learning more."

"I thought you were finding us allies, or was that just a way to save some dignity as you stormed off?"

"I did not storm off." Her tone was brittle, eyes narrowed. "And given that I've made the effort of coming back, the least you could do is listen to what I have to say."

The least she could do was give him some support and guidance, some encouragement even, instead of striding back in telling him what he'd done wrong and how she was going to fix it, trying to grab control of the situation. She might not have said it yet, but he could see the way this was going, the insistence that others should hear her out whether or not she heard them.

Raul took a deep breath. He'd known that this moment was coming, had prepared the words he needed. Still, forcing them out felt almost impossible.

"You may be my mother, you may have been a minister, you may be the smartest person I know, but none of that entitles you to my attention, especially not after what you did. Right now I'm listening, so make the most of it, but don't go mistaking what it means."

The two of them stared at each other, both perfectly still, though Raul's heart was racing and the blood rushing in his ears. He could hear his people heading into action down the trail, people who trusted him even though his own cause was built on falsehoods. He was as bad as she was.

No, not as bad. He'd accepted the necessity of a terrible compromise, while she'd woven a web of lies. That difference, and the voice of the people depending upon him, helped him hold his ground and hold his silence.

"Fine," Prisca said at last. "For the greater good."

She opened a pouch on her belt, took out a sheet of fine cloth, and unrolled it to reveal a map.

"You remember how Balbianus died in the wild?"

"I do."

"Pulling together the different accounts, I think that the Withered Hills are where it happened, and that there's a reason why he went there."

"Because he was being hunted by the old earls, to get revenge for replacing them."

"No, that story came centuries after the fact, probably conflating him with the earlier death of Lady Betrona. Balbianus went to the wildest place in his whole kingdom to work magic."

Raul gazed at the map. Caught between the questions he had about its contents and the curiosity he couldn't help feeling about the story, he almost forgot that nothing here could be trusted, that he had to be wary of every word.

She was waiting for him to ask a question, and once upon a time she wouldn't have had to wait. Now he held his silence, forced her to choose what came next.

"How does magic work?" she asked.

"I'm not the one being tested here."

"Just tell me, in your own words, how do you understand it?"

"It's about connections," he said, not quite able to resist showing off his understanding, still hoping that his mother would smile in approval. "Sharing the truth of things. An ox is strong, so etching it into the handle of a hammer lends

Drusil strength when she's beating iron. It's not making a new strength but drawing it out."

"That's right. But as you practise further, you'll start to realise that those connections are made possible by boundaries. If, by pulling on that strength, you drew it into everything around you, then it wouldn't matter—everything would be stronger, but compared with each other, they would all remain the same. That image of a bull pulls strength into the hammer and holds it there, separate from the air, the anvil, the iron you're beating. The nature of a hammer as a tool means that strength transfers to you, but no further. That simple charm draws a line through reality. Understand?"

"I think so."

"Good. Now, the late King Cataldo hypothesised that all these boundaries are, on an intrinsic level, offshoots of one great barrier, that between our real, messy world and the realm where the . . . the . . ." Her eyes narrowed and she tapped a finger against her knee. "Something like the original versions of things are found."

"Their fundamental forms." This was a lesson he remembered.

"Yes, exactly, that. And in certain places, the boundary between our world and that of the fundamental forms is weaker. Balbianus, presumably without understanding this later theory but holding a firm grasp on the learned practicalities of power, had identified something important about the wild. For some reason, possibly related to the relative absence of human civilisation, the boundaries are thinner there. Not just the boundaries between things within this world, but the boundary between our world and that of the fundamental, defining abstractions, the ideals of an ox, or a hammer, or even a kingdom. Do you understand?"

"I think so." Raul looked around, picturing where the boundaries were between one thing and another—the forest, the river, the mountains, the sky. Without hedgerows or walls between fields, without roads or town walls, with low clouds blurring the edges of the high peaks, it was easy to imagine that things were less separated here, and this wasn't even the true wild.

"That lack of boundaries could make magic harder to control, but it could also make it more powerful." Prisca tapped the map again. "I believe that's why Balbianus went there, for the potential to utilise greater power. He tapped into the essence of the land and the people, binding them together with his death, a single vast charm written in blood by the dagger on which he died."

Raul fixed Prisca with a hard stare.

"That's what you want from me, is it? To go and die for some magic to rebuild the kingdom?"

"Fire and fury, no!" She shook her head, looking genuinely alarmed. "You're far too...too..."

"Too precious?" The barbs of disdain hurt Raul even as he dragged them up from the depths. "You're going to pretend that family means something now?"

At last, her expression faltered. Raul wouldn't have gone so far as to call it shame, but at least she showed a little of the discomfort she deserved.

"Am I really that bad?" she asked quietly.

"You tell me. What were you going to say?"

She took a deep breath and clasped one hand around the other, stilling it.

"I was going to say that you are too important to the cause to be thrown away. Your death would undermine everything I've spent these years building, and while that's not the only reason it matters, I won't patronise you by pretending it's not a factor."

That was an answer he could believe, and it hurt less than it could have. The fear of hearing her say what he really meant to her had been more of a burden than the half confession itself. Now that was done, the fear unravelled from around his heart and he sat back, leaning on his hands, ready to listen.

"If this isn't about sacrifice, then what is it about?"

"The dagger."

Laughter burst out of Raul, so loud and heartfelt that birds took flight from a reed bed across the river. The whole thing was so absurd, he couldn't help himself.

"You built your last conspiracy around a sword, and now you're going to use a knife? What, you found a blacksmith who gives bulk discounts on fake artefacts?"

"Don't play the fool," she snapped, fixing him with a glare. "This one is real. I've found enough reliable accounts to say that it's in a shrine in the wilderness where he died, a place the early monarchs took pilgrimages to but one that's barely visited now. That knife is more than just a blade. It's the tool with which this nation was cut from the womb, saved from the forces that threatened to choke it off at its birth. It embodies the story of our people and it's soaked through with the power that made us. If you can retrieve it, then you can tap into the essence of the kingdom and the strength of your heroic forebears. With that sort of power, you'll drive the Dunholmi clean out of our lands, leave nothing but dust and the rust off their horseshoes."

The fierceness of her tone, the absolute conviction of her words, sent a surge of energy through Raul. He rose to his feet and paced back and forth, while Prisca kept him fixed with a steely gaze.

"Trust me, this is more than just a symbol," she said. "It's the magic that bound Estis together once, and could bind its people around you again, give them the strength and courage they need to—"

"Enough." Raul held out his hand. "I get it. I need to think."

Whatever she'd meant to say next, she held it behind her folded arms, sitting straight-backed and watchful.

The riverside ground was soft beneath Raul's feet, the grass full of life despite the frost they'd faced that morning. At first, it sprang back after each step, but as he strode back and forth, trying to order his thoughts, the trampled stalks started to wilt.

He didn't trust Prisca, *couldn't* trust her, but the two of them shared a cause. She would use him and his people if she could, but she wouldn't waste their efforts, wouldn't put them in danger unless there was a real chance it would free Estis. Victory meant that much to her.

And she was right. Amazed as he was at how many rebels had gathered to him, they were still weak and wary, uncertain of him and of their own capabilities. The Dunholmi had a hard core of noble warriors raised to fight; an army of levies who'd spent years trudging through the weary, toughening work of soldiering. They had weapons, armour, and feed for their warriors and their steeds. All the swords and spear tips that Drusil had forged couldn't save the rebels if they didn't find a way to match that. Robbing the pay wagon was meant to tip the scales just a little, let them buy more iron and persuade more people to come fight, but even that had failed.

She was probably right about the magic as well. It fit with what she'd taught him in the past and with what he'd learned since. It felt like the clanging of a hammer in Drusil's smithy, the embodiment of magic through the tools that shaped the world.

If there was any chance that this might work, he had to take it.

He stopped, took a deep breath, and faced her.

"I'll do it," he said. "I'll go find Balbianus's dagger. Maybe I can even do something with it out in the wild, use those thinner boundaries like he did."

"Exactly." Prisca got to her feet. She was almost smiling. "We find the dagger, we work magic at the temple, we tie you to Balbianus, to the kingdom, to the cause, and we gain so much power."

"Not we." He shook his head. "You want me to use this thing? Fine. But I'm not working with the woman who lied to me my whole life."

She snorted and waved a hand toward the rebel village.

"That's rich, given what you're doing here."

"This is temporary, to keep people motivated until we win."

"You tell yourself that. But unless you want me to expose that lie, you'll take me with you."

This time, his laughter was bitter. "You wouldn't spoil my story. You're too invested in it."

She frowned, lips pressed tight together, shoulders hunched.

"Fine, I won't, but if this is about practicalities, you should still take me. I've been traversing this country as long as you've been alive, I know the tracks and trails better than anyone, and you'll need that to find our way."

"We have other people who know the country."

"And do they know magic? Can they read the signs in the flight of birds or the ashes of a fire? Can they help you understand what this blade can do, once you find it?"

Now it was Raul's turn to frown. She was right again. While he'd learned a lot about magic in the past few months, it was still so little compared with what there was to know, and no one else in his life knew these things like Prisca did.

"Fine. You can come as a guide, but I'll be making the decisions. If you start arguing, or trying to get around me, or to manipulate anyone who comes along…"

"I know, I know, you'll send me back."

"If you're lucky."

Now she really did smile as she laid a hand on his arm and looked up into his eyes.

"I know it's hard to believe, Raul, but I really am proud of you."

He shook off the hand and turned away.

"You're right—it is hard to believe."

Chapter Five
For Luck

The first light of a muted dawn was seeping out of the east as Raul stood on the trail at the top of the rebel village, watching the grey outlines of trees emerge from the gloom on the slope above. Prisca had wanted to take a different route out, up a gentler rise on the other side of the river, but while she knew the lands of Estis better than Raul, he'd spent months in this area and he knew its ways better than her. He also needed to assert some authority, before she started trying to take charge or he bowed to her will out of force of habit.

A bird gave a single tentative chirp, then subsided, apparently deciding that the dawn chorus should wait. Leaves rustled in the wind coming up the valley, warmer than the winter winds that had blown out of the north the past few days. Was that a good omen or a bad one? Raul couldn't tell without looking at the books he'd left back in his hut, and he wasn't going to ask Prisca for the same reason he hadn't let her set the route. Later, once they got going and he felt more confident in his position of command, he would look to her for guidance. But not yet.

"Are you all right?" Yasmi asked softly, laying a hand on Raul's arm.

He nodded, then realised that she might not see the movement. "I'm fine. Short on sleep, I suppose."

"You're the one who said we should leave at dawn."

"I don't want to waste the light."

"Or the opportunity to make all this more dramatic."

"That's not the point."

"It should be." He could just make out the way she turned her head, looking toward the group of shadows waiting by the riverbank. "Your life is a performance, and there's always an audience."

Raul rubbed the back of his neck. "I suppose. I just wish I knew how to play for them, how to make people believe in this as much as I do."

"They believe in you."

"They believe in the idea of me. Then they see the reality and things start falling apart."

Another shadow detached from a nearby tree and stalked over to them, walking stick in hand, a bow strapped to the pack on her back.

"We should get going," Prisca said loud enough for everyone to look around.

"Valens isn't here yet," Raul replied, turning to face her squarely.

"All the more reason to leave. The last thing we need is to drag a one-handed drunk around the wilderness."

"That's not your decision." Yasmi took her place at Raul's right-hand side, arms folded. "And you're the one who got his hand cut off."

"He made his own mistakes in that fight."

"You made it happen."

"Young lady, I—"

"Enough," Raul hissed. He could see some faces now among the other group, make out expressions of concern, Biallo leaning in to whisper something to Drusil. "If you don't want to spend time with Valens, you can stay here."

"I see." Prisca turned away from him, walked back to the tree where she'd been waiting, and set to adjusting the straps on her pack.

"Thank you," Raul said.

"I know how to play the supporting part." Yasmi's voice sank so soft only Raul would hear. "She's right, though. I know Valens is strong and experienced, but right now he's like a lead who can't remember their lines. Look at what's happening—we've not even set out and he's already holding us up."

"I said dawn. He's not late yet."

"Isn't he?"

Raul tugged at the sleeve of his tunic, making sure there was no gap between it and his fur-lined gloves, and stared down the track back into the settlement. Yasmi was right, his da should be here by now. If Prisca had pulled something like this, he would have been striding away already, forcing her to catch up. But that would have defeated the whole point of bringing Valens along. This was a chance to remind him of who he could be, to give him a sense of purpose beyond the next tankard or plate.

When he'd been young, Raul had dreamed of being as smart as Prisca, as strong as Valens. Now a whole nation was relying on him to show real smarts and strength, and he was starting to doubt what those looked like.

The people waiting to see them off were growing restless. Raul walked over to them, beaming with a confidence he didn't feel, lifting his head and chest like Yasmi had taught him.

"Are you all ready for what you need to do once we're gone?" he asked.

"Ready as we can be," Biallo said. "But don't you want us attacking the Dunholmi?"

Raul hesitated. He knew that he was likely wasting time, having the rebels stay hidden while he was gone, and he knew that without purpose some of them might leave. But he didn't know where they should be striking either, and he didn't want to give orders that could easily go wrong, leaving others to die without him.

"Find more recruits." It was all he could think of to say. "We need numbers to fight a war."

"Especially with people deserting us." Biallo scowled.

Behind him, others exchanged uncertain looks, and Raul worried that they might lose more than they gained in his absence. But he had to do something, and he could wrap his head around Prisca's quest into the wilderness, not like trying to keep all these people happy.

"Focus on those who want to fight," Raul said. "You'll find them."

"And arm them." Drusil tapped one hand against the palm of the other, hefting a hammer that wasn't there. "Most of the armour and weapons are stowed in the caves, but we've packed what we can for the other groups."

"Tenebrial and the team are hitching up the first wagons now," Biallo added. "Nice as it's been to live under a roof for a while, I'm looking forward to getting back on the road. They say that if players stay in one place too long, we turn into stone."

"Only in the head." Drusil tapped a knuckle against Biallo's forehead and they all laughed. Perhaps some bonds might hold even as the community scattered.

"Remember, take your time; spread the departures out over a few days," Raul said. "I don't want everyone sitting here waiting, but if the Dunholmi see a big caravan heading out of the hills, they might investigate."

Drusil snorted and slammed her fist into her hand. "Let 'em."

"You'll all get a chance to fight soon enough." Raul raised his voice, drawing everyone in. "When we return, I want you all ready, and new bands gathered around you. An army of rebels spread across northern Estis, armed and eager, ready for the fight. Can you be that for me?"

Some people cheered, some mumbled or clutched themselves nervously. It wasn't the chorus of affirmation he'd hoped for, but at least he'd tried.

Drusil rummaged in a pouch, then held out her hand. Dark strands dangled between the paler shapes of her fingers.

"Made these for you, one each."

Raul plucked one of the amulets from her hand, a disk the size of a large coin with a leather cord running through a hole on one side. He dangled the disk from that cord and held it up to catch the light creeping over them. The shape of a swift gleamed, its lines indented into the steel and filled with blue enamel.

"For speed...and for luck."

"Thank you." Raul tied the cord around the back of his neck, then slipped the charm inside his tunic. It was like the welcoming hands above the doorway of the inn where he'd grown up, or the eyes on the posts of their huts, and it should have been reassuring, a sign that the world was on his side. It should have been even more helpful to a leader trying to rebuild his people's knowledge, the ancient charms and signs that they had used for centuries, the more scholarly magic that the occupiers had tried to take from them. But the further he delved into those books, the less certain he became about any of this. There was a deeper essence to the world, and those who understood it could tap into the true nature of things, but what were the odds that the small gestures he'd grown up with really worked? If only one in ten of the magic lanterns Drusil forged could summon light, then what were the odds that this small token did anything at all?

If those doubts bothered Drusil, they didn't show. She held a charm out to Yasmi like it was the most important thing in the world, and even offered one to Prisca, who took it with a small, respectful bow of her head.

That left one more for the man who was walking up the track, a sword at his waist, a round shield at his side, and a pack strapped to his back, shoulders hunched beneath a weight that was more than supplies for their journey. Valens's freshly shaven head was bowed, and though it could have been to talk with Efron as they walked, it was a posture he'd been wearing too much lately, as was the slight wobble of his steps.

Instead of greeting his da with concern, Raul forced a confident smile. It was light enough now for everyone to see him. No time for doubt.

"I knew you wouldn't miss the chance for adventure," he said brightly.

"Adventure?" Valens looked at him, one eyebrow raised. "Is that what this is?"

"Of course! It's a quest, like in all the old stories. Out there in the world is the weapon we need to defeat Count Alder, to cast out the forces of Dunholm and make this our country again. King Balbianus left it for us, a gift down the generations, and we're not going to let him down."

Valens stood close enough for Raul to smell the beer on his breath. At least it was only beer this time; Efron had kept his man somewhere close to sober. It wasn't perfect, but any belief Raul had in perfection had been shattered in the palace in Pavuno. He would make do with good enough, and the way to get Valens to that point was to drag him along now, give him purpose and time away from a bottle, find the man that a younger Raul had admired. The man he still admired, but who had lost himself along the path to freedom.

"You sure you want me for this?" Valens asked, holding up his stump. "I'm not what I was."

"Even with no hands, you could outfight half the people

in this country," Raul said. "We need your strength and your skill if we're going to survive in the wilderness."

The words were a lie, but he truly did need this to work, and he leaned into that truth, filling every word with meaning as he laid a hand on Valens's shoulder.

"Please, Da. Not just for me, but for Estis."

"For Estis," others echoed.

That was enough to put stiffness into Valens's back.

"For Estis," he said, chest swelling.

Drusil held out the last of her charms. "Here."

Valens took the metal disk in the palm of his hand, ran his thumb across its face, stared at the shape of the bird.

"That's good work," he said. "Thank you."

While the others watched, Efron took the charm from Valens's hand and tied it around his neck, moving as solemnly as a squire armouring a noble for war.

"There," the ageing actor said and patted the larger man on the chest. "All set." The two of them looked into each other's eyes. "Don't get yourself killed."

"I'll try."

"Promise me."

"I'm a warrior. I can't make a promise like that."

"Well." Efron swallowed, rubbed the back of his hand across his eyes. "I'll miss you."

There was an awkward pause. For a moment, Raul wondered whether his da could even find a way to say a thing like that.

"I'll miss you too," the big warrior mumbled, then leaned in for a kiss. Some knot in the air seemed to unravel, and even as he looked away, Raul relaxed.

"Are we quite done here?" Prisca asked sharply.

Raul didn't bother to respond. Instead, he held out his hand toward the crowd, which had been growing with the light.

"Who has a knife?"

Dawn gleamed like a shard of ice along the dozens of blades they hurried to hold out. Raul scanned the crowd and picked out a young woman near the back, Tola, a recent arrival who struggled to hold her sword straight in the fighting line. With a nod, he took the blade from her trembling hand.

"I leave a part of me with you," Raul said, tapping his chest with the pommel. "And I'll be back for it, like I'll be back for all of you."

He tugged his left sleeve up, exposing a finger's width of flesh on the back of his wrist. There was a pinch of pain as he slid the knife across it, just deep enough to draw a thin scarlet line.

"Blood for luck."

"Blood for luck," the crowd murmured, fingers extended.

"For Estis!" He punched the knife into the air.

"For Estis!" This time there was more of a cheer, and a few birds fluttered from the nearest trees.

Raul handed the knife back, straightened his pack, and signalled for his companions to join him. The towering bulk of Valens; Yasmi graceful in loose clothes and her belt of shifter masks; Prisca clutching her walking staff as she watched the patterns of birds in flight.

They took a few steps up the trail to a low cairn, a small shrine to a local god of trees who was supposed to protect this valley and the people passing through. Raul took an apple from his pack and left it by the stones, an offering in hopes of guidance. He didn't know if the god would hear him, never mind respond, but he needed all the help he would get.

"How are the omens?" he asked quietly.

"Better than I expected," Prisca replied.

"Well, then." Raul looked at his da, this broken man he hoped to bring back whole, and then at the woman he'd always called Ma, but whose voice now felt like a knife to his heart. He couldn't trust her, but he didn't have to keep beating down her pride. "Why don't you lead the way?"

Chapter Six
Tooth and Claw

Yasmi bounded along the steep trail, rotting leaves soft beneath her paws. Every breath swelling her chest brought the scent of the forest, of pine trees, moss, and the afternoon's rain. Water still dripped from the branches above, fat drops sliding off her fur. The whole forest seemed full of wonders, as if a veil had fallen away to reveal a world she'd never known.

As a human, she would have lost her footing by now, missing a step in the shadows and the gloom of the fast-falling dusk. But as a wolf, everything stood out as clear as day, her eyes picking out flickers of movement at the edge of her vision, ears finding every drip and cracking twig, a chorus of scents filling the gaps between her other senses. How had she never noticed how rich this mask could make the world? How could she have been so lost in her performances that she had missed it?

The deer was small and spindly-legged, springing over boulders as it bolted away from her. What it had in lightness, she had in power, muscular legs flinging her forward, bounding unstoppably over rocks and fallen logs, snapping closer to her prey with every moment. A wild thicket of brambles rose ahead, and the deer turned rather than tear its skin open on their pointed thorns. Yasmi cut across the angle of its turn, pulled her legs in, then pounced, flinging herself through the air. In that moment, there was only the soaring arc of her body. No audience, no cast, no directions, just her own power and potential.

The deer let out a panicked cry as Yasmi's claws caught its flank and the two of them went tumbling down the slope, sliding through a slick of half-rotten leaves, slamming to a stop with the deer trapped between her and a tree trunk.

Yasmi pushed herself up, forepaws on the deer's chest. She bared her teeth, took a breath rich with blood, felt the triumphant beat of her heart and the stuttering pulse of the deer. Its back was twisted, but it still gasped and twitched one of its hooves as if trying to run on its side.

That movement stirred something else in her. Looking into its wide, dark eyes, hearing desperate, snuffling breaths, her chest swelled with pity instead of pride. The poor creature. She ran a paw softly across its cheek, feeling every strand of fur, every frantic, panicked movement as those eyes went even wider.

She hesitated, claws bared at the deer's throat. She could do this. She'd done it last night and the night before, proving that they could eat as well out here in the wild as they did at the rebel camp. Gods be cursed, she'd even killed human beings, helping Raul rescue his parents from the palace in Pavuno.

So why should she struggle now? She took a deep breath and slashed her claw across the creature's throat, a gift of mercy, as the poet Humdal had said.

The blood running across the deer's fur cut sharp through the soft scents of drizzle and mulch. She licked her lips in anticipation. But there was another scent too, the rich and tickling smell of woodsmoke, not coming from back where her companions were making camp for the night. This fire was up ahead.

Setting aside the part of her that longed to sink its teeth into the deer, and the more refined but equally hungry part that wanted to drag it back for cooking, Yasmi stepped off her prey and crept between the trees, soft paws finding the silent spaces where she wouldn't disturb leaves or twigs. She slid through the forest, a ghost-grey shadow, seeing everything and seen by no one. Her snout twitched in the breeze as she followed the smoke, which was soon joined by the sweaty scent of horses and a medley of smells that spoke for humanity.

Her route took her at an angle down the slope, to the edge of a clearing beside a small but lively river. Orange flames flickered at its centre, a campfire ringed with round stones from the stream bed. Three warriors sat by the fire, roasting rabbits and a duck. Two more were tending to the horses tethered under the far trees. One last warrior sat by the river, her boots beside her and her feet in the water. Bows and quivers rested against the saddles they'd set back from the fire, and all of them wore sabres with blue tabards over their chainmail.

Yasmi's throat tightened, breaths coming as strained as the muscles she held tensed, ready to leap away. Slowly, she slid back into the woods, then turned, picking up speed as she left the clearing behind. There was no matching orange glow in the forest ahead of her, thank the muses, no smell of smoke yet to give her friends away. Still, anxiety clawed at her mind. What if the scouts had spotted her? What if they heard something? What if they'd been sent to chase down the little group, and more were closing in from the other side?

Using every ounce of her newfound strength, she dashed over a ridge, down a slope, and approached another clearing. Raul crouched in the middle, flint and steel in his hand, striking sparks onto a pyramid of tinder that damply refused to burn. Valens sat nearby, shoulders slumped, head bowed. Across from him and the would-be fire, Prisca watched the proceedings with a look of disdain.

"Almost got it," Raul said, looking up with a smile as Yasmi ran over. "Did you bring us something to cook?"

Yasmi set a paw to her snout and jerked it back, pulling the mask away from her face. She was well past the point of worrying about who saw her shifting; that taboo had been broached many performances ago. As her face came away in her hand, her body twisted, joints popping, bones buckling, flesh folding into a different shape. In a moment, she crouched beside Raul, her fur replaced with a shifter's loose grey clothes.

"Dunholmi war scouts," she said quietly, not wanting her voice to carry. "Six of them in a clearing, that way." She pointed with a bloodstained finger.

"Are they coming?" Raul drew his sword as he rose, moving protectively between the enemy and the rest of them.

"Not yet. Not the ones I saw."

"How far?"

"Less than a mile."

With his off hand, Raul rubbed his jaw while he stared into the woods. Then he nodded decisively.

"No fire tonight. We've got plenty of roast boar left from last night to eat, and we'll be warm enough if we find somewhere sheltered. We keep our heads down, stay out of sight, and if they're still there in the morning, then we'll find our way around them."

"That won't work," Prisca said.

Yasmi glared at the older woman. She couldn't say that she expected a better attitude from her, but it would have been good if she at least realised that no one but Raul wanted her there.

Raul, his back to his mother, took a deep breath before he turned to face her with his reply.

"Why not?"

"The terrain narrows here, at the entrance to the Withered Hills." With a stick, Prisca drew swift lines in the dirt beside the unlit fire. "Thanks to the rock formations, the river veers from side to side across that narrow space. The only places with tree cover the whole way along are the upper slopes, and while Yasmi could manage those as a monkey or a wolf, and you might be limber enough to climb, I'm not fit enough, and anyone trying with one hand would take a fall."

"Sounds about right," Valens said in a flat voice that made Raul scowl.

"So we find another route," Raul said.

"That would mean doubling back to the start, wasting our

effort so far, while these scouts nip at our heels." Prisca sat back. "Besides, I thought you liked fighting the Dunholmi."

Somehow, she made that statement sound like an accusation, or perhaps a challenge. Yasmi wanted to shove her advice back down her wrinkled throat, but she was right. Those slopes were too precarious.

Yasmi closed her eyes, trying and failing not to think about the prospect of more violence. Her fingers ran across the contours of the wolf mask and a small part of that anxiety turned into excitement. Enough of it to stiffen her sense of purpose.

She opened her eyes and looked at Raul pacing back and forth. "Well?"

"We'll wait until it gets properly dark," he said. "Take our packs and stow them closer to their camp. You've seen more of these woods, and you'll be able to see better in the dark, so you can lead us."

"Are you sure you want to put your fate in the hands of an imitation monster?" Yasmi asked, holding up her mask.

"I'm putting my fate in the hands of a real hero, someone with the courage to do what's needed."

Her heart swelled at those words, and at the look he gave her. They were words he could have used with anyone, the sort of language the playwright Tenebrial had been writing for him, but the look in his eyes told her it was more than a performance.

"That gets us close," Raul continued. "Then we'll attack. How should we handle that, Da?"

"Me?" Valens looked up.

"You've got ten times more experience in war than the rest of us put together. How would you attack the camp?"

"I don't—"

"Yes, you do. Come on."

"I suppose..." The old warrior got to his feet, ran a hand across his head like he was sweeping the dust from an old inscription. "We creep in silent, take the lookout first and the others while they're asleep."

"How terribly heroic," Prisca said.

"War isn't heroic." Valens rubbed his crumpled brow. "The plan probably won't go right, so we have a backup." He pointed his stump at Yasmi. "You turn into something scary, an ogre. Get around the horses and panic them into the middle. Make enough chaos so the other side can't use weight of numbers."

"And then?" Prisca's tone was still scathing. "I trust that your tactics come down to more than loosing anarchy and relying on fortune to see us through."

"It's a brawl in the woods, not the Battle of the River Teff. Tactics only take us so far, then it's who can murder the others faster."

"What a noble sent—"

"Enough," Raul snapped. "Prisca, you stay quiet and guard our supplies. Your bow's not going to be of any use in the dark." He nodded decisively, then went to refasten his open pack. "Let's do this."

———————— • ————————

Valens crouched in the darkness, counting heartbeats until the time came to attack. This wasn't going to work, and he should know, it was his plan.

He'd made strikes like this before. At Rustling Bend, in the last year of the war, he and Fabia had led a small band along a river's hidden shallows, slipped into the camp of Dunholm's Saditchi allies, slit the guards' throats, and set their supply wagons on fire. With only one warrior dead and one injured in the aftermath, it was a tiny price to hold up a siege column for another month, and though it hadn't saved them, it had been his last real moment of hope, with only the false hope of Prisca's plan after that.

But he'd been nearly twenty years younger then, with two hands to fight with and Fabia at his side. Now he was an old, lumbering man, with his sword in his off hand and a shield strapped to his useless fighting arm. Time and Count Alder had blunted him. This was going to go to shit.

He shook his head, trying to shake that thinking. Defeatism got people killed, and right now the people at stake included his son. If Raul wanted him to fight, then he would fight as hard as his broken body let him. It was the least he owed the lad.

Counting down was an instinct born of long practice, one he could easily keep up while he watched the camp. Even as his mind wandered, he was judging the moment. At four hundred and ninety, he checked the straps on his shield, then drew his sword.

Five hundred. Enough time for the others to get into place, out there in the dark.

In the deeper darkness beneath a tree close to the riverbank, Valens rose to his feet.

The glow from the remnants of the campfire held his attention. It seemed brighter than he'd expected, and as the only light in the dark it was hard to look away from. A whisper of a voice reached him, too quiet to make out the words. He squinted at the low shapes of the sleeping Dunholmi, the silhouette of the lookout against the glow from the fire. Were they awake and talking to each other? If they were, there was nothing to be done about it, except to move quietly as long as he could and quickly when he had to.

One careful footstep after another, Valens emerged from beneath the tree. If he was lucky, its outline would hide his shadow until he was close. If he was really lucky, the sentry would have fallen asleep.

He hadn't felt lucky for a long while. In the old days, he might have made an offering to Laughing Loftus before he set out, but even if the gods hadn't abandoned Estis, he was sure they'd abandoned him.

Closer, closer, shifting into a low crouch, following instincts older than adulthood. No one was born to fight, he'd realised that running the inn, but you could be raised to any trade and he'd learned his well. He turned the sword a little to keep the moonlight from gleaming too brightly along its edge, to stop the straight shadow standing out against the softer shapes of nature.

Closer across the soft, mossy ground. From the corner of his eye, he could just see another movement, Raul making his approach from midway around the clearing. On the far side, a horse snorted, then fell silent.

Another step, and another. As Valens shifted his weight, the ground gave way beneath him. He sank halfway to his knee in soft mud and the softer, deceptive plants that had grown over it. He froze, pulse drumming in his ears, staring at the sentry. Had they heard anything?

There was that whisper again as he looked at the fire, still too soft to make out. But the sentry hadn't shifted, and no one else was moving under their bedrolls. Just Raul creeping ever closer, and he'd be on his own if Valens didn't keep going.

He moved his other foot forward, checked that the ground there was solid, then heaved his leg out of the morass. The mud clung to him and for a moment he thought that he was going to lose his boot, but what happened was worse. His foot came free with a sloppy squelch like a blade drawn from someone's guts.

This time, the sentry moved, head whipping around and then freezing in place. Valens couldn't see the warrior's face, but they'd clearly turned his way.

If they'd seen him and he stayed still, he was leaving them vital seconds to prepare. If they hadn't seen him and he moved, he was giving the raid away.

This had been easy at Rustling Bend.

Then he saw the other movement, Raul rushing the sentry from the side. Almost there when they looked back. Raul's blade swung, a black line against the amber-lit camp. The sentry shouted a moment before the blade bit, turning the shout into a scream.

The war scouts bolted upright. One stumbled over his blanket, but another was straight into a crouch, sabre in hand, while the rest went for their weapons. Valens bellowed as he charged toward them, hoping to draw attention away from Raul. That was a desperate hope when his son was already close to the fire and someone had kicked its banked coals to a brighter glow.

Blades crashed as Valens ran. He felt ungainly, one foot sodden and slippery with mud, sword and shield on the wrong sides. He almost lost his balance but kept moving as two of the scouts turned to face him.

Then came the whinnying shrieks of horses crying out in alarm. Whatever shape Yasmi had chosen, it had done the job. The horses galloped into the firelight, two of them dragging branches behind their reins, scattering warriors and hot coals. Valens dodged as one thundered toward him, and it was like the old days again, Dunholmi cavalry bearing down on the honest infantry of Estis. With a war cry as incoherent as it was fierce, he charged.

A horse slammed into him, knocking him off his feet. He brought his shield up, bracing it with both hands, and a hoof hit so hard it dented one board of the shield, but better that than Valens's head. He rolled aside and the horse galloped past, vanishing into the night.

A Dunholmi scout charged, sabre swinging. Valens brought his sword arm around, ready to take them first. Except that it was his shield on that arm, not his sword, and all he could do was block. His other hand was empty, his blade abandoned when he'd braced his shield, and his belt knife was on the wrong side. As he twisted around, trying to reach for it, the Dunholmi hacked at him again and again, driving him back across waterlogged ground that gave beneath his feet, throwing him off balance, leaving him exposed.

A grey shape bounded out of the moonlight, knocking the

Dunholmi off his feet. Hot blood spattered Valens's cheek as the wolf ripped one throat open, then sprang on to take the next, letting out an exhilarated howl as she went.

With a grunt, Valens heaved his foot back out of the mud and looked around for his sword, but it was impossible to spot on the ground in the dark. At least he could find the larger shape of the war scout's body, a last few breaths still gurgling from a torn throat. He fumbled around by their side until he found their sabre, gave it a test swing, and stomped determinedly toward the scattered embers of the fire.

"Da!" Raul exclaimed. "Are you all right?"

"'Course I am." Valens peered around, looking for someone to hit. That felt like the best, the only thing he could do right now, but the only person he saw standing was Raul. "Did you get them all?"

"Me?" Raul laughed. "Hardly. One or two. Most of this was Yasmi. You should have seen her, Da, leaping from one of them to the next, all claws and teeth and that. They never stood a chance."

"Well, that's..." Valens looked around at the savaged bodies. "That's good."

It was, wasn't it? After all, this was war. Any fight you walked away from was a win, doubly so when the enemy didn't get to run. Six fewer war scouts. Six fewer occupiers. Six fewer chances that someone would tell Count Alder where they were going. And Yasmi was one of the rebels; this was what they did.

Yasmi, who he'd known since she was a tiny lass singing choruses from a wagon-bed stage.

Yasmi the entertainer, who brought people light and hope.

Yasmi, Efron's daughter.

This had to be good, because this was Raul's plan, and this was how they won.

Then the wolf was beside him, prowling out of the darkness so quietly he never saw her coming, just realised that there was a lighter shadow beside him now.

She raised a paw and that shadow shifted, the lines of the wolf writhing into those of a human, a sight that twisted up his guts.

"That was amazing!" Raul exclaimed.

"Yes, I was amazing!" Yasmi laughed and took an ostentatious bow. "But then, aren't I always?"

The two youngsters laughed as they hugged, slapping each other on the back, and even in the light of the dying embers, Valens could make out their grins. He remembered being that young and excited for action, for victory, and for other things. He didn't belong in this moment.

"You two clear the fire," he said. "Don't want that spreading. I'll let Prisca know we won."

Still carrying the sabre just in case, he headed for the woods. Behind him, Raul and Yasmi chattered excitedly as they stamped out patches of smouldering grass.

Then came the other voice, the one he'd heard before. Quiet still, but clearer.

"Don't scowl like a kicked priest," the voice whispered, and its familiarity reached down through the years to halt him in his tracks. "'Any fight you walk away from is a win,' remember?"

Valens stood, the sabre hanging loose in his hand, water seeping into his boots from the waterlogged ground. Everything else in the world seemed to fade away. Everything except that voice.

Trembling like a levy on his first battlefield, Valens whispered her name.

"Fabia?"

Chapter Seven
Not Like Home

Raul woke with an ache in his legs and a sharper pain in his hip. The hip was easily solved, as he rolled off the stone he'd rolled onto in his sleep, then rubbed at his flesh through the blanket and the clothes underneath, finding nothing sore enough to make a bruise. The duller ache, though, the one running from his hamstrings all the way down to his calves, was harder to shift. He stood to shake it out, but as the blanket slid aside, the cold hit him through his shirt and hose, and he ended up shivering instead of stretching, clutching himself as his breath frosted.

"Get your tunic and cloak on," Prisca said quietly. "We can't be slowed down by you catching a cold."

She sat on the far side of a ring of soot-blackened stones, feeding twigs of growing size into the flickering beginnings of a fire. A pot full of water and herbs hung over it.

There was no point making himself miserable just to defy her, so Raul pulled on the rest of his clothes, then rolled up the blanket and tied it to his pack. It wasn't fully light yet, the sky a murky blue between glowering grey fields of cloud, and if he couldn't see any sign of Valens, he could at least leave Yasmi to sleep a few more minutes. After all, it had been a late night.

He looked across the clearing to where they'd left the bodies of the war scouts. Scavenging creatures had found them in the night, leaving strings of guts and trails of blood across the mossy ground. Crows perched on their heads and hands, pecking at every exposed inch of flesh, tearing away their clothes and jabbing through gaps in their armour. Raul turned his gaze down and away, one hand pressed to his stomach. The wind seemed brisker today, though the trees were barely moving, and he reached for his gloves to keep out the cold.

"We should bury them," he said.

"And lose half a day of travel, when we don't know who else is in the vicinity or when this group's absence will draw someone's attention?" Prisca shook her head. "Don't be a fool."

"Don't forget who's in charge." Raul's nostrils flared as he glared at her. "You threw away your right to tell me what to do."

Two of the crows cawed and flapped their wings hard, fighting over a morbid morsel of flesh. Yasmi groaned into the pillow of her cloak.

"Well, then." Prisca peered into her pot, which was starting to steam. "Should I look for a shovel?"

Raul sighed. He hated that she was right almost as much as he hated to leave those bodies for the crows. The Dunholmi did terrible things, but from what Alder had said, so had Raul's people once upon a time, and even the worst person in the world deserved some empathy in the end. But they did need to get moving, and it would be a nightmare to dig graves in this waterlogged ground, using only the trowel that they'd brought to forage for roots.

"What are you infusing?" he asked instead.

"Fennel, pepper, and…" Prisca frowned. "And some other enlivening herbs and spices, to get us started for the day. Though it's mostly about the warmth."

"And reading the leaves after?"

"And reading the leaves after." She nodded. "Tasseography is one of the weaker forms of divination, but the further into the wild we go the stronger the signs should become. There's no point in wasting an opportunity for guidance when it comes along."

Valens walked out of the trees, surveying the landscape as he came. He reminded Raul of how he'd looked when they were raising rebellion in Pavuno, head held high and eyes alert, hand never far from a weapon. Raul smiled at the sight.

"No more scouts hiding out there," Valens said. "Horses are long gone too. Maybe they'll get lucky, or maybe the local wolves will eat well tonight."

He set to packing up camp, while Yasmi dragged herself grumbling from under her blanket. By the time they were ready, so was the infusion, along with oat cakes and strips of cooked venison that Prisca heated by the fire. There wasn't time to cook Yasmi's catch from the previous evening, so they butchered it for the best parts and bundled them up in a sack, which Valens strapped onto his pack.

"Can you read the entrails?" Raul asked as Prisca drained the last of her drink.

"You can eat an animal that's been sacrificed for its signs, but not the other way around."

"Why not?"

Apparently there was still something left in the cup, because Prisca raised it one more time, then licked her thin lips before answering.

"That's a complicated question connected to intention and the way that an essence signifies itself."

Not long ago, Raul would have asked her to tell him more, eager to get past the complicated words and understand how the world worked. But he'd had enough of Prisca's superior tone for one morning.

"Nearly ready?" he asked, looking around.

"'Ready as a scarlet messenger waiting on my lord's will,'" Yasmi said, with her performing voice and a small flourish of the hand. "*The Leaping Lovers*, act three, scene two."

"Da?"

"Hm?" Valens turned from staring at the trees. "Do you hear something on the wind?"

Raul tilted his head and listened, but all he could hear was the rattling branches and the crows cawing as they fought over their blood feast.

"I don't think so. Why, do you?"

Valens tossed his empty cup down with the others at Prisca's feet. "Must be the trees."

Prisca glanced into the empty cups, shook her head, and stowed them away. A pot full of water quenched the fire, then they all shouldered their packs, Raul feeling the weight down through the ache in his legs. As he winced, Valens looked pointedly at him.

"I've told you before, stretch out after a fight. It makes everything better."

"So you don't ache this morning?"

"Oh, I do." Valens shook his head. "But that's me getting old."

———————•———————

The sun was probably at its peak when they reached the head of the valley, though it was hard to tell. With growing banks of cloud looming over them like the mountains to east and west, Raul could only guess at the time by the levels of light and how hungry he was. They stopped long enough to quickly eat cold oat cakes and relieve themselves behind the trees, then carried on up the ridge.

The going was steep, and at times he had to grab wiry bushes or lean into rocks to avoid overbalancing and rolling away down the slope, carried by the weight of his pack. The others were struggling too; even Valens was puffing and panting as he stomped his way up the slope. Prisca advanced with silent, scowling determination, leaning heavily on her staff, while Yasmi made up for that quiet with a string of the most vivid curses Tenebrial had ever written into his plays. A pair of cats, twice as large as the usual farmyard mousers and with long fur in streaks of grey and yellow, watched them judgementally from a rocky ledge, but Raul suspected they were more interested in the meat on Valens's back than they were offended at Yasmi's language.

The trees that managed to cling to this rocky slope were smaller and less healthy than those in the forest they had walked through for the past three days, most of them bent in line with the prevailing wind. Raul grabbed one as his foot slipped on loose stones, which went bouncing down behind him. Then the tree creaked and shifted, more rocks breaking loose around its roots, clattering as they tumbled away. He yanked his hand off the slowly falling tree, wobbled, realised that he had to fall forward or back, so flung himself onto the rocks as the tree tore loose and went sliding down the slope, narrowly missing Valens.

"Sorry!" Raul called out from he lay pressed against the slope, looking back at his da. "Are you all right?"

"Just keep going," Valens called back. "The sooner we find somewhere flat, the better."

Going upslope added to the ache in Raul's legs, and now his shoulders were bothering him as well, thanks to the pack pressing on them for hours on end. The supplies they'd packed for the journey had barely seemed enough, given how long they were planning to travel. Now they seemed far too much.

But he was the leader. He couldn't complain, couldn't rely on anyone else to motivate him or to sooth his strains. It was his job to show that this could be done. So he pushed himself up into a crouch, grabbed a jutting rock above, and climbed again.

"Come on, country boy," Yasmi said as she passed him on his left. "You should be in your element out here. Weren't you the one who grew up like a goat, roaming dirt tracks in the hills?"

Despite the cursing, she grinned as she looked at him, eyes bright and cheeks flushed. Her movements were smooth, agile, ascending the slope like she was born to it. Fresh energy surged through Raul and he pushed himself upward, scrambling from one rocky protrusion to the next, trying to catch up with her.

"You know you're not really a mountain lion, right?" he asked.

"I am an actor—I can be whatever I want, and I'll do it a lot more convincingly than you could." She patted the masks on her belt. "If I wasn't carrying this pack, I'd show you just how convincing."

"I don't need masks. I'm a hero, remember?"

Spotting a cluster of tougher trees, he veered off to the right, aiming to use them to overtake her. But Yasmi had reached a zigzag trail left by some wild animal and she went running up it, back and forth across the slope. It looked a lot easier than hauling up hand over hand, but Raul's route was more direct and he was feeling determined. He flung himself forward, ignoring his aches, almost running up the slope as he pulled himself from one tree to another, up and up and onto the last few feet of slope, his breath grating in his throat. Then he was at the top of the ridge, and he flopped to the ground, chest heaving, exhausted but satisfied.

A moment later, Yasmi sprang into view, staring down at him.

"As heroic as a drowned rat on a riverbank," she said, shaking her head.

"But I got here first."

"Only just."

"I'm the real mountain lion! Roaaar!" He swatted at her leg, fingers curled clawlike.

"Oh no, the wild beast has me!" Yasmi laughed and sank to the ground beside him. "Still, I stand by my earlier stance. You're the country boy, you have an unfair advantage. This is your home ground."

Raul released himself from the straps of his pack and sat up, rubbing at his strained shoulders. He looked back along the valley they'd ascended, a spike of treetops stabbing into the foothills and mountains above. Then he turned to look ahead, along a rocky defile between the sloping flanks of two mountains, a bleak ravine in which nothing seemed to live. While the path ahead was more gloomy, the one they'd passed through was the one that unsettled him more.

"This isn't my sort of land," he said, looking out across the treetops. "It's…"

What was it?

That valley should have felt more comfortable, more like home. It was certainly more familiar than Pavuno had been, with trees instead of brightly painted houses, winding trails instead of straight dirt roads, no wharfs stretching their grasping fingers into the river to catch trade as it passed. Living in the rebel village, it had been good to be back to something more like what he knew, a place with space to be by himself, with burbling brooks and the autumn smell of fallen leaves, a place where the first sound in the morning was birds, not a hauler's wagon creaking and rumbling out of a warehouse. But as they'd come up the valley, he'd become more aware that something wasn't the same.

"There are no fields," he said. "No meadows. I mean, there are plenty of woods back home, you've seen them. But there are open spaces too, places for grazing sheep or growing corn. Here, most of the open spaces are the ones where nothing can grow. I haven't seen a fence, a wall, even a proper trail since we left camp. I know how to live around farmers, not around wolves." He touched her arm. "With one important exception, of course."

Her hand met his, fingers not quite curling in around each other. "You do seem more comfortable out here, though, more yourself. Perhaps that's just about getting out from under other people's plans."

She scowled as the tapping of a stick and the thud of footsteps approached. Valens appeared around a protruding rock, and then Prisca came up behind him, the two of them walking the last few strides to the top of the slope.

"Well." Prisca peered along the cleft behind them. "This is every bit as delightful as I remember."

"You've been here before?" Yasmi asked, pulling her hand away from Raul's. He sat up, tense, seeing her eyes narrow.

"I've crossed most of Estis in my time, and not the well-worn routes you players stick to." Prisca tapped her staff against the ground. "That's why I'm leading the way, remember?"

"If you've been here before, and Balbianus's knife is so important, why didn't you get it from its temple then?"

"Two reasons. One, I've been here, not all the way through the Withered Hills. We still have a way to go yet. And two, I didn't know that the knife was still around. Now I do. That's what study will do. Perhaps you should try it."

"Prisca," Raul said, his chest tightening around the growled word.

"Honestly, can't I even offer a suggestion for self-improvement?"

"Yasmi's not the one who needs to improve." Raul stood up and pulled his pack back on. "We should keep moving."

"I need to catch my breath."

"No, you don't."

————————•————————

The mountain pass was bleak, but at least it was easygoing, the ground solid underfoot, nothing to block their way and the loose stones too visible to trip them up. Raul strode purposefully along, unwilling to relent in the pace he'd set at the start, even as his weary feet made their discomfort known. Footsteps echoed from the slopes on either side, while a wind blowing straight along the gap blew his hair around his face.

His da marched in step beside him, arms swinging and stance steady. He'd cleaned the mud from his clothes as best he could and straightened his tunic before they set off so that even with the stains and sweat, he looked the smartest he'd done in months. Raul smiled to himself. So far, his plan was working.

As if in response to that thought, Valens started humming. It was a steady tune with a beat to match the rhythm of their feet.

"Is that a marching song?" Raul asked.

"Seemed fitting."

"What are the words?"

Valens snorted. "No one wants to hear me sing."

"I used to like it when you sang me to sleep at night."

"Only because you didn't know better." Valens smiled a soft smile. "Still, those were good days, eh?"

"So are these. I'm glad you're here."

"Me too." Valens took a deep breath and stood straighter, then started to hum again, picking the pace up so that they marched faster down the pass, forcing Prisca and Yasmi to keep up.

Halfway along, Raul stopped, peering at a shape looming over the far end of the defile. When it first appeared around the curve of the rocky slope, he'd assumed that it was an outcrop, but the closer they got, the more its straight lines and stacked blocks forced him to see it differently.

"It's a building," he said quietly, knowing that any sound might carry to whoever occupied it. "Who'd build up here?"

"Dunholmi fort," Valens growled. "Could be where those scouts came from."

"It's not the Dunholmi, and it's not even a building anymore." Prisca strode straight past, her staff clacking against the ground. "It's a remnant from the Earls' Wars. A beacon tower for signalling down the gap. Apparently, there was one at the other end as well, but that was made in a rush out of wood and it burned down the first time it was lit. Did the job it had to, I suppose; no one in the area could miss the signal."

They approached the stones in the day's final fading light. The peak to their left had already cast the defile into shadow, and that somehow made the remains seem to tower higher, uneven stacks of rock looming over them like angry giants.

Part of the building had fallen, leaving a scatter of blocks around its base. Raul ran his fingers along one of those blocks, feeling the carvings that had run down the outside of the tower and that reminded him of the repeating carvings of winds and crops at the Temple of Yorl in Pavuno. If you repeated an image enough times, it would stop being a thing and become a pattern, something you could see other images in. In that way, the carving was like divination, one thing becoming another, shapes you could read the world in.

"This should keep any rain off our heads," Raul said, peering through a doorway into the tower, then up at the thickening clouds. "And we can light a fire inside without being seen."

"A fire made from what?" Prisca asked distractedly, looking up at the sky. "All we have here are rocks."

"There are some bushes a little way downhill." Yasmi, having removed her pack, took the monkey mask from her belt. "It'll be an easy climb with four hands and a tail. I'll see what I can get for us."

As she donned the mask, she curled over and seemed to shrink, while fur sprouted and a tail uncurled from her waist. Lips peeled back from a wide grin in a face that was more unsettling for being closer to human. Some of the masks seemed to make her grow, expanding into monsters of muscled beasts, while the monkey made her smaller, an agile shape bouncing away down the slope beneath the tower.

A score of birds, alarmed by the monkey's sudden approach, fluttered into the air and swooped around, following the wind along the face of the mountain.

"Dusk is a good time for divination," Prisca said. "Day

shifting into night as the sun touches the earth, one set of creatures hiding away while others emerge. There's power in liminality, in the spaces of transition, an opportunity to read secrets that the world wants to hide."

Raul knew that she was working on him as much as on the world, that her soft words were a hard hook to draw him closer, to get him used to listening again. But a long day of walking and climbing, on top of a night of violence, had burned out the energy that would have fuelled his anger. While he was proud of what he'd been learning without Prisca's help, he wasn't too proud to admit that he could learn more with her help than from a bunch of books.

"How do you spot them?" he asked. "Those signs in the dusk?"

"If not for the clouds, I'd say shadows. Watch where they point, use that to pick out what the world wants you to see. Tonight, though…" She raised her staff, pointing with the flint end. "Look at those clouds. What do you see?"

When Raul had been little, this had been a fun game, squinting and twisting his head to find the most exciting, most dramatic images. Lions, tigers, and dragons; castles and sailing ships; heroes out of legend. But divination wasn't about making the world fit the shape you wanted. It was about accepting the shapes you found there. He let his mind rest, sank into the weariness of the day, and gazed with detachment at the clouds above.

"I see a willow," he said. "A wheel turning. And an animal… a horse maybe?" He laughed. "A sword, but I always see swords."

"That's what comes from Valens's stories." Prisca's voice

was softer than usual, more like how she'd been in his earliest memories, or how he'd wanted her to be. The version of Prisca he'd written over reality. "But that doesn't mean it's not real."

He pondered at the connection between Prisca's own words and his thoughts. Had she somehow led him into what he was thinking, or was it a connection drawn from the power of this passing time, when day and night touched, sharing meaning from one to the other? If he was finding that power, then he wanted to make the most of it.

"What do they mean?" he asked. "Those signs."

"That depends. Can you see an order in how those birds fly past the shapes?"

He hadn't even realised that the swooping, repeating pattern of that fight had touched on all the images he'd seen, but she was right, they were connecting. The flock would pause for a moment by the valley side, then follow a distinct curve across the sky.

"Wheel first," he said, watching them, "then willow, then horse, sword last. What does it mean?"

"A wheel can mean commerce, change, disappointment if it's broken. But it can also mean a smooth journey. Where is it?"

Raul pointed. "Over there."

"Then that's our best direction to set out tomorrow. How about the willow, what do you think that could mean?"

"To watch out for a willow?"

"Think less literally. It could mean grief, but we're heading into another wooded area, so most likely it stands for a river, and we should watch for that."

"The horse?"

"What do you think, Raul?"

"The Dunholmi often ride, but you said to think less literally."

"This time, I think your direct approach works. Not a surprise to learn that we should be wary of the Dunholmi, they have outposts in the Withered Hills. Was the horse far from the other signs?"

"All the way over there."

"Not an immediate threat, then. Good. And what do you make of the sword?"

Raul swallowed. He could think of one very obvious and very important connection, and he really hoped that this wasn't about the sword he'd had. If the fake relic that he'd lost to Count Alder mattered, then that could be a bad thing. His cause was still tangled in the prophecies Prisca had forged, ones featuring that sword. If people got too focused on it, if they started to see how he wasn't living up to those prophecies, then all his plans could start to unravel.

He didn't want to think about it, but he had to.

"Could it be about the sword you gave me?"

It was almost dark now, so he could only just see Prisca pursing her lips. Then she shrugged.

"A sword is a symbol of violence. Yes, that could technically be the one you had, but given everything else we're doing…" She patted him on the shoulder. "I wouldn't worry about it."

His weary shoulders sagged in relief. It felt good to find meaning in the world, but he could live with a lack of clarity this once.

"Thank you," he said. "For helping me find the way."

"My pleasure. Perhaps, as we're going along, you'd like me to teach you more? If that's not too much like I'm taking charge."

He couldn't quite tell if that was meant as concern or another of her verbal jabs. Maybe it was both, just like dusk could be day and night, and a wheel could be a smooth journey. Maybe sitting in the space between meant he could get back to learning from her without worrying about who that put in charge.

"Thank you," he said. "I'd like that."

Chapter Eight
Living With the Flow of the World

"I thought the Withered Hills would be..." Raul looked around. "Less alive."

The trail looked like it should be a difficult one. Twisted trees reared over them from both sides, windblown branches clawing at the air, and roots crisscrossed the ground like bulbous veins. But somehow those branches managed to sway away as they approached, revealing that they weren't as closely grown as they appeared, while the solidity of the roots proved easier underfoot than the mud of the previous valley. A smooth journey, like the omens had promised. At least, so far.

"Some people say that this land is the most conducive to life in the whole country," Prisca said, surveying the thick undergrowth to either side. Few of the plants here had shed their dark leaves or died away for winter. "Others say that it's the most deadly."

"So which is it?" Raul asked.

"Both."

A fly buzzed across the path. Raul swatted it away and resisted the urge to ask for more information. If Prisca had something to say, she would say it either way. He wasn't going to let her think he should be grateful for that wisdom, and he knew she couldn't resist showing what she knew.

"There are no towns up here," she said. "No villages. Not even fields. Life, but no civilisation."

When Raul didn't respond, she fell silent again.

The tangled trail stretched out behind and ahead of them, Valens's heavy footsteps thudding along, Yasmi's lighter tread with him. From branches above to roots below stretched the trunks of trees, their bark ranging from cracked white through sandy yellow to deep reds and smooth, dark browns. Between them stood long grass, splayed ferns, and rambling thorns, still as the surface of a midwinter pond. New life grew across the trunks of fallen trees and drifts of old, dried leaves.

As they crossed a ridge, the forest opened up before them, revealing blackened ground from which charcoal stumps protruded like broken limbs. Raul stared, dumbstruck, while Prisca crouched to scoop up a handful of ash.

"Who did this?" Raul asked. The forest had been a place of intimidating shadows and uncertainty, but this was worse.

"No one, I suspect." Prisca watched the ashes trail through her fingers. "Fires happen in forests, especially ones that go untended. Lightning strikes, brings down the tallest tree, that ignites the leaf litter, and you get a blaze that lasts until the wind changes or the rain comes."

"That's usually in summer," Valens said, having caught up with them.

"So was this fire." Prisca held up her hand, showing how some of the ash had stuck in a dark, muddy glaze. "Look, it's already growing back."

Sure enough, green shoots peeked through some of the heaps of ash, and even from the burned remains of trees. New life amid loss, hope amid devastation. Just like their rebellion. The thought made Raul smile.

Still, he walked faster to get across that devastated ground and was glad that they were soon back under the living trees, sheltered from the wind and the thought of the flames blazing through.

They kept walking north, or as close to north as the trails let them. It was downhill so far, into a bowl between the mountains behind them and those slicing off the horizon. Forested slopes and rocky promontories filled most of that space: the Withered Hills.

"Do you hear that?" Yasmi asked as they walked on through the forest.

"Hear what?" Raul looked back over his shoulder.

Her head was tilted on one side, eyes narrowed.

"Rustling in the trees."

"I've been hearing rustling the whole way." He pointed at the branches above the trail. "It's windy up there."

"But not down here."

She was right. There was a stillness close to the valley floor that went beyond the sheltering of trees. The air was thicker, oozing like sap instead of flowing like water.

He held up a hand and they all stopped. Without their footsteps in the way, he listened for what Yasmi had heard. Was that a low rustling or a trick of his ears, making the high branches sound closer than they were?

"Da, can you hear anything?"

Valens, who had been staring down at the roots, raised his head. His expression went from weary blankness to a frown, then to a slow nod. His stump touched the place where his sword used to sit, then after a heartbeat his hand found the place where it was now.

"Left of the trail," he said quietly. "More than one."

"Wild animals, maybe?"

Valens shrugged. "I'm no hunter."

"Lucky for you that I'm here, then." Yasmi lowered her pack and took the wolf mask from her belt. She smiled at Raul, her eyes shining in the broken light that fell through the overgrowth. "I'm getting good at telling scents apart, let me see what I can sniff out."

Raul couldn't keep from returning her smile, but he couldn't shake off his wariness. He remembered the war scouts around the embers of their campfire, the Dunholmi outposts scattered across the countryside, the regular patrols that had passed through the Vales. If he and his family could get here, then so could the occupiers, and with their horses they could move faster.

"I don't want one of us to get caught on their own," he said, careful to make it one of them, not just Yasmi. The last thing he wanted was for her to think that he was protecting her more than anyone else.

"Trust me." She leaned toward him, hands clutching the mask, bouncing off her toes like she might take off at any moment. "This predator can take care of herself."

Why did those words set Raul on edge? He couldn't tell, and he shouldn't let the spiked feeling in his guts get in his way.

"We'll keep walking," he said, voice still low in case someone was listening. "You see if you can sniff out what that is. If someone's following us, then you follow them for a bit, come back and tell me who it is before the afternoon's out."

"That's not long." Yasmi glanced up, mask almost on her face. The sun was halfway across the sky on what would be a short day.

"It'll be long enough for a wolf like you."

Raul slapped her on the arm, the rebel leader passing on his bravado, pushing past anyone doubting themselves or his plan. The twist in Yasmi's smile told him that she, proudly, recognised the tricks she'd taught him. The mask slid into place, her body twisted and dropped, and then she was bounding off into the trees.

Somehow, a root had got hooked over one of the straps from Yasmi's pack. As Raul lifted the pack, the root slid off and slapped back into the dirt. Instinctively, he started shifting the weight of his own pack, ready to bear the burden of both; then he thought better.

"Could you carry the extra weight?" he asked, holding it out toward his da. "You're the strongest one here."

Valens swung the pack around like it was nothing, settling it over one shoulder next to his own. Then he set off again, striding purposefully along the root-paved path, leading them deeper into the Withered Hills.

Before, Raul had just been walking along, like he might have walked across the hills back in the Vales, bringing home firewood he'd gathered or chickens traded from one of the neighbouring farms. Then, his head had turned as he walked, looking for anything interesting to keep him entertained. Here in the wild, the same motion was a defence mechanism, watching for danger in the shadows between the trees. If they were being pursued by some wild creature, then he needed to be ready when it tried to make a meal of them. Though his da seemed more purposeful since setting out into the hills, Valens wasn't as alert as he'd once been, his expression sometimes becoming blank and distant, and he was vulnerable to attacks from the right. But an attack by a wild bear or wolf wasn't the worst prospect facing them. What made Raul's shoulders tighten and the hairs stand up on the back of his neck was the worry that Dunholmi scouts might be out there, watching and listening, following their path, sending messengers to call more forces down. He set his hand to the pommel of his sword and kept walking, alert to every rustle of undergrowth and whistle of wind, every chirp of the birds overhead.

They found the stream as the light was faltering and Raul was wondering where to camp for the night. Looking back, the peaks flanking the pass were closer than he wanted, but his feet ached and he couldn't imagine how they would navigate this terrain in the dark. When the trail emerged onto the bank, offering fresh water and a patch of softer, moss-strewn ground beside, it seemed like the perfect spot.

"A river among the trees," he said. "The omens were right."

"Not a difficult thing to predict up here," Valens said as he crouched to dip his hand in the water. "And not much of a river."

"They were more right than you think." Prisca pointed to the opposite bank, where the limp branches of a willow trailed across the dirt and into the water. Between its roots, pale curves of human bones protruded from the dirt. "A river in the woods, grief, even the willow itself. I've never seen a sign find its mark with such precision."

Her distant, distracted tone made Raul tense.

"Is that good or bad?" he asked.

"Maybe neither. Maybe both." She shrugged. "Maybe just a sign of how the walls of the world are thinner here, the abstractions of a symbolic realm crudely intruding upon reality."

"They're old," Valens said, peering at the bones. "Don't need to worry about what put them there."

Raul, who hadn't got as far as that worry, stared across the water at the bones. Who had those people been, and why were they buried out here, tangled in the roots of a tree instead of laid to bed in grave dirt or sent aloft on a funeral pyre? That thought left him feeling queasy, wanting to get out of there as fast as he could. But that was childish fear talking, and he had to be an adult. No, more than an adult—a leader. And as a leader, he knew they needed somewhere to rest.

"Seems peaceful," Raul said, purposefully taking off his pack and laying it against the bole of a knotted oak that stood opposite the willow. "It's cold again, so we'll gather wood while there's still a little light, get some stones from the stream and—"

A howl rang through the trees, making Raul's heart race. Something burst from the bushes on the opposite bank and fell thrashing in the stream.

Raul drew his sword. Valens had his in hand already, and Prisca was grabbing the bow off the side of her pack while the thing twisted and writhed, flinging water about. Raul craned his neck as he took a step closer and realised that it wasn't just one shape. There were two creatures, human and beast, wrestling for dominance.

No, not for dominance: for life or death.

Yasmi, the wolf, was flinging her weight onto a man, pinning him in place and bringing her teeth to bear. For his part, the man was desperately fending her off, pushing her head back with one hand while he tried to crawl back up the bank, gasping for breath whenever he got his head above water.

"Yasmi!" Raul shouted. "What are you doing?"

She didn't respond, just kept battering at the man with her paws, pressing him down beneath her weight. She snapped at his arm, and he got it clear just in time. As he managed to wriggle free, her claws came out, raking across his shoulder.

"Yasmi!"

Raul flung his sword aside and charged in. He didn't know who the man was but he wasn't armed, and if he was an enemy, then this was a chance to question him, a chance they would lose if Yasmi tore him apart. Raul slammed into lean muscles wrapped in sodden fur, shoving her off. She steadied herself, turned, and stared at Raul, teeth bared, a growl rising from her throat.

"Please, Yasmi." Raul held up his hands. "It's me."

The growling faltered, then faded away. The wolf lowered her head, paused for a long moment, then walked over, water running from her fur, to press against him.

"That's it." Raul ran a hand slowly along her back, like he was soothing an agitated hound. Yasmi stared past him at the man, but at least she didn't attack. "That's it. You got him. It's all good."

Together, they walked out of the stream and stood dripping on the bank. Yasmi reached for her face, pulled away the mask, and twisted back into humanity before sinking onto the moss-covered ground.

The stranger stood with his hands raised, Valens's sword pointing at his guts. He was shorter than Prisca, but a lot more muscular, his wet woollen tunic clinging to a solid frame. Shoulder-length hair was plastered to his scalp and the side of his face, and lively eyes peered out from beneath bushy brows.

"He was following us," Yasmi said, her voice shaking.

"Why?" Raul asked, looking the man in the eye.

"Why are you here?" the man replied.

"You may want to reconsider your attitude," Prisca said, "considering who here is armed."

"No, wait," Raul said. Being Prisca, she was right in the wrong way. This man hadn't drawn a weapon in spite of what was happening, and that was important. "You live around here?"

"Aye, so's said."

Raul pushed Valens's sword gently aside, then held out his hand. "My name is Raul Warborn."

The man looked at that hand, looked at Yasmi, looked at Valens's sword, finally looked Raul in the eye and shrugged.

"'Course you are." He slapped a hand against Raul's chest, then against his own. "Nice to meet you, Warbur. I'm Lestavo." He had a thick accent, sounds stretching out like he had to drag them from deep inside. "Is yon dog girl fixing to fray my throat again?"

Yasmi, her hands clutched tight around the wolf mask, shook her head, the movements short and sharp.

"Well, then." Lestavo took a fistful of his tunic and wrung the water from it. "Best we get a fire started, so?"

———————————————•———————————————

Raul waved a hand in front of his face, trying to waft the smoke way. He'd given up on moving out of the smoke's path. No matter where he sat around the fire, some breeze pushed it toward him, leaving him sneezing and his eyes watering, the taste of ashes on his tongue.

To his left, Yasmi sat subdued, legs crossed and the wolf mask cupped in her lap. Valens was quiet too, staring at the well-gnawed rabbit bones and the leaf platter charring in the fire in front of him. Prisca stared into the fire, but with the flickering expression that came from trying to read shifting signs. That only left Lestavo, a roasted rabbit leg in his hand, to chuckle as he watched the struggle between Raul and the smoke.

"You're town folk, so?" Lestavo asked, waving the meat at Raul. A pair of tiny wooden charms rattled against his wrist: a fleet-footed hare and an eagle with its piercing gaze.

"I'm from the country. Just not this bit of it." He glanced at Prisca, then focused on Lestavo again. "I thought no one lived up here."

"Ha!" Lestavo barked his laughter and spittle flew from his lips. "So's said by those as don't know. But there's real living up here, not your bricks and fields, living with the flow of the world."

"How do you get shelter if you don't use bricks and stone? How do you feed yourselves without fields?"

By the flickering yellow light of the campfire, Lestavo ripped away a strip of meat with his teeth.

Raul laughed. "I suppose I'm just so used to my sort of life, I can't imagine yours. But then, I couldn't imagine city living a year ago."

"That so, Warbur?"

Lestavo held slender bones out toward the trees, scraps of meat still hanging off them. A rodent scurried out, rubbed its head against Lestavo's hand, and took the bone between its teeth. Lestavo scratched the top of its head, then left it to vanish into the woods.

"Aren't you worried that thing might come back and steal your supplies?" Raul asked.

"More worried something might die for nowt," Lestavo said. "No tree grows alone."

Raul stared at the strange man with his matted hair and worn woollen clothes, damp rising from them in a faint haze of steam. Even after Lestavo had insisted there was no house nearby they could shelter in, Raul had half expected him to run off and find one rather than sleep in the cold. But if Lestavo was making plans to get away, he showed no sign of it.

"Doesn't anyone come up here and try to build?"

"Oh, aye, but rock don't take root around here. Look at yon heap of square stones at the valley mouth. Us five together couldn't shift not one of those, but they still fell. The Withered Hills resist."

Resistance. That was the sort of talk Raul was used to, the sort he could use to connect with his curious companion.

"We resist as well." He tapped his chest. "Fight back against the Dunholmi invaders. Do you know them?"

"All dressed in blue, heavy on the horses?" Lestavo rubbed a thumb against his eagle charm. "Aye, we know them well. Smarter than the stone men, they know to work with wood, though they don't understand why. Every spring, they come up here, fixing to tame the hills. Every summer, they get a little further than the one before, raising barns and fences, sending wagons full of timber south. And every autumn, the wild wrecks their wooden huts, sends the horses mad, packs them off where they came from." He grinned. "I told you, the Withered Hills resist."

Raul smiled even as he shivered. He'd changed into what dry things he had, but there was no spare cloak, and he couldn't do without it in this cold, so now everything was damp. Still, that thought of resistance warmed him, the idea that even the land could fight back against the invaders.

"A little further every year." Prisca pierced Lestavo's mirth with the glare of an eagle diving on prey. "So they're gaining ground against you and whoever else lives here."

"What of it?"

"If you don't fight back, then that's how they'll win, slicing your land away piece by piece. You seem like a man who esteems his freedom, but you're going to lose it soon."

Lestavo wiped his stubbly chin, then picked a fragment of food from between his teeth and flicked it into the fire.

"Not our land to lose," he said. "We just live here."

"So you'll let them take it?" Prisca's tone sharpened with scorn, which Lestavo returned with a visible sneer.

"You city folk think you're smart, so you do, but you don't understand nowt. They keep fraying away the hills a little at a time. Soon they'll draw Jarrag's attention, and the trees'll cut them down for a change."

"Who's Jarrag?" Raul leaned forward for the warmth of the fire and the chance to hear a story. Smoke billowed in his face and he flapped futilely at it again.

"He's the god of these parts, and one you'd best not cross."

"He has a shrine, doesn't he?" Prisca said without any of Raul's eagerness. "Probably the only stone building that stands for miles around."

"So you do know something. Not much, though, if you think Jarrag chose walls over a cave."

"And there's a dagger in this cave?" Raul asked, leaning further forward still.

"Aye, so's said."

"Have you seen it, when you go there to pray?"

Lestavo drew his head back and looked at Raul like he was the strangest creature he'd ever seen.

"Did I say something wrong?"

"You don't pray to Jarrag, don't say no to nowt he calls for and don't ask for owt he don't offer first. Not if you're fixing to live."

A log cracked and fell, flinging a swarm of sparks into the darkness. Raul scowled, remembering the flies that swarmed around bodies hanging in the streets of Pavuno. Count Alder was a man to demand and punish, a bully and a tyrant. Raul wasn't going to start a fight if he didn't have to, but he wasn't going to let anyone treat others with that sort of cruelty.

"We'll see what this Jarrag has to say," he said. If the local priests were using cruelty and their master's name to keep people obedient, then maybe the Dunholmi weren't the only people who needed to be overthrown. "Then we'll decide how to deal with him."

"You've a strong spirit, Warbur, least you have right now. I wonder how these hills will shape it."

Raul reached for something bold to say, something about how he and his companions weren't going to let the hills change them, how they were strong in spirit and righteous in purpose, a stirring speech stealing snippets from Tenebrial's plays. But who was he looking to inspire around this fire? It would just be a way to chase off his discomfort at being judged by Lestavo, and the man had the right to judge strangers who came tramping into his homeland.

Though that wasn't the only thing making him uncomfortable. After a long day's walking, he'd drunk too much water from the stream, and if he wanted to sleep, then he needed to deal with that. He got up, crossed the open ground of the riverbank, and headed for the trees.

"Don't—" Valens began.

"Go out of hearing, I know," Raul called back, and smiled. At least his da was paying some attention to the world.

He walked far enough between the trees not to be heard relieving himself, but not so far that he couldn't catch a little of the firelight. When he was done, he turned back and started heading toward the light, stepping carefully so as not to trip on roots. A shape moving in the darkness jerked him to a halt, grabbing for his sword.

"It's me," Yasmi said, her voice the creaking of a brittle twig.

"Oh." Raul felt his cheeks warm. "I didn't know you were out here too. I didn't mean to . . ."

"It's not that." She moved closer, placing herself so that a flicker of firelight through the trees illuminated one side of her face. She cleared her throat before she spoke again, whispered words to keep the others from hearing. "Do you trust that man?"

"I don't know." Raul shrugged. "He's done nothing bad so far. If anything, he's the one who should worry about us." He touched her arm. "What's the matter? Is this a wolf thing, like he smells funny or something?"

Her fingers tightened around the mask that she'd been holding most of the evening.

"Don't be stupid. I'm not the wolf right now."

"But you were earlier, you could have smelled something then."

"I did. That's why I followed him. That's why I dealt with him."

"And that was great, thank you." He fished around for something he could say to lighten the mood, to ease the tension between them. "You probably didn't need to rip his throat out, though."

Even as the words came out, he knew he'd chosen wrong. What could have been light teasing in a cosy tavern took on a different tone in the icy dark of this strange forest, their breath fogging the air between them.

"So I should have left him to leap out and murder you all?" Yasmi snapped. "You could at least show some gratitude."

"I said thank you."

"And now you're telling me I shouldn't have done it. Are you feeling small because the actress protected you?"

"I didn't say that!"

"But you're thinking it."

"Stop putting words in my mouth."

"I thought that was what you kept me around for, so you'd know what to say."

"I can find my own words when I…" He stopped, took a deep breath, noticed the way that his fingers had tightened on her arm, the way the mask was rising toward her face. Slowly, he let go, exhaled, drew another steadying breath. "I really do appreciate what you did, and if you thought we might be in danger, then it was better to attack him than give him the chance to ambush us."

Her head sank, chin pressing against her chest. Raul caught the flicker of movement as she turned her gaze toward the people around the fire.

"I'm not sure that is what I thought." Her voice was a

whisper again. "I'm not sure I was thinking at all. I'm so alive when I'm the wolf, it's like a surging force I don't want to resist. I could feel the forest flowing through me, the howling in my ears. It wasn't even a choice. I had to do it." She looked up at him, and her lower lip trembled in the moment before she spoke. "This isn't like wearing the mask in the theatre or to fight the Dunholmi. What's happening to me, Raul?"

Normally, he wouldn't have dared to touch her masks without permission, but he wrapped his hands gently around hers, pried her stiff fingers off the carved and painted wood, then hooked the wolf back onto her belt. It was strange how ordinary it felt. Whatever power the weirdwood prop had, he didn't feel it, just the craftsmanship of the carved fur.

"It doesn't matter what this is, you're strong enough to deal with it," he said. "I believe in you."

She blinked, then laughed, and though the laugh was only half humour, it filled him with relief.

"You're such a farm boy," she said. "Honestly, it's a good thing it's adorable, because otherwise it would be infuriating."

"Thanks, I think."

He grinned as she wrapped her arms around him, and he hugged her back. Resting his chin against the top of her head, the scent of her damp hair mixing with the earthy smell of autumn leaves, everything in the world felt good for a moment. Then he noticed how badly she was shivering.

"We're both cold," he said. "And it's only going to get colder tonight. Do you want to share our blankets for warmth?"

"That's one way to talk a girl into bed," she said, with a slyly mocking tone.

"I didn't mean…My parents are…I just mean because our bodies are warm and…"

"I know. And better you than Prisca; those bony elbows would keep me up all night." She unwrapped herself from his arms, took a step back, and smiled. "You go sort out the bedding. It's my bladder's turn to answer the call of the wild."

Chapter Nine
Pity

Nothing reminded Valens of the value of roads so much as going without them. On roads, even ones full of potholes and rain gullies, he could get up a decent, steady stride. No need to think, just march along to the next skirmish, the next siege, the next poorly laid out army camp sprawling across the fields of some poor village. It meant he could look around, pay attention to his surroundings. Less chance of an ambush or of walking into the back of an officer and ending up digging latrine pits. But in the Withered Hills, he didn't even have the footsteps of other soldiers to march in, just rocks and roots and trails that turned into tangles of thorns. His determination to keep up the pace and be Raul's dutiful warrior ran up against the resistance of the world.

At last, the twisted roots they'd been walking over half the morning gave way to dirt and ankle-high grass. The branches were thinner too, and though the sunlight didn't warm him, it at least softened the cold. He raised his gaze, taking in the plants that grew between tall, scattered trees, clusters of six-foot leaves like green swords stabbing the sky. Black flowers peered slyly between them, things that shouldn't have bloomed anytime, never mind on the brink of midwinter.

Strange place, but he'd seen worse. At least it wasn't on fire.

The local, Lestavo, was up front, annoying Prisca by not answering questions the way she wanted. Raul and Yasmi were behind them, the lad not leading for once. Was it good or bad that things seemed stilted between the younger pair today, between the sidelong smiles and the long glances? He wanted Raul happy, but things could get messy when comrades started tangling limbs, and you didn't want messy on campaign. Besides, he didn't want to think of his son having that sort of life.

As for himself…

He had to admit, it felt good to be out and moving. The hunger that came with rationing food hadn't lasted long as he slipped back into the mould of old habits. The trek was tiring, but satisfying. The weight of a pack on his back and a sword against his hip made him smile, even if it was the wrong hip. This was the work he was made for. Maybe he could be useful again, even if he hadn't been against those war scouts. He scowled and kicked the dirt. Things had been so much easier when he was sitting on his drunken arse all day in the camp.

The others' conversation passed him like birdsong. When you'd got no privacy, you learned not to listen, to leave your comrades something of their own. There was comfort in their chatter, though, the sound of family, if that was still what they were, and if not, then the sound of his warband.

He looked around while he could, hand resting on his sword, stump on his belt. Between those striking leaves and the strange flowers, something was coming toward them. Flashes of striped, yellow fur, a glimpse of a glittering eye.

Not something—some *things*. The one that had caught his eye and at least two more ahead, given away by the swaying leaves. He looked over his shoulder, saw two more prowl onto the trail from behind, just like he would have done.

"Ambush," he growled, drawing his sword.

The others turned to look at him. He pointed back, then into the undergrowth, and ahead to where more were emerging in front of Prisca and Lestavo. Seven at least, cats as big as hunting hounds, with broad faces and long canine teeth, their fur streaked in yellows and browns. They sniffed the air and one of them made a low rattling sound as they closed in.

The worst thing you could do when surrounded was stay still. That way, you ended up with no space to manoeuvre, or even to swing a blade. Let the enemy tighten the noose and you'd swing.

Ignoring Lestavo's frantic clicking noises, Valens pivoted and lunged at the cats to the rear. No battle cry to give them warning. A swift, sudden attack for advantage.

It wasn't his old familiar sword, but Drusil was a good smith. The blade hit the first cat as it twisted away, steel slicing through fur and flesh, then cracking bone. The creature's voice was a stuttering shriek as it stumbled, bleeding, into the undergrowth.

The other one tensed, body low, legs drawn in, ready to pounce. Valens's backswing wasn't elegant and it wasn't accurate, but it didn't need to be. It forced the creature back, that coiled power unravelling as it tried to avoid a gutting. It bared its teeth and made a sound like slingshot rattling off shields, and a curve of dark fur on its forehead drew in.

"Good kitty." Valens bared his own teeth. "Come closer, I'll give you a proper petting."

This felt good. This felt right. This was who he should be. No complex schemes, no hidden villages, no serving ale to farmers from the country's arse crack. A man, his comrades, and their swords. Blood and fury.

People were shouting, like people always did. Plenty of growls too, and a grey shape diving off the trail as Yasmi turned wolf. An arrow hissed past and plunged into one of the creatures with a thwack. The beast kept running, but it wouldn't get far with blood spraying from its hip.

The cat facing Valens backed away and he stomped toward it. Something flashed in the creature's bright white eyes—fear, anger, or desperation—then it flung itself at him.

This wasn't how beasts were meant to act, and it threw Valens off. His sword came up, a deep slash across the cat's chest, but he couldn't stop the weight of it slamming into him. He staggered, tripped on a root, landed with a bellow of pain as his back bent over his pack. Rolling half over, he raised his bloody sword between him and the cat. Instead of advancing, the creature dragged itself to its feet and crawled off the trail, leaving a sticky crimson streak across the greenery.

Valens looked around. The fighting was done. Raul stood with his sword in a strong defence, blood oozing down the blade and dripping from the cross guard. Prisca had her bow out, arrow nocked but not drawn, turning slowly as she surveyed the forest. Yasmi padded out of the trees, long tongue lapping across her muzzle. They'd fought and they'd won, even him with his ageing body and his missing hand. He picked up a thick leaf from the ground near his knee and wiped the blood from his sword, feeling like a warrior again for the first time in too long.

The bodies of impossibly large cats lay dead and dying, but not as many as he'd expected from the sounds of the fight. In the middle of it all stood Lestavo, one hand pressed to his brow, slowly shaking his head.

The heavyset man looked at Valens.

"Why'd you do that?" he asked quietly.

"To protect us." Valens glared back at him.

"We were safer before."

"Horse shit." Valens steadied himself using his stump and pushed himself up to his feet. The stump hurt when he used it like that, the wound not old enough to really deaden, and it wasn't as steady as using his hand, but he didn't want to let go of his sword. More of those cats might still be out there. "It was an ambush."

"Oh, was it so?" Lestavo snorted. "Yon creatures are touched by Jarrag. Did you not see the mark?"

He pressed a thick finger against his forehead, forming a curved V. Valens remembered the dark shape he'd seen on the face of the cat, realised that they'd all had them, wondered if he should have known it meant something. But fur was fur, animals had shapes like that.

"They were surrounding us." He tore leaves from the

nearest plant and wiped the blood from his sword as he stepped closer to Lestavo.

"They were sniffing, looking, listening, seeing us for *him*." Lestavo moved too, stepping up to Valens as their voices rose. He might be two heads shorter, but he wasn't backing down. Valens would just have to make him. "Jarrag sees everywhere in the hills, but the claws let him look up close and see your soul."

The memory of those white eyes staring at him made Valens shiver. He could believe that the creature had been staring through his skin, but an ambush was an ambush. Besides, what was the god going to do, stop answering prayers he'd never made?

"I'm a warrior. I did what was needed. If I didn't, we'd all end up dead."

A snort from Prisca whipped Valens's head around.

"Don't you start," he said, pointing his sword at her. "You might think I'm only good for fighting, but you brought me into your schemes for that."

"You *were* good at fighting. Now…" She shrugged. "Did you see many cripples in your old fighting lines, Valens?"

"I'm not a cripple." He said it as a weapon to fight back, not because it felt true.

"Really? Then please, provide me with a better word for a man who can't serve his own food without help."

"Prisca." A steel edge lay beneath the quiet of Raul's voice. "I told you before we left…"

"Yes, yes, don't upset the old man." Prisca put on her least convincing smile. "I'm so frightfully sorry."

"I'm not old," Valens snarled, heat rising through him, fingers tightening around the sword's hilt. "And I'm not crippled, or any word you find for it. Otherwise, why have you brought me along to protect you all?"

He pointed at Raul, the best proof in the world of his own worth.

"To protect us?" Prisca's laugh was colder than the winter wind that blew down the trail, snatching up the scent of freshly spilled blood. "Sure, that's why you're here."

"By Yorl's eye, it is!" The thunder of Valens's voice scattered the birds from the trees. The sword in his hand quivered as he stopped himself halfway to Prisca.

"Da." Raul stepped between them, laying a cautious hand on Valens's chest. Behind him, Yasmi crouched where she'd just transformed, holding her mask an inch from her face. "It's all right. No need to fight."

"Tell her," Valens growled, pointing past him at Prisca. "Tell her why I'm here."

He felt so childish, like the father-son roles of a decade before had been reversed, but he couldn't help himself. He needed other people to know that he was still a real warrior, because then he might believe it himself.

Raul turned to face Prisca, but there was a moment of hesitation in the movement, and in a terrible instant of realisation, all of Valens's pride fell through that gap.

"You didn't need me, did you?" he muttered. "You think *I* need *this*."

"Da, I..." Raul turned back, his voice flat, eyes dull.

"I'm here out of pity."

Valens's shoulders slumped. His sword hung limp by his side. Unable to look Raul in the eye, he stared at the ground.

"That's not it," Raul said, but the boy had never been a good liar; Valens had just wanted to believe. "You're here to keep us safe."

"By starting pointless fights?" Valens turned away, nearly tripping over a dead beast as he went. "I'll be back."

He stomped along the deer trail that passed for a path, those stupid roots pressing into the bottoms of his feet and threatening to turn his ankle. That should have been a sign, when he couldn't even walk straight without looking up. No point blaming the world around him when he was useless enough on his own.

He clenched his hand around his sword handle so hard his knuckles went white. An urge to slash out with it, to hack down leaves just to see something fall, rose through him. But that was childish behaviour, petty, pointless at best. At worst, a way to damage a good sword. He pressed the feeling down like he was swallowing bile, the bitterness leaving a trail through his chest. Branches shook overhead as the wind rose around him, grey clouds rolling out of the north with the promise of a storm.

He should go back before those clouds reached them, but he couldn't bear to see the others yet. Couldn't face Prisca's condescension or Raul's disappointment. He stared at a spot where roots grew over the blackened tree stumps from an old burn, trying to master his thoughts and his breath.

Then he heard the voice, almost lost in the wind at first but emerging more clearly with each word.

"What the fuck are you playing at?"

Valens spun on the spot, looking for any sign of her. But there were only the trees and, down the trail, glimpses of the comrades he'd abandoned. Of course she wasn't here. She'd been dead for nearly twenty years.

Still, it sounded so real…

"Fabia?" he asked quietly. "That you?"

Memories came flooding back. The two of them sparring for hours when they first took military indenture, battering each other black and blue so that they could beat the rest. Celebrating around a campfire after the Battle of Pennington's Rest, singing and drinking and shouting nonsense while the sun sank and came up again. At night on the walls in Pavuno, her face falling as the first breach crashed down. That last moment in the streets, leaving her to die because something mattered more than them.

Or so he'd believed.

"What, are your ears as shitty as your spearfighting now? Of course it's me."

The voice, the words, the memories, all of it fitted: either he was hearing her or his mind was as fucked as his body.

He didn't know how she could reach him, but he knew Fabia, even now. If she'd pushed her way back up the river of death, then she must have done it for a reason.

"Why are you here?" he asked.

"This place you're in," she said. "This ugly forest full of weird trees. It's powerful. That's why you can hear me, after all these years."

"All these years?" He frowned. "Have you been with me all along?"

"Let's not piss around with that now. There'll be time later."

She had. All these years, he must have carried her ghost, and he'd never known. Had she been trying to talk and he hadn't listened?

"Sorry I lost your mourning ring," he said. When he closed his eyes, he saw his own hand lying in a pool of blood, the jet ring black around a pale finger. The last time he'd seen it. The last time he'd been his whole self. Anger curled like a fist in his stomach. "That fucker of a count, he was better than I thought."

"Yeah, yeah, yeah, you lost your hand. I lost my whole body, remember?"

In spite of the pain and grief, Valens laughed. Maybe because of it. This was what his family and Efron's actors didn't understand. You couldn't make the pain and loss go away by treating it with respect. You laughed and spat in death's face or you sank into the mud like a thousand other lost warriors before you.

"That's better," Fabia said. "Less self-pity, more action. I need your help with something, yours and Jarrag's."

"The hill god?" If she'd been there to see, Valens would have stared at her in confusion. "What can I do with him?"

"Bring me back from the dead."

———————————•———————————

Count Alder galloped up the valley, the thunder of hooves all around. He let his cloak flap out behind him to add to the drama of the ride—better to intimidate these people into submission if he could, and if they stood their ground, he'd ditch the cloak before the real fighting began. His chosen guard galloped along behind, while Captain Brook led riders from the local garrison up the far bank of the river. The infantry levy weren't far back along the narrow, hidden valley, and though he hoped he wouldn't need them, he wasn't going to assume that the day was already won. Even ignorant Estian peasants could put up a fight. That was why all of this was necessary.

The gap between the woods and the river widened, allowing a few of his chosen to catch up and ride beside him. On the far bank, Brook waved her spear, its blue pennant flapping, and pointed to something ahead. Alder rounded a bend and saw it: the unmistakable shapes of houses, small and crudely constructed from local timber, little better than barns.

This was it.

He raised his own spear and the rider next to him blew a horn. A string of notes rang up the valley, powerful and aggressive, the bellow of destruction about to descend. The chosen roared a battle cry. Alder braced the spear under his arm and set his heels to Fellstride's flanks, calling forth a final burst of speed.

He'd expected to see panic, a rush of desperate little people grabbing cheap weapons or running for their lives. He would run them down, trample bodies beneath his hooves, strike the fear of Dunholm into these rebels, fiercely question the trembling survivors for details on their leader. But as he charged into the town, the only movement was a herd of pigs trotting hurriedly into the forest and a flock of birds wheeling into the air. The charge slowed to an uncertain canter as no one emerged to challenge them.

If this was the rebel camp then where were all the rebels?

In an open area in the middle of the settlement, Alder slowed Fellstride to a gentle trot and circled, looking for signs of what had happened. His troops, well trained in his moods and methods, spread through the houses and trees, some of them riding, others dismounting to take doors. Nobody split into groups of less than three. They were competent and confident, but he'd made sure never to foster a level of self-regard that might turn into complacency. Leading a soldier was like training a horse—you didn't want to let any instinct become too exaggerated.

Amid the banging of doors and the scuffling of feet, Alder examined the ground around him. This place looked like some sort of square, an open expanse in the middle of the rebel camp. The grass was trampled, indicating heavy use, and worn away in patches. Were those blocks of bare ground where rebels had stood on parade? No, the spacing wasn't right. Benches around tables, perhaps, and the feet under them. The ashes in the middle were from a cooking fire, and a few bits of wood protruding around the edges might have been pegs broken while packing up fast. An important shelter and meeting place that had been taken down.

The rebels weren't just hiding. They had moved on.

Straightening in the saddle, he rolled his shoulders beneath his chainmail and looked around, hiding his frustration. He'd seen the original Countess Alder, his grandmother, scold her heir for showing a temper in front of his troops, and his father's inability to master those suppressed moods had caused half his trouble at court. Brennett Alder wasn't going to fall into that trap. Besides, he'd just sharpened his sword; he didn't want to blunt it hacking up trees in a temper tantrum.

"My lord." Captain Brook hurriedly strode around one of those rickety houses, sword in hand. "We found a few."

Behind her came two soldiers in the livery of the Pavuno companies, warriors provided by powerful local merchants to prove their loyalty. Between them they dragged a woman in a rough woollen robe with muddy boots under her long skirts. She looked pale beneath her red hair, and flinched as one of the soldiers leaned in close.

"There are four of them," Brook continued. "One with a broken leg, two sick with fever, and her."

Alder swung his leg over the saddle and dropped to his feet. Fellstride pawed briefly at the ground, then stood silent, motionless except for the rise and fall of his sleek flanks.

"It's a charming village you have up here," Alder said, smiling at the captive. "But it seems a little large for four."

"It's the harvest." The woman forced her gaze up to meet his. She was trying not to shiver, in spite of the cold and the weapons pointed at her, but her stiffness accentuated the trembling movements that remained. "It wasn't good, so most people left."

"The harvest." Alder nodded. "I see. But these woods look rich with life, plenty of game to hunt, and you could gather nuts or berries or whatever it is that woodland folk do." He raised an eyebrow in Brook's direction. "Is mushroom picking a thing?"

The captain shrugged. "I grew up on fish and river weed, my lord."

"I may not know these woods, but I do know when I'm being lied to." Taking a silver officer's knife, he sliced open the pouches on the captive's belt with a brief flick, then watched what fell into the mud. "Herbs, bandages, small bottles—that makes you a physician, or what passes for one out here." He nudged at a clay figurine with his toe. "Or some sort of practitioner of magic, but that would be illegal. You weren't breaking the law, were you?"

"A physician. Exactly." The woman's voice rose, sharpened by fear as she stared at the silver blade. She'd probably never seen anything cut so easily before, and now its edge gleamed at her in the cold winter sun. "The figure is just a charm, for luck."

"Your people aren't meant to work magic." Alder's boot slammed down, shattering the figure, and his voice became a growl. "You look to me like a diviner, and that figure is part of your craft. Were you trying to connect to the essence of your patients and make them better, or to someone else so you could curse them?"

The woman took a deep breath and closed her eyes.

"If you're going to kill me, get it over with."

How very noble, but not bait that Alder would take.

"I'm not going to kill you. At least not here, not now. Them, on the other hand…"

The remaining captives were being brought out, carried on improvised stretchers of branches and blankets. Two trembled and twitched. The third had a splint bound to his lower leg, and a yellow-green stain on the bandage said it wasn't healing well.

"This is a rebel camp, and I should string you all up with your guts dangling. But I don't want to hurt this land any more than I need to, and physicians are in short supply, so I'll execute the others and leave you to watch."

"Please, no, my lord," the physician said, her eyes wide again, hands clutched together. "Take me instead."

"Three lives for one? Why would I agree to a trade like that?"

"I'll tell you the truth."

"Go on."

She looked down. Who could blame her? She must feel a kinship with the dirt right now.

"The others left days ago, spread out to other places. Waiting for the winter to pass and our leader to return. These three were too sick to move, so I stayed with them."

"Where did the others go?"

"I don't know."

"Brook, fetch some rope."

"Please, no, I swear, I don't know where they've all gone! No one told me because I didn't need to know."

"Then these three don't need to live."

In Brook's fingers, the end of a lasso had already become a noose. She looked up, eyeing the branches swaying over their heads.

"That one looks sturdy," Alder said, pointing.

"Please, my lord!" The physician sank to her knees. "These people don't deserve to die."

"Then make better choices." He glared at her. "It's not something your people are good at, but if you won't bend to kind words, then you will bend to the whip."

"I know where our leaders have gone."

"Where?" Alder raised a hand, halting Brook as she slid the noose around a fever patient's neck.

"North, into the Withered Hills." The physician pointed up the valley.

"Who went that way?"

"Raul, who leads us. Yasmi, who aids him. His parents too."

"The old warrior and the grey-haired diviner?"

The physician nodded. Alder smiled. This was perfect. Take out those four and the rebellion would fall.

But it made no sense.

"There's nothing of value up there, no towns or villages to rally around them, not even a taxation post to attack at this time of year. The most they'll find is a logging camp, and even those are quiet in the winter. Why did they go that way?"

"I don't know, my lord."

"Two more ropes, please," Alder called out. "Let's get them all done at once."

"By Yorl's blind eye, I swear I have no idea! Please, don't kill them."

"Why would I listen to someone who's useless as well as a rebel?"

The physician sank to her knees, hands clasped in supplication—to Alder himself or one of the local gods? It didn't matter, no one here would be listening to her prayers.

It didn't matter much either why the rebels had headed

for the Withered Hills. This was a chance for him to catch up with the ringleaders and rein this rebellion in before it reached a gallop. Catch them in the wild, away from their supporters, and deal the death blow where no one would see. No heroes, no martyrs, no grand stories to stir people up. The whole embarrassing business swept away at last.

Alder hadn't been this far north before, but he'd been assiduous in his study of the territory he governed. Some nobles treated governorships as an inconvenience, a duty they sent a subordinate to fulfil while they spent their days cosying up to King Lorrin. But while the king's whims could make someone powerful, they could destroy them too, whereas good governorship, truly controlling this land, could give Alder a secure power base, one from which his uncle couldn't afford to dislodge him. So he'd taken the time to study the terrain and its people, carefully examining maps and travellers' guides from among the books he'd confiscated. On open ground, he could have relied on speed of horse to catch up with the rebels, but the route up the valley had been difficult enough this far; it would become impassable to riders over the rocky ridges between here and the Withered Hills. The route around to Fort Sawblade and the logging camps was longer but far easier, especially with the roads he built for the timber wagons. If they set off now, they could be at the fort by dusk tomorrow, but not if they dragged along the local troops and the infantry levy.

"Brook, gather the chosen to ride out," Alder said, sliding the dagger back into its sheath. "The rest of you, start tearing these hovels down. You're going to be building yourselves a nice warm fire tonight."

"And the prisoners?" Brook gestured with her rope.

"Down to the cells in Pavuno, I think. No point in throwing them away when we can squeeze them for knowledge." He swung into the saddle and Fellstride shook his head, tossing his mane about. Alder patted his neck. "That's right, my friend. It's time for some real riding."

Chapter Ten
Rain Like Tears

"What do you mean, you don't know the way?"

Prisca's voice was a blade slashing at Raul's nerves. Even directed at someone else, that sharp snap of anger left him raw with pain, shoulders rising as he flinched. It was no way for a hero and leader to be, but he couldn't help himself.

Lestavo, on the other hand, seemed indifferent to Prisca's fury. He shrugged and scratched his stubbly chin, looking up at her like she was one more interesting tree to point out.

"What do you want me to mean?" he asked.

"That is a singularly useless question."

"Maybe to you, but I don't hear owt wrong with it."

Prisca's lips squeezed together so tight that they seemed to disappear. Fury radiated from her across the clearing, even more icy than the wind snatching their words away. She and Lestavo stood staring at each other, caught in an intellectual impasse.

If they were going to find a route, then someone else needed to step in.

"I think what Prisca's trying to say—" Raul began.

"I don't need anyone to speak for me."

"Fine." He heard his voice hardening and fought back the urge to argue. "What I want to say to Lestavo is that he lives around here, so we thought he'd be able to show us the way through the woods."

He gestured around the clearing, taking in the trees, the undergrowth, and the lack of any clear path except the one they'd come in by. There were gaps in the undergrowth, ferns and brambles and stranger plants trampled by animals passing through, but nothing wide enough to show humans passing, and absolutely no sign of which way would be best. Yasmi was in her wolf form, sniffing around the edges of those trails, but improved senses couldn't do much if you didn't know what you were looking for. And while Valens was standing by one of the trails, one hand rubbing back and forth across the scars and stubble on his head, he had the distracted look he'd worn for a day or two.

"I don't know the way," Lestavo said. "Never do."

"But you said that you travel all through the hills, that no one's seen more of them than you."

"Aye, I've seen the oldest, gnarledest trees and the tiniest seedlings, the rock shaped like a dragon and the one like nowt you've ever imagined. Been to this side and that, round and round, back and forth."

"Then how do you not know the way?"

"Withered Hills is always changing. The trail you find one day will be nowt but trees the next."

"That's…" Impossible? Not if this place really was

connected to the essence of the unknowable wild. But was it something people could live with? "How do you find your way home?"

"Home's where I make my shelter. This ain't town land, remember?"

Raul sighed. If anyone really could live like that, never settling down in one place, it was Lestavo. The spot he'd found for them to camp the previous night was the most shelter they'd had since they set out, a cosy nook under interwoven branches that kept off the night's rain. Maybe the little man just drifted from one place to the next, seeing what was new. But that was no help to Raul.

And then, as if the world had heard his thoughts about shelter, a fat drop of rain dashed itself against his cheek.

"I'll work out the way," he said. "By reading the signs."

"You will?" Prisca raised an eyebrow.

"You think I can't?"

More rain pattered down, a slow rhythm of isolated drops that left dark streaks down their tunics. Prisca clenched her jaw and Raul braced himself for one more fight, but then her expression softened.

"Will you let me help?" she asked. "I can teach you more about what to look for."

Raul hesitated, then nodded. After all, wasn't this what she was there for?

He set his pack down under a tree, out of the growing rain, pulled off his gloves, and rummaged around until he found a small wooden bowl with animals entwined along the sides. One of the older rebels had carved it for him, a gift to thank him after he'd saved her husband from being lashed by the Dunholmi. A small thing, but handmade and heartfelt.

"This represents us, the rebellion, and our quest," he explained, holding it out for Prisca to see. "And the animals around the outside represent the wild. I think those connections will make it useful."

"Could be," Prisca acknowledged. He would have to drag any real agreement from the ground of her stubbornness.

"Leaves from the wild." He took some off a bush, their bitter scent mixing with the fresh smell of rain on the forest, and shredded them into the bowl. "Water as a medium, because it's what I have." He poured from his waterskin. "And something from me, and my connection to Balbianus, whose shrine we're looking for."

He bit the inside of his lip just hard enough to get the taste of blood, swilled it around the inside of his mouth, and spat into the bowl. With two fingers, he stirred the mix, fragments of leaf swirling in the water, then tipped it out at the base of the tree. Rushed and improvised as it was, the whole thing felt right, and he smiled as he saw the clusters of green sticking to the inside of the bowl, leftover signs of what had gone. Prisca leaned in for a closer look, seeking signs in what he'd done.

"That one looks like a hedgehog," Raul said, pointing to one of the shapes. "And there's a boat, maybe, or a fish." He looked around, hoping for a rustling as a spiked shape emerged from the undergrowth, or maybe the bank of a stream he'd missed before. "But what does it mean?"

"It means that you've let your thinking get warped." Prisca tapped a finger against the bowl. "This won't help at all.

You're making shapes you want to see, instead of reading the signs that are in it."

"But I've seen you do things like this before, with the bowl and the knife and the milk and…"

Raul choked on his own words as they caught in his throat, unable to express the frustration he was feeling.

"You've been spending too much time with Drusil." Prisca took the bowl from him, shook out what was left, then placed it on the ground in the rain. "Her smithing is very clever, and it has its uses, but it's all about forcing the essence of the world to your will. Divination works the other way, letting the world show itself to you. It takes subtlety and patience, qualities you seem to have lost."

Raul had thought he was past caring what Prisca said, but those words hit like a punch. He'd thought he was making progress with his divination. He'd even thought, as they spent time together, Prisca might come to appreciate that. But apparently he'd failed.

"We'll give the bowl five minutes in the rain, then see what we can read in the water," Prisca continued. "I really don't think that bowl is suitable for our purposes, but we will make do with what we have. I used to use a…" She frowned and folded her arms, clenching fingers tight around her upper arm. "You don't need to know that. Focus on the bowl."

Now she didn't even trust him to absorb the lessons she was teaching. Raul sank to the ground with his back against a pine tree, wrapped his cloak around himself, and huddled down hidden from his mother's gaze.

The downpour was growing heavier, hammering at the

leaves, a trickle of water breaking through the needle-furred branches above and pouring into the ground a hand's breadth from Raul's toes. Across the clearing, Valens and Yasmi had also taken shelter, the wolf curled up two trees over from the big warrior. Lestavo, in contrast, stood in the rain, head tipped back and mouth open wide, tongue out to taste the falling drops.

"Nowt like the flavour of rain off a northern storm, so?" he called out.

Raul hated that he couldn't even join in with the man's smiles and laughter, but he felt squeezed by a hard fist, his soul buckling, and it was hard to find joy in that moment. He stared at the bowl. He'd failed.

No.

No, he hadn't failed. Prisca hadn't even given him the time or opportunity to work it out.

"You didn't have to do that." He forced the words out.

"What?" Prisca looked around, frowning again.

"I said you didn't have to do that, just throwing away the signs I found. We could have tried to work them out."

"A waste of both our time."

"You don't know that!" He was on his feet, cloak falling back as he waved his arms around. "You didn't try—not to read the signs and not to help me. How am I meant to learn anything if you're too busy proving how much better you are?"

The tree he'd been leaning against shook and more water fell around them, bringing loose pine needles and broken twigs.

"I taught you what you know," Prisca said, her voice growing quieter as Raul's rose. It wasn't a soft quiet, but a steely one, the silence of a bared blade. "And I am going to teach you more, once you show that you're ready to learn."

"That I'm ready to learn? When are you going to be ready to teach?"

He wasn't sure it even made sense, but it felt like it did, like everything she said was wrong so he had to push the opposite way. There was a squealing and rustling as small creatures pounced on each other in the undergrowth. From deeper into the wilds, something growled.

"What do you think this is, you ignorant child?" Prisca pointed at the bowl. "I'm trying to teach you, to make you into a better…a better…" She stood frozen for a moment, then her arm swung around and she pointed at him. "You have years of my teaching to work with, all the time and effort I've channelled into your education. The least you could do is show some respect."

"Respect, for the woman who lied to me my whole life?" Raul snorted. "Sure, I'll do that. Let's see what I can learn."

He strode out into the clearing, indifferent to the rain hammering down on his head and the others watching him. He picked up the bowl and stared at the water collecting in it, the last fragments of leaf floating around inside, the way the surface shifted as raindrops hit. He stared at the shapes forming there and barked out a bitter laugh.

"You know what I see?" he shouted. "A hedgehog. A hedgehog and a fish." He whirled around, water slopping over the sides of the bowl. "I was right."

"Stubborn is not the same as right." Prisca snatched the bowl and looked at the water. "I don't see any hedgehog, or fish, or anything that matches what you said. What I see is the impossibility of reading anything from the world when you don't even have the patience to wait for a bowl to fill."

He opened his mouth to answer back but the words didn't come out. What if she was right? He hadn't waited, and now she would have to start her work again. What sort of a sign was a hedgehog anyway? It was a ridiculous animal to read anything into, and he felt stupid for saying it.

But that stupidity was no match for his anger. He wasn't going to keep listening to her if she wouldn't listen to him. If the only way he could become a proper diviner was by thinking like Prisca, then maybe he shouldn't be a diviner at all. And if learning to channel essence like Drusil wouldn't work right, then . . . there had to be other ways he could save Estis.

The rain was a torrent soaking through his cloak, through his hose, through his boots. It turned the clearing into a quagmire, tufts of grass standing stranded amid a rising tide of mud. It shouldn't have been possible for the ground to soften so fast, but already it was sucking at his feet. Raul lifted one foot, then the other, and pushed his sodden hair back from his face. He wasn't going to let himself sink.

"If you don't think I'm good enough to work with the signs, then I'll stick with the role you wrote for me," he said. "The warrior hero. Maybe I'll cut my way through the forest until I find the temple. It's got to be better than waiting around, right?"

He turned. The others were watching: Lestavo still standing in the rain, Yasmi in human form next to Valens. Unable to bear the concern in their faces, he turned again and pointed north, to where a jagged pair of rocky hills rose above the rest.

"That way," he announced.

"Raul, don't be an idiot," Prisca snapped. "Come back here."

"No."

"I apologise if I was less than sensitive." Her tone sounded like anything but an apology. "However, there are larger issues at stake here than your hurt feelings. If we're going to take the opportunity that has arisen, then we need to keep our faculties about us, and we need to think it through every step of the way."

"No. We're going that way." He looked around. He'd left his pack under the tree. He'd have to go back and fetch it, but he didn't want it to look like he was coming back to her. Instead, he called across the clearing. "Yasmi, can you please get my pack for me?"

Yasmi and Valens exchanged a look, then she dashed for the pack, while Valens stepped more slowly out of the shelter of the trees.

"Don't be ridiculous, Raul," Prisca said. "You can't just pick a direction and walk in it."

"Why not? It's what Lestavo does, and he knows this country better than any of us."

"Is so," the little man said, bobbing his head. "Nowt wrong with following where the wind takes you."

"This is not about the wind!" Prisca yelled, her temper finally edging out her fake calm. "This is about the fate of *nations*, and I need you to listen to me while there's still... while I can manage to..."

Prisca pressed a hand to her brow like she was trying to squeeze the words out of her head.

"What?" Raul growled. "While you can still control me?"

Valens stepped between them, hands raised to either side like he was holding fighters apart in the street.

"You're both tired," he said. "Cold. Hungry. Saying shit you don't mean. We'll find somewhere to rest, sort this out tomorrow."

Raul sagged. His da was probably right. And while he couldn't bring himself to offer anything like an apology now, maybe he'd be able to say sorry later, and even to listen. Shelter, food, a warm fire, that all sounded like a good idea, and with Lestavo's help they could surely find it.

"No," Prisca said. "No rest. No waiting. Raul, you need to listen to me now."

He wrapped his right upper arm in his hand, where his fake birthmark lay hidden under his sleeve. "Like you decided what I needed all those years ago?"

"You need to learn from me now, because I won't be able to teach you much longer."

"Prisca," Valens said, his voice more sad than angry, "not now."

"Yes, now. Raul, my mind is going. That's the price of divination. Slowly, over time, the power wears away canyons in your consciousness. For some diviners, strange smells appear, or their sense of taste fades. Sight or hearing can be blunted. Tempers shorten."

"You're using magic as an excuse." Raul clung to his anger, because it was easier than facing the chasm that opened up at her words, the gap she was carving through his life.

"Then your concentration goes," Prisca continued as if he

hadn't spoken, "so that it's harder to stick with a task. Everything becomes a strain, even forming sentences, because you lose words. Imagine how that must feel, Raul, to build a life around the workings of the mind and then to have it unravel.

"I've held it off as long as I could, but now I'm running out of time. Another year, maybe two, and it won't just be words. I'll forget my craft, then who I am. I'll be undone. Everything I've learned, everything I've built my life around, the future I had planned for our people, all of it depends upon passing this on to someone else.

"I need to teach you now, because it's my last chance."

She fell silent, arms hanging limp by her sides. The rain ran down her face like tears and plastered her clothes to her body, accentuating her scarecrow frame. Still, she stood proud, eyes locked with Raul's, begging him to understand.

His throat thick with emotions, Raul strode across the muddy clearing and wrapped his arms around his mother. He held her tight while the rain washed over him and the grief washed through him, clinging to this woman who had raised him, exposed now in her fragility.

Then, before she could respond, he let her go and stepped back.

"You just told me that divination is destroying you, and so you've got to teach it to me?" He shook his head, anger sinking into resignation. "That may be the most selfish thing I've ever heard."

Chapter Eleven
Crossroads

The first difference Yasmi noticed about the new area they walked in was a scattering of scarlet berries in the undergrowth. Even she knew that it was the wrong time of year for raspberries, but there they were, plump and ripe as if it were the height of summer. As she walked closer, she realised that the air around them was warmer, heated by a steaming spring and sheltered by lines of strangely flat fir trees. Her hand slid toward her masks—the wolf's keen senses would understand this place so much better—but words should probably come first.

"Did someone plant these?" she asked.

Lestavo looked up from the figure he'd been making from sticks and grass as they walked. He looked at the berries she'd singled out and nodded eagerly.

"That's so, aye."

"They're part of a farm?"

"Nowt like that out here." He broke a thorned twig off one of the bushes and started weaving it into his doll.

"But the people who live nearby grow them?"

Lestavo chuckled.

"No one lives in one place. You move or you die."

"So why plant them?"

Lestavo tilted his head on one side and scratched his chin. "Why's anyone plant anything? To eat."

"But if no one lives here..."

Lestavo put his doll away and started plucking berries, his movements nimble despite the thickness of his fingers in their rough hide gloves. He passed a handful of berries to her and headed for the next patch, never clearing a whole plant, always leaving some and moving on.

"You're thinking like town folk," he said, dropping a few frost-chewed berries in the dirt. "Out here, we plant one place, eat at another. Seeds I dropped might feed me, might feed someone else, so?"

Despite her misgivings about their growth, Yasmi's belly gurgled at the sight. Long days of walking and low rations were reshaping her in ways she didn't like. She popped one of the berries into her mouth and the flavour was so intense, a sharp and delicious sweetness, that it made her jaw ache. She followed it with another and another, forcing herself to eat carefully, to draw out a pleasure that was all too rare in the Withered Hills. The words to "The Scarlet Sailor" sprang to mind, and she hummed the cheerful tune as she ate.

> *There once was a sailor sailed a scarlet sea,*
> *To treasure 'cross oceans so vast,*
> *But her boy was tender as landlubbers be,*

Too timid to run up the mast.
Then came a Saditchi vice-commodore,
His hands worn from winding his rope,
Who said to the sailor he'd show her fresh shores,
If she cared to ride on his boat . . .

The crackle of breaking undergrowth announced the others' approach, and she turned with a handful of berries, offering the brightest smile she could.

"Look what we found!"

Neither Valens nor Prisca looked up, each caught in their own misery. She wouldn't have minded so much—each had brought this on themselves—but their misery had spread to Raul, who had walked with the same slumped posture all morning. It hurt to see him like this, her bright farm boy brought down by the people who should have lifted him up. How could he even grieve for Prisca's sickness when she kept picking fights with him? At least he looked up now and smiled as he met Yasmi's eye.

"I didn't know these grew here," he said, taking one of the berries and popping it into his mouth. His smile widened. "Wow!"

"Looks like there's folk nearby," Lestavo said, peering at some bushes on the far side of the patch. "You want to see them?"

His tone told Yasmi that he wanted to, and she wasn't sure they could say no without losing the closest thing they had to a guide. Besides, she could do with some more cheerful company. Maybe it would even help with Raul's mood.

"Yes, please," Yasmi said. "Especially if they can help us work out which way to go."

With Lestavo in the lead, they walked more purposefully than they had before. He led them along something like an animal trail out the far side of the berry patch. Beyond that was a region of tall grass, each stalk an arm's reach higher than Valens, with thick fluffy seed heads running down their full length. It was like walking through clouds. Yasmi laughed as the pods tickled her face, and she followed Lestavo's lead in tugging off a handful of that fine fluff. It was soft against her palm, with none of the seeds she'd expected to find. But then, what sort of plant put out seeds on the edge of midwinter?

Lestavo frowned as he rolled the stuff back and forth between his fingers. His sudden hunched, defensive stance made her wary.

"What's the matter?" she asked quietly, her hand settling on her wolf mask, the grass strands abandoned.

"Not a good sign when grass goes bad," he said, clutching his wooden hare charm as he picked up speed. "Best we get out fast."

Yasmi fought back a laugh. How bad could grass be? But Lestavo knew this place, even if he didn't know the route they needed through it, and years on the road had taught her to listen to the advice of local people. If you were performing in a new town every day, you didn't have time to learn which taverns served the best wine, or which bakers mixed chalk with their flour.

Something brushed across her boot. She looked down, muscles tensed, half expecting to see a snake, but there were just roots running between the strands of grass. Several of them were tightening around her ankle, and her throat went dry as she stared at the sight.

She wrenched her foot free and half ran after Lestavo. Some of the grass swayed toward her, and she didn't know whether it was the wind, but she whipped a long knife out of her belt and slashed the stalks down, grateful to Drusil for teaching her to keep the blade sharp.

"The plants!" she shouted. "They're moving!"

Footsteps sped up behind her. Prisca hissed and snapped an angry curse.

A thick green tendril whipped across the path, straight toward Yasmi's face. She caught it, a stinging slap against her palm, and pulled out a knife even as it wrapped around her wrist and pulled. Before the plant could drag her off balance, she slashed out and the tensed cord gave way, spattering her with sap.

"Keep moving!" Lestavo shouted. "Almost out!"

Yasmi looked back. Raul and Valens had slowed down to fight the flailing vines, but for every one they cut down three more slid from the undergrowth, reaching for them from every direction like withered fingers.

"Listen to the man!" Yasmi snapped. "You can't fight the whole forest."

Her hand was at her belt, but she knew there was nothing there that could help. Plenty of forms that would let her run faster, keeping herself safe, but none that could mow down the menace closing in on them.

Pale, seedless strands burst from the grass, forming a cloud around Raul and Valens. Then there was a flash.

"Run!" Yasmi screamed.

Wrenching themselves free from the tangling plants, the two men raced toward her. Fire flashed through the pale cloud, fast catching up on them. There was sizzling and a charred smell. Raul shoved Valens ahead of him, and the fact that he could move the veteran at all spoke to how much Raul had grown, and how much Valens had faded. Their swords lashed out as they passed, fending off clawing plants, rushing to stay ahead of the fire rolling through the air. All four ran together, following Lestavo's voice, until they burst from the trees into a blackened stretch of open ground. Behind them, the fire reached the edge of the cloud and blazed out. In the moment before it vanished, Yasmi could have sworn she saw a face grinning from the flames.

Standing in a mud made of ashes, they stopped to catch their breath.

"Too short to reach us?" Yasmi asked, watching creepers twitch in the tree line.

"They don't like this." Lestavo stamped a foot in the black ooze, then flicked three fingers at the creepers and laughed. "Ate it up already. We're safe now."

"You are, Lestavo," a voice said. "What about yon town folk, though?"

Yasmi turned, reaching for the wolf. Across the ashen ground stood a dozen people all pointing bows at her. Some of them were dressed in animal hides dyed in shades of yellow and green, some in pale clothes that seemed to have been made from panels of giant leaves. All had fur or straw showing at their necks and cuffs, signs of warmer layers beneath, and several had protective charms around their necks. The heads of their arrows were black, chipped stone instead of steel, but they still looked as menacing as any villain. In the middle of the line stood a short woman with her grey hair shaved away on one side, showing a pattern of crosshatched scars.

"Don't play the raven, Ferra," Lestavo said, walking toward her. "They're wanderers, same as us."

"They're nowt like us," the woman said, still eyeing Yasmi with suspicion.

"No blues, so." Lestavo plucked at his clothes. "No sawing and building and burning. These ain't road's teeth, just town folk travelling."

"You're too trusting," Ferra said, but she slid her arrow into the quiver on her belt.

"Must be, to trust thee."

The two of them slapped each other on the chest. Along the line, the other strangers lowered their bows. Yasmi straightened from the animal crouch that she'd been dropping into and took her hand from her masks.

"Where you fixing to lie tonight?" Lestavo asked.

"Not next to you again," Ferra replied. "You snore like rocks smashing."

"Not even if I dreamed you up a new verse?"

"Not if you told me a whole new poem."

"What about if…" He pulled out the strange little doll he'd been making, and the twitch of his hand made it move like a living thing. Ferra rolled her eyes.

"We're by the Seven Wells these few weeks," she said. "And don't tell me that's too long one place, fifty of us has to go slower than one."

"Got space for five more tonight?"

Lestavo's smile would have been hard for anyone to resist. Ferra sighed with as much affection as resignation.

"Always."

———— • ————

Yasmi couldn't have called the place a village, even if its inhabitants did. It was too strange for that. Instead of houses, there were round baskets wider than wagons and enclosed hammocks like giant bean pods slung between the trees. Supplies hung in nets from the branches; pigs and goats milled around an enclosure of tautly strung ropes; children sang intricate, ever-changing songs and built towers of sticks while adults gathered nuts and wove baskets from long leaves. They didn't fix their attention on the new arrivals sitting around the campfire, but they all looked over from time to time, the adults with suspicion, the children with wide-eyed curiosity.

"Heading for Jarrag's lair?"

Ferra paused plucking tubers from the fire and looked at Raul. Her gaze was as steady as Lestavo's was light. If he was a banner blowing in the breeze of the Withered Hills, then she was the steady pole holding the likes of him from flapping away. She reminded Yasmi of Valens, but the way he'd been before, not the sagging shoulders and slack features of the man staring into the woods, looking like he was listening to the wind.

"There's something there we need," Raul said. "To drive out the Dunholmi."

"Ah, so there's bad blood between you and the road's teeth."

"The road's teeth?"

"They've been biting at what lives," Lestavo said. "Building their roads and their towers, trying to make this into town land."

"Well, we're going to get rid of them."

"Are you, now?" Ferra had rolled blackened tubers across the dirt, so that they each had one resting by their feet. Now she dug short fingernails into the skin of the last one and cracked it open, revealing the soft, steaming flesh inside. Yasmi followed her example, enjoying the warmth of the lump in her hands and the slightly sweet smell that billowed out with the steam. The flesh, once she'd given it a moment to cool, was soft, fluffy, with a wholesome flavour nicer than anything else she'd tasted since they set out on their quest, not to mentioning blessedly warm. She found herself thinking of all the comforts she'd left behind, first to become a rebel and then to follow Raul into the wilderness, forcing herself to believe that the price had been worth paying. Soft beds, good wines, spiced food, and all the possibilities of the theatre's extensive wardrobe, reduced to memories and hopes.

While she ate, the conversation moved on. It seemed that Lestavo wouldn't be coming with them any further, and Ferra wasn't interested in offering someone to take his place. Raul, being Raul, didn't match the look of frustration on Prisca's face, and that was probably for the best. Real support wasn't won by anger or cajoling, but by showing what you had to offer, and what Raul had to offer was himself.

"All right if we take food from places like that berry patch?" he asked, gesturing back the way they had come.

"Aye, in the Withering you take what you need, but no more," Ferra said, scraping the last edible flesh from its blackened shell. "And you lay the way for who passes through later."

"I can't promise that we'll plant the right things in the right places, but we'll try."

"That's how anyone starts."

"And we can give you something more valuable in time," he added. "No more of the Dunhol—the road's teeth. We're going to drive them out of all of Estis, from here to Pavuno to the Vales."

"All of Estis, eh?" Ferra's eyes narrowed. She tossed the blackened remains of her food into the fire. "Well, there's a thing."

"To do that, we need to find this shrine of Jarrag's. Can you point the way?"

A look passed between Ferra and Lestavo, her expression flickering through frustration and indulgence while he simply beamed, looking pleased at the novelty he'd found.

"Two clear routes from here." Ferra pointed toward two gaps between the densely grown trees on the north side of the clearing they sat in. "One's a well-worn deer trail, the other follows a slow stream. Which one you think takes you right?"

Raul licked his fingers with a thoughtful expression as he eyed up the two openings. To Yasmi, they both looked the same, nothing but open mouths framed by the long teeth of branches. Near them, the children had gathered and were making dolls from materials plucked off the plants, sweet playthings unlike the one Lestavo had made as they walked.

"Is this a test?" Raul asked.

"So's said." Ferra smiled, no more friendly than those forest maws. "Those who can pick a path might pass through the Withering without ruining our lives, and for them folk I might send word ahead to help. Those who can't, though…"

She drew a knife from her belt, a hand's length of dark stone chipped to a wicked edge with a handle wrapped around in leather. She plunged it into another blackened tuber sitting in the embers at the base of the fire, then started slicing it into pieces.

If the gesture troubled Raul as much as it did Yasmi, he didn't show it.

"A test," he said, smiling. "Quests should have tests."

"And forking paths," Yasmi added, because it was nicer to think about a story than the slicing motion of the knife. "But how are we going to pick the right one?"

"Could we judge which path's more worn?"

"Only if we knew how many people went our way."

"And you don't know anything useful about plants to help us?"

Yasmi laughed. "Less than you, country boy."

Ferra rose, chopped-up tuber in hands, and went to share it out among the children. At least there wasn't any urgency to their decision.

Around the fire, Valens was scraping the last he could out of his tuber and peering hopefully into the heaped embers it had come from. Prisca and Raul were looking into those embers too, and Yasmi shivered as she realised what they must both be thinking. What better time than this for divination, to find signs and direction in ashes or flames or the way the birds flew? Except that divination was ruining Prisca's mind, and now Raul knew that it would ravage his too. Slowly, perhaps, but inevitably, and that wasn't something Yasmi wanted to support.

She flipped through the masks on her belt, painted wood clacking. She paused at the wolf, feeling the lure of those sharpened senses, the athletic stride, the freedom she felt as she bounded through the trees. Just thinking about it left her breathless, stomach fluttering like leaves in a spring wind. But what she needed now was a view to the horizon, and the wolf couldn't help with that, so she reluctantly moved past and picked out the monkey.

"I can climb above the canopy," she said. "See what's ahead."

The look of relief on Raul's face stirred something like autumn brambles in her chest, sweet fruit and barbed thorns. If she was thinking like that, then she'd definitely been playing too many of Tenebrial's overwritten parts.

"That's a great idea," Raul said, sitting up straighter, smiling more brightly. "Can we help?"

"I doubt it." Yasmi raised the mask, overcoming the tightness that rose in her chest at the thought of shifting in front of others. It didn't matter how often she did it, it still felt wrong. "Just wait, I'll be back soon."

Then the mask was in place and her body buckled. Fur prickled as it slid through skin and clothes; muscles ached then eased as they knotted and reformed; her balance shifted as her legs and back rearranged themselves. There was a moment of tension and release at the base of her spine, then she swished her tail from side to side, tossing leaves around. It wasn't the wolf's body, so lithe and strong and right, but it would do.

The children stared at her, eyes wide. Most of them clapped and cheered, but one poor little boy burst into tears. Not the worst audience she'd ever had. She waved a small paw at them before bounding across the clearing and flinging herself into the trees.

She grabbed a low branch, used her momentum to swing herself past, and let go, stretching out for the next one. Though she hadn't spent much time in this body, it felt deceptively familiar, like her own limbs were showing her what to do. The secret was not to get stuck on working with the tree whose top she was aiming for; going back and forth with branches from its neighbours would get her to the top sooner.

Just like the wolf, the monkey sensed the world differently from the human. Instead of blood and sweat, the scents of leaves and fruit dominated. She noticed the different creaks of the branches she swung from, the way the wind moved different parts of the canopy, larger shapes that might have been predators. The cold was harder to accept, her fur not thick enough for the winter weather, but there was satisfaction in being this body, in its bounding movements. Not quite the power that gave her so much comfort as the wolf, not its strength and ferocity of purpose, not the richness of blood and the hunt. Something more playful, closer to human and all the more alien for it.

Despite under- or overreaching a couple of times and having to adjust her course to avoid a fall, she soon reached the highest branch that could hold her and paused for a moment, swaying above the forest, her giddy laughter becoming a chitter that expanded as it echoed around her mouth and then burst out, scaring away nearby birds. She shook with that laughter more than the cold.

Big soft lips pressed together as she forced herself to focus, looking across the greenery. This tree was higher than the rest, and she should be able to see where they were going, but where were the two paths? Where was the deer trail? Where was the stream?

Scowling, she twisted around, the treetop shaking under her. Had she got turned around as she ascended? No, the clearing was there behind her. Twist back again, squint, tilt her head, try to pick out anything that could be the path, any sign of which way to go.

She hooted in frustration, beat a loose fist against her chest. Stupid woods. Stupid humans. Stupid cold. She couldn't stay up here, she would turn into an icicle. After one last look around and a snort of disgust, she swung to a lower branch and went scrambling down the tree, dropping the last dozen feet to the ground.

"Well?" Raul asked eagerly. He'd moved away from the fire, leaving the others behind so that he'd be there when she got down.

She resisted the urge to throw dirt at him and instead grabbed the fur around her face with long fingers, hooking the mask away. Her tail curled in, back straightened, joints rearranged themselves. The exhilaration was gone, leaving only frustration, but at least her human travelling clothes were warmer than the monkey's fur.

"Useless," she said, waving the monkey mask. "This forest is too thick. Next time I'll stick with the wolf."

"Would that help finding the way?"

"That's not the point."

She hung the mask back in place and headed over to warm her hands by the fire. It was one of Raul's better qualities that he didn't ask what her actual point was.

Standing as close to the flames as she dared, she tried to shake off the shivering and the tension that had gripped her body, from her clenched teeth to her curled toes. The wolf would have helped her somehow, even if she couldn't see how, standing here in her human body. The confidence it provided as she bounded through the woods, the certainty in her knowledge of the world and in her own choices, that made a difference none of the other masks did.

Old, half-rotted leaves whispered under Raul's feet as he came back to the fire. He stood over them, looking into the flames, while she sat scowling, arms folded across her knees, spine tight with discontent.

"Did any of you keep anything from those big cats we fought?" he asked.

Reaching around himself, Valens pulled a furry ear from a pouch and handed it sheepishly to his son.

"It felt a bit like old times," he said. "So I thought..."

"That's perfect." Raul peered at the fur, then walked around the fire so that it was between him and the openings into the woods. "I just needed something connected to Jarrag, a bit of the creatures people say are his."

Even down here in the shelter of the trees, the wind conspired to blow smoke from the fire into their faces. Her eyes watering, Yasmi looked up at Raul, saw the determined expression on his face, realised what he was about to do.

"You don't need to do divination," she said. "There are other ways to find a route."

"It's a test. If we wait too long, we'll fail."

"Then get Prisca to do it."

Yasmi looked at the older woman. She ought to volunteer. After all, it was her mind that would be worn away, or it was her son's. She sat silent, watching him.

"I can't ask other people to do what I won't," Raul said.

The wind went still and the smoke drifted upward again. He took a deep breath, then flung the ear into the fire. It crackled and hissed, releasing an acrid smell that made Yasmi gag. The smoke darkened, then shifted, and for a moment it seemed to point toward the left-hand path, before it blew back in their eyes again.

"That one." Raul pointed. "The stream."

Ferra looked from the smoke to Raul, then placed herself between him and the children.

"Back in the season, a lot of town folk died for the sake of magic," she said. "Some Withering folk too. Why should I stand for it around me and mine?"

Raul hung his head. "I should have thought before I acted."

"That's more than most would confess." Ferra raised an eyebrow. "So, now you've had a breath of thought, would you do it again?"

Yasmi knew what an honest answer would sound like, that he was fighting for his people and he couldn't afford to give up the weapons he had. Then there was the easy answer, saying no to appease a stranger. But in the pause Raul took to think, she could see that neither of those was enough for him.

"When you're navigating the woods and hills, you look for signs in the landscape, don't you?" he asked. "Things that you've learned to watch for since you were young, that help you navigate the world."

"Aye, so's said."

"I'm learning to navigate my world, one full of hidden meanings and unseen dangers, and I use the signs that I have. It's not good for me, but it's how I find a way of fighting that gets fewer people hurt."

Ferra looked from him to the fire and back, then ran her hand through one of the children's hair. Squirming under that touch, the boy wriggled in closer to her.

"You carry a lot of weight for one so young," she said.

"I do the best I can, and I'm trying to do better every day. If that means not using divination around your people, then I won't."

After a moment's thought, Ferra shook her head.

"There's worse powers in the wild. Just have a care with it."

"Thank you." He pointed at the path the smoke had picked out. "Did I read the signs right? Is that the way we should go?"

"Aye."

"So I passed the test?"

"So's said." Ferra walked over to them, and for a moment Yasmi thought she would ruffle Raul's hair, like she'd done to the boy. "I'll put word out through the Withering, let folk know why you're coming, that you've something to you. Maybe they'll help." She shrugged. "Maybe they won't, but it's better than nowt."

"Thank you." Raul beamed. "Before we go, can you show

me a few things we can do along the way, to make sure we're giving not just taking?"

"Aye, that I will, *Raul Warborn*."

Raul smiled as he and Ferra slapped each other in the middle of the chest. But Yasmi couldn't find the pleasure he did in the moment. Her fingers tightened around the wolf mask as she stared into the opening that gaped for them.

———————————— • ————————————

Yasmi had seen puppet shows down by the Golden Ocean, but she'd never seen one like Ferra and Lestavo's people put on that night. A show in which everyone was a performer and there was no space for an audience, only the four outsiders standing off to one side, trying to follow a story that wasn't being told for them.

"Which one's the hero?" Valen asked, brow furrowing as he watched.

In the light from nets full of glowing moths, puppets which had seemed crude during the day were revealed as wonderful, intricate creations. Their faces and the patterns of their clothes were marked as much by shadows as by the pieces that cast them, and their shapes were as varied as any cast Yasmi had known. These creations of lumpen wood and woven grass came alive in the hands of their creators, moving like real people around the clearing, interacting with animation that would put most theatre troupes to shame.

"I don't think there is a hero," Yasmi said. "Or perhaps it's all of them."

The interactions between the performers were chaotic, but everyone clearly understood their part and she thought she could see a pattern emerging, like the first notes of a familiar song from the corner of a crowded tavern. Every time two or more puppets met, they would interact: a conversation, a fight, even a dance. The tension of the moment would rise and then break, the figures bowing before they moved on. When one of them started a new interaction, they carried words or actions from their previous partners woven through their own. It should have reduced the art of the event to mush, everyone drifting toward a single indistinct performance, but instead it made everything more interesting, more distinctive. While the performers integrated ideas from each other, they never lost their own identity, finding ways to transform the gestures others had invented.

She could learn so much here, if only she had the time.

"What's it about?" Valens asked.

"Community," Yasmi said.

"And things they've seen," Raul added, pointing to a pair of puppets who were conversing nearby. "This one's talking about the burning grass and that one's dancing like a rainstorm."

"You can't dance like a rainstorm," Valens said, then his eyebrows rose. "Or maybe you can."

"Is Lestavo playing us?" Raul asked, pointing across the crowd.

Their travelling companion was one of the most animated performers there, his puppet leaping, striding, and careening from place to place, bumping into others and tripping over roots, raising peals of laughter. His interactions had the sublime clumsiness of an expert tumbler, the ballet of absurdity, and he managed to swing seamlessly from one encounter to the next. He was the best-performed puppet in the place.

He was also the only one who never learned. The others picked up pieces of his mannerisms, played with them, integrated the things they liked, but he blundered on regardless, a thread of havoc stumbling through the cloth of the performance, a jester with a face of thorns.

"I believe he is," Prisca said. "And it is not a complimentary portrayal."

Yasmi sighed. Trust Prisca not to understand that any presence in the play was a compliment. These people hadn't owed them the hospitality they offered, and they certainly didn't owe them attention.

From somewhere, a consensus emerged and the play drew toward an end. The puppets came together, dancing in circles in the soft white moth light, all except for Lestavo, who, just as the play reached its peak, walked his puppet into a tree. Then they took those wonderful, intricate puppets and trampled them into twigs around the roots of a tree.

There was laughter and cheering, a moment of shared warmth, and though Ferra kindly waved the guests over, Yasmi knew that they weren't really part of this.

"Why did you end it like that?" Yasmi asked. "Breaking the things you made?"

Ferra looked at her like she was an idiot, and perhaps she was.

"Everything breaks in the end," Ferra said. "No good clinging to the past. Our old story feeds the tree and we move on to the next."

Chapter Twelve
The Plunge

The river crashed over the rocky edge, tumbling and thundering into the depths, throwing out spray in a cloud so dense that the chasm seemed filled with fog. Valens felt dizzy looking over.

So much for divining the right route.

He stepped back and squatted with his back to a rounded rock. When you were on the march, you took rest when you got the chance. If that meant five minutes sitting in the dirt waiting for orders, so be it. There might not be officers here, but the principle stood. He wasn't in charge. He wasn't even useful. He was here to feel better about himself, and not even getting that right.

At the edge of his attention, the others were talking, Raul speaking softly as he probed for gaps in Yasmi's and Prisca's frustration. At least the girl had the goodness to turn her anger inward, though it might have been better if she hadn't; Prisca would have preferred a good fight to the caution they showed around her, the careful attempts not to upset somebody sick. They'd find some pointless task to flatter her ego next. It was what they knew.

"Well this is shit," said a voice on the wind over his shoulder. Valens didn't look around. He knew better by now; there would be nothing to see. "I mean, real prime shit, like you'd get from a Dunholmi officer's horse. Oat-fed shit from a well-exercised behind."

Valens almost smiled.

"Are you going to help?" he asked. No need to creep off for a conversation, the others had their backs turned and wouldn't hear him over the waterfall's roar.

"'Course not," Fabia replied. "Benefits of being dead, no one expects you to carry their pack."

"Any excuse." He drummed his fingers against the hilt of his sword. "Don't we need to get through so this god can bring you back?"

"They'll find a way. That's what they do, right? Prisca and Raul to do the thinking, Yasmi to keep them motivated, and you playing the two-legged mule, carrying heavy bags and light expectations."

"Sounds right."

He wrapped his hand around the leather protecting his stump, felt lingering pain from the pressure. Would it stop hurting one day? Any of it?

Voices were rising. Valens dragged his attention out of the dirt.

"…underestimated the challenge inherent in crossing this terrain. We're not even halfway to our destination and problems like this will only become worse as we approach midwinter." Prisca glared down into the chasm like it had pissed on her boots. "Perhaps it would be prudent to turn back, marshal our resources, and try again in the spring."

"Leaving the Dunholmi in charge for another half a year?" Raul asked. "Leaving our people to fight alone when the campaigning season begins?"

"If need be, yes. We must accept certain setbacks for the greater good."

Raul paced back and forth along the lip of the chasm, staring into the gloom. "What do you think, Yasmi?"

"Whatever you do, I'm with you," she said. "I know it's hard to judge right now, but…"

"Are you saying that my mind's impaired, girl?" Prisca snapped.

"That's not what I meant."

"Really?"

"Can't you just…"

"Prisca's right." Valens hated to say it, but not as much as he hated their looks of surprise that he'd spoken. Still, he pressed on. "This whole country's against us. What's the point in fighting it?"

"Arsehole," Fabia whispered over his shoulder, but there was no malevolence in her tone. She understood.

Raul stopped his pacing and looked from Valens to Prisca, then to Yasmi, who shrugged apologetically. Then he turned his back to them all and stood staring over the precipice, hands clasped behind him. Framed by the fog of the falling waters, he'd never looked more like a hero, and Valens had seldom felt more like a failure. He should be backing the boy, but he couldn't find the will.

Overhead, crows flew in formation, a dark V against the sky like the mark on the giant cats. This place made Valens shudder from deep inside.

"Things like this are how the Withered Hills defend themselves," Raul said. "Terrain so difficult that only the locals can manage it. But that defence can't hold forever. The Dunholmi are encroaching, year by year. Road's teeth eating up the land.

"In all the plans we made, we never thought about the people living here until we had to. The rest of Estis, the town people and country people, we abandoned the Withered Hills to the wild, and then we abandoned them to the invaders. I won't abandon them again. Once I get Balbianus's dagger, get control over the power of the land, I won't just drive the Dunholmi back—I'll tame this place, make it somewhere people can settle in peace, instead of carrying their whole lives in rolling baskets from one clearing to the next, hoping that the seed they scattered years ago has given them enough food to live."

He pointed to some vines growing over the trees they'd come through.

"We'll make cords, lower our packs as far as we can, then climb down after them. It won't be easy, but if we wanted easy, then we'd still be in the Vales, selling ale to travellers and listening to Old Wellic moan about the frost. Is that what you want?"

Prisca scowled but didn't reply. Yasmi smiled, her hands clasped together, halfway to applause.

"That's more like it," Fabia said in Valens's ear. "The kid's got fire in his belly, what happened to yours?"

"Quenched in blood," Valens replied.

"What's that?" Raul asked, looking at him.

The crows were flying lower, and the mist rose in long curls behind them, cold wet claws from the depths.

"Nothing." Valens set his pack aside and pulled out a knife. "Let's get on with this."

———————————— ● ————————————

Water ran in a slow trickle down the side of Valens's face, gaining momentum as tiny droplets found each other. It tickled as it ran down his cheek, and he leaned his weight against the rocks so he could let go for a minute and brush the distraction away.

Below him, Prisca and Raul were making their way down slowly. The cliff face had just enough of an angle to give them places they could rest in the irregularities of the rocks. Turned out that was a good thing. Clinging to slippery stone made the climb tougher and slower but moving away from the water took them to an even steeper climb, with chunks of dirt that risked giving way beneath their weight. No one had said that Valens was going down last because they expected him to be slowest, and he didn't need them to say it, but it turned out that they were the ones going slow. He might have a lot of bulk to carry but that meant he had the muscles for the climb too, and he knew how to use them. He didn't even have to think about it all that much now that he'd got into the rhythm, just move his hand down to a lower hold, put his weight there, feel his way with one foot then the other, and repeat.

It had taken him a good ten feet to remember the real trick of climbing, that it was in the legs, not the arms. It felt wrong, when your hand had all those ways to cling on, and when the rocks it clung to were closer to your face. But there was power in your legs, and they could take the weight better, even as they started to ache from the long descent.

His fingers closed around a rock near his shoulder. He found a good grip, shifted his weight, then reached down with his foot until it found an inch of protruding stone, something solid enough to hold him. His other foot slid into a crack in the rock face, then he was back to his hand again.

He'd never wished that he was a shifter, but he wouldn't have minded a bit of the agility with which Yasmi had scrambled down in monkey form, retrieving a stuck pack on the way past. Only commanders talked up the virtue of hard work; ordinary warriors understood why the easy way was better: save your strength, because you'd need it.

Hand down, fingers hooking into a gap, testing what it could take, weight shifting onto it. Foot out, then settling on an outcrop the size of his head. Other foot down beside it, check balance, move on...

Still, it felt satisfying to test his body's limits, to use the strength he'd built and the skills he'd learned, to prove what he could do. Prove it to himself as much as the others. Drag himself out of the sucking dirt of defeat.

Hand down to a pointed rock. Shift weight onto it. One foot down, leg tensing, then the other.

Except that they didn't need him now. Maybe they hadn't needed him ever. Prisca had wanted someone to retrieve a baby, back when the city fell, but after that had she kept him around for anything beyond his silence? She certainly hadn't listened to his ideas, not on anything that mattered. Now Raul was in charge, and the boy really didn't need Valens holding him back.

Hand down. Foot. Foot.

Fabia said that she needed him now to bring her back, but without him would she even be dead? Fixing what you broke didn't make you useful, it just meant you weren't making things worse.

Hand. Foot. Foot.

He was even less useful in the Withered Hills than he was elsewhere. He didn't know half the plants or animals, could barely even find a good spot for shelter at night. Too used to relying on supply wagons and raiding farmers' barns or buying what he needed when they'd been in the inn.

Hand. Foot. Foot.

Maybe he should stop at the bottom here.

Hand.

Tell the others to go on without him.

Foot.

Stop holding everyone back.

F—

His toes slipped on wet rock, leg kicking out over the void. The sudden lurch of his weight almost wrenched his hand away and pain jolted through the joints of his arm. He swung between his handhold and remaining foothold, flailed for balance with his other arm, brought his foot around in a desperate lunge for another rock.

His foot landed. There was a scraping sound. He hadn't tested his weight, just like he hadn't on the rock he'd slipped off, or a dozen more before that. A chunk of stone as broad as his chest broke away from the cliff.

"Raul!" he bellowed as the stone fell, smacking off other rocks, tumbling end over end toward his son.

Raul looked up, eyes wide, then flung himself sideways, into the waterfall. The rock plummeted through the place where his head had been and cracked against the rocks as it fell past Prisca. There was a splash as something dropped into the pool at the bottom of the cliffs.

"Raul!" Valens screamed.

His foot was back on the rock, fingers clinging so tight they went white. Yasmi ran toward the pool, but all Valens could do was stare in horror and fear.

The edge of the waters stirred. Yasmi reached down and helped a soaking Raul drag himself out. The water ran red from the side of his head and he clutched his left arm close to his chest, but at least he was moving.

Valens turned his gaze away to stare at the cold grey rock face. He didn't feel empty anymore, but like a thin hide drawn out to dry across rocks, stretched so tight it was almost tearing open. Ice-cold water dappled his hand, his face, the exposed side of his neck. Water his son might have died in, thanks to his carelessness.

He pushed all other thoughts from his mind, put his whole focus on his hand and the next rock he moved it down to, testing his weight and his grip before he made another move. When his foot descended, it was with a careful, probing touch.

Hand, weight, wait a moment in case something shifted.

Foot, weight, wait.

Foot, weight, wait, pause and scan the rocks below, looking carefully for the next place he might move down.

Inch by tensed, aching inch, Valens made his way down the cliff to see the damage he'd done.

———————•———————

Raul huddled by the fire, a blanket wrapped around his shoulders. Even after changing into dry clothes, he was shivering hard. When he raised his fingers to feel whether his hair had dried out, he instead found the sticky mess where blood from the scrape on his scalp had oozed, and he winced at his own touch.

"Are you sure you don't want to bandage that?" Yasmi asked.

"Da and Prisca both say that it's better to let this one take care of itself, and they know more about wounds than I do."

"That's certainly true." She took a pot off the fire and poured a sharp-scented infusion into wooden cups. "Here, the herbs might help; it'll warm you up, at least."

"Thanks." He took the cup and sipped. It tasted bitter, but as the first mouthful went down he felt an urge to drink more. That was probably a good sign.

"How's your arm?"

He flexed the fingers of his left hand and held them out to

examine against the light of the fire. Smoke swirled up the chasm above them and into the night sky, amber sparks disappearing into the stars.

"Aches a bit," he admitted, "but I can still use it."

"And you still want to press on?"

"Of course!"

"Of course."

She reached around him to take the edge of the blanket and wrap it tighter about his shoulders.

"You're ridiculous, you know that," she said, looking him in the eye. The flickering firelight softened the contours of her face, made the hair falling to one side of her face into a golden haze. "After a fall like that, anyone with any sense would at least pause and take thought."

"I can't. I've got to keep playing the part, remember? Heroically pushing on."

"I think you're taking this performance too seriously."

"I've watched your troupe rehearse. It doesn't count as serious until someone's screaming or throwing props at other people's heads."

She laughed at that, and the sound made him feel warmer.

Footsteps crunched across the pebbles by the side of the stream. Valens approached, sword and shield at the ready. Raul squirmed at the wariness in his expression, which seemed much more about Raul than about their surroundings.

"I checked a mile downstream, no one's there. Same up the dry side of the chasm." Valens stood stiff-backed, head held straight. "What else should I do?"

"Rest," Raul said. "Sleep. Be ready for tomorrow."

Valens didn't quite frown, but a flicker of something crossed his face.

"You sleep," he said. "I'll keep watch."

"I'm not sure we need a watch tonight." Raul nodded to a bundle of blankets and travelling clothes from which soft snores were emerging. "Prisca read the signs."

"Can't be too careful."

Valens settled into a crouch with his back against a boulder and his sword across his knees. Were his words a reflection on Prisca's weakness, or of this new demeanour that had come over him since their descent? Good as it was to see him emerge from the slumped weariness with which he'd been facing the world, this new Valens put Raul on edge. He wasn't quite the man he remembered or had been looking for. A version of him, but tense as a bent branch, moments away from snapping.

Raul took a deep breath. He should trust his da. Valens hadn't meant to dislodge that rock, and he had come this far.

Setting aside the empty cup, Raul stood up. Aches ran the whole way down his legs, a memento of their climb. He winced and rubbed the back of his thigh.

"I'm feeling it too." Yasmi stood beside him. "Why don't we go for a walk, stretch them out before bed?"

"Does it count as a bed when we're sleeping in blankets under the stars?" Raul asked, heading away from the fire.

"That's as close to a bed as I've had half the nights of my life," Yasmi replied, settling in step with him. "Touring the land, sleeping in wagons and under trees, looking up at those twinkling lights, and running through my lines for the next day."

"I would have liked to do more of that with you. Travelling with the theatre, painting scenery, seeing places I'd never been."

"Trust me, you soon start wishing for stability and a proper bed."

They were near where the waterfall hammered down into the pool. Yasmi slipped her arm through his, and they steadied themselves against each other as they made their way across a beach of worn, rounded rocks, heading for the tall willows that hung over one shore.

"Careful," she said as he wobbled closer to the pool. "That's your only set of dry clothes. Much as I'd love to watch you run around naked, you'd be frozen long before we found this wild god's lair."

"Does that mean we're sharing a blanket again tonight?" he asked, hopeful and uncertain. "For the warmth's sake, I mean."

With all the walking, he should have fallen straight into an exhausted slumber every chance he got. But the last couple of nights, lying beneath their shared blankets with Yasmi curled around him, he'd lain awake for a long time, listening to her every soft breath, trying to make out the curve of her face in the starlight.

"For warmth's sake," she said. "Just don't keep me awake with your shivering."

She pushed aside the dangling willow and Raul followed her through. Closed off in the shadows beneath the tree, he looked for her in the darkness, reached out a hand and found hers. She turned toward him, and he could just make out a hint of her hair, the curve of her hip, a ghost of her smile.

"I'm so glad you're all right," she said. "You scared the

words out of me, falling like that." She hugged him tight and he wrapped his arms around her. "Don't do it again. I couldn't stand losing you."

"I, um, that's…" Words clogged in his throat, half-formed things. He couldn't even order the thoughts queueing up behind them. His heart was full of the warmth of her, the scent of her, the press of her body against his.

Her fingers ran up his cheek, stopped below his ear, cupped his face.

"That is, I mean, well…"

"Raul…"

"Yes?"

"You're not very good at this, are you?"

"I don't know. I haven't ever…that is to say…" He was meant to be a hero, and here he was stumbling over himself at the touch of a woman. He was glad that the darkness hid his blush.

"That's not quite what I meant, but I suppose it's still true." She slid against him as she rose on tiptoes, and then her lips were brushing his, as soft as her fingers. A rush ran through his body like sunlight bursting from the dawn. He didn't dare move, didn't dare breathe, not wanting anything to end this perfect moment.

"There." She kissed him again, more firmly this time, and he sank into it, letting himself get lost in her presence, in the warmth rising from inside him. "How's that?"

If he tried to put a sentence together, he'd only get in a deeper mess, so instead he pulled her tight against him and kissed her right back.

Raul didn't know what he was doing, but his instincts gave

him a good lead. He ran a hand down her body then back up again, ran it through her hair, drew her against him while the kiss deepened. She wrapped one leg around his and her fingers pressed into his back. The taste of her was exquisite, and his whole body surged with an excitement that he could feel her matching, her movements urgent, her body insistent, a moan rising from her throat. That hand on his back slid down, pressed his hips hard against hers, and he would have felt embarrassed at what she might feel there, except wasn't that the whole point of this? His own hand went to her waist, to the edge of her tunic, crept up inside…

Yasmi paused, leaned back, laid a hand against his chest.

"Raul." His name passed her lips as a low, ragged wisp of breath.

"Don't you want to?" He withered in disappointment.

"Oh, I do." She patted his chest. "Believe me, I really do."

"Then what is it?"

"Raul, we're in the wilderness in the middle of winter, sleeping on frosted, rocky ground under the trees, so close to your parents that we can hear Prisca farting in the night. There are ticks and fleas and gods only know what else living amid the twigs and dirt clinging to our blankets. Even if all of that didn't make this the least romantic setting ever, I've needed to keep a soft cloth between my legs for the past two days, and that's messy enough to deal with this far from clean linen and a proper chance to wash."

"Oh." He almost scratched his head but stopped himself before he touched the raw scab there; one more reason why she was right. "Um, is there anything I can do to help with that last thing? I might have another shirt you can tear up if you need rags, or..."

Yasmi laughed and pressed her head against his chest.

"Of all the boys I've known, only you would respond like that, instead of backing off like they'd been burned."

"It's just one of those things, isn't it? I mean, Prisca explained how bodies work when I was just a child."

"I bet she did."

Yasmi, laughing, looked up at him. His eyes had adjusted to the darkness enough to see hers, and they shone with all the light he could ever want. This might not be everything his body was demanding, but it was enough to make him happier than he'd ever been.

He leaned over and kissed her again, tender rather than urgent, holding her close instead of squeezing her tight.

"When this is over," she whispered, "we are going to have so much fun."

———————————— • ————————————

Valens tensed his legs and tightened the grip on his sword, ready to leap into action, but the crunch of pebbles was just Raul and Yasmi returning.

The two of them were holding hands, the boy grinning like an idiot and the girl not much better. Watching them curl in together under their blankets, with soft whispers and half-hidden caresses, Valens was torn. Half of him was happy for them both; the other worried that this might mean they let down their guard.

Who was he to criticise anyone for that? He had a long hill

to march up before he could claim the high ground. He was going to do it, though. He was going to pull himself together and protect his son. He was going to bring all the strength he had to this fight.

The wind whispered past his ear.

"About fucking time," Fabia said.

———————— • ————————

When Count Alder had seen the state of the logging camp, he'd assumed that it was run by an incompetent. His predecessor had given too many positions to obsequious nonentities, leaving Alder with the challenge of digging them out like stones from beneath a horse's shoe. Captain Thorn had been put in place just before Alder's arrival, and could easily have been a parting shot, one last mess left for him to clear up.

An hour in Thorn's company taught him otherwise. The rough buildings and rougher-looking warriors weren't a reflection of poor planning or discipline, and it was probably only the captain's will that kept this place from falling apart.

Still, what he saw was frustrating. The horses reverting to untrained instinct. The saws and shovels that rusted up no matter how well they were kept. The ramshackle roofs that would have leaked if not for the moss growing between their shingles. The map that was mostly blank space.

"A generation in the Withered Hills, and this is as much as we know?" the count asked, and a gold bracelet rolled around his wrist as he stabbed at the parchment Thorn had laid out for them.

"A generation?" Thorn shook his head and chewed on the wad of leaves he kept in his cheek. "All of this was done since I took over from Sedge, and I've lost thirty war scouts getting this far."

Thirty Dunholmi scouts lost in the space of three years, and still only the roughest understanding of the terrain. Alder had known that things weren't good up here, but this was worse than he'd imagined.

"What was Sedge doing all these years?" he asked.

"Thought he could clear the woods a bit at a time." Thorn spat into the stained clay pot in the corner of the room, to Captain Brook's clear disgust. "You do that, it grows back just as fast over winter. So instead, I've gone deep." He ran his finger along three straight streaks on the map. "Driving solid roads hard, then scouting out around them. We still lose some progress every winter, but we're getting there. One toward the southern gap in the mountains, one toward this central river where I'm hoping to build docks, and one toward the gold."

"Gold?"

"A group of scouts found it in this chasm." He tapped a less even line that trailed out at the ends. "There are strange floods in this land, and our theory is that there's a valley whose entrance gets clogged with fallen trees and weird growth. Wouldn't happen most places, but everything grows so cursed fast here. Every so often, that dam breaks and the water stampedes down the valley, carrying chunks of gold out of the hills with it."

"And after the waters are gone, the gold remains."

"Exactly. But once we get established up there, we can tame

the waters to drive pumps for a proper mine. We're almost there. The road takes us to the chasm, and the ground's flat enough there for a mule train. Give me another year, and I'll make this land pay."

A gold mine opened up all sorts of possibilities. Funds to reinforce Alder's position in the north. Tithes to the palace that would buy him more favour with King Lorrin. Perhaps even licensing out the running of the site, putting another of the noble houses in his debt. Alder looked at Brook, who gave a slow, reluctant nod.

"Sounds good," she said.

"It does." But for now, he had to focus. Deal with the rebels, then plan for the next steps. "Captain Thorn, the people I'm after must have come north for something that could help their cause. Do you know what that might be?"

Thorn spat again, leaving a string of dark saliva down his jaw. The man was as foul and belligerent as any mule, but like a mule, his sturdy work had its uses.

"Not a clue," Thorn said, wiping his chin with the back of his hand. "But if they're coming from the south, they'll have to follow the chasm to reach the high hills. That's as good a place as any to catch their trail."

Spurs jingling at his heels, Alder walked to the window. The shutters were open, revealing his warriors in the middle of the logging yard. They were mud-spattered, some slumping wearily from a long, hard ride. If he told them to, they would ride back out through the gates with him now, straight on to intercept the rebels. And in doing so, he'd blunt their wits and their fighting ability, as well as wearing out the horses.

Rest tonight, ride tomorrow, as his grandmother had said.

"Are you from the Umber Plain branch of the Thorn family, Captain?" Alder asked.

"I am." Thorn's voice grew lower, darker. Floorboards squeaked as Brook stepped away from the wall.

"I always thought that it was a shame, the whole family being punished for one man's misdeeds."

Thorn spat into the jar. There was a long pause.

"It's how I came here."

"And that has worked well for me, but it needn't be the end of your story." Alder turned to meet Thorn's leaden gaze. "Estis is a wild steed, and I have been given a free hand to break her. Help me catch these rebels and we both get our shot at redemption. A man of your skills shouldn't be wasted in the wilds like this."

Thorn stared right back at him, like few would have dared. Then he took a pouch from his belt, stuffed a rubbery leaf into his mouth, and held the pouch out toward Alder.

"I'll get saddlebags packed," Thorn said. "It's going to be a long ride."

Chapter Thirteen
Casting for Signs

The bear roared as it lumbered across the chasm toward the man and woman trapped at the cliff face. Stones tumbled down the cliffside, clattering to the ground around them, and the man flinched as one hit his shoulder.

"Hey!" Raul yelled, running toward them. "Get away from them!"

He'd hoped that, together with his companions, he might be able to scare the bear off. Yasmi might have been more intimidating in her ogre form, but the wolf was nothing to be messed with, and Valens with his sword in his hand was enough to send most people running. Instead, the creature turned to face them, rising on its hind legs. It was nearly twice as tall as Raul, a black V shape in the paler brown fur of its belly, teeth like a saw blade made of stone and a red gleam of madness in its eyes. Suddenly, this didn't look like such a smart idea, but if it was that or let the bear kill those people, then smart didn't matter anymore.

"Spread out," Raul said. "We'll try to get someone around to attack it from behind."

Valens put on an extra burst of speed, circling around to the left. Yasmi growled, then bounded to the right, moving between the bear and its prey. That left Raul in the middle, facing the creature head-on.

An arrow whistled past and buried itself in the bear's shoulder. It didn't even flinch. Prisca might as well have been throwing acorns.

The bear battered its chest with its paws, turning its roar into a low ululating sound that felt like something uncanny rising out of the earth. From the woods at the top of the cliff, other voices replied. Raul didn't want to be here if they found a way down.

The bear thudded back onto all fours and ran at Raul. He forced himself to hold steady, to meet its charge with one of his own, sword raised and out to the side. A moment before they would have collided, he sidestepped out of its path, bringing the sword down. His blade slid off matted fur, not even leaving a scratch.

Bellowing, the bear slowed and turned its path. Raul was on the inside of the arc and he lunged, trying to stab it in the flank, but a paw the length of his forearm knocked the blade aside and he had to fling himself back to dodge claws like blood-crusted sickles.

A howl cut across the air, and Yasmi leapt, a flying streak of grey burying claws and teeth in the bear's haunch. It lashed out with its back leg and she went flying, skidding to the ground in a spray of loose stones.

Prisca had stopped shooting now that they were so close, but Valens was circling around, trying to trap the bear between him and Raul. He lunged, body turning into a single muscular arc with the sword blade at its tip. The bear's claw swept down and he caught it on his shield, somehow took the weight of the blow as he kept moving, thrusting the blade in under the bear's arm.

Another roar and a spray of blood this time, crimson against the pale grey of the frosted riverside stones. Claws hooked onto the shield, twisted, forced Valens to stumble aside.

While the creature was looking at Valens, Raul took his chance to attack again. This time, he swung with the direction of the bear's fur, sliding between the thick hairs rather than trying to hack through them. His sword sliced the flesh close to the creature's neck, lodged in the dense muscles, and he yanked it free with a spatter of blood.

A paw backhanded him, flinging him into the shallows on his back.

He almost pitied the bear, caught between Yasmi and Valens as they approached from different sides. Both moved slowly, made wary by the blows they'd taken, but carefully too, not giving the bear a chance to move out from between them. Its head turned back and forth, trying to watch both assailants while blood streamed from the wound Raul had left, a sticky trail down its leg that left paw prints on the ground.

Raul got to his feet, shook the dizziness from his head, hefted his sword. The bear was moving slower now and the other two were closing in, ready to make their move.

"Stop!" he called out. "Back off."

Valens did as he asked, stepping sharply back, but the wolf kept advancing, teeth bared, growling with menace.

"Yasmi!" Raul snapped. "Back!"

Her gaze darted to him, then to the bear. Still growling, she took a single step away.

The bear turned its attention toward Raul, who raised his sword and flicked the blade toward it.

"Come on," he called out. "Walk this way. Move that leg a lot. Let the blood flow."

Sure enough, it lumbered toward him, movements becoming slower as the blood flowed faster from its wounds. Its legs wobbled. As it came within reach, it took a deep, bubbling breath, then its forelegs crumpled and it sank to the ground.

Raul's chest tightened as he lowered his sword.

"Sorry," he said. "I wish it hadn't been like this."

Eyes stinging, he laid his hand on the bear's muzzle, felt the trembling of its body and the slow pulse of its veins. Lips rolled back and hot breath washed over him, stinking of rotten meat. The bear's eyelids flickered, almost closed, then went wide, a dark flash in them.

Roaring, the beast reared up, claws raised, about to come crashing down on Raul.

He brought his sword up, both hands on the grip, a scything arc that slipped through the fur of its belly, through thick hide and the soft flesh beneath. A torrent of guts flopped across Raul. The bear teetered, swayed, and thudded down sideways, shaking the ground.

Blood dripped from Raul's sword. It dripped from his hand. It dribbled from his hair down his face and dripped off his nose. He lowered his arm and a length of bear intestines slithered wetly over his shoulder to flop on the ground. More hung in a loop around his neck. An organ he didn't recognise lay across his boot, oozing yellow-green goo. Every breath he took was full of the stench of blood and torn bowels. He struggled to keep from puking straight across his shoes. The bear's empty eye stared up at him like an accusation while more blood dripped darkly from between its teeth.

Yasmi padded over to sniff at the mess. For a moment, he thought that she was going to take a bite, and that made it even harder not to be sick. But she wrinkled her muzzle, leaned back, raised a paw to her ear, and transformed back into herself. Her eyes sparkled with excitement, as they always did after she spent time as the wolf, but there was something else in her expression. Lips pressed together, she stared at him.

"What?" he asked, struggling to read her expression.

"Nothing." She shook her head.

"What is it?"

"I can't…" She pressed her hand to her mouth, stifling a laugh.

"You look ridiculous," Valens said, grinning as he wiped his blade.

"Like a mad butcher took over the decorations for a harvest festival," Yasmi said. "Strings of guts instead of flowers, everything painted the most flamboyant shade of red."

Raul wished that he could join in their laughter, but he felt grotesque, and the bear was still staring with its dead eye. He shook off the coils of guts and stepped away carefully so as not to slip.

The couple they'd rescued watched wide-eyed as he approached, their arms wrapped around each other.

"Please, don't hurt us," one of them whimpered.

"We'll build your roads," the other added. "We'll cut your wood. We'll show you the trails. Whatever you want, just please don't hurt us."

"I'm not going to hurt you." Raul reached out a hand, realised how he looked, drew it back. Setting his sword aside, he held his arms wide and tried his best not to look intimidating despite the dead monster dripping off him. "And we're not here to make you build roads either. We want to stop the road's teeth."

Slowly, the man and woman released their grip on one another. His clothes were stitched from fur and hide, hers from strips of broad, sturdy leaves. Behind them were a selection of hollow gourds strung together on vines. Their eyes were still wide, hands trembling, and the man kept looking over his shoulder like he was hoping a hole would open in the rocks behind him, but the woman stared steadily at Raul.

"You're the ones Ferra sent word about, so? The folk looking for Jarrag's Rest."

"That's right."

How had word got ahead of them? Had Ferra sent runners along secret ways? Did they use carrier pigeons in the Withered Hills, perhaps? Was there a magic that let them talk from tree to tree?

Then he realised how ridiculous he was being. Local people just knew their way around better. They'd get where they were going faster than him and his companions, and they probably shared news in the same way that they shared food and places of shelter—with a thoughtless generosity at odds with how little they had.

"You could help us fight the road's teeth," he said. It made sense. His people and these people had a mutual enemy.

The woman shook her head.

"Yon fray's not for us."

Even back in Pavuno, not everyone was ready to face the fight, and they saw the Dunholmi occupation every day. These people could mostly avoid it, and it was going to be hard to convince them that the world as they knew it was in danger from the men with the horses and roads. No time for a conversation like that now when he was soaked in blood and starting to shiver as it cooled.

"Can you at least tell me if we're heading the right way for the shrine? Jarrag's Rest, that's what you called it?"

The woman nodded. The man pointed on down the ravine, which was narrowing as it went along, the steep sides reaching for each other.

"Nowt good there," he said. "Less you have to, don't go."

"I have to, for the sake of the whole country."

The man shook his head like he'd heard that someone was dying. Perhaps he had, but that was a risk Raul was willing to take.

For now, he needed to get clean. With sticky red steps, he headed for the river. The two strangers picked up their strings of gourds and hurried away.

"Raul?" Prisca called out. "A moment?"

She was standing by the bear, along with the other two. Steam rose from the mess Raul had left, the bear's heat escaping into the cold of the world. Was that its life leaving its body forever, its spirit vanishing like water from a pot that had boiled too long? A towering, terrifying creature, and Raul had reduced it to this.

"Can it wait until I've cleaned up?" he asked, the sharpness of Prisca's tone pushing him into the shrill, nervous justifications of youth. "I'm covered in this mess."

"And you might be covered in more before we're done." Prisca prodded at the bear's side with her staff and more guts slopped out. "This is a valuable opportunity for a lesson in reading entrails."

Raul took a deep breath, barely noticing the stench around him anymore. He wanted to feel clean. He wanted Yasmi to look at him like she had done last night, instead of like he was the clown in a travelling show. He wanted to get going to reach Jarrag's Rest. But it had never even occurred to him that they could read the signs in something like this, and he couldn't help his curiosity.

"Will that work?" he asked. "Reading something I've killed in a fight?"

"Divination is about the confluence of circumstances. Given your and this creature's relative roles in our endeavour, I think we could learn things here that won't be visible any other way."

Raul hesitated. He'd never even thought about bringing together the things he did as a warrior and a diviner, but there were unexpected possibilities here. Not pleasant ones, but nothing about fighting was pleasant.

Then he remembered what else he'd learned about divination recently, and he took a step back.

"You still want me to do divination, even after you've admitted that it's ruining your mind?"

The level of disdain clawed coldly at his insides.

Prisca's hand trembled as she brought it to her brow. Her hawk-like features were frozen, pale as the snow-capped peaks beyond the canyon's end.

"I understand how that could seem hurtful." She stared at the bear while Raul stared at her. "But I did not mean it that way. What I'm suffering from now is the outcome of a lifetime of divination, decades of magic wearing channels through my mind. It has taken this long for me to feel its effects, but even if they had come sooner, the price would have been worth paying for the things it has let me do." Now she looked him in the eye. "For the help I've given others."

Raul swallowed. He'd thought about the price, but not what it bought, and he'd been so sunk into his anger at her that he'd become blind to the good she'd done. It didn't make up for everything else, but it was enough to make him consider what she said, and he had to admit that he was curious about what they could learn from a bear's entrails.

"You're saying that I should join in, because it will only ruin my mind later?"

"It's not just about timing. Use the gift lightly and its price might never catch up with you. That's your choice, Raul. What you do with it depends upon what you want to achieve."

Raul looked down at that heap of innards, red oozing from a wobbling pink heap. The bear seemed almost to merge with the ground, the curves of stones and intestines almost indistinguishable now both were painted with blood.

"What if I read it wrong?" he asked. "What if I miss something important?"

"The signs are always ambiguous. Nobody reads them perfectly every time." Her lips rose in something close to a smile. "Though I come close."

Raul looked at the others. Valens stood straight and still, waiting. Yasmi looked at him in concern, then let out a deep breath.

"Whatever you decide," she said, "I'm here for you."

It made him miss the days when other people made decisions and he followed them. But he'd had to take responsibility for pushing them in the right direction, and now he had to take responsibility for the tools he used to get them there.

Besides, he was very curious about how this would work.

"Let's do it."

Prisca drew a short, sharp knife from her belt, its edge gleaming in the cold light.

"To deliver meaning, entrails have to be cast with intention," she said, severing the intestines at the point where they emerged from the bear's belly. "For larger beasts, that used to be done by suspending them over a prepared area, so that the diviner could slit the belly and let them drop. Circumstances are different here, so we'll need to work together." She wiped the knife clean, put it away, and looked at Raul. "Ready?"

The two of them slid their arms under the heap of guts from opposite sides, then carried them to a large, flat boulder that the river had to bend around. In some ways, this was different from any work of divination that Raul had done before. In other ways, it was comfortingly familiar, listening as Prisca explained the connections between the messy world they lived in and a higher order, the way that those connections could be revealed through the purposeful use of random patterns. In another life, these were things that the royal cabal of Estis would still be studying, that Raul himself might have gone to learn about if he'd been very lucky. But in this life, Dunholm had torn down Estian scholarship for fear of how the magic might be used. All that remained were folk customs, hidden books, and a pair of cold, weary travellers trailing bear guts around in the wild.

"Ready?" Prisca asked as they raised the guts as high as they could.

"Ready."

"Three, two, one, now."

They let go. The guts fell onto the stone, blood spattering, rolls of intestine slithering out like snakes. Prisca folded her bloodstained arms across her chest, and the two of them stared down at what they'd done.

"What do you see?" she asked.

"Me?" He had expected her to find the patterns then point them out.

"You made the sacrifice, that makes you more connected. The lead diviner. What do you see?"

He smiled at the thought that he was the lead diviner, acknowledged by Prisca of all people. Then he forced himself to focus on what he could see in the mess they'd made.

"A horse's head," he said. "And a small circle. A ring maybe, or a bracelet."

"What does that mean to you?"

"Count Alder. Horses for Dunholm, and maybe a bracelet he wears, or their crown, something of his I'm sure."

"So he's coming?"

"And soon. The horse is moving fast. Look how its mane blows back." He pointed, but when he looked at Prisca, she was looking at him instead of the entrails. "Don't you think so?"

"I think that you're better at this than you used to be. Or perhaps I underestimated you before." Coming from her, that was quite a concession. "What else?"

"A doorway. The entrance to a house, maybe?"

"Don't think so literally." Though it was a criticism, her tone wasn't harsh. "There aren't many houses out here, so think again."

"A narrow way through. Something opening or closing. That fits better, doesn't it?"

"It does. We must always be careful to strike the right balance between bringing our own insights and being blinded by our assumptions. That's part of the diviner's art, and one where I think you're improving."

"Thanks, M—" He caught himself on the edge of a word that she'd never liked, and that tasted like bile on his tongue these days. "Thank you, Prisca."

"That's quite all right. Now, given what we've seen, the two of us should get cleaned up quickly, and then we should get moving. Apparently Count Alder is on our tail."

———————————•———————————

Valens marched along the riverbank behind Raul, keeping pace with his son and captain, almost too eager to leap into action when the lad called on him. The stony banks of the riverside crunched beneath their feet, making it harder to listen out for threats, but he kept his eyes peeled, watching left and right. There was danger in these hills, danger that had been here before them and danger that was following in their footsteps. Jarrag's creatures ahead, Count Alder and his riders behind.

He flexed a hand that wasn't there anymore, could almost feel the ghost of a finger brushing against the cold, hard jet of Fabia's mourning ring. He'd worn it for so long, every detail of it was perfect in his mind. Its smooth texture beneath his thumb. The way it dug in just a little when he formed a fist. The pressure he'd had to apply to get it past his knuckle on the rare occasions when he'd taken it off.

That had to be the ring that Raul had seen in the bear's entrails, riding toward them in Count Alder's pouch. The Dunholmi lord had turned Valens's most precious possession into a souvenir, a token of his own success. But Valens would show him. He would take the ring back and take his pride with it. He would show the horse lord what a real warrior was.

The crunch of their footsteps echoed from the sides of the narrowing valley as they marched on into the dusk.

Chapter Fourteen
The Crossing Point

Raul opened his eyes and looked out from under the granite overhang into the narrow, rocky valley. The rain that had woken him was still hammering down, a flicker of movement in the dark before dawn, a blurring of night. Other sounds beneath the falling rain, swirling and swishing and the clatter of stones, told him that the river was rising, swollen by the rain running off the hills. He hoped that it would still leave them enough space to walk along the bank, because there was no way they could climb up the cliffs. Not unless something was very different up ahead.

Yasmi sniffed and pressed in closer against his back. Under the blanket, his hand found hers.

"Your fingers are cold," she whispered.

"So are yours. So is everything here."

"Could we light a fire?"

"With what?"

There was a rustle in the darkness, then a series of soft sounds as Valens drew and checked the edge of his sword and knife before rolling up his bedding. Raul smiled to himself. It was good to hear those movements, to witness his father finding himself again. Not the routine Valens had back home, one of brewing and baking and serving customers, but a routine for a man of war, which was what they needed now and what his da needed to be.

Raul wormed his other arm out from under him and touched the amulet strung around his neck, felt the outline of the swift that Drusil had given him. Maybe they'd found some luck after all.

"Do you think we can find holly?" he whispered.

"What for?" Yasmi replied.

"Midwinter's day. You're meant to wear holly to prick the frost if it grabs at you. It makes for a milder winter."

"No holly out here." Prisca didn't bother keeping her voice down. "We will have to make do with the charms that we have." Now she was moving around too, making rustling sounds. "If you're all awake, then we should get moving."

"In this?" Valens snorted.

Raul stared out into the rain. The darkness was just starting to fade from black into grim grey, and he shuddered at the very thought of emerging from beneath his blanket, of losing what little warmth he had. But Prisca was right, they should get moving. If Count Alder really was on their tail, then this weather wouldn't stop him. Raul took a deep breath and closed his fingers around the edge of the blanket.

"Please, no . . ." Yasmi groaned.

Raul pushed the blanket off and, his whole body clenching against the cold, reached for his cloak and boots.

The rain, so cold it was a moment away from snow, rattled against Raul's hood and streamed down his waxed cloak. Even wearing a thick, dry pair of socks, he could feel the cold creeping into his feet, and that cold would be joined by damp before they made camp for the night. This seemed to be his days now, always wet, always grey, always cold. Days of rain-slicked stone.

The Withered Hills had been so full of life when they first arrived, and it grew in abundance on the slopes rising ahead, past the end of the chasm. But this part was like a scar across the landscape, pale and hard and dead. Aside from short, wiry plants clinging with desperate tenacity in the cracks between stones, the only life was in the river and along its banks. Even some of that life was disappearing beneath the swollen grey tumult as the waters swelled, rising up the stalks of reeds, drowning riverside burrows, carrying away rafts of flat round lily leaves. Frogs hopped out ahead of currents that threatened to slam them against upraised rocks. Fish, their scales glittering like blades, leapt and thrashed as they were swept along, their fates no longer their own.

Was that what had happened to him, swept up in the rising current of the myths that Prisca had woven, caught in a story that wasn't his own? Or had he chosen this life, this chance to make the world better? He couldn't tell anymore.

Ahead, the river swung in one last loop, veering right to the far wall of the chasm, then left again, across their path, to disappear into an opening in the rock face, with a roar that indicated a waterfall somewhere in the darkness.

This was it: they had no choice but to cross or turn back.

If they'd had to try to swim through these raging waters, it would have been no choice at all, because the currents would certainly have swept them into oblivion, but an unexpected source of hope stood out on the last stretch: a single vast slab of stone wide enough to carry a wagon, straddling the river with its ends set on heaps of boulders on either side. It was the roughest bridge Raul had ever seen, but it was definitely a bridge.

Equally undeniable were the figures standing on the bridge, out in the open despite the hammering rain. There were a dozen of them, one in the centre taller than any of the rest by a head and a half. In the gloom of a cloudy midwinter's day and the blur of rain, it was hard to make out details, but they were all carrying staffs or spears and all facing the direction from which Raul and his companions came.

"Who wastes time putting guards in the middle of nowhere?" Prisca asked in the tone she reserved for idiots and people who interrupted her work.

"Someone who's found a bottleneck," Valens said, his hand on his sword. "How do you want to approach this, Raul?"

The one thing Raul didn't want to do was to stop walking, not with the rain pouring down and the prospect of Count Alder following along behind them. He kept plodding forward, water dribbling past his face, contemplating what lay ahead.

"Let's find out what they want first," he said. "Then we'll decide."

It wasn't as though they could get around the bridge guards, or creep up on them—the travellers were as exposed as the bridge itself in this broken, barren chasm. And there lay one more reason why Raul didn't want to pause, though he didn't want to worry the others if they hadn't worked it out for themselves—a place like this had probably been made by a river, one far bigger than the one that remained. In this pouring rain, it wasn't wild to imagine that river forming again, as water built up in the hills or burst from the banks of another waterway, or if the river they were looking to cross got just a little higher. Once the water started rushing down this valley, there would be no getting away from it. It didn't take a reading of the omens to see that outcome.

At the near end of the bridge, rocks had been arranged to make a set of steps, uneven but serviceable, wide enough for two people walking close together—or for a horseman, a nervous part of Raul's brain pointed out. He resisted the urge to glance back as, by unspoken agreement, he and Valens led the way up those steps. His da had strapped his shield onto his right arm, but while his hand hung ready by his belt, he hadn't drawn his sword.

Reaching the top of the steps, Raul stood facing the strangers on the bridge. They wore cloaks made from large yellow leaves, each one as long as Raul's arm, stitched to overlap, and those strange clothes looked like they were keeping the rain out far better than his own cloak. While the rest of their clothes were obscured, he caught glimpses of armour woven from reeds, with fur and straw protruding at its edges. Most of them, men and women alike, were as tall as Raul, and the giant in the middle must have been nearly seven feet tall. She was the one who stepped forward, carrying a staff thick as a small trunk, to stand glaring at him.

Despite the rain, Raul pushed his hood back, not to improve his vision but to show his face. The towering warrior did the same, revealing a curving black V drawn in tar or sap on her forehead—the mark of Jarrag.

"You shall not pass," she rumbled, and slammed the end of her staff against the stone. Raul felt the vibration through the soles of his boots.

"I don't want to cause trouble," he said, "but we have to come through."

"Then you have to fight me."

She shrugged her shoulders back and her cloak fell away, revealing an intimidating body broadened and given strange edges by cages of wicker armour. A bark charm in the shape of a mountain hung around her neck.

"Let me, lad." Valens stepped forward, starting to draw his sword, but Raul touched his arm and he froze.

"No, Da," Raul said. "I have to deal with this."

"I know I'm not the warrior I was, but—"

"It's not that."

"What, then? Building the legend?" Prisca snorted. "It is not as though there are plentiful witnesses out here. Moments like this are what lies were invented for. Let your father face the monster and we can decide how to tell the story later."

"Not that either," Raul said. Or at least, not just that, though he had to admit, the need to reinforce his act as the chosen one had become a habitual part of his thinking, something that sent his thoughts flowing down unexpected channels, not always ones he would have foreseen.

"Honestly, Raul, must we—"

"He said that he's doing it," Yasmi snapped. "If you're not going to back him up, then why are you even here?"

With Prisca, there might be a dozen different answers, but Raul knew she couldn't say them out loud. Valens was simpler. His hand slid from his pommel and he stepped back.

"You've got this, lad," he said. "Remember to guard your left. Do us proud."

Raul set down his pack, slid off his own cloak and passed it into Yasmi's outstretched hands, leaving him as exposed as the guardian he faced. Then he stepped away from his friends and advanced, hands still not touching his weapons, until he stood so close he could almost have touched the towering figure. He looked up into a face made by fighting, the nose crooked and jaw scarred, into eyes as fierce as the heart of a fire.

"Why?" he asked, just loud enough to be heard over the rain and the river's rush.

"What?" The woman's brow crumpled, twisting Jarrag's sign.

"Why can't I pass? And why does that mean I have to fight?"

"Jarrag says you can't pass until you fight for it."

"Fight you?"

"So's said."

Raul kept staring up at her. Maybe this was a fight he could win, but he wouldn't bet on it. She might be big, but the way her staff tapped against the stones told him that she wasn't slow.

"Why are you fighting for him?" he asked.

She held out one hand, palm up. "We do as Jarrag says, he shows us where shelter and food lie." The hand flipped over. "We don't, we get frayed by his beasts."

"You mean his priests bring—"

"I mean what I say. Jarrag gives, Jarrag takes, and Jarrag ain't gentle about it."

Raul hesitated. He understood that gods made a difference in people's lives, that was why they made prayers and offerings. But the only people he'd met who claimed to speak for gods were priests, and even they did it by reading the signs. Here, a god seemingly touched directly on human lives.

Perhaps it made sense. In old stories gods walked the earth, handing out favours and punishments, and just because people didn't talk about it anymore didn't mean it couldn't happen. Prisca had said this was a thinner place, one where unusual powers could intervene. Perhaps a god could make himself heard more directly, even a cruel and ruthless one.

"You have to fight me to stay safe?" he asked.

"So's said." The warrior's voice was sharpening with impatience, eyes narrowing as the rain ran down her face.

"And I have to fight you to get past?"

"So's said."

"Do I have to win?"

She blinked. "Eh?"

"To go past, do I have to win, or just to fight?"

The warrior looked back over her shoulder at her comrades. Two of them shrugged; a third laughed.

"Jarrag only said fight," one said.

"Well, then…" Raul raised his fists. "This is me fighting you. Now hit me."

The warrior looked at him uncertainly, then drew her arm back. It was all Raul could do not to flinch as her fist swung straight into his face. Even if he hadn't decided to fall, that blow would have taken him down. He sprawled on the wet stone, head spinning, one side of his face throbbing. He was almost glad of the rain soothing his cheek.

"You win," he called out. "Now can we pass?"

A huge hand grabbed the front of his tunic and hauled him to his feet. The guardian looked at him with her brow still furrowed, face lowered so it was only inches from his own. Rain dripped from the charm hanging around her neck.

"Why did you do that?" she asked. "I see your sword, see your arms, see you could put up a fight."

"I could, but I didn't come here to hurt you. This seemed like the least bad thing."

The guardian chuckled, then slapped Raul in the chest.

"I'm Ovida," she said. "What's your name?"

"Raul." He returned the gesture, cheeks reddening at the thought that he was touching a woman's chest. Back home, that could have started another fight, but the boundaries of the personal seemed different here. "Raul Warborn."

"Good name." Ovida nodded. "Come, best we get out this rain. Sky really doesn't like the hills today."

Raul retrieved his cloak and pack from his companions, then the four of them followed Ovida and her people down the far side of the bridge and a little further along the chasm. Around a bend stood three round wicker huts with flat roofs woven solidly into the walls. Smoke rose from under a disk that capped the middle of the roof. Ovida pushed aside a heavy blanket to reveal a small doorway, and one by one they ducked inside.

The first thing that struck Raul was the heat. The interior of the hut was warmer than anywhere he'd been since they left the rebel camp; he could almost feel the rainwater steaming off him. What light there was came from a low fire in a metal dish hanging in the centre of the room, directly below the outlet for smoke, and from jars of glowing insects. Overlapping patterns of shifting light cast strange shadows from the wooden hooks and leather straps that lined the walls, and for a moment he feared that this was a trap, that their hosts would grab and bind them as they came in. That worry fell away as Ovida hung her cloak from one of the hooks, bound her staff behind the straps, and set a shallow pan of vegetables on the fire.

"Come," she said. "There's nowt to fear."

An hour later, Raul's stomach was pleasingly full and he was almost feeling dry. He listened to Ovida and Valens trade stories about fights, while trying to work out where the air current came from that kept smoke and steam rising to the centre of the room and out, keeping the place from becoming muggy as a swamp in the summer. There seemed to be something in the weave where the walls and floor met, though even when he pulled back the furs he was sitting on, it was hard to see details in the dim light. In the background, the hammering of rain against the hut had quietened to a soft but persistent rattle.

"Did you ever see a place like this when you were walking the country?" he asked Prisca, who sat next to him, still holding a half-empty bowl of fried roots, staring into the fire.

"Hm?" She blinked, then looked up at him. "What? Oh, no. Most of Estis has found more civilised ways to live."

"Civilised, so?" Ovida, sitting cross-legged at the far side of the fire, leaned forward to gaze intently at Prisca.

"I don't mean it as an insult. Most people simply prefer refinement and comfort when it's a possibility."

"If you don't call this comfortable, you can step out."

Ovida's companions laughed, and one of them thumped the entrance blanket with a stick he'd been carving.

"Everything is relative."

"Prisca," Raul said, hearing the sharp tone in his mother's voice and the growl in Ovida's. "Why don't you eat your dinner while it's hot?"

"I am not a child, Raul, and I will not be..." She pressed her lips together, face crumpling in frustration. "Will not be talked down to."

"You lost your words there?" Ovida asked.

"Not at all," Prisca snapped.

Ovida's expression grew distant, and her voice with it, as she gazed into the fire.

"Don't think it's the first word you've lost either, so?"

"I don't know what you mean."

"Jarrag does." Ovida pointed at the flames. "He told me."

Prisca didn't move, but Raul, who had grown up around her moods, saw the tiny movement as her jaw clenched. What was she supposed to say, that she didn't believe in messages from gods hidden in the flames of a hearth fire? As a diviner, she could hardly deny that there were signs in the world any more than she could deny the influence of a god whose temple supposedly held a weapon that could empower their rebellion.

The fire crackled. Rain rattled against the wicker walls.

Almost everyone was watching Prisca, but Raul turned his gaze away, the only thing he could do to ease her discomfort. He saw Ovida's eyes narrow as she watched the flames again, and her nod of acknowledgement toward the fire before she returned her gaze to Prisca.

"Jarrag says he can heal you, if you want."

Prisca's lips parted. For a moment, there was a softness to her face, somewhere between fear and hope. Then her shoulders tightened and the hardness returned.

"No," she said.

"You don't think Jarrag can do it?"

That drew more laughter from their hosts, some of it with a bitter edge.

"Whether he can do it or not, I'm saying no."

"You don't want to pay his price." Ovida leaned forward. "That's smart, but you can talk it out. If Jarrag's fixing to make friends, maybe he'll take owt you're willing to give."

"Still no."

Raul laid a hand on Prisca's forearm. She flinched, drawing away from his touch, pulling in tighter against the wall, away from all of them.

"Just talk to him," Raul said softly. "Surely if there's a chance to heal your mind, you want to take it?"

"I won't be that old woman, bent by age and stumbling on my own feet, about to have a fall."

"But you are getting older, and the divining's wearing at your mind, you told us that. If someone can help you . . ."

Without even looking at him, Prisca jerked to her feet, grabbed her cloak, and stormed out of the hut. Raul stared at the heavy blanket as it fell back into place. For all the angry words between them, he still loved his mother, still wanted her to live a long and healthy life, still wanted to go after her now and make sure that she was safe. But he was the one who had driven her out into the rain and the falling night.

Yasmi, her expression blank as only an actor could make it, took her own cloak down from the wall.

"I won't be long," she said, and followed Prisca out.

———————————●———————————

It was almost night outside, the last light of the shortest day vanishing not into a dramatic sunset but into the grey gloom of a cloudy dusk. Yasmi strode across ground littered with round stones, rain pattering against her cloak. Prisca stood in the middle of the chasm, her back to the huts, looking like a scarecrow—stiff, slender, and dishevelled.

"What in Yorl's name is your problem?" The words rose in an angry growl from deep inside Yasmi. She was done watching this woman hurt Raul. "All anyone's doing is trying to help you, and you're treating them like shit."

She grabbed a bony shoulder and yanked Prisca around, ready to keep yelling into her face. Instead she froze, aghast, at the sight of something she'd barely thought possible.

Prisca Servita was crying.

There was no drama to it, no huffing breaths or red cheeks, no tremor in her lips, barely even a shift in the creases of her face. But tears, as undeniable as nightfall, were running from her eyes.

"Do you know, girl, how hard I have struggled for control over my life?" Prisca asked. "Not to be pushed into mediocrity by older siblings who thought they knew best? Not be twisted into the purposes of a hundred schemers at court? Not to become one more in a million conquered souls when our kingdom fell?

"Now this thing, this sickness, it has its claws in me, slicing deeper into my mind with every passing moon. I accepted this price long ago, knowing it would one day destroy me, but that doesn't stop me from fighting back every day, grappling for focus, forcing myself on. If I am going to die in here"—she tapped the side of her head—"then I am going to do it on my own terms. I will not have my course determined by gods or physicians or some boy who suddenly thinks he knows best."

"That boy is your *son*, and he loves you, whether you deserve it or not." Yasmi hadn't meant to say that last part, but she couldn't help herself. A quote from Rolla's speech in *Golden Roads* sprang to mind, all about family at its complex bonds, but she bit it back. Prisca didn't deserve the beauty of Tenebrial's words. Even in the face of the older woman's anguish, Yasmi couldn't let her own anger go.

Prisca blinked. She swallowed. With a steady hand, she wiped the tears from her face, and it was as though they had never been.

"You're right." She looked up at the darkening sky, and Yasmi wondered whether she was looking for omens or just making night an excuse to cover herself in a blanket and pretend to sleep, a tactic Yasmi herself had used in her younger days. "We should go in, before Raul and Valens barter away half our supplies for goodwill and a new sword."

She brushed past Yasmi and stalked back toward the hut, but hesitated halfway.

"Thank you, Yasmi," she said, without turning to face her, and the words shocked Yasmi almost as much as the tears had done. "I needed to be heard, and I needed to be told."

Yasmi's anger finally started to fade.

"I'm sorry this is happening to you," she said.

Prisca bobbed her head, then started walking again.

"There's more ground to cover tomorrow, we should all get some sleep."

Chapter Fifteen
Into the Underworld

Helping pack the huts the next morning reminded Raul of travelling with the theatre troupe the previous spring, loading the wagons again after each night's performance, ready to roll on to the next village. Except that this time, instead of packing everything as tightly as they could within a small space, the trick was to bind Ovida and her people's possessions tightly behind the straps on the walls while spreading the weight as evenly as they could. Judging burdens by weight without considering size made for an interesting challenge, as did working out how to strap the bulky objects down. How did you balance pans against embroidered blankets, a lute made from a huge dried toadstool against a collapsible weaving frame?

Then came the part that was entirely new. With the aid of ropes hooked onto the walls and roofs, they hauled each hut in turn up onto its edge, the wicker creaking as it went, so that the buildings became giant wheels. The ropes were removed and reattached on the disks at the centre of roof and floor, then hooked onto harnesses that the villagers wore over their shoulders, everyone checking and adjusting each other's straps. Raul tried to help again but was brushed off, the views of an uninformed outsider more hindrance than help. He stood silent through a long discussion about one of the ropes before Ovida decided that it was too frayed and needed to be replaced.

For the first hour of the day, Raul and his companions travelled alongside the strange village, wheel huts rolling across the stones of the chasm floor, rumbling and bumping, dragged by the villagers and their ropes. He offered to help again, but Ovida shook her head.

"Best we do it ourselves," she said with forced patience. "It takes practice, working as a team, knowing when to turn, so."

She pointed to the smaller hut, which was rolling on ahead of the other two. As they approached a boulder, the team dragging it changed their path without pause or apparent discussion, altering their route with perfect and unspoken coordination, each pulling at a different angle to turn the hut's path without tipping it over. There was more to life out here than Raul could have imagined.

"Once we beat the Dunholmi, we can come back," he said. "Help you build large, secure houses, places you'll be comfortable, with proper farming, drainage and irrigation."

Ovida snorted. "What good's stillness? The wild and its creatures would eat us."

"We'd show you how to build proper defences, to keep it safe until we can drive those creatures back."

"You fixing to put us in clothes like yours too?" she asked, shaking her head. "This is life in the Withering. No call for another."

She didn't sound angry, but her tone was firm enough to put him off saying any more.

Animals and birds appeared from time to time, travelling beside the travellers or even approaching them. A boar let Ovida pet its bristled head while its piglets trotted along behind. A raven settled on her shoulder and she took a string from around its leg, ran the knots between her fingers, nodded and tossed it away.

The sun was shining, but the clear sky left the land even colder than it had been the previous day. Rocks that had been dark with damp were now slippery with ice. Every step was taken with caution, slowing their progress even more than the huts did, and Raul caught himself looking back nervously over his shoulder, wondering how much ground Count Alder and his mounted warriors might be making.

Around midmorning, the end of the chasm came into sight. Between two rocky crags, the ground split. On the right, it rose into a rough sort of ramp toward the lower slopes of one of the mountains. On the left, it descended into the gap where overarching rocks met, a pool of darkness as thick as any ink Prisca had ever brewed.

"You want Jarrag's Rest, that's your path," Ovida said, pointing into the darkness. "Through the earth itself, to find the true heart of the wild."

The first of the huts was already heading the other way, slowing as its team dragged it up the ramp. The path was rough, angular blocks of stone almost breaking their momentum, but they kept moving, while the other two huts waited at the base. Some of the stones looked so angular that Raul would have assumed they were carved by people if he'd seen them anywhere else. But wasn't that the nature of the wild, that nothing was like it should be?

Ovida reached out to tilt his head, examining the place where she'd hit him the day before.

"You heal fast. There'll be nowt left of yon bruise in a week."

"I guess you'll have to hit me harder next time."

"Way you're headed, there won't be a next time." She laid a hand on his shoulder. "You've good sap in your veins, Raul Warborn, but don't try taking root in the wrong season. You fix to hurt our land, we'll fray you hard as any road's teeth."

As she rejoined her people at the ropes, Raul and his companions headed down toward the looming cave mouth. The rocks around the edges were in layers whose broken ends gave them the appearance of jagged teeth, as if the land itself had opened wide and was preparing to swallow them. Raul opened his pack and took out an iron lantern with an image of the sun stamped onto its side. Valens, who carried the largest pack, did the same.

"I didn't know that you'd brought Drusil's lanterns," Prisca said, failing to hide a note of annoyance.

"I've been saving them until we needed them."

"It's not as if they're going to run out."

"We don't know that." Raul opened the shutters of his lantern and light shone in a beam ahead of him, without any fire to make it. "No one else can make these, only one in ten ever works, and Drusil's only been making them a few years. How do we know how long they'll last, especially in a place like the wild?"

"Fine, but couldn't we have brought more?"

"Only one in ten, remember, and Drusil's been making other things. I left the rest for the folks we left behind. Two lanterns between four of us is plenty. I'll lead the way, Da can bring up the rear, you'll have enough light in between. It's not like you're a frail old lady who might stumble over her own feet in the darkness and take a fall."

It only felt half good to say a thing like that, to let a little of his frustration out. The other half felt guilty, more so when, to his surprise, Yasmi responded with a soft "Raul…"

He sighed. Now wasn't the time for any of this. "Come on."

Their footsteps echoed back to them as they advance down and into darkness, those echoes coming faster and clearer as the walls closed in. However Raul angled his lamp, whichever way he set his shutters, no end was visible to that darkness, so he focused on the ground in front of him, on finding his footing and moving as fast as he safely could. At least down here the rocks weren't slicked with ice. For the most part they weren't even wet, despite the drips from occasional stalactites. After a while, there were fewer loose rocks, and the ground became almost smooth underfoot.

"This is better, isn't it?" he said, snatching for something that might lighten the mood. Leaving behind the daylight when they finally had a sunny day hadn't helped with the cold and weariness that were a part of his life now, completely inescapable.

"It's exactly what we needed," Prisca said. "An entrance to a realm where mortals might suitably face a god."

"'Into the underworld with you,'" Yasmi added in her reciting voice. "'To rip Sathin's divine glory up by the roots and wear it as thy triumphal crown.' *Queen Carletra*, act four, scene two, though Tenebrial keeps adding new scenes to that one."

"Not quite what I meant," Raul said, ducking under a low-hanging row of stalactites. "In fact, I'd rather face a god in the light where I can see them."

"Gods are like legends: they're powered by belief," Prisca said. "A place like this encourages people to fear the divine, and fear is a powerful form of faith."

"All the more reason why I'd like daylight. If we've got to take something from this god, I want him weak."

"What if that weakens what you take?"

"This is a better story too," Yasmi said. "Raul Warborn in the underworld, a prince descending into darkness to bring back light to the world. It'll remind people of the heroes of legend, especially once Tenebrial makes it into a play to go recruiting with in the spring."

Raul tried to imagine himself as the hero of a play, with audiences cheering for him just like he'd cheered for so many imaginary monarchs and imitation heroes through the years. The idea was absurd, but that didn't stop him from smiling at the thought.

Then the shadows from his lantern cast a shape like a face, just for a moment, on the wall ahead, and his mind came back to the worry that had kept him awake half the night.

"This god, why do you think he offered to heal Prisca? It

doesn't make sense, when he had people trying to stop us on the bridge the same day."

"Gods are fickle," Yasmi said. "Or at least, that's what Tenebrial says when my father asks him for more consistent characterisation."

"They're also powerful," Prisca said. "And power comes from strategic thinking. After seeing us get past his guards, perhaps he decided to try a different approach."

"But a different approach to what?" Raul asked.

The echoes of their conversation ran ahead of them as they kept walking, through tunnels that narrowed and widened, twisted around corners, rose and fell.

"Have you ever heard of a god acting like this before?" Raul asked. "Harsh and fickle."

Prisca's laughter was as savage as any wild beast. "Have you ever listened to a priest? Do as Yorl says and he'll send you love and gold, defy him and you'll drown in blood. Avgar likes puzzles as much as revelations, and Selthin's a walking brawl."

"Laughing Loftus seems friendly."

"Not if you read the old stories and see what he was laughing at."

"But they always want something, even if it's just offerings at the temple. What could Jarrag be trying to get out of all this?"

"Maybe it's a test of character," Yasmi said. "In *Sisters in Sorrow*, the priest of Avgar says that the nation is being tested by war, to find out whether it's strong enough."

"But what would Jarrag be trying to find out? If he could

see that Prisca's sick, then he already knows more about us than most people do."

"You have a theory," Prisca said.

"What makes you say that?" Raul didn't mean to sound defensive, but he couldn't help hearing it in the echoes of his voice.

"Because you're disagreeing with ours. So, what is your hypothesis?"

Raul hesitated. He wasn't really convinced of the idea himself, but something about it felt right, and it seemed unfair not to expose his own thoughts after criticising other people's.

"I wondered if he's offering us what he thinks we want. So he offered me a challenge like something out of a legend, because I'm on a quest, and he offered Prisca a cure for her sickness."

"Interesting." Prisca's staff tapped against the ground between her footfalls, a sharper rhythm than the rest. "He could be laying the foundations to striking a deal, winning us around so that we'll pay his price for the power of the wild."

Raul's scalp prickled. He didn't like the thought of owing something to a strange god, especially one whose creatures had been attacking them since they came into the Withered Hills, one that was only offering them good things after violence had failed. That was how tyrants behaved.

"If that's the alternative, maybe we'll have to call that power for ourselves," he said.

"I would say that some prices are worth paying to avoid violence, but that logic is why so many of our contemporaries became collaborators." The tapping from Prisca's staff stopped briefly, then started up again. "Of course, this is all hypothetical. So far, we've only seen evidence of attempts to please two of us."

"Maybe not. Yasmi, Da, can you think of anything the god's done that offers something you want?"

When he looked back over his shoulder, he saw Valens frozen in his tracks. He thought that his da was about to answer the question, but instead he held up his stump as he slowly turned his head, looking back the way they had come.

"You hear that?" Valens asked, his voice low.

They all stood silent, Raul holding his breath, afraid of how loudly it might echo back.

"Hear what?" Prisca whispered after a moment.

"Footsteps behind us, distant." Yasmi's hand rested on her wolf mask. With her head tilted to one side, her eyes looked almost yellow in the lamp light. "No, not footsteps."

"Hooves." Valens pointed past Raul, further down the tunnel. "Move."

They picked up their pace, rushing along the tunnel as fast as they could in the dark. Yasmi was soon beside Raul, bounding confidently over raised rocks and ducking under dips in the ceiling, while Prisca's staff and the thud of Valens's footsteps followed not far behind.

The tunnel was broadening and there were no more downslopes, only upward ones. It was hard to judge, but Raul thought that they might even be higher now than they had been when they came in. Then he rounded a corner and there was light up ahead, faint against the rock of the tunnel. Another turn and it clung clear on the wall, then sky appeared above and ahead, as bright and blue as when they'd headed in that morning. With one last burst of speed, they rushed out of a tunnel mouth and onto the upper slope of a green valley, with a lone trail leading down through densely grown bushes and trees. It looked just like the Withered Hills had when they first arrived.

So much for entering a realm where he might face a god.

To either side of him, Prisca and Yasmi paused, catching their breath. Raul looked back and felt like his stomach was sinking all the way down that valley side.

"Where's Da?" he asked.

Chapter Sixteen
Dying in the Dark

It was pitch black in the tunnel, no light in either direction. Valens had picked a place too wide for him to feel the walls on either side, wide enough to swing his sword but not for his pursuers to ride past. A perfect place to fight.

"At last," Fabia said in the back of his mind. "Time for some proper action."

The worn leather of his sword grip was smooth and familiar against Valens's hand. He would have preferred his own old sword, the one he'd carried through so many campaigns, its grip moulded to the shape of his hand by years of sweat and swinging blows. He'd lost that sword in the throne room of Pavuno on the same night he'd lost his hand, the same night he'd lost the ring, but a warrior had to adapt, and any weapon made him feel more whole. Silent and unseen, he raised the sword, swung it through the air, felt its balance and weight. Good enough to kill a count. Good enough to give his son time to get away. Good enough to reclaim what was his.

"Remind you of anything?" Fabia asked.

"Of course," he whispered back.

Darkness and horses, like the night that Pavuno fell. That night, he'd left the wall while others fought and died, and then Fabia had held the enemy back one last time so that he could get away, so that they could fulfil Prisca's plan. This time, it was his turn to make a stand. Valens didn't plan on dying, though.

Light was growing on the tunnel wall, back the way he had come from, the first sign of an unseen lantern. Then the pursuers rounded the corner, chainmail and horse tack gleaming, the light of oil lamps illuminating blue surcoats edged and belted in white. Count Alder's guards, and at their head, his dark hair almost scraping the ceiling, was the unmistakable figure of the count himself.

The riders trotted toward him, seeing only what was illuminated by their own pool of light. If he could have done, he would have lain unseen until he was close enough to kill them, but there was no chance of that here, so instead of buying himself an advantage, he would buy Raul time.

There was just enough light now to see the outline of his lantern, hanging from an outcrop of the rock wall. He reached out with his sword, slid the tip under the lever that opened the shutters, and flicked it back. Light poured out, brighter and steadier than anything from the Dunholmi riders, the light of an Estian charm illuminating a warrior of Estis, driving back the darkness.

Count Alder raised a hand and his men came to a halt. The sounds of clinking harness, snorting horses, and muttering men indicated scores more warriors behind. Good that Valens had met them here, where they couldn't use their numbers against him.

The count's expression shifted from surprise to recognition. "Valens, isn't it?" he asked. "Prisca Servita's hired muscle."

"I'm no one's to hire."

"And the muscles don't show so well either. Have you put on weight while you recovered from your injuries?"

While he spoke, the count looked around the tunnel, assessing the space just like Valens had done. If he stayed on his horse, he wouldn't even have space to swing his sword, so Valens wasn't surprised when he dismounted. His leading warriors, a short-haired woman and a leather-skinned man, did the same, passing their bridles to the riders behind them and stepping clear of their horses.

"Did Prisca leave you here to buy herself time?" Alder asked. "Or was it the boy? From everything I hear, your false saviour is still the figurehead, but I have trouble believing a royal minister would let an untested youth take charge."

Angry answers bubbled up in Valens: about how he didn't follow Prisca's lead, about how Raul was a better leader than this fool would ever be. But he was steady, a sword in his hand, and he could tell he was being baited.

"I'm here for my ring," he growled.

"Your ring?"

"My mourning ring. You took it with my hand. I'm taking it back."

Alder laughed. "What makes you think that I have your ring?"

"Trophies." With his sword, Valens pointed at the gold

bracelet on the count's wrist, once a symbol of authority on the Earls' Council of Estis; at the sword on his hip, the straight blade with a ruby gleaming red in its pommel, the sword Prisca had made for Raul. "You're the sort of gods-cursed show-off who keeps souvenirs of his kills."

Alder laughed again and Valens gritted his teeth. He wasn't going to let this bastard get to him, not while he was advancing down the tunnel, half a dozen warriors dismounted and with swords in hand behind him.

"I admit it, I do like my souvenirs. I still have the antlers of the first stag I ever hunted, hanging in a hall back home. But I only do that for opponents who matter, and you, Valens, don't matter at all."

Valens's hand was so tight around his sword he could feel the lead weighting under the leather of the grip. His nostrils flared as he took deep, snorting breaths, fuelling the fury in his chest. That ring wasn't just for him, it was for Fabia, and for every other warrior who'd died on the walls while he ran. If that didn't matter, then nothing in his life did.

The flames in the Dunholmi oil lamps flared, and a voice hissed in the air over Valens's shoulder.

"Lousy fucker," Fabia said. "He's still trying to bait you."

Valens took a step toward the count.

"You're lying," he rasped.

"Believe what you like." The count shrugged. "I expect that ring was tossed into a muddy pit along with your hand, and with all the other rebels you got killed that day. Really, you people should be more careful."

A roar ripped its way out of Valens's throat, filling the

tunnel with his ferocity. He flung himself forward, sword swinging.

The count's sword, Raul's sword, flicked out, deflecting the blow as the count stepped aside. He was good, not trying to block all of that strength, using his agility against Valens's power. But Valens had agility too, even if he wasn't as fast as he'd once been. His own sword whipped up, got in under Alder's guard, forced the count to leap back. Alder lost his footing on the rough ground and went sprawling.

Valens grinned. This was how it should have been last time.

Alder's chosen warriors sprang forward to protect their lord. Not the two who had taken the lead with him, but others rushing past. Always the way: officers and aristocrats leaving the hard, dangerous work to the grunts.

Sabres flashed silver against the darkness. The tunnel was wide enough for two of them to attack at once, but that left each with less room to manoeuvre. Valens blocked one strike with his shield, parried the other, then lunged. Chainmail screeched across his blade and a shudder ran up his arm as the steel rings parted, then the flesh underneath. He yanked his sword free and a warrior fell, blood bubbling through his last breaths.

The other one swung low, trying to get up under Valens's shield. Valens blocked the blow, kicked away her overextended leg, slashed her throat open as she fell.

More were coming, warily this time. Those at the front had round shields now as well as sabres, and spears were thrusting over their shoulders from the second rank. He realised with alarm that he'd only got lucky so far. These weren't just sword-wielders, trained for flashy fighting. They were proper warriors, battle-hardened and disciplined, and now they'd had time to organise.

He hunched, making himself as short as he could to stop the spears from stabbing at his face. As one of the sabres swung, Valens batted it aside, hit the warrior in the arm, felt the satisfaction of snapping bone and flying blood. But even as he withdrew another blade caught him on the forearm. A glancing blow, barely pain, but now his own blood was flowing and it would only be time before that slowed him down. Better to do what damage he could now.

"Get the fuckers!" Fabia bellowed, and Valens roared as he flung himself into his enemies. His shield slammed into theirs and he knocked them back, the front rank into the second, all of them into the mass behind. There were grunts and curses and a clatter of weapons on stone as, just for a moment, he turned their numbers against them, slashing at the jumble of bodies, forcing them into each other's way.

A move like that couldn't last. A spear slid over the top of his shield and glanced off his shoulder, almost drawing blood. Another one struck his sword arm close to where the sabre had hit, and he cursed as he stumbled back, the blood flowing faster. Someone kicked his leg, just missing the weak point of his knee, and he wobbled as he took another step back. The Dunholmi, reformed and braced against a charge, advanced down the tunnel toward him, a bristling mass of gleaming points. He backed past his lantern, abandoning it to the rock and his enemies, parrying their attacks as he went.

So much for Fabia's ring. So much for revenge on Alder.

All he could hope was that he'd bought Raul enough time, though he was painfully aware of how little had passed, and of how fast a horse could go once they got out of these tunnels.

Blades clanged. Warriors shouted their anger and their orders. The echoes resounded like a field of thousands, like a whole pitched battle, not just a score of desperate people dying in the dark.

Valens raised his shield, blocking two spears at once, deflected a sword blow, parried another, saw a third coming too close for him to stop, felt the horror and relief that this must be the end.

With a crash, another blade blocked the blow. Raul, sword in hand, stepped up beside Valens. From somewhere behind them, light was glowing.

"What in Yorl's name are you doing here?" Valens asked, the words sour in his mouth. "You're meant to get away!"

"Did you really think I'd leave you behind?" Raul lunged, but the Dunholmi ranks were steady now, and the warrior facing him easily turned the blow aside.

"You have to! The quest, the country..."

"I'd die for those." Raul parried an attack, took a step back, and Valens, with the instinct of discipline, stepped back with him. "But I won't give up my da."

Pride and gratitude grappled with impending grief in Valens's heart. Now they were both going to be caught or killed, and it was his fault. But what was he meant to do, ignore Fabia's talk about the ring and the chance to let the others get away? Give up the best chance he'd had to make good for the failings of his past?

He blocked a sabre thrust and Raul's sword hit that warrior's outstretched arm. The sabre fell.

They were a good team, father and son, but it wouldn't be enough.

"Go," Valens said. "Please. Someone has to get away."

"We will. Back again, and get ready to run."

They stepped into a wider space and the air currents shifted around them. There was a rumble. Fragments of stone fell from a crack in the ceiling.

Valens risked a glance over his shoulder. An ogre loomed, long arms reaching up, warty fingers plunged into a place high on the wall where the seams of rock met. Light from their remaining lantern shone past her from where Prisca stood in the narrowing of the tunnel.

The Dunholmi hesitated, staring past Valens at the ogre.

"Yasmi, now!" Raul yelled.

The ogre roared. Its muscles bulged as it strained against the stone. With a crack like artillery stones striking fortress walls, dark jagged lines raced across the ceiling and chunks of rock started to fall.

Raul grabbed Valens's arm and dragged him past Yasmi, toward the light. As they reached Prisca, she turned too, and the three of them ran for their lives. Behind them were shouts of alarm and pain, the whinny of panicked horses, then only the thunder of falling rocks, a sound that buried everything else.

They ran out of the tunnel and into the light, emerging onto a valley side. Valens, sword gripped tight, turned to face the tunnel mouth and the dusty wind billowing out of it. A four-legged shape rushed toward him and he raised his shield, but it wasn't a Dunholmi rider. Yasmi, her wolf fur covered in rock dust, came to a stop next to Raul.

"Do you think that got them all?" Prisca asked.

"I doubt it," Valens said. "There were a lot."

"But it will stop them," Raul said. "They'll have to find another way around, and that will buy us time."

Valens hung his head. He should have trusted his son. The lad had achieved what he supposedly set out to do, only better, and without leaving anyone behind.

"Don't worry," Fabia whispered in his ear. "You'll find another chance to prove yourself."

"Maybe," Valens mumbled. "But we're never getting that ring."

———————————•———————————

Yasmi winced as Valens rubbed a stinging green pulp into the scrapes across her knuckles.

"Hold steady," he said. "It'll help you heal."

"I believe you, but that doesn't stop it from hurting." She looked past him to the tunnel mouth. "That was a stupid thing you did."

His brow furrowed but he didn't speak. Just because she could feel guilt radiating off him didn't mean that she was going to let him off lightly. Not like Raul was doing.

"You put him in danger. Put all of us in danger."

"We're already in danger."

"Well, you made it worse."

He took a deep breath, then finally looked her in the eye. "Sorry."

She flexed her fingers, easing the improvised salve into every crease and crack. Blood darkened the treatment in places, but nowhere near as much blood as stained the bandage she'd bound around Valens's arm first.

Valens reached inside his tunic and took out his charm from Drusil. The day was nearly done, but there was enough light to make the blue shape of the swift gleam on the pale metal disk.

"For speed and for luck," he said. "We've not had much of either, have we?"

"We're still alive, and we've come a long way. I'd say it's working."

Did she mean it, or was she just resisting being drawn into one of his low moods, maybe trying to keep him out of it too? It hardly seemed fair that dealing with Raul's parents was so much like managing children, but they were who they were; growing up in an age of war couldn't have been good for anyone.

She pressed a hand against her chest, felt the matching charm under her clothes. Did she feel lucky? She'd certainly felt fast at times, but that was mostly in her wolf form. If only they could all shift and race away across the Withered Hills.

"Your eyes," Valens said. "Do they usually do that?"

"Do what?"

"Turn yellow."

To her relief, that was when Raul and Prisca approached.

"What do you think, then?" Yasmi asked. "Is this a suitable

underworld to face a god in, or do we have to keep walking and hope that the scenery changes for the next act?"

She looked down the valley. It was cold and bleak, stretches of bare trees alternating with bands of dark green firs, all of it broken by rocky crags. But it was hardly the underworld her imagination had conjured as they headed into the tunnel. She had half expected to find Jarrag's shrine down there, and though she wasn't disappointed to be back in the light and fresh air, it felt anticlimactic.

"Raul and I have been discussing this," Prisca said. "The nature of the terrain, the deeper presence it represents, and how the world works in a place like this, a wilderness where the barriers are thinner. He has speculated that there is a way to find what we need here; in a sense to make it. It is an unusual approach, but there might be a theoretical grounding to justify hopefulness."

Valens pressed his finger and thumb to his forehead.

"Meaning what?"

"Meaning they think they can change the scenery," Yasmi said. "Right?"

Raul crouched over the wooden bowl of salve, picked up a cloth that Valens had used to clean his injured arm, and wrung it out. Red dripped into the green, darkening it.

"Blood for luck," he said.

"I didn't think that saying was meant to be so literal," Yasmi said, thinking back to a similar act as they'd set out. "At least, not all the time."

"This is a thinner place," Prisca said. "Words, acts, charms, the boundaries between them aren't as strong, and we can use that."

Yasmi tugged at her tunic, bringing the collar up as hairs rose on the back of her neck. Like anyone, she'd lived with the charms and rituals of everyday life. Offerings of food to the small god of crossroads to keep the journey safe. Looking for a rabbit's foot or outstretched hands as a sign of welcome over a door. Three taps of her foot before the start of a performance. There were a few things with more power to them, like her masks and Drusil's lanterns, or the incredibly sharp edge of a Dunholmi officer's blade, but for the most part, magic was muttered words and small signs that might or might not have made a difference, things that you did to be on the safe side. With Raul and his family, they were becoming more.

Her fingers felt for the swift beneath her tunic again, instinctively reaching for one charm to protect her from others.

"How is this going to work?" she asked.

"Look out across the valley," Raul said, dipping his finger into the bowl. "Pay attention to the cold and the dark, the wildness and the danger, the winter closing in."

Yasmi did as he'd asked. It wasn't hard. One glance down the slope told her how desolate this place could be, while the wind blowing icy against her cheek was a sharp reminder that they were only one day past the longest dark of midwinter, and that the season would keep getting colder from here. She hunched over, arms wrapped around her knees, holding as much warmth to her as she could, and that difference between herself and the world only made the Withered Hills more dour and menacing.

Raul ran his finger across his own forehead, marking his

skin with the green ooze. He drew the shape of an eye, like the ones that they'd carved on the doorposts of buildings in the rebel village, except that instead of being crossed through, this one had lines radiating out from it and a pupil so wide that it almost filled the eye. Prisca nodded approvingly at his work, then let him draw the same mark on her, and after that he did it to Valens. At last he came to Yasmi.

"Keep watching the valley while I do this," he said. "Remember to see the wildness."

"I can hardly miss it," she replied as a hawk dove into the trees, screeching as it fell on its prey.

Raul's finger was warm and gentle running over her skin, but the salve was thick, greasy, and cold, a cloying ooze that made her shiver. As Raul drew, the shadows deepened and the wind rose. Dark clouds rolled in across the mountaintops. Things skittered and shrieked in the undergrowth. With a grown of strained timber, a dead tree fell, its bone-pale branches snapping as they hit the ground.

"We've found the wild heart of winter," she said as the wind flung her hair around and snowflakes hit her cheek, stealing away her precious heat.

"Not found it," Raul said. "Made it." He tipped the remaining salve from the bowl and stood beside her, staring out across a desolate scene. "Welcome to our underworld."

Chapter Seventeen
Word of God

The good thing about walking down the valley side, into the brooding shadows between the trees, was that it gave them shelter from the wind. It might also provide good inspiration next time Yasmi was called upon to paint the backdrop for a scene set in a haunted forest. Aside from that, there was nothing appealing about the place. The ground underfoot was uneven and hidden by shadows, so that she almost tripped every third step. The twigs and fallen pine needles crunched so loud that she was convinced there must be bones underneath. Movements among the trees left her jumping at the darkness, expecting some wildcat or overgrown bear to leap out at her at any moment. The only contrast from the darkness was the pale clumps of snow that periodically accumulated on the branches above before falling onto their heads. She couldn't even work out a safe way to flee, because every direction looked equally menacing.

But if Raul said that they had to face this, to tap into the power that they'd come here for, then she trusted him, and she would be here no matter how miserable and menacing it got.

That didn't mean she had to suffer in silence.

"This has to be the single most ghastly place in the world," she declared.

"I've seen worse," said Valens, a few steps down ahead of her on the steeply sloping trail. Past him, Prisca was leading the way, while Raul brought up the rear.

"What could possibly be worse?" Yasmi asked as something scuttled through the undergrowth to her right.

"Scarlet Marsh four days after the battle. Sunken bodies rising swollen and bursting in the midsummer sun. The whole place stank like a rotten wound. Look down in the wrong place and you saw the half-eaten face of someone you knew, flies tunnelling in behind his eye."

A life spent telling stories encouraged an active imagination, and Yasmi gagged at the images Valens had summoned.

"Fine," she said. "It's the second most hideous place in the world. Happy now?"

"I can tell you the second, if you want. And the third."

Yasmi paused to let her stomach settle and to adjust her cloak against the cold.

"That's enough war stories for today. Enough for the rest of my life, in fact. When we get back, I'll be asking Tenebrial to write more peaceful plays."

The slope was getting gentler, to Yasmi's immense relief; if they weren't going to stop until someone tripped, then she wanted them to fall flat, not go rolling and bouncing down for half a mile, breaking a dozen bones along the way. Even Prisca didn't deserve that.

A clearing opened up ahead of them. On the one hand, Yasmi was relieved not to be so hemmed in and shrouded in shadow. On the other hand, the opening that let in washed-out grey light also let in wind and snow. White drifts formed at the bases of some of the trees.

Prisca paused at the edge of the clearing, looking around, and the others gathered around her.

"Are we stopping here for the night?" Yasmi asked.

"No shelter," Valens said.

"At least we'd see the monsters coming."

"They'd see us frozen stiff."

She scowled. He wasn't wrong.

"If we're still moving, then let's get on with it," she said. "Which way?"

With a jerky movement, Prisca stalked across the clearing, toward one of the larger gaps between the trees.

They followed her across the open ground, wind flapping their cloaks, and then back into the relative shelter of the woods. There was almost no light now, so Raul took out the remaining lantern. By its light, Yasmi brushed the snow from her windward side, then followed Prisca deeper into the trees. Even held high by Raul's long arm, the lantern cast as many deceptive shadows as patches of illumination, but it was better than stumbling around with nothing.

"I really think we should stop soon," Yasmi said as she stubbed her toes for the third time. "Preferably before one of us breaks their neck."

Valens grunted.

"Oh, don't tell me it could be worse," she said. "You probably sneaked into a black stone castle on a moonless night to fight warriors dressed in the deepest, darkest velvet."

"I was going to say I agree."

"Oh. Well. Thank you."

Prisca stopped again. She was running a hand down the trunk of a tree, looking from something there to the animal trail they'd been following, which split at the tree to go two different ways.

"Have you found something, Prisca?" Raul asked, leaning in to peer at the same bark as her. "A sign of where we might find shelter?"

The lantern was turned to illuminate the path, so Yasmi only just made out the tiny movement of Prisca closing her eyes, the way her shoulders slumped. She remembered arguing with the older woman in the pouring rain, the desperation in her voice as she'd talked about the sickness slicing away parts of her mind, her fierce determination to deny that mental spectre its victory.

Denial wasn't always a fight to the death. Sometimes it was a lie you tried to tell yourself. The lie that you were fine. The lie that you could still do what you could when you were young.

The lie that you knew what you were doing.

She sighed as she laid a hand on Prisca's shoulder.

"We're lost, aren't we?"

Prisca's nod was the smallest, most broken thing, but it was enough to draw a curse from Valens.

"I thought I could follow the signs. Not just divination, but things I've learned for navigating woodlands. There's something about different lichen, where and how they grow. I thought I knew it, but what I'm seeing here doesn't make sense. Years of experience, always certain in my path, and now I feel like I'm trying to read the world through a fog."

"Maybe that's just this place. We're in the deep wild now, right, the place where the barriers fade. Maybe that makes the signs less certain."

To Yasmi's surprise, Prisca's hand rose to her shoulder, her fingers settling for a moment over Yasmi's. It was like being touched by a cold, old statue; she had no idea how to respond.

"No," Prisca said, more firmly than before. "This is me."

Yasmi looked at Raul, saw the worry in his eyes. He'd been so certain in the face of the river guards and of Count Alder's troops, but his mother's sickness left him at a loss. She remembered that feeling all too well, seeing her own mother's bright smile falter as sickness took her, blood flecking her lips as she lay trembling under sweat-soaked sheets. She had always thought that her mother was taken from her too soon, but now she saw that no time could be long enough.

"Maybe we can stop here," Raul said, looking around. "Make a shelter from some of those fallen branches, set out again in the morning. It'll be easier to think these things through once you're rested, and I can help."

Prisca swallowed, opened her eyes, and her fingers tightened on Yasmi's just a little as she braced herself.

"No," Yasmi said. "If Prisca's brought us this far, then there must be proper shelter nearby." She slid her pack from her shoulders and held it out toward Valens. "Hard to see the last signs in the dark, but I can use other senses."

Cold swept over her as she handed her cloak to a grateful-looking Raul, but that cold wouldn't plague her much longer. She took the wolf mask from her belt, fingers tingling at the texture of its weirdwood fur. Just touching it made her heart beat faster, and there was a thrill of anticipation as she lifted it to her face.

She slid the mask on and the transformation rushed through her. Not just the twisting of muscle and buckling of bones, the sweet embrace of thick, warming fur, but the shifting of her mind from one state to another, the sharpening of senses. As she landed on all fours, she heard prey fleeing through the undergrowth, smelled deer trails from earlier that day and boar from the night before. She felt the call of the moon even through the clouds, a throbbing in her mind whose precise position pinned the whole world in place.

She was herself again. Her true self. Her chosen self. Every movement was a reminder of her strength, powerful muscles flexing as she turned her body, raised her head, sniffed the air.

She smelled humans, and she smelled fire.

With a growl, she set off toward those scents.

Before, there had only been cold and darkness, but now there was so much more. The clear shapes of trees and the trails between them, illuminated by the light that filled the world even at night, light that only a human would miss. The rich tapestry of smells, animal trails crossing like fascinating threads, each telling a tale of who had passed and when. Old leaves lay soft beneath the pads of her paws, released the gentle, familiar scent of the earth, gave way with a satisfying crunch as she dug her claws in.

A lifetime of masks and pretence had done nothing to prepare her for how real the world could be.

In the distance, other wolves howled. She flung her head back and joined them, bodies separated by miles of wilderness but voices and souls becoming one. When she looked around, she was surprised by the way her companions stood back, watching her uncertainly. But of course, they couldn't feel it like she did. They were only human.

A rustling in the woods. Hooves, not quiet enough to fool her. The scent of a deer, fresher than the rest. She licked her lips and tensed her legs, ready to spring off the trail and race after it, to feel the rush of the hunt, to taste blood, rich and hot.

Then Raul spoke, and though she missed the words, his voice drew her back. She sniffed, found the human scents again, and followed them on down the trail.

———————————•———————————

At the sound of voices and the crackling of flames, Raul laid his hand on his sword. Maybe the people up ahead would be friendly, but between Count Alder's troops and Jarrag's challenges, he wasn't going to bet his family's lives on it, especially not with the way Yasmi's fur bristled as she led them through the dark woods, toward that growing light.

Behind him, Prisca narrowed the shutters on the lantern, turning its pool of light into a narrow beam along their path. A minute later, as more firelight illuminated the trees, she shut it entirely. Valens strapped his shield into place. Moving more cautiously, they followed the wolf down the last few strides of the trail.

Yasmi had stopped at the edge of a clearing, and the three of them gathered in the shadows behind her, staring out at the structure in front of them. Its stones were like those that stood on the high hill above Old Wellic's place back home, silent sentinels older than any of the local farms. Unlike those stones, which people could dance around with ribbons on a midsummer's day, these jammed in tight together, forming walls. Except that they were the most useless walls Raul had ever seen. There was no roof to keep the rain off, no gate at the opening to keep animals in. Just an oval ring of rocks packed tight as teeth in a mouth, and in the middle, a single stone three times Raul's height, jutting out like a grotesque tongue. The whole place was illuminated by a bonfire burning at the foot of that stone. Chanting rose from around the fire.

The snow that was still falling on the surrounding woods left this place untouched. It was as if the heat of the fire melted the flakes away before they could reach the clearing, except that the place was far too large to be warmed by a fire that size. Was this the thinness of the world again, the fire's effect exaggerated in the wild, or was something else going on?

The shaggy fur around Yasmi's neck rippled as she turned her head, yellow eyes fixing on Raul. Her growl was soft and questioning.

"It's the best shelter we've seen so far," Raul said. "There can't be any harm in asking."

He set one hand on Yasmi's cloak, rolled up and flung over his shoulder, the other hand on his belt, thumb thrust through, well away from his sword. Smiling his friendliest smile, he stepped out from under the trees and headed toward the opening in the stone wall.

The entrance was a squared arch, two standing stones and a flat one capping them. Images of a hearth fire and a shield were carved into the stones; charms for comfort and shelter, though Raul didn't feel either of those now. He paused in that rock frame and looked into the enclosure.

Seven people stood around a fire at the foot of the tallest stone. They all wore cloaks of red and yellow fur, brighter than the fur of any animal Raul knew. Each of them had a dark V marked on their forehead and a black streak on each cheek. Three of them stood to each side of the fire, and the last one, a middle-aged man, stood on a rock platform at its far side, at the foot of the standing stone. He stared through the tops of the flames at Raul, and the red light in his eyes seemed to be more than just a reflection.

"Raul Warborn," he said, and the other six joined in, their voices joining in uncanny unison. "You come to my temple at last."

Raul swallowed. If other priests were right, then he'd been in the presence of gods before, when he visited the Temple of Yorl or made an offering at a roadside shrine. But he'd never experienced anything like this: a god speaking through his followers, addressing him directly. His mouth felt dry and he almost stepped back, away from the threat and the promise of power.

But people were counting on him, and he had to see this

through. Hand clenched by his side, he squared his shoulders and took a final step through the doorway, inside the ring of stones. Immediately, his skin prickled with sweat from the heat of the place, as if he'd stepped from the middle of winter into a summer's day.

"Are you Jarrag?" he asked.

"I am," the seven figures chorused, and the six flanking the fire turned to face him. They all had the same light burning in their eyes. "And you are in my domain."

"This is where you keep Balbianus's blade?"

Even the laughter of the seven was synchronised, making a jolly sound into something disturbing. Raul's hand tightened on his belt as he looked around for any more of them. His companions had come into the enclosure, but they stood silent to either side, waiting for his lead.

"Here?" The seven each raised a hand, gesturing around the circle as one. "No. This is not my rest, just one more shrine among many. A place to root my power."

Raul swallowed. He'd never spoken with a god before. He'd made offerings and prayers, like anyone did, without ever really expecting an answer. At least, not one that came so clearly and directly. As far as he knew, this didn't even happen to most priests. Cirillo, the High Priest of Yorl in Pavuno and therefore by default the most powerful priest in all of Estis, had to follow the signs of divination to work out what his god wanted. Yet here was Jarrag, the god of the Withered Hills, talking directly through human mouths.

Was this a sign of great promise or a terrible threat? One thing it couldn't be was mundane.

"I am the heir to King Balbianus." For all Raul knew, Jarrag knew that was a lie, but he couldn't publicly let down the facade. "I've come looking for the power he found in this land, the power that built a nation and that can make it free again."

"You've come to save Estis," Jarrag said from seven mouths. "Or the North March, as some call it."

Raul had been wondering if he should sink to one knee or perhaps make an offering to the god. Those words decided him against it.

"Estis," he said firmly. "One kingdom, free of tyranny."

"And you its true king?"

Was Jarrag mocking him? Did it know?

It didn't matter. Raul's goal was the same. He stepped closer to the fire. His companions spread out, watching, ready to act.

"The dagger. The power of the land. We're here for it. Will you hinder, or will you help?"

The seven shrugged as one, tipped their heads, and grinned so wide the firelight shone off their teeth.

"We shall see."

With a whoosh, the fire flared to the height of the stone, before subsiding to mundane flames. The seven slumped, and when they raised their heads, they weren't moving together anymore.

While the others huddled together at either side of the fire, exchanging worried whispers, the leader walked around to Raul.

"I'm Issol," he said, and placed his hand against his chest, where a charm in the shape of a snowflake hung against his robes.

"Raul." He imitated the gesture.

"I know." Issol rubbed at the black V on his forehead, turning it into a grey smear. "Knew before Jarrag told me."

"How?"

"Heard from Ferra."

"But she's…" Raul gestured in what he hoped was the direction they'd come from.

"Aye, well, we've ways in the Withering." He pointed to a stone bench at the side of the enclosure, where three pigeons sat in wicker cages.

"Messenger birds?"

"Among other ways, aye."

Raul wanted to ask about those ways, but there were more urgent questions.

"Are you priests?"

Issol's lips fluttered as he made a dismissive sound.

"So's you'd call it out there." He waved a hand. "But these things work differently here. Jarrag demands and we obey— or we feel his fury."

"You're saying he'd kill you if you didn't do this?" Now Raul's hand was on his sword, fingers tightening.

"He'd take his price. But he provides too, for those as serves."

"Like Ovida and her people."

"Aye, and like us here." Issol plucked at his bright furs. "Plenty of warmth comes from Jarrag."

Beside where Yasmi was sniffing at the caged pigeons, Prisca had sunk onto the stone bench. Her head hung heavy, arms limp in her lap. Further in, some of the other priests were stretching a hide roof between the stones.

"We could use that warmth tonight, and a sheltered place to sleep. Could we stay here with you?"

"Aye, I was fixing to offer. Ferra says you're proper folk, not road's teeth."

"That's good of her. We have some food we can share in return."

"Seems fair." Issol waved a hand. "Gather your people yonder and we'll see to you."

For a moment, Raul wondered whether this was a good idea. What might they owe a god once his priests had given them shelter? But no one could claim a debt on you that you hadn't agreed, and Issol had been offering to share. Besides, they hadn't rested since before the tunnel; even Valens was starting to sag.

"Thank you. It's very kind. I hope we can return the favour one day."

"Favours pass on, not back." Issol headed for the fire. "Come."

"In a moment."

Raul waved at Yasmi and Valens to follow the priest, while he headed over to Prisca. He thought that she might be sleeping already, but she raised her head as he approached.

"There's food and shelter," he said, crouching in front of her. "You can get a proper rest."

Prisca nodded and braced herself, preparing to rise.

"This reminds me of the old days," she said. "Those rare moments when King Cataldo's coven tapped right into the essence of the world and made powerful magic happen, not just divination and charms."

"You were part of that?"

She shook her head. "I was better at divination, and some-one needed to focus on that. None of us can be everything."

"Perhaps I could learn those things to save us."

Her hand seized his wrist.

"No, Raul. Not you."

"I know there's a price, I've seen how it's hurting you, but maybe it's worth paying to save Estis."

"Maybe it is, but that's not what you're here for. If you want to learn a little divination, that's fine. Play around with Drusil's smithing charms if that makes you happy. But we need a king: a warrior, a leader, someone to rally a fallen nation. Remember your destiny."

"It's not a real destiny." He shook off her hand. "You made it up, remember?"

"That doesn't matter. You still need to fill that role. The whole rebellion is built around you."

"And it could still be, even if I do things differently." He rose and stepped away from her, scowling. "We're not working your way anymore."

"You still need something that *works*." She stood too, her exhaustion gone, glaring. "Cataldo tried to be the sorcerer king and look where that got him. Where it got all of us."

"I'm not Cataldo."

"No, you're Balbianus reborn." One stick finger prodded him in the chest. "Don't ever forget that."

"How could I?" He slapped his upper arm, where he'd been branded as a baby. "You left a mark I'll never forget."

Prisca opened her mouth to speak, then shut it again. Raul

didn't know if she'd lost her words or decided it was better to hold them, but whatever her reason, she turned without a word and stalked off to join the others.

With deep breaths, Raul calmed his racing heart. They were into the heart of the wild and in contact with Jarrag. That was as much his doing as Prisca's, and when the time came, he would solve this his way, just like he'd beat Count Alder. Right now, though, his stomach was rumbling and his feet were wet from rain and snow. Noble stands were all very well, but they wouldn't keep you dry and fed.

Feeling the weariness of long days walking, he headed for shelter and rest.

Chapter Eighteen
The Howling of Wolves

The howling of wolves filled the air, calling from one side of the valley to the other, sounds splintering and merging between the trees until their separate voices became a single hunting song rising and falling but never fading into silence, as though the snow and the wind themselves were howling their hunger. That sound wrapped itself around the trees that lined the route, thick trunks only a few feet tall that ended in fists of knotted bark made by generations of pollarding, from which fingers of wood stretched bare toward the sky. And through it all, snow drifted from an ice-white sky, flakes circling in a dwindling dance on the slow, broken breeze.

Raul shivered and shrugged his shoulders, trying to settle his back so that his cloak would sit better against it and keep out those chill currents, which seemed to rise from the earth as much as they swept out of the sky.

"Do those wolves belong to Jarrag?" he asked, his words frosting in the air.

"Belong?" Issol laughed the same laugh Raul had heard from almost everyone they met in the Withered Hills. It wasn't cruel or judgemental, but it marked the object of amusement apart. "Only thing anyone owns here are memories, Warborn."

"But are they working for him, like you were?"

Past encounters with fierce cats and a vast bear, their fur marked with Jarrag's black V, seemed to mark Issol's words out as a lie, or at least naivety. Surely those were a sign of ownership just like the Dunholmi heraldry on banners and uniforms back home, the mark of a lord demanding obedience.

"Reckon they're working for Jarrag like they do. Like any does when he calls, 'less they want to be frayed by another."

"So you do what he demands out of fear? That doesn't sound like a good way to live."

"Do you live without fear?"

"No, I suppose not."

Their boots and those of the others behind them scrunched in the snow as Raul pondered that point. He felt like there was a difference between accepting the everyday reality that the world could be fearful and accepting the menaces of some dark and threatening force, and with enough time maybe he could work out a way to express that difference without falling back on Prisca's help, but even if Issol wasn't right it was interesting to hear what he said, to look at the world through a different perspective, even if it was a bleak one.

Despite the cold, Issol had taken off his outer gloves, revealing thin, fingerless ones underneath. He twisted strands of fur and dried grass together, and Raul recognised the beginnings of a puppet, like the ones that Lestavo and Ferra's people made.

"Could you teach me to do that later?" he asked.

Issol frowned. "We've already shared sustenance and shelter, best you don't push your luck too far."

They emerged into a gap in the forest, a place where the trees had been reduced to scorched stumps and the blackened posts of charred trunks. Not the first time he'd seen a place like this, but the previous times they hadn't been draped in snow, black protrusions piercing the blanketing white shroud.

The footsteps behind them stopped. Raul turned to see his companions and the two more locals who walked with them standing at the edge of the open ground. Valens was pointing to a cluster of burned remains that stood closer together than the rest.

"Dunholmi watch tower," he said.

As Raul looked his perception adjusted. He recognised the regularity in the shapes of the posts, disrupted by fire damage, and the distinct squares in which they were laid out, the same shape and size as ones he and his people had torn down.

"They've been this far?" he asked.

"Once." Issol held up a finger. "Didn't go well."

"You drove them out?"

"The wild did, for now."

"For now?"

"Road's teeth are like rain, they come and they go, some times heavier than others."

"But they're not here now."

"Not as I've heard."

They walked on across the open ground. The snow lay more evenly here than between the trees, so they couldn't pick a path through the shallower patches, but had to trudge nearly knee deep through it. Raul wondered whether it would have been like this if he hadn't made them see the wild more clearly. Were their perceptions really making this place grimmer?

"You're further than them now," Issol said, putting his puppet away as they walked past the burned remains of the watch post. "Further than any road's teeth's come in my lifetime."

He smiled that knowing smile again, the one that all the Withered Hills folk seemed to share. Raul felt like he was meeting different versions of the same person over and again. Was that about this place, or was it about him walking into a land where no one was like the folks back home, where a thousand variations of accent and mannerism all seemed the same to his ignorance?

The howling of the wolves, voices fracturing and combining, came louder across the open expanse of snow. Grey bodies moved beneath the trees.

"Have you tried to drive them out?" Raul asked. "The Dunholmi, I mean, not the wolves."

"Why would we fix to do a thing like that?"

"Because they're trying to take over your land."

"Can't own land."

"They'll try, and they could do a lot of damage along the way."

Issol, gaze drifting down to the snow, made a clicking sound with his tongue.

"Some good stands of tree and fruit been lost and not come back after they cut through," he admitted. "Some herds and packs not roaming so far, not growing so big, not carrying as much meat and hide as we'd like."

"And people?"

His thoughtful look became a frown. "Some hurt, or gone, aye, but that always happens when town folk come." He looked pointedly at Raul.

"We're not trying to do what they are. Do you think that Count Alder and his people would have avoided fighting Ovida on her bridge?"

If Issol had a response, it was cut off by the crunch of snow as footsteps hurried to them from behind, Yasmi rushing up to Raul's side.

"The wolves," she said, her voiced raised in a way that was as much excitement as alarm.

Raul looked around. "I don't see them."

"You don't hear them?"

He didn't. Even though they were almost at the trees again, he didn't hear a single wolf.

Yasmi closed her eyes and took a deep breath, head rising as if she was sniffing the breeze. When she opened her eyes again, they were yellow, and she bared her teeth in a feral grin.

"They come."

One of the people who had been with Issol at the shrine tugged at his sleeve.

"Come," she said, hurrying past. "Away from these."

The woman hurried toward the trees, another of the travellers following her. But as she stepped into the shadows, a wolf burst out, leaping onto her. She screamed as she fell, and her companion stumbled back as more wolves poured from the forest's edge, five of them falling on the screaming woman.

Raul drew his sword. Prisca's bow creaked. Valens stepped up beside him, shield raised, while Yasmi pressed a mask to her face and sank into her own wolf form.

"Get behind us!" Raul shouted.

Issol and the remaining locals hurried to do as he said. They carried staffs, but those wouldn't be enough to protect them against the dozens of grey bodies emerging into the clearing, prowling forward with teeth bared. Yasmi growled, a sound of rasping menace, but those wolves didn't respond, only stared at her.

"Back," Valens said. "Get some space."

The band of travellers retreated toward the centre of the clearing. The wolves followed, nearly a hundred of them now, some leaving a red trail in the snow.

"I thought that you served Jarrag," Raul said. "Why would he kill your friend?"

"I told you, we're not his," Issol said, his voice shaking. "We serve him when he demands, but he doesn't care for us any more than for a tree or a rock or a gust of wind."

"And why do this?"

"Blood and fire. What else would Jarrag want?"

The wolves spread out, forming a circle, ringing them in. Each of the creatures had a familiar black mark on its fur.

"He's testing us," Prisca said. "Trying to find out how we'll respond to each challenge."

"By dying," Valens said, his head turning to survey the shapes closing in on them.

"Not funny."

"True, though. We can kill a lot of these, but they'll keep coming. One slip and that's it."

Yasmi was still growling, and now the other wolves echoed that sound. It was a low noise at first, barely audible, but with each step they came closer the rumbling rose louder.

Raul pressed a hand to his chest, fingers pressing against Drusil's charm, hoping that it could somehow bring them the swift passage it was meant to represent. But even speed wouldn't do them much good now. They needed safety where they stood, like the snail shells people hung around the necks of children in times of danger.

"We need a sheltering charm," Raul said.

"Much as I admire your dedication to the craft, even I don't think that charms are going to protect us now," Prisca said. "What we need are walls."

"Well, we don't have walls." Raul slid his sword back into his scabbard.

"And the world doesn't have a charm that could protect us without them."

"Not the world we know, but maybe this place."

Raul bent and thrust his arm into the snow. With small steps at first, he moved between his companions, drawing a spiral through the frozen white, all the way down to the black of the scorched ground below. Even through his thickest tunic and fur-lined gloves, the numbing cold crept in, but he kept going, stepping in a wider and wider spiral.

"Stay," he said as Valens moved to protect him. "I need you not to disrupt this."

"The wolves…"

Raul was all too aware of the wolves, as he exposed his back to those growling, staring beasts, knowing that if one leapt, there was nothing he could do to stop them. He instead focused on the land, on the power of it that he'd been feeling since he came into the Withered Hills, on the stronger, darker version of it that they'd made themselves see. He drew that power through him as he thought about a snail's shell and what it represented, sheltering a soft body from a hard world. The same struggles from tiny beasts to whole kingdoms, and all the people in between.

He kept his other hand pressed to his chest, to the medallion hidden under there. Drusil's charm seemed so tiny by comparison with what they faced, but it reminded him of what he and the blacksmith had done together, of the feeling that came as he worked the essence of the world into steel. Humble objects could become more than they had been, whether it was a lantern, a doorpost, or a stretch of snow.

The wolves were still growling, but they didn't advance. Raul could barely feel his arm, but he kept dragging it through the snow, marking off the entrance to the shell and the body of the snail below. With every movement, he felt himself connecting more deeply with the wild land he was marking, felt himself becoming one with it, not forever but for long enough. Not owning, not serving, but directing it for a moment.

The world hardened around him. Loose snow at the edges of the charm turned into solid ice. A coating of frost crackled across his clothes, gleaming like armour. Falling snowflakes paused above the charm, then whirled away as if the wind itself was held at bay.

At last he stopped, stood, stared back at a wolf with blood dripping from between its teeth. The creature looked at the charm large enough for seven people to stand inside. It jerked its head, raised a paw, and instead of attacking scratched irritably at the black V in its fur. Then it turned and trotted away, and the others followed, a stream of fur flowing out of the clearing.

Raul sank to his knees. Snowflakes swirled again, and the frost no longer gleamed on his clothes. Was the world growing grey, or was it just him? He felt as though the same numbing cold in his arm was oozing through his mind.

"What's the matter, lad?" Valens knelt beside him, face full of concern. His da, so huge and powerful, seemed as tiny as all the rest, as insignificant as the one last furry shape leaping out of their circle and chasing after the rest.

"Yasmi!" someone yelled, but Raul barely registered the word.

He was land.

He was power.

He was safety.

He sank into his da's arms and into darkness.

———————•———————

The pack howled and Yasmi howled with it, their voices uniting in a wonderful whole, a fierce chorus in which all belonged. A song that set her soul alight, not constrained by melody and cadence like human singing, not held back by petty passions and the desire to entertain. This was the music that roared from within, that flung her feelings into the world and dared it to respond. A sound that left her trembling, ecstatic.

Her strides were longer than they had ever been, her muscles more powerful, her movements more sure. The rise and fall of the ground, broken branches, hoops of roots, none of it stood in her way. The wind and the snow brushed past her flanks, barely ruffling her fur. She bounded through the trees and nothing could stop her. She was invincible.

The world whirled past, and with each vaulting movement, she encompassed it. The earth. The sky. The woods. She embraced its vastness, and instead of dwarfing her it made her greater because she was a part of it. She was the wild heart of life, fierce and free.

The warmth of the other wolves was all around. Not just the heat of their bodies but the heat of their souls, of spirits united. A herd of deer fled before them, thudding hooves and desperate breaths. The pack turned to follow Yasmi's path, cutting their prey off in its flight, running and roaring then ripping into flesh as they dived on the slow ones, dragging them down in the snow. She drew her legs in and leapt, a movement made up of her whole body, an arc of menace and muscle that slammed into the largest deer and flung it to the ground. It thrashed under her, snorting in panic, flailing with hooves that could break her skull. Claws bared, she slashed into its flank, pouring all her power into those attacks, feeling flesh rend beneath her strength. The smell of blood was overwhelming, hot and rich, her heart beating faster, and when the deer went limp, she howled in triumph, victorious and proud.

She tore its body open, feasted on its hot, soft, salty innards, felt satisfied in a way that she hadn't in so long. She was wolf, and everything before that felt thin, distant, empty. If she wanted, she could call it to mind, but the shapes of that life were insubstantial as fog. As long as she was here, now, with her pack, nothing else mattered.

Muzzle dripping, she raised her head, licked her lips, and looked around. There was another scent on the wind, among the trees and the snow and the blood, a scent that also made her think of pack.

A wolf approached, big and black, eyes glowing with Jarrag's fire. Was he here to challenge her, or to tell her something?

She didn't care. He was welcome to the remains of her feast, as the rest of them were, and he was welcome to whatever Jarrag wanted. Yasmi was no one's to command. Not her father. Not her pack. Certainly not some god, a thing without body or blood. Hadn't she shown them her strength and what it could do?

As she stalked away, wolves called out to her. The voices of the pack combined again, and she joined them, a howling chorus rising all around, filling her chest and making her heart beat harder. The urge to stay was strong, but she didn't need to be here to be who she was. The strength was hers, not theirs.

She prowled away, following the other scent.

Chapter Nineteen
Wrapped in Ice

Raul woke to scraping, the crackling of a fire, the shaking of branches in the wind, and a throbbing in his head. He was lying on a heap of what felt like old, dried-out leaves, which rustled when he shifted in the blanket wrapped tight around him. The smoke didn't smell like a fire made from good, dry wood, but like whatever half-damp rotten remnants someone had forced into flame.

With a groan, he opened his eyes and looked around. Across the low and struggling fire sat his da, sword laid across his knees and whetstone in hand, watching him. The limited light of the fire cast Valens's face into shadows that exaggerated his wrinkles and hid his eyes. A rough lean-to of branches gave them some shelter from the snow that was falling past its open end, pale flakes against the gloom of night, but the shelter was barely tall enough for Valens to sit upright by the fire, never mind for either of them to stand.

"How are you feeling, lad?" Valens asked.

"Like I drank too much cider at the harvest festival," Raul said, pressing a hand to his head. At least that last icy stab of pain he'd felt had been replaced by something more muted, something he could think through. "How long have I been unconscious?"

"The rest of the day. You've just missed dusk."

"Where are the others?"

"Prisca's taken her bow hunting."

"And Yasmi?"

"Not seen her since she ran after the wolves."

Raul sat up, which made his head throb harder.

"We have to go find her. What if she's in danger?"

"Out here, that girl's safer than any of us. Especially if she's still a wolf."

Raul took a breath to argue, but his da was right. Yasmi could take care of herself. His mother, on the other hand...

"Why has Prisca gone hunting?"

"Because foraging failed. We couldn't find any roots or berries under all this snow."

"Couldn't Issol and his people help?"

"They went soon as the wolves did, took their dead with them. I'm not going to stop someone dealing with that."

"Can she even hunt?"

"She can use a bow." Valens waved his stump. "More than I can do."

Silence fell. Raul didn't have the energy right now to argue with his da's self-pity, and besides, the words didn't have the bitterness such comments had held before. At least the breath carrying those words hadn't frosted as it emerged; this small shelter with its dripping roof and cramped space was holding enough heat to save them from that.

"Couldn't hunting have waited?" He looked anxiously out into the snow. While Prisca had roamed the country alone throughout his youth, she'd always returned to the inn for winter. He didn't like the idea of leaving her out in the dark, especially not now that she was getting old and forgetting things.

"Needed food. Ours is nearly all gone."

"I thought we'd been careful."

"We have, but we're a long way from home, and we didn't bring that much. A lot's gone. Some's spoiled. I didn't pay enough attention to what's left."

"*We* didn't."

"If I'd—"

"Da, enough." Raul reached out his hands to warm them over the fire. "We're doing this together, remember?"

Footsteps outside the shelter made Valens reach for his sword, but Raul, weary and aching, was too slow to get his before he saw who it was.

Bending over to fit under the low roof, Prisca sidled into the shelter.

"Any luck?" Raul asked, hopeful despite the fact that she was only carrying her bow and arrows. Maybe she had a brace of rabbits strapped to the back of her belt or a fat bird in a pouch.

"Do I look like I've had any luck?" Prisca snapped.

"I didn't mean to…" Raul's voice trailed off. "I was only asking."

"And I was only saying." She scowled as she settled by the fire, midway between him and Valens. "We're going to be hungry tonight."

Valens held out a strip of dried beef to each of them. "Here, make the most of it. We'll try again in the light."

The meat was salty and satisfying. Raul tried to eat it slowly, but he was so hungry that his jaw ached at the taste and his belly echoed that ache as the first mouthful went down. The reminder of what he was missing made things worse in some ways, the absence adding another layer to the ache, but he couldn't stop himself from chewing and swallowing like his life depended on it, and as it went down he felt some of the pressure in his head ease. He was on his last mouthful before he realised that his da wasn't eating.

"What about you?" he asked.

"I'll be fine," Valens replied, running the whetstone over his sword.

"Idiot." Prisca held the remains of her meat out to Valens.

"Said I'll be fine."

"Fire and fury, do we have to have more foolishness? The boy keeled over today, we can't have you doing the same because you've starved yourself."

Valens's face screwed up, lips squeezed tight, but after a moment he took the offering.

Prisca shifted her attention to Raul.

"What you did today was very impressive."

Raul sat up straighter and his head brushed what passed for a ceiling. He hadn't felt impressive a minute ago, but Prisca didn't give out praise that wasn't earned.

"It was just a charm," he said. "Only bigger."

"That's how these things work, from Drusil's lanterns to battlefield rituals. Taking the concept inherent in our interaction with the world through charms, then finding a way to expand upon it, whether in scale or duration or something else entirely."

"I couldn't have done it somewhere different."

"That's often the way. During the war, King Cataldo's coven worked a ritual that opened up the ground and swallowed half an enemy charge, but that was only possible because we were in a place associated with mouths at a time of day for eating and on ground where we had ascertained that there were openings underneath. It was perhaps the most impressive work of craft I have ever seen, and sadly not replicable.

"It's the same reason why every spy and brothel madam in the world doesn't carry a silence charm like the one the queen gave you. Often, a thing works once and never again. I don't hold with Rabollio's hypothesis that there's an element of expenditure, that doing a thing once makes it impossible forevermore, but the difficulty of reestablishing the exact circumstances is often insurmountable."

"I meant I couldn't do it if we weren't in the wild. I feel the land here, that power in it you talked about. That...thinness."

"Could replicate what you did today next time we're in danger?" Prisca raised an eyebrow, and Raul thought it might even be a question, not a challenge. Still, he couldn't give the answer he wanted.

"I don't know."

"Then we are in for some very interesting times."

From outside came softly padding steps and a low growl. A long, furred face emerged from the darkness, grey fur turned amber by the coarse light of the fire. The wolf that was Yasmi sniffed suspiciously at the edges of the shelter, then stepped inside.

Raul held out his hand to let her sniff at him, then ran that hand over her fur. This wolf act was becoming more convincing every time. When he shuffled along his improvised bed to make space, she didn't remove her mask before climbing on and curling up beside him, her head leaning against his leg. A low, satisfied rumble drifted from her chest.

"Aren't you going to join us?" he asked. She stared up at him like it was a stupid question. "No, I suppose you're better off like that, with the fur to keep you warm."

Looking more closely, he noticed dark flecks on her jaw and larger streaks matting the fur further down. As his thumb ran across one of them, he felt something sticky and starting to harden, caught a little of a salt scent.

"Is that blood?" he asked.

Yasmi growled low and rested her head on his thigh, rough tongue rolling out across the nearby fur.

"It's not yours, is it? No, of course not, but let me help get it out."

He brushed at one of the larger lumps, and it caught on his fingers, tugging at Yasmi's fur. She jerked up, tail out, snapping her teeth at him. Raul drew back, hands raised, looking at her in alarm. In a moment she had gone from a gentle lapdog to a ferocious beast glaring at him with angry eyes. His hollow stomach clenched as he listened to the growl seeping from between her teeth.

"I didn't mean to hurt you," Raul said. "Could you maybe change back to yourself, so we can talk?"

The wolf kept on growling, yellow eyes flitting from Raul to Prisca to Valens, his hand around the handle of his sword. Yasmi looked ready to pounce.

"Please?" Raul asked.

Teeth still bared, the wolf brought one foot up to the side of its head. It hesitated, then there was a tugging motion and its face fell away. In its place, Yasmi crouched with her back badly bent in the cramped corner of the shelter.

"I was myself," she said.

"What?"

"Just now, I was myself. All my life, I've been playing roles, putting on performances, inhabiting other people. But out here, hearing the call of the wild and letting myself respond to it, choosing a life that follows no one's script, I'm as strong and as powerful as I've always played at being. What could be more real than that?"

"Oh, I didn't…"

In truth, Raul didn't know what else to say. The thought that the wolf wasn't really Yasmi had been a source of comfort as she'd become more wild. He didn't like the idea that the woman who meant so much to him was also the creature that brought wild animals down with its bare claws and came back matted with blood after running with its pack.

He patted the space next to him. Warily, she drew herself out of the corner and sat down. The confines of the shelter didn't allow much space, but they managed to sit without touching, both staring into the fire. Part of Raul wished that she would move closer and lean against him like she'd done before, but another part was glad that she didn't—he wanted to be with the woman, not the wolf.

Despite everything that the day had held, it had been a short one, and none of them was ready to sleep yet. All four travellers sat wordless around the fire, the only sound the scraping of Valens's whetstone across his blade. Raul half expected Prisca to call an end to that steady scraping sound, but it seemed like even she thought that was better than silence.

After an hour there was movement from outside, where the snow was falling ever more thickly. This time, Raul got his sword into his hand quickly. If it came to a fight, the shelter would collapse straight away, and they'd have to be careful about the fire, but at least they were ready to face a threat. Right now, it seemed like they would all rather face a threat than each other.

"It's me," Issol called from the darkness. "You fixing to stay in your leafy little hole, or you want to come somewhere with a proper roof and food?"

It wasn't a question that even took any contemplation. The four of them gathered the few things that weren't already packed, doused the fire with snow, and followed Issol into the cold, their remaining magic lantern lighting the way. Issol, dressed in thicker clothes than when they'd last seen him, led them on a steady march through the trees, back along a trail he'd left through the snow. Raul hoped it was a good thing that he didn't say much, that if he'd been angry at them for his companion's death, then he wouldn't have come back.

After another long stretch of snow crunching beneath

their feet and billowing into their faces, new shapes emerged among the trees ahead. Some were curved domes, while others had straight sides and slanted roofs, and all were taller than a person. Raul thought that they were all covered in snow, but as they followed Issol through a tunnel entrance, pushing aside hanging cloth doors with goat charms carved in their frames, he realised that the walls he passed weren't just covered in snow, they were made from it, the snow packed down hard and tight, then wiped with water to make a sealing film of ice. Even when they walked through another door into a wicker interior reminiscent of Ovida's rolling home, he caught a glimpse of ice walls forming a layer around the outside, mountain charms carved into their edges to help them endure.

Raul started to relax as the warmth of the place melted away the frost that had filled his flesh. His cold feet tingled, and he stumbled as he followed Issol through a series of interconnected spaces, built of different forest materials and in different styles, occupied by an equally eclectic range of people. Pigeons cooed from cages high on one wall, and a parrot squawked in Raul's face. A band of kittens watched him with curiosity from a woven bowl while their mother cleaned the fur along their backs.

"Warbur!" Lestavo called out as they entered the largest hut yet. Raul blinked in surprise, then smiled as the short, muscular man strode over to greet him.

"How did you get ahead of us?" Raul asked as they slapped chests in greeting. "What is this place?"

"Bit of a gathering, so," Lestavo said, waving around the

room. "Good to come together when weather's its worst, easier to make it through together."

"You have places where you gather when it snows?"

"Places? No. Folk just find each other, like you've done now."

"Actually, Issol found us."

"The same is the same."

Within a few minutes, they were all sitting around a fire, along with some of their hosts. Aside from Issol and Lestavo, Raul recognised faces from groups they'd met along the way, though he didn't know their names. He felt even more embarrassed about that once they pressed a bowl of hot stew into his hands.

"You realise how absurd it is to keep rebuilding these places again and again?" Prisca was saying, several seats around from Raul. He would have said that she was arguing with Issol, except that Issol showed no sign of arguing back, just nodded and smiled and ate his food while Prisca talked. "It is manifestly a waste of effort when you could instead build more... more..." She scowled. "Longer-lasting places, ones that will hold together when you need them."

"Everything changes," Issol replied. "Try to stop that and you get stuck, same day and day again."

"Certainty. Stability. The opportunity for progress."

"If you say so." Issol was twisting strands of fur into features for a puppet, its face long and pointed like a wolf's.

"Don't play the fool. Ignorance is not a virtue, especially not once someone has taken the effort to enlighten you."

"Isn't it?" Issol nodded again. "Well, then."

"Are you even listening?"

"Are you?" Lestavo called out. "We've told you and told you, your walls and your roads, that's not how we live."

"But you could!"

"Aye, so the road's teeth always say."

"This is…is…is…" Prisca's fingers curled into a claw as if she was trying to snatch something out of thin air. At last, she gave up and slumped against the wall, head hanging. "It's stupid."

"See, the Withering way wins in the end." Issol patted her shoulder, his expression still kind. It was strange to think that only a day ago he had embodied a god who would later try to kill them. Raul struggled to understand the sides here, how people fitted in, but he was very grateful for the warm bowl in his hands and the energy that came back to him with each mouthful of stew.

If he was going to wrap his head around the wild, then he needed to take a lesson from what Prisca wasn't doing and accept that these people really were happy with their lives, but that didn't mean he shouldn't try to share something that might matter to them.

"We might not be like you," he said, "but we're not like the Dunholmi either. We're connected to this place because it's where the Kingdom of Estis was born, where our leaders come from. It's at the root of what makes us, and we've not come to conquer but to look for what we need to become free.

"The Dunholmi are different. I've seen them beat and kill people who wouldn't obey, seen them tear down the things that matter to others just to break their spirit. If you let them keep coming into this land, they'll tear down more of the trees, hunt down more of the animals, and soon this way of life you have will be gone."

"It's not for us to let or not let anyone in," Issol said. "Not our land."

"But our home." Lestavo slapped a hand to his chest. "Don't play the worm, Issol. You know they're changing the wild."

"The wild is change."

"Not like this. They're fraying at it."

"And it's healing."

"Not healing as quick as it's dying. Too long since you've been south, you've not seen what I have. 'Less we change something, we're going to lose, and lose faster with each year that passes."

Issol chewed at a thumbnail as he stared down at his wolf puppet.

"Aye, maybe," he said at last.

Raul licked the last of the stew from his lips and carefully set his bowl aside. There was an opportunity here to make stronger allies, to get help not just in this quest but in the war with the Dunholmi. Not just the strange, scattered, disorganised people of the Withered Hills, but the power that watched over them, for better or for worse.

"You're a priest of Jarrag," he said. "Why don't you pray to him for help?"

Issol snorted with laughter.

"Pray for help?" he asked. "That ain't Jarrag's way." The fire in the middle of the room flared. "See, he's listening and even he's laughing at you."

"But you said that he gives people what they need. Why else would you follow him?"

"I told you, we don't follow, we obey when we must and we avoid when we can. If he offers, we take, but we do it careful and knowing it could be snatched away. You don't pray to Jarrag; Jarrag preys on you."

Raul had never thought much about the gods and what they were like. He joined in prayers on festival days, gave offerings when they were called for, and tried not to curse too much. The most he'd seen of their presence had been visiting the Temple of Yorl in Pavuno, where Holy Cirillo had helped them read the future. But even there, what he'd seen and heard had been a different relationship to the god, one made of respect, admiration, even a distant sort of love. Cirillo was clear on the fact that Yorl cared for his people, even if he didn't always show it in the clearest way, and as far as he'd heard, it was the same with the others, from wise Avgar to the jovial Laughing Loftus. You cared for a god and they cared for you.

If Jarrag cared, then it wasn't the sort of care Raul would want for anyone.

"Never mind Jarrag." Lestavo waved a dismissive hand. "We need to help ourselves. There are folk who listen to you, Issol, for who you are and for how Jarrag touches you. If you say a move needs making, those folk will make it, and we both know that moment's past due."

Issol's sigh was so weary that Raul might have thought he was the one who had marched across half the hills. The priest waved a hand at a nearby doorway, fingers shaping signs in the air, then took a thin string from his pocket and quickly tied a series of carefully spaced knots. By the time a young woman appeared through the doorway, bringing a caged bat, the knotting work was done. Issol reached through the bars of the cage, wrapped the knotted string around the bat's leg and tied it in place, then nodded to the woman. She headed out again, carrying the cage.

"If they'll move for me, then they'll move now," Issol said. He looked at Raul, then at Lestavo. "You two had best be right, or I've just called the ravens down for good folk for no reason."

"You ever know me to be wrong about owt that matters?" Lestavo asked.

"Often." Issol sighed again. "But I think not this time."

Prisca had risen from her seat.

"I've not seen a messenger bat before. Might I be permitted to watch the procedure for its release?"

"Aye." Issol gestured out the door. "Back where we came."

Raul leapt up. He had a thought, and he couldn't think of anyone better to share it with than his mother. "I'd like to see it too."

As they hurried out of the room, he leaned in close to Prisca and spoke in a hushed tone.

"What makes a god?"

"This hardly seems the time for a lesson in theology, especially not one that could fill entire libraries."

"A different question, then: are you sure that Jarrag really is a god?"

They hurried through another of the wicker-lined rooms, nodding in greeting to the people they passed, and entered a tunnel of packed snow, alone again.

"I'm asking because—"

"Yes, I see it." Prisca's tone was sharp with annoyance. "Now that you ask, the distinction is obvious. I should have raised this myself by now, instead of becoming trapped in the image this creature has crafted and the language of ancient texts."

"So what do you think?"

Raul pushed a heavy sheet aside to reveal the young woman with the bat. She had set its cage down on the ground and was unfastening the lid. It was colder here, only one last hanging door between them and the cold outside.

"Going out?" she asked.

"Actually, we came to watch the bat go." Raul peered into the cage. It wasn't often that he saw one of these creatures so close. "What a funny face it has."

The woman laughed. "Reckon she thinks the same, seeing you stare in like that. Still, if you want a proper close look, you can take her out."

"Really?"

"Sure. Wrap your hands around her wings like this." The woman mimed cupping the bat. "Don't squeeze tight."

She eased the lid of the cage open and Raul slid his hands inside. Carefully imitating the movement he'd been shown, he wrapped the bat in his hands, lifted her out, and examined her crumpled face and wide ears.

"How can you tell if she's happy?" he asked.

"Same way as with anyone, you get to know them." The woman took hold of the edge of the hanging door. "Ready?"

She pulled the heavy cloth back and a blast of icy air blew in. Raul stepped into the wind and snow, into the dark of the wild, bare trees twisting upward around him. As his hands opened, so did the wings of the bat, and with a soft flutter she flew away, vanishing into a night as dark as her fur. He imagined her in flight, rising across the forests and hills, carrying the message that Issol had wrapped around her leg, a creature on her own quest. Then the cold kicked in hard enough to make him shiver and it was time to head back in.

The woman with the cage was already hurrying away, back to her own life. Prisca stood staring at the wall, and the vacancy of her expression sent a jolt of alarm through Raul, but then her head snapped up, expression as sharp as ever.

"You're right," she said. "I've compared Jarrag with all eight of Im-Abrakti's possible definitions of divinity, and the only one he matches is the weakest. We're not dealing with a god."

"Then what is he?"

"It may not matter. He has enough power to leave these people trembling in fear. If he has Balbianus's blade, then we need to deal with him."

"But how—"

"Raul, your curiosity does you credit, but I'm exhausted in body and mind, and now you've thrown me a new challenge that I need time to process. Give me until tomorrow, at least."

"Sorry, Prisca."

The look she gave him wasn't quite a smile, but there was something tender in it.

"You don't say sorry so often these days, Raul, and I think that's good. You don't owe the world an apology for being you."

He had no idea what to say to that, so he simply followed her back through the improvised village, along ice tunnels and through movable homes, back to the place where they'd eaten. Their hosts were gone, leaving only Valens and Yasmi.

"Issol's people have gone to make up poems together," Valens said. "They didn't say we couldn't come, but…"

"But we weren't invited either." Yasmi stretched. "And while I've dabbled in metre, I doubt any of you know an iamb from a trochee. We'd end up as awkward as peasants trying to dance at a royal ball."

Raul was surprised by how disappointed he felt, facing this reminder that they were outsiders, an intrusion on the life of the Withering. However warmly they'd been received, they didn't quite belong.

"They brought fresh bedding so ours can air and dry," Valens said, pointing at heaps of furs. "I'm here, Prisca's there. I put you youngsters together."

Raul barely remembered the last time he'd been warm enough to strip off most of his clothes, not to nestle down in the same layers he'd been sweating in all day. Yasmi did the same and they both crawled under the furs dressed only in their underclothes. By the light of the dwindling fire, she smiled at him, and he smiled back. He brushed a fleck of something dark from her cheek.

"What is it?" she whispered.

He rubbed it between finger and thumb, dried blood crumbling, and thought of the angry beast that had snapped at him before.

"Nothing," he murmured back, then pulled the furs up, forming a soft shield between them.

For the first time in many days, they didn't fall asleep wrapped around each other.

Chapter Twenty
Shattering

The whole world was icy white, buried so deep that everything but the trees and hills had vanished from view. Valens had never seen so much snow in a single place. They'd had to tunnel up and out from the entrance to the hut where they had been staying, digging up into the dazzling light of day. Trapped between a white world and a blue sky, he hunched over in his cloak, glaring at the hostile ground.

"I feel like a fish in a frozen pond," he said. "Why couldn't we stay inside?"

"Because there are fires inside," Prisca replied, "and one of the few things we know about Jarrag is that he sees through fires."

Valens wasn't surprised that she had a good answer, but he still resented it. This weather was made for resentment. Most weather was, when you were on the march, but the cold was making him particularly miserable.

Raul and Yasmi didn't look any happier than he felt. The

two of them stood stiffly, an arm's reach between them. Yasmi was straightening her clothes and staring at the ground, while Raul looked around at the strange scene that had swept over the landscape, and although neither of those things was out of character, the way they didn't meet each other's eyes was. Valens wondered if he should try talking with Raul about it. That felt like something a father might do, but it also felt like something a son might resist. Gods be cursed, but he missed the simple days of conspiring to bring down an empire.

"Fine, we need to talk out here," he said. "Let's get it done, before one of my fingers freezes off. It's not like I've got many to spare."

That got all their attention, with looks of horror and uncertainty.

"Yes, I'm joking about it," he said. "*You* still can't."

A flock of birds flew past overhead, and Prisca looked up with a familiar expression of calculation.

"Enough looking for signs," Valens growled. "Get on with this."

"Trust me, we'll need all the signs we can get." Prisca met his gaze. "We've built our mission on a lie."

"I know that." He gestured at their younger companions. "They know that. It's the whole point of our rebellion."

"Not our lie—his." She pointed toward the most dramatic peak in the visible hills. "Jarrag's."

Valens pressed his thumb and finger against his brow. His head was starting to ache already and the conversation had barely begun.

"Go on," he muttered. "Teach us a lesson."

"There's no need to…" Prisca stopped and took a deep breath. "Fine. Raul, why don't you start?"

"Me?" Raul looked around, uncertain.

"Yes, you. What did you work out yesterday?"

"That Jarrag isn't a god."

"How can he not be a god?" Yasmi looked at them in confusion. "He has priests and he gives them visions through the fire. He's sent storms and wild beasts against us. He spends all his time controlling these poor people. The role couldn't be more clearly written."

As far as Valens could tell, she had a point, and Raul seemed to think so too, judging by the uncertainty of his expression and the way he stared at his feet, struggling to muster a response. In the distance, the flock of birds had almost disappeared, leaving the sky starkly empty.

"Yes, there are signs that fit, but there are others that don't," Prisca said. "And what we may be getting into is a question of how one defines a god, though that is hardly pertinent to our current circumstances. What matters is that the gods as we are used to them nurture, protect, and at times even serve their congregations, albeit in a distant and abstracted way. Jarrag is not only empowered to intervene more directly in the world, he does so capriciously and cruelly, abusing rather than nurturing. He is grounded in the world and in this place in a way that even local gods as we know them are not, and I suspect that his frustration with this has bred a pettiness in him. This is why we've struggled to find a consistent pattern or motive in the way he responds to our presence, alternating acts of violence and promises of wish fulfilment. To seek consistency in this would be like looking for consistency in the whims of a small child."

Valens's heart sank.

Wish fulfilment. That meant something to him. Right now, he almost wished that Fabia would speak, to tell him they were wrong. But out here, in the place they'd come to get away from Jarrag, she had also fallen silent.

"This land, its power, and this being that calls itself Jarrag are not one, but they are deeply intertwined," Prisca continued. "And that presents a further problem.

"The stories that drove us here say that, in this place, King Balbianus found a way to control the power of the land, and through it to unite Estis," Prisca said. "I put it to you all that there is no possible way that Balbianus could have controlled the power of this land, because that power is wielded by Jarrag, and Jarrag concedes power to no one.

"Whatever power Balbianus obtained here, he obtained *through* Jarrag, not his own efforts. The power found here, in the spiritual heart of Estis, in the place where our nation was born, the power that can be drawn out in the wild, where the walls of reality are thinner, that power *must* be obtained through a bargain with Jarrag, and so it is such a bargain that we must seek."

"Wait a moment," Yasmi said. "Didn't Raul use that wild power when we met the wolves?"

"He tapped into some source of power, yes, and directed it through a very impressive adaptation of a charm. Given months or years and a team of scholars, we might refine that achievement into something we can use in the wider world. But as we all know, we don't have years. What we have is the forces of Dunholm breathing down our necks, both here and elsewhere in Estis. We must utilise tools suitable to our circumstance."

"Of course." Yasmi spread her hands wide, head on one side, with a knowing smile. "What is a quest if not a shortcut, a way for the heroes to grab what they need quickly instead of putting in the years of work for real change. Honestly, it's a tribute to Tenebrial's writing that I didn't see it before."

Prisca's smile was cold as stone.

"You're right, despite your mocking tone. This is a shortcut and it's one we desperately need. I suspect that it's one that our monarchs have taken before. Remember, the early rulers of Estis used to take pilgrimages to this place, following in Balbianus's footsteps. How much would you wager that they each made a deal while they were here, power from Jarrag in return for something else? For some reason, that tradition ended generations ago, but now we will revive it and make a deal of our own, or at least Raul will, and we will return to our cause stronger than ever."

"I don't like it. This feels too much like selling ourselves from one dictator to another." Yasmi looked at Raul with concern. "What do you think?"

Raul hesitated, and Valens was glad of that. He didn't see how any response to this could be both certain and right.

"Maybe we can make a deal," he said. "Can we trust him?"

"Given the right circumstances, a suitably binding arrangement, terms agreeable to both parties, then—"

"No." Valens was surprised by his own firmness, but there was one thing here he finally understood. "We can't trust him."

"How would you know?" Prisca snapped.

Valens closed his eyes and took a deep breath. Before he could admit what he'd worked out to the others, he had to admit it to himself, and that hurt. In his mind, he rubbed his finger against a jet mourning ring, and it felt as real as if the hand and ring were still there. But they weren't, any more than Fabia was. He opened his eyes.

"The fucker's been lying to me."

They must have heard the pain in his voice, because both Raul and Yasmi looked at him with an all too familiar concern. Unable to bear those looks, he looked at Prisca instead, facing his old co-conspirator and the mind behind all his worst decisions. His old anger flared again, an anger that scorched him as well as her, the same sort of anger he felt toward Jarrag.

"Since before we came into the hills, I've been hearing a voice." He tapped the side of his head. "The voice said it was Fabia, said I could bring her back with Jarrag's help." He snorted. "Like you said, he offers us what we want, and he hurts us. Got me with both at once. Must have read my thoughts somehow, found her there, worked out how to talk like her. And I believed him. Even did what he said and almost got you all killed in the tunnel." The corners of his eyes stung. "Cursed old fool that I am."

"Oh, Da," Raul murmured. "I'm so sorry."

"Don't be." Wrath boiled inside Valens, driving everything else away. Anger at the violation of his mind and at the violation of Fabia's memory. "But know that if he'll lie about that, he'll lie about anything. We can't trust him, and we can't trust this place."

Silence fell. The icy wind blew into Valens's face, making his eyes sting again. A dot emerged out of the southern sky, a small bird flying toward them.

"That's useful to know," Prisca said in a voice that held much more unspoken. "But still, if we want his power, we may have to make a deal."

Valens hated that she said it, but not as much as he hated that she was right.

———————————•———————————

Count Alder leaned back in the saddle, finding balance as Fellstride worked his slow way down the stony trail that flanked the narrow but fiercely flowing stream. Awkward though it was, the two of them could have taken this terrain at twice the speed, but it was important to set an example of caution. They'd already lost two horses and a rider to the uneven ground and steep slopes over the high ridges, on top of their casualties in the tunnel, and while doubling back had allowed them to meet oncoming reinforcements and fresh supplies, morale mattered as much as manpower. They could make up speed when they got to flatter ground, and even leave the supply train with its mules behind as they manoeuvred to overtake the rebels, and when he faced those rebels he wanted his chosen guard to feel as invincible as they did parading through the streets of Pavuno. He wanted the will to win.

Downhill, where the trail reached the edge of the snow-swathed forest, Captains Brook and Thorn had dismounted and were peering at the slush and dirt. Melting water dripped from the branches so swiftly it sounded like the pattering of rain. The weather was changing again, one more reason why Alder hated the North March, a place as inconsistent as it was grim. Fortunately, being a governor wasn't like being a rider: he didn't have to love this place to rule it well. If anything, this part of the March needed to feel a firmer hand.

"What is it?" Alder asked, swinging out of the saddle.

"Someone's been through." Brook pointed at a muddy puddle in which the vague shapes of footprints were just visible. "Enough of them to be the rebels we're after."

"Too many." Alder crouched to look more closely at the footprints, and at others leading away. "This isn't just four people, it's a whole warband. Or it was until they split, one group following the stream into the woods, the other skirting their edge."

"Could they have left the trail on purpose, something to misdirect us?" Brook asked.

Thorn spat a dark wad of chewed leaf into the undergrowth, then shook his grizzled head. "Not how these people live. Their trails are part of how they hold their communities together. They'd as soon cover their tracks as I'd ride my horse to collapse."

Alder ran his gaze across the trees. Snow bore down their branches and lay in deep heaps around their roots, a fallen mass of white but nothing compared to what lay beyond, the thick fall that they'd seen spread out below them as they crossed the ridge. Was that the reason he felt uneasy, because snow was meant to be worse higher up, across the peaks of the hills and mountains, not in the woodlands below? Had this inversion of the world shaken him, or was there something else, something he'd seen but not seen, a small detail like the stumbling of a hoof or a courtier's stiff smile which would later become the omen of something worse ahead? Snow could provide trails to follow, but it could conceal as well.

Fellstride snorted and tossed his mane, watching the rocks above the tree line. A black point moved, the tip of a raven's wing perhaps, or maybe…

"It's an ambush," Alder said quietly. He set his foot in the stirrup, deliberately not looking at the rocks or the oddly positioned heaps of snow. "Be ready to move on my mark."

The other two mounted. Perhaps that alerted the ambushers, or perhaps it was simply time for the trap to be sprung. Arrows hissed out from amid the rocks, some rattling against armour, others thudding into the ground.

Leaning low over Fellstride's neck, Alder spurred his steed into the trees. That would be where the rest of the ambush lay, but it was also the only way he could gain momentum, could make any use of the advantage he had, could perhaps catch someone by surprise. He drew his sabre, ready for the fight.

Snowdrifts burst into clouds of white as buried wicker shelters were flung open. People sprouted as if from the ground, raising weapons as they came. The nearest held a bow, but was too close to use it before Alder hacked him down. Another lunged with her spear but made the mistake of targeting man instead of horse. Alder deflected the thrust and kept his blade swinging around in a wide arc, using the advantages of height and momentum to cleave the warrior's skull open.

Arrows hurtled past, flying in both directions. One hit his shoulder, its obsidian tip shattering against the fine steel of his chainmail. A warrior armoured in scaled lizard hide swung a long black blade like a strange scythe. This attacker was fast and skilled, moving with nimble lunges despite the ungainly weapon. In a more even fight, Alder would have wagered on him. Alder parried once, twice, shiny black chips flying as his blade hit the gleaming obsidian. On the third parry the black blade cracked; half its length spun off through the air and buried itself in a tree. Alder's strike missed the man, but it barely mattered. He was disarmed and retreating, and a Dunholmi arrow punctured his throat as he hesitated.

By now, Alder wasn't alone. Eight of his chosen were with him, Brook at their head, while others headed through the trees around their flank, moving to split the ambushers and pin half of them against the stream bank.

A woman with grey hair aimed her bow at Alder, steady as the tree she stood against. He tugged at Fellstride's reins too late. The arrow slammed into his chest, the force of its impact almost flinging him from the saddle. But the pain was a broad and bruising impact, not the sharp stab of penetration, the arrow breaking against his armour again. The woman watched for a moment, then shouted a command and vanished around the tree.

"They're running," someone yelled.

"Pursue?" Brook asked, twisting in the saddle to address him.

"No." If they'd been in the open, then Alder would have relished running these attackers down, giving Fellstride free rein as his sabre slashed left and right. Here, they couldn't see what lay ahead, whether it was traps, another ambush, or just rough terrain. He couldn't take that risk. "Regroup at the woods' edge."

It was a victory by numbers. They'd lost two dead and five injured, most of them from Alder's chosen band, while killing ten locals in return. No prisoners to question, though. That was one frustrating part of the whole business, and a victory by numbers wasn't much of a victory when they had fewer than two hundred in total and the enemy might be as populous as the Withered Hills.

While others tended to the wounds and the bodies, Alder stood with his captains by the stream.

"Is this how they usually fight?" he asked, holding up a broken obsidian blade.

"They don't normally fight at all," Captain Thorn said, shifting his chewing leaf from one cheek to the other. A dark stain crept from the corner of his lips. "From what I've seen, some arm themselves like this, some with wood, some with bronze or better. It depends on what they've found."

Alder tapped the flat of the blade against his palm. It was as sharp as any sword, sharper than some they gave the infantry levies. It might shatter against steel, but if it had hit cloth or exposed flesh, it would have sliced him open as easily as an officer's blade.

"Does this mean they've sided with the rebels?" he asked.

Thorn chewed contemplatively, spat into the stream, wiped his stubbly chin with the back of his hand.

"Could be, my lord. Could be they just don't like us being here."

"Either way, they're organising." Alder ran his thumb across the edge of the blade, contemplating the sorts of people who armed themselves this way. "To gather this many, to know where we were coming and lay the ambush. It's the first time we've seen that. Something's changed."

The broken blade had told him everything it could. He tossed it into the stream, watched it vanish into the churning current. Losing the rebels in the tunnel had been a serious setback, and now he needed to find their trail again. But his forces were over the high hills now. They had horses, they had numbers, and they had better weapons than anyone who lived around here. If the locals chose the wrong side of this fight, then he would rein them sharply in, and if they took the bit, then he would find his prey all the sooner.

One thing was certain: if the sophisticated schemes of Prisca Servita hadn't hurt him, then these barbarians and their primitive weapons certainly wouldn't.

Chapter Twenty-One
Bargaining

Raul raised a hand above his eyes to fend off the glare of sun and snow as he watched a flock of birds swirling through the air. They swooped and soared in long ribbons of movement, forming patterns that reminded him of the steady flowing of a stream. Perhaps a sign that a thaw was coming, to melt away the ice, or a symbol of a clear current carrying him to his destination. Good omens for his journey, unless he'd just imagined them. So many things could look like flowing currents if you squinted at them right. Was he just seeing what he wanted to?

Suddenly, the birds scattered, flying apart in a hundred directions, the mass of the flock melting away and taking his doubts with it. For all her flaws, Prisca had taught him well. Divination was so interesting and satisfying, he had no trouble concentrating on what mattered, finding the shapes amid the chaos of the world. Maybe this was a sign just for him, but it was surely a sign.

The icy surface of the snow crackled under his boots as he strode toward Issol and his people, who were examining the tops of a cluster of trees where they protruded through the white drift. The group's expressions were downcast.

"What's the matter?" Raul asked.

Issol prodded one of the branches with his toe. It was broken. So were others, now that Raul looked closer.

"These were good fruiters in summer," Issol said. "If this snow and wind has done more like it, next year will be hard."

"This is because of us." Raul crouched to look at the broken branches more closely.

"This was Jarrag stirring up the wild."

"But we stirred up Jarrag."

"Aye, well." Issol closed his eyes and took a deep breath, then let it go along with his scowl. "You've brought harm here, it's true, and some spoke verse last night on how we should leave you to freeze. Withering ways can be as hard as they're welcoming."

"But you're not doing that?"

"Others spoke for connection and you being part of the world, that we should fix to care for those who came. Once we brought our lines together, that was the rhythm they settled in, so here you are."

Raul smiled. "Thank you for standing up for us."

"Who says I did? Kindness and softness got to be wound together, like grass and stick make a puppet stand."

"Oh." Raul looked out across the pale expanse. "Thank you anyway. And sorry for bringing Jarrag's anger down on you."

"Jarrag makes his own choices."

Raul ran his fingers over a branch, felt the roughness of its growth, the bent and snapped parts where it had broken, but the flex and give of it too, the life that had been here and would now fade from everything but the heart of the tree. Maybe even from that, if the damage was too much. Growth and destruction, life and death, the same things that the whole world was made of but raw and exposed, that was the nature of this place. It was what made it so easy to read the signs and to pull out the power that lay behind the everyday. He'd opened Drusil's lantern last night, just for a minute, and it had shone brighter than he'd ever seen before.

The Dunholmi came to this place and saw something they needed to tame. Perhaps the old kings and queens of Estis had seen the same thing, acted in the same way, but Raul wouldn't. This place needed to be treasured and preserved for what it was, not what others wanted it to be. What was the kingdom without the wild?

"When we get home, I'll send someone with supplies," he said. "To make sure that you don't go hungry."

"Ferra's told me of the last time help was sent." Issol shook his head. "We don't need teaching how to build your walls, or how to fish your way."

"I know. You have your way of living and we have ours. If we ever do want to learn from one another, it shouldn't be us telling you what to do. But we have plenty of food we can send for a tough year." Plenty was a lie. Running and hiding, far from their home farms, the rebels had just enough to see them through, and they should be saving supplies for the campaigns ahead. But judging by the looks on their faces, these people needed it more. "Don't repay the favour but pass it forward, right? Think of this as me sowing seeds for a good crop."

Issol chuckled. "You learn quick, don't you?"

"I try."

"But I don't think you came out here for dead branches, so?"

With the broken end of one of the branches in his hand, Raul straightened up to face Issol.

"I want to talk with Jarrag," he said. "Can you arrange that?"

Issol looked around at the men and women around him. They seemed even less happy than they had before, but when he nodded, so did they. Even in a community that flowed like the river, without hierarchy or command, some voices meant more than others.

"See that hill?" Issol pointed to a high point in the expanse of white, about half a mile away. "Bring your people and bring firewood from our stores. I reckon Jarrag might be fixing to talk with you too."

———————————•———————————

Down in the settlement under the snow, Valens sat with his back to a wicker wall, eating porridge by the light of glowing moths trapped in finely woven cages. Across the unlit firepit, Prisca sat with her walking staff laid across her knees, staring into the ashes. Yasmi lay curled up by the door, a pool of grey amid the other furs. Valens couldn't blame her for slipping back into wolf form; it looked warmer and more comfortable than any sort of clothes. The only sound was his spoon scraping the last vestiges of oats from his bowl.

Yasmi's head rose, and a moment later the curtain shifted aside as Raul stepped in. He smiled uncertainly down at her, and for a moment the two youngsters looked into each other's eyes, but then both looked away.

Setting aside his bowl, Valens watched silently as Raul approached the firepit and crouched facing his mother.

"Reading the signs?" he asked.

Prisca didn't respond.

"Prisca?"

Still no response. Valens's eyes narrowed as he watched. What was she playing at?

"Ma?"

"Mm?" Prisca slowly raised her head. "Oh, Raul." She blinked. "What are you doing here?"

"Are you all right?"

"Of course I am."

There was her familiar tone but blunted a little. The way she held herself, she seemed smaller and more vulnerable than usual, but Valens didn't trust any of it.

"Were you reading the signs in the ashes?" Raul asked, sitting down next to her, his voice soft and expression concerned.

"That's right."

"What did you see?"

"I saw . . ." The staff trembled in Prisca's hand, and her voice fell again. "Raul, I don't remember. I was looking, and there was something, and then you were here, and . . ." She took a deep breath. "Very occasionally, it's more than words I lose."

"It's all right." He wrapped an arm around her. "You're still the smartest person I know."

"Thank you, but that's not going to last, and we both know it." She swallowed. "If you see something strange, if I look blank or don't make sense, please tell me. Having this happen is bad. The idea that I might not know it's happened, that's a thousand times worse."

"Of course."

"And if you could find a way to tell me without doing it in front of others, that would be a mercy." She trailed a finger through the ashes. "I can't stand the thought of being pitied."

It all seemed so real: the weak old woman voice, the hunched shoulders, the downcast gaze. Valens almost wanted to believe it, rather than believe that she was lying to their son again. But he'd already fallen for one lie lately, and Prisca was a better liar than any fake god. Still, he held back, watching her, watching Raul, not wanting to say anything that might hurt the lad.

"Don't worry, Ma, I'll be careful." Raul squeezed her shoulder. "How are you feeling now? Could you read some signs for me?"

"Of course."

"Great, then I need you to come outside." He looked around, catching Valens's eye and finally Yasmi's. "We're going to talk with a fake god, and I'm going to be too busy to look for the signs in his flames."

"Just give me a minute to collect myself," Prisca said. "And Raul, please, don't—"

"Don't call you Ma, I know."

"Actually, I was going to say please don't worry about me. I'll find a way through this, with your help."

She squeezed his hand and he smiled wider than Valens had seen in a long while. Then Raul headed out the curtained door, Yasmi padding after him.

Valens rose. His legs ached from walking long leagues and his back ached from nights on rough ground, but none of that was why he frowned and clenched his fist as he stood over Prisca.

"The little old lady act doesn't suit you," he growled.

"I don't know what you mean." Prisca's joints clicked as she stood to face him. "Or rather, I know, and I refute it. Do you really think that I would demean myself if I didn't have to?"

"Maybe you're telling the truth. Maybe the years with you have made me too cynical. But maybe this is just a way to bind that lad close and control him."

"That is an outrageous accusation."

"Fuck your outrage. If I decide that you're manipulating that boy, then I won't hesitate before I cut your throat. By Yorl's eye and Laughing Loftus, I swear it."

They stared at each other; her face was as blank as he had ever seen it, while he could feel his nostrils flaring and his eyes bulging with fury. Whether she was hiding pain and confusion or the careful workings of a manipulative mind, she kept it shuttered behind a courtier's pose. This was what made her formidable. It was why he had followed her, and why he would kill her if she betrayed the boy.

"If you're quite done posturing," she said, "our son is waiting for us to help him save the kingdom."

Stick tapping against the woven floor, she stalked out of the room.

As Valens stared down into the cold brass bowl of the fire-pit, Fabia's voice whispered faint as old ashes over his shoulder.

"After everything we've been through, now you don't trust me?"

Valens laughed bitterly. It was that or kick the firepit across the room, and this wasn't his home to wreck.

"I lived with a better liar than you for eighteen years. Did you really think I wouldn't work it out?"

A desperate, scarred corner of his soul hoped to hear a denial, the possibility that this really was her, that there was a way to heal his deepest wound.

He'd always been a fool.

"Ah, well." The voice shifted, Fabia's tone giving way to something just as forceful but more masculine. "I had to try."

"You tried to poison me with my own worst regret. If I get the chance, I will destroy you."

Jarrag laughed. "You can try, little man, but who are you to defy a god?"

No one who asked questions like that deserved an answer. Valens snorted and stalked out of the room.

———————————— • ————————————

They lit the fire at noon, on a hilltop shovelled clear of snow. Issol scraped sparks from a piece of steel engraved with a charm of the sun, and Raul wasn't surprised to see flames flare instantly despite the damp, rising quickly through a pile of wood twice as tall as he was. Magic had more power here in the wild, whether it came from a charm or a fake god. The fire stretched eagerly toward the sky, its hot colours bright against the clear blue. Branches further up the heap crackled and popped as the heat dried them out, ready for the flames to consume them. Steam and smoke billowed on the breeze, a vast imitation of the onlookers' frosted breath.

Seven figures stood around the fire, Issol and six of his people. Further out, in front of the banked snow, locals watched with protective charms in their hands, only Lestavo looking more curious than wary. Between these two groups stood Raul and his companions, Yasmi still in her wolf form.

Issol used a stick to scoop the first ashes from the base of the fire, then used those to draw dark Vs on his forehead and those of his companions. As each one was marked, they shrugged off their cloaks to stand dressed in only thin trousers and tunics.

"Do you need to do that?" Raul asked. "I don't want someone catching a sickness from the cold because of us."

Issol plucked at Raul's cloak. "You'd do well to do the same, so."

Now was no time to hesitate, when they were already putting so much trust in Issol. Raul unfastened a clasp and let his cloak fall to the floor, then tried not to shiver as the cold clawed at him. At least his breath had stopped frosting as the fire grew in intensity.

Behind Raul, Yasmi growled. Glancing over his shoulder, he saw her shoulders hunching under her fur as she glared into the flames. Prisca was staring into the fire too, and the intensity of her gaze told him she was looking for signs already. Valens was watching Prisca and Raul instead of the flames, but his hand was on his sword, as if steel could strike down a shape in the fire or a mere human could kill a vengeful god.

Except that this wasn't a god, and whatever it was, it needed people. If it didn't, then why did it put so much effort into bullying and controlling them, and why was it coming now, a presence Raul could feel moving through the world, like a flood wave washing along the valley and sweeping up into the flames?

Fire flared so bright that the noon sky seemed dark by comparison as Issol and the six other priests turned to face Raul.

"We meet again, Warborn," the seven said as one. Flames shifted in contradictory winds and elements of a face emerged within the glow. A wide mouth, fire-red lips around an ash-black chasm, each tooth a flame; eyes like glowing coals. Was this really Jarrag, whoever and whatever Jarrag was, or just a mask in a play, one more story designed to shift its audience through fear to obedience? "Have you come to pray to me?"

"Not to pray," Raul said. "To bargain."

The crackling of flames became the cackling of laughter. A wave of sizzling heat hit Raul and he understood why they had cast aside their cloaks.

"Gods do not bargain," the voices of the possessed chorused.

The wind turned. Smoke billowed black into Raul's face. He kept his eyes open even though they watered, held his ground though he struggled not to gasp and retch. If this thing could put on a front, then so could he.

"Monarchs do not bow the knee," he said through the taste of ashes. "As heir to Balbianus, I have a duty to maintain the dignity of his line as well as his kingdom."

"Ah yes, *Balbianus*. I remember. A long time ago, now. I made him, and his kingdom."

"That's not the story my people tell."

"Maybe not the *common* people, but those who mattered knew." Fire eyes narrowed. "You didn't know. What does that say about you, Warborn?"

It would have been satisfying to snap back that Raul knew what it said—that he was a fake, just like Jarrag, and that it was time to cut through the lies. But he had a story to maintain, upon which liberation might be built, and so many people were counting on him. So he held his face steady and he held to the words he'd worked out, because the thought of letting all those people down was more than he could bear. He put on the show.

"It says that I have come back from nothing, just like Balbianus did. It says that I have his strength of will as well as his blood. It says that I'm worthy to take his dagger."

"A dagger? That's what you're here for?" The chorus of coordinated laughter was even more unsettling than the words. Even at their best, Yasmi's acting troupe couldn't time laughter to match up like that.

"His dagger and the power of this place."

Around the hilltop, the banked snow was melting, running in rivulets down the snow that remained and forming puddles around their feet. Steam rose as the ground closest to the fire dried out. Raul pulled out the charm that Drusil had given him and clutched it tight, a reminder of the people he was here for, something to hold him steady as sweat broke out across his brow.

"I can give you power, little man, but it comes at the same price Balbianus paid."

"What price is that?"

The air seemed to grow even colder as the god's response built up in the seven gathered figures, smiles spreading across their otherwise blank faces.

"War. Leave these hills to me, but push your kingdom outward. Use the strength I give you, and let me see it through the fires you light as you go.

"The price I demand is *blood*, Warborn. It is always blood."

Of course. Raul should have known. Jarrag loved nothing more than cruelty and control. What could suit him better than forcing others to carry pain and violence before them, turning them into tools of that same cruelty? Was this how he gained his strength, or was it some twisted pleasure? Whatever the answer, the question curdled in Raul's guts. This was the force he was meant to be bargaining with.

"I won't do it," he said.

"Think carefully, Warborn. With my strength, you can free your people. More than that, you can strike your enemies so hard that they will never come for you again. If you truly are a king, then you have a duty to your nation and to your people."

"Even if I thought that my duty to others ended at a border, it wouldn't matter. The violence we carried into the world is why other countries rallied against Estis. If we become what we were before, then we'll call the same disaster down on ourselves again. I'm not here to remake what was broken, but to build something better."

"You think that you can defy me and live?" The seven priests flung their heads back as they roared the words. Flames stretched so high that Raul couldn't see where they ended.

"I don't know," he answered. "But I have to try."

The answering roar came together in a sound of pure fury, the priests' voices in tandem with the soaring flames. The fire blazed so bright Raul could barely see, and his skin hurt at the heat.

Then shadows fell across him. Valens's shield above his head. Yasmi as an ogre standing between them and the fire, her vast and hardened body sheltering them both.

There was a flash that forced Raul to close his eyes, and a scorching wind blew across them, tearing at his shirt. But the ogre's body was like a mountain in the path of a storm, sheltering him from the worst of that billowing rage. He could stand because the ogre stood over him, bearing the heat and the pressure, her furious bellow louder than the flames.

When the wind had passed and he opened his eyes there were ashes on cracked ground where the fire had been, grey flakes floating through the air, and seven limp bodies groaning on the ground. The ogre sank to her knees, one fist planted on the scorched ground, heaving and groaning. Her whole back was blistered and black.

"Yasmi?"

His heart beating slow and heavy as a funeral drum, Raul reached out for the ogre. She ran a warty hand up the side of her face and the mask came away. To Raul's huge relief, she was still standing, her grey shifter outfit barely touched by the heat, but the mask was half burned away, weirdwood crumbling to pieces in her fingers.

"I don't suppose I'll be performing this role again," she said, cradling what remained. Charred lumps broke from the edge of the mask, pattering like tears into the dust. "At least it had a grand finale. Everyone loves a heroic sacrifice."

"Sorry," Raul murmured. He knew that her masks were more than just tools, more than the most expensive pieces of costume that the players owned. They were a legacy, passed down to Yasmi by her mother, and now this one was gone.

She sighed and met his eyes just for a moment. Her grief was there for him to see, but she held herself steady. "All things pass."

Then she looked away.

"What now?" Valens asked, running a hand across the charred surface of his shield.

"That depends." Raul turned to Prisca. "What did you see?"

"A fist for strength," she said. "A knife within its reach. Horseshoes and a standing stone to either side."

"Strength." Raul nodded. "Not a surprise. I can't make a deal on the terms Jarrag offered, and I don't think he'll compromise. Caught between him and the Dunholmi, we have to take what we need."

"That was also my interpretation."

A rising hubbub of voices made them all look around. Issol, his priests, and the rest of the locals were staring down the hillside. It took Raul a moment to realise why.

The snow was gone, drifts deeper than doorways melted away in moments. In its place, rivers ran through the wilderness, racing around trees, parting and reforming in crisscrossing braids like coloured threads in a tapestry. As they watched, the soil was washed from around the base of a broad, bare-branched oak and the ancient tree came crashing down, to be carried away on the current.

"This whole place is broken," Yasmi said, and blackened wood snapped in her hand.

"It is what it is," Issol said. "Wild and ever changing."

"Changing, aye," Lestavo said. "But never as fast, as hard. Never fixing to fray half the withering folk in a single flash."

"Aye." Issol's voice came slow as mud, dragged down by reluctance. He ran his fingers across his forehead, wiping the ashen V away. "There'll be many lost today."

"I'm so sorry," Raul said, laying a hand on Issol's shoulder.

"Don't be sorry." Issol turned to Raul, his expression stern. He took a leather cord from around his neck and held it up, a wooden charm in the shape of a snowflake hanging from it. "Here. For protection from Jarrag's fire. It won't do nowt against his beasts, and it can only hold back so much heat, but it might help your strength last."

He hung the charm around Raul's neck. Others of the seven approached, holding out similar charms to Yasmi, Valens, and Prisca.

"Are you sure?" Raul asked. "It could be dangerous for you, crossing him like this."

"And this ain't dangerous?" Issol gestured toward the waters flowing past the hill, carrying broken trees and the bodies of drowned animals. A flood washing across the land. "The Withering is all about change, so go make it change again for us."

Chapter Twenty-Two
Aftermath

Yasmi folded her spare shirt around the scorched remains of the ogre mask and placed it carefully in her pack, laying other soft layers over the top before putting in the food supplies that Issol's people had given them for the journey. The wind was blowing her hair around, whipping strands loose across her face, but she didn't try to tie them back.

"How are you doing?"

She'd heard Raul coming, but his hand on her shoulder still made her flinch, not just from the memories of fire and destruction but from memories of the expression on his face when he'd seen her as the wild, bloodstained wolf, of the way her exhilaration had crumbled to dust in the face of his disappointment.

"I'm fine." She dressed her face up in her brightest smile before brushing her hair back and turning to him. "Just burying one monster before I get back to playing another."

She laughed. That was what people expected, what they

wanted, for everything to be good. If she could stay the bright, playful actor she'd been before, then perhaps she could dissipate the tension she felt growing between her and Raul, the crack in the solid ground of their connection. And yet, when he smiled, seemingly taken in, she felt as though the ground under them was cracking wider, like it had under Jarrag's fire.

"Lestavo says that he's going the same way as us, a few of the others too," Raul said. "I'm not sure whether they're coming to help, to watch, or just because that's where they want to go next, but they can help find the best route."

"The more the merrier. You know I love an audience."

He grinned, and it finally lifted her spirits a little.

"Which way are we going?" she asked, stowing the last supplies in her pack.

"Toward that peak." Raul pointed to a mountain that rose pointed as a blade from the forest ahead, a shape so dark and narrow it felt unnatural. She was getting used to the strangeness of the wild, even starting to find comfort in it, but there was nothing comforting in that sight. "Apparently it has the thickest, tallest forest across its lower slopes, and Jarrag's Rest lies up a rocky trail beyond them, a path those royal pilgrims used to take."

Yasmi hefted her pack, contemplating its weight and the journey ahead. First they would have to cross the mud-slicked plateau, ground turned into a thick swamp by the floodwaters, waters which still rushed in feverish streams across it, cutting ever deeper channels through the muck. Then there would be the forest and whatever threats lay within it. After that, perhaps a climb up a mountain, which one of their troupe would have to perform one-handed. And finally, at the end of it all, a battle against a fake god to seize what they'd come for.

What joy.

"When this is over, we'll have the makings of a fabulous play," she said. "*Warborn in the Wilderness*, a tale of heroic struggle against the odds. Perfect for whipping up support. I expect that Tenebrial will write you some marvellous speeches."

Down in the mud, Issol and his people were dragging together what remained of their former lives. At the base of the hill, some of them were stitching new tents from parts of ones that had been torn apart, while others were draining the mud from the few rolling huts that hadn't been smashed open or washed away. Issol himself was among those scattered across the open expanse, wading through the mud to find scattered possessions and drag them back in. It was amazing that they had spared a kind word for the outsiders in their midst, never mind any of the precious food stores that remained. The guilt she felt at not helping them with the task was balanced against the dreadful thought of fishing around in that thick, cold ooze, while the journey ahead gave her all the excuse she needed not to join in. At least she recognised when she was making excuses—Raul was far too good an influence.

Issol, standing proud even in this drudge work, was a distinctive figure at the far side of the flat expanse, near the edge of the surviving trees. There were others with him, tossing lines of poetry back and forth, too distant for her to make out the words, just the rhythm it set for their work. That rhythm was broken by exclamations of excitement as they spotted something in the muck. All of them bent down, sank their hands in, strained and grunted as the edge of a rolling hut started to emerge.

Behind them, something moved in the trees. Yasmi took a deep breath, caught the barest hint of a scent that she hadn't known she would recognise, and set her pack down, leaning forward as her hand reached for her waist.

"Cats," she growled.

The creatures crept out of the undergrowth, the black Vs on their mottled yellow fur just visible at this distance. Not cats like she knew them back home but like they'd met early in the hills, creatures of fangs and claws large enough to take a human down. They prowled toward the unknowing people heaving the hut out of the mud.

"We have to protect them," Raul said, drawing his sword, just like she'd known he would.

Yasmi didn't even have to think. She was in motion already, sprinting downhill as she raised the mask to her face. The shift into wolf form became a leap, hurtling into the mud flat without hesitation, letting her body find its strength and the confidence that came with it, heart and paws both hammering. This time, she ran beside Raul and Valens, her pack on the hunt. The same sense of shared power and purpose she had known with the wolves, this time with the people she loved.

Mud flew from her feet and spattered her fur as she hurtled across the flat ground in long bounds, never slowing enough to sink. As they approached one of streams, she sprang over it with ease, tense muscles releasing like the string of a bow, flinging her across the gap. She didn't just jump; she soared.

Issol and his people had heard Raul's shout of alarm. They pulled together, drawing weapons, trying to keep the edge of the half-raised hut between them and the beasts. But the cats had heard too, and now they rushed from cover, more than Yasmi had seen at first, a pack of their own rushing to grab their prey while it was alarmed and unready. Their excitement was a scent as sharp and clear as anything else in the air, and she howled her fury in response.

She ran faster, the breath rushing harsh and hot in her chest. One of the cats was charging at Issol. She leapt just as it did, unfurling herself in a bound like nothing she'd ever known, and as she soared through the air all her worries vanished in the exhilaration of a perfect, deadly form fulfilling its purpose. She collided with the cat in midair, slamming it off course, the two of them tangling together as they smashed into the edge of a hut, wicker snapping along with several of the cat's ribs. They rolled into the mud, clawing and biting, but though the cat was as big and strong as she was, Yasmi was agile, certain, graceful. She relished the movements of her body as she slid under a thrashing paw and ripped the cat's shoulder open. It fell back, screeching in pain, and the rich smell of blood made her mouth water. If the cat was prey for a meal, then she would have finished it, but instead she turned to the rest.

Raul and Valens dashed the last few yards through the mud and hurled themselves into the fray with her. The world was claws and blades, mud and blood, bodies stumbling and thrashing around as they sank hip deep into the ooze. It was dreadful and desperate, but it made her heart swell with each flashing moment. The mud was a weight clinging in her fur, yet her body felt light, and she sprang from one movement to the next, snapping and slashing, gouging and rending.

The beasts were strong and they were ferocious, but they were driven on by fear of punishment and it showed in the way they fought. They flinched from physical threats, because why accept one pain just to avoid another? Yasmi and her pack fought out of love and loyalty, out of a desire to protect, and so they hurled themselves again and again into the danger, knowing it was worth the risk. Raul darting and lunging, Valens slashing and roaring, while she clawed and snapped and tasted blood and fur. They were one. They were invincible.

And then it was over, Jarrag's beasts fleeing through the mud, out into the trees and away. Yasmi vaulted up onto the half-raised hut and shook the worst of the mud from her fur for all that it was worth, then lifted her head and howled, filling the sound with her breathless excitement and unstoppable ferocity. One last threat to send the beaten on their way.

Maybe the journey ahead would be hard and unpleasant, but it could be much more than that too. Her chance to be herself among her people, to embrace her own strength.

She howled again, this time for herself, and it was a sound of joy.

———————— • ————————

Fellstride snorted and shook his mane, his leg shifting under Count Alder's hand. Even with several of the chosen holding him in place, even with Alder himself treating his wounds, the horse resisted the pain of treatment, wanted to break free and run. Alder didn't blame him. Even the smartest steed couldn't comprehend the world the way people did, couldn't understand that its shock and pain would carry it to something better in the end.

There had been a lot of shock and pain.

"Hold steady, old friend," Alder said in his most soothing voice as he tied a bandage tight around a poultice on Fellstride's wound. "We're almost done."

Fellstride snorted again, but didn't move anymore. He trusted Alder, even though Alder had brought him into this. Now it was Alder's turn to repay that trust. With the bandage in place, he took the reins and set to stroking Fellstride's face. The horse leaned in, pressing his head against his palm, seeking reassurance.

"How many have we lost?" Alder asked quietly.

"Four warriors, with three more wounded," Captain Thorn replied. "Nearly half the horses. Only one mule, but that's mules for you."

Alder looked around. There was no way they could light a funeral pyre in this sodden land. Digging a grave pit had been hard enough, but he'd insisted and no one had disagreed. Some of them had lost friends and many had lost loyal steeds as the vast expanse of snow had melted into a flash flood, flinging bodies around, flooding lungs, breaking necks. His own side ached where he'd slammed into a tree, and his palms were raw from clinging on. The salve he'd made for Fellstride stung in the creases of his fingers.

"Have you seen anything like this before?" he asked.

Thorn took a dark leaf from a damp pouch hanging off his belt, shoved it into his mouth, chewed thoughtfully, and finally shook his head.

"Bad rains up here last winter," he said. "Strangest and strongest I'd ever seen, like nails of water hammering out of the sky. Worst thing I've seen since the war, and it wasn't a match for this."

The war had crossed Alder's mind too. This had to be magic, arcane work by the old Estian elite. Like the field of teeth. Like the grass of the Long Plain withering in an enchanted summer heat. Somehow, Prisca Servita had brought their cabal back together, or something mimicking it. That must be why she was out here, hunting down some source of power. It certainly wasn't for the sake of the locals with their stone blades and woven armour; when it came to recruiting allied troops, there were better places to look.

This was why it wasn't enough to stop these people now. Loosen your grip on the reins and they would canter off into dark magic and destruction. They had to be held down forever, nailed into place for the good of everyone else.

"So you don't know how quickly the land will dry out?" he asked.

"If all I saw was this, I'd say never." Thorn spat into one of the many small streams running down the hillside they'd dragged themselves onto, the closest thing for miles around to solid land. "But in this place, who knows."

Still stroking Fellstride, Alder turned to look out across the sea of mud and broken trees, then back up the hills. The ground was more solid up there, and hopefully it would be more normal over the ridge and down the far side. The whole world couldn't be flooded.

"The horses can't make it through this quagmire," he said. "I won't risk breaking good steeds, and I can't wait here while those rebels find ways to stir up something worse. We'll send the horses back with the wounded and however many are needed to lead them."

"And the mules?"

"We need to carry supplies somehow. The mules will manage."

If they didn't, they were only mules.

"Not that many supplies to carry." Thorn stared steadily at the count, in a way that captains didn't back home. Without breaking that gaze, he spat more dark juice into the mud.

"Are you suggesting that we turn back, Captain?" Alder stepped away from Fellstride, one eyebrow raised. "I may be battered, cold, and sodden, but I am still the governor here. I am still of the royal line of Dunholm, and I do not recommend crossing me."

"Just saying, we don't have the supplies for the stomachs, and this isn't good land to live off. I'm cold, battered, and sodden too, and I'm not keen to add starving to the list."

Alder gritted his teeth, took a long breath, and let the anger go. Thorn's outspoken behaviour helped explain his family's downfall, but the man was right, and a good leader didn't let pride get in the way of that.

"Take a count of what we have left, decide how many you think it can feed, and let me know. We'll decide who to bring and who to send back based on that."

"Very good, my lord."

"This might help." Captain Brook strode up the slope toward them, a huge fish hanging from a spear over her shoulder. "There were rivers around here before the flood, and the fish that lived in them are scattered, confused, some of them stuck in shallower water than they're used to. It's a good time to get a catch in."

"Do we have many experienced fishers?" Alder asked.

"I'll count that too," Thorn said, then spat one last time before walking away.

Brook shot Thorn a less than friendly look, then dropped the fish at Alder's feet and bowed her head. "My lord."

"You're from the eastern water lands," Alder said. "What do you make of this?"

"May I..." She gestured with a knife at the fish, which lay on the ground, a pale, dead, graceless lozenge of flesh as long as Alder's leg.

"Go ahead. I don't want to stand in the way of fresh supplies."

"The water's coming down off the hills and will be for a few more days at least." She knelt by the fish and slid her knife in, then ran it along its belly, opening it up like a blood-slicked book. "Aside from existing rivers and streams, it's cutting other channels through the land, blocking our way."

"Could we use them for travel? Boats have to be faster than walking through this mess."

"The channels aren't deep, and they won't last." With a series of deft slices, she flicked the fish guts aside. "But they could carry shallow-bottomed boats." She lopped off the head, then looked up at him. The fish's beady dead eye seemed to be staring too. "I spotted some locals a mile down from us turning the remains of their homes into oared craft. It's ingenious work, not something we could do ourselves, but by the time we gather the troops it could be done."

Alder rested his hands on the swords at his sides—his own sabre and the flashy blade he'd taken off the rebel boy. Back then, he'd been in control of the situation, able to predict which paths his opponents were most likely to follow. The steady, trudging quality of the way North Marchers thought had made them so much easier to manage than the courtly intrigues of home. That was the mindset he had to capture now.

He looked the way the rebels' trail had led them before the flood. That trail might be gone, but its direction was clear, and there were few markers in the landscape that anyone could care about. No towns or cities where they might be looking for friends. No mines or plantations. Just the chaos of hills and woods, with a single mountain standing out amid the rest.

If he was establishing a source of power in this landscape, somewhere a local cabal could gather and where visitors from distant lands could find him, he would put it on that mountain.

"Do any of those channels head north?" he asked.

"I'm sure I can find one, my lord. I got my start hunting Saditchi smugglers down delta canals, work like that gives you a sense for where the water flows."

"My uncle offered me a governorship in the deltas." Alder thought back to his days at court, conversation layered with meaning and consequence. "A life of hunting smugglers and pirates down by the Golden Ocean, readying our garrisons for the day when Saditch stops being our friend."

Brook looked at him, one eyebrow raised. "Why didn't you take it? It's warmer down there, more comfortable living."

"Because that comfort was a trap. King Lorrin wanted me content, counting off the years drinking wine and eating figs. What better way to neuter a noble house?"

"So you chose this instead." Brook waved her knife at the sodden wilderness.

"I chose the chance to become more than I was, to make myself useful to the king instead of harmless."

"Did it work?"

Alder gave her a lopsided smile. "We'll see."

He turned to Fellstride, who leaned in toward him with a contented snort.

"I'll have to leave you out of this fight, but don't worry, we'll be back." He nodded to Brook, who was standing with the perfectly filleted fish in her hands. "Find someone to cook that, then gather enough warriors to seize the boats. The last few days have been a long ride, and our troops deserve a chance to feast once the fighting's done."

Chapter Twenty-Three
Some Life Goes On

The trees were closing in, but Valens didn't mind so much anymore. Better the trees than the snow or the mud it had left behind. He was even getting used to walking over the roots that crisscrossed the trail. They might make it uneven, but at least they ensured that it was solid, that puddles were just puddles and not long stretches of swamp trying to suck him under. He'd finally found the rhythm of the place, a way to keep a good pace and keep marching even as branches hung into their path and the trail rose and fell beneath his feet. A steady rhythm but a slow one, and that might be a problem in the end. They'd been weary from walking even before the fire and the flood, and dealing with that had taken more out of them. Aching legs moved slower. Wet boots led to slow, uncomfortable steps. To top it all, they were heading uphill, and that was always more of a grind.

He really must be getting old, though, if it slowed him down this much. Back in the day, he and Fabia could have...

The thought trailed off, incomplete, interrupted not by the thought of Fabia but by the memory of the voice pretending to be her. He ground his teeth and stamped down hard with each step, as if Jarrag might feel those pounding at him through his connection with the land. Whatever else happened, he would have a reckoning. By Yorl's eye, he swore it.

Glaring into the woods, he sought any sign of movement, any glimpse of an attacker he could take his wrath out on, but there were only the trees, their trunks growing thicker the further he went, the drifts of old pine needles rotting around their roots, and an occasional bird flitting darkly from branch to branch.

At the front of the group, Raul and Lestavo were talking as they went, easy as old friends. Lestavo moved more lightly and easily over this ground, as did the two other locals in their furs and their packs of interwoven leaves, but they seemed content to stay at the visitors' pace. Valens watched them warily. They seemed to be friends now, but one was from the priests who had carried the voice of Jarrag at the fire, and the false god might not be the only one telling lies. These people might be all friendship and sharing, but when the moment came for blood, there was still a chance they'd fall back on their deal. He'd seen it before, a local guide disappearing in the night just before the enemy struck. He wouldn't fall for that again.

Step after step, root after root, tree after tree, on they marched, Valens's damp feet increasingly sore.

He didn't realise that trouble was coming at first. It was just another movement over their heads, another bird flying from branch to branch. Prisca, ahead of Valens on the trail, stopped to stare up at it. He shoved her in the back and she had to lean into her staff to avoid falling over.

"Keep moving."

"Look at that." She pointed. "Don't you think that's a bad sign?"

"I don't read omens." He deliberately didn't look up, just gave her another shove to keep her moving.

"I'm not so addled that I would count on you to divine even the simplest of fortunes, but I would have hoped that what passes for a military mind could assess the potential of an attack."

That got his attention, and his hand went to his sword as fast as he raised his eyes.

It wasn't just one bird, not even a few. Scores of them sat on the branches up ahead, all poised and pointing their way. When Valens looked back, he saw the same behind. Rows of feathered bodies, from the tiny brown blobs of sparrows to sleek black ravens to a pair of kestrels, all staring his way, wings rising as if readying to take flight. There was a black V on one of the kestrels' heads, just large enough for him to make it out.

"Lestavo." Valens raised his voice to carry up the path. "You seen birds do this?"

Still watching the birds behind them, Valens didn't see the others look up, but there were no more footsteps, and a low growl told him that Yasmi had shifted.

In the branches, the birds perched silent and unsettling, their unwavering gaze sending a shudder through Valens. This wasn't how creatures were meant to act. It wasn't how anyone or anything was meant to act.

"Don't reckon I have." Lestavo made a series of clicking noises, then whistles and hoots. There was no response from the birds. "Strange, so? I wonder what they'll do next."

"I don't." Valens swung his fire-blackened shield around and slid his arm through the straps. "It's an ambush."

One of the kestrels screeched, and with a sound like a sudden fall of rain, the birds swept from their branches. Valens ducked, drawing in like he was back in the shield wall, bracing for the impact of a charge. But the birds swooped past, only a wren flying too close and spinning off as it struck the rim of his shield. He whirled around, realisation dawning a moment too late.

"Raul!" Valens bellowed, shoving past Prisca and up the slope.

At the front of their group the air was thick with feathers, hundreds of birds swooping and soaring, rising only to dive back down, wings stretched wide and claws out. At the edge of the vortex, Yasmi snapped and slashed, trying to snatch birds out of the air, but most moved too fast for even the wolf to catch. The others were indistinct shapes hidden inside the storm of beaks and feathers.

Sword drawn, Valens strode into that chaos. Bodies battered against his shield, fragile forms breaking and dropping to the ground until they realised what was happening and changed course to fly around him. He tried to cut them out of the air, but they were small and fast, almost impossible to target. He slashed two down by luck rather than skill, but by then his advance had stalled thanks to the scores of birds flying straight down the path at him, forcing him to stop and raise his shield, to dodge and slash, and still to take a step back as claws shredded his sleeves and sliced his exposed skin. One, two, three birds in a row caught his cheek, small wounds accumulating until blood ran down his neck. One almost caught his eye. He crouched into the shield defence again, waved his sword wildly at any passing shape, cursed himself for not getting close enough to protect his son and leader.

There had to be something he could do. Bodies were breaking against his shield again, the birds trying to drive him back by the sheer mass of their attack, some slipping past close by and scratching at his legs. A swift swooped past, the tips of its claws scratching his scalp. Valens laughed bitterly at being attacked by the same shape as the charm he wore.

Then the idea came. It was stupid, desperate thinking, not solid and practical, but it couldn't be worse than this.

He dropped his sword, reached inside his collar, and drew out Drusil's swift charm. *For speed and for luck*, she'd said. Speed and luck seemed like what he needed. He swung the charm around until its cord was wrapped around his fingers and the metal disk lay against the back of his hand. Then he peered out across his shield.

As a crow swept in, Valens shot out his hand, catching a bird between thick fingers. It squawked. He squeezed. Bones crunched. Wings flopped. He cast it aside and looked for his next target.

A pigeon flew at him. He grabbed it, crushed it, flung it underfoot, snatched a sparrow as it flashed past.

The birds were still coming, but their bodies were piling up around him, around Yasmi, around the central vortex of conflict, a whirl of feathers that seemed to be shrinking. He stamped fragile bodies underfoot as he advanced, his shield sheltering him on one side while on the other he grabbed whatever came closest.

A kestrel shrieked as it dived toward Valens. He tried to grab it, but it was too big, too powerful. Its claws cut painful gouges down his wrist, but he returned the favour, yanking at one of its wings. Instead of soaring, the bird spiralled through the air and thudded into one of the towering trees.

At last, Valens was almost where he belonged, in the heart of the battle. Birds flew at him from every direction, but they were getting in each other's way and so close together he didn't even have to look for targets, just grab whatever came close. Another step forward and he could make out human shapes, the locals huddling together close to the ground, but where was Raul?

Yasmi plunged past him, snarling, snapping birds out of the air with her teeth. Maybe it was that animal sound, the sight of a known predator, the scent of something fearful, or maybe the birds had just had enough, but as she bounded into their midst the feathered bodies scattered. With one final desperate flutter of wings, they disappeared between the trees and Yasmi chased after them, snarling ferociously.

"Where's Raul?" Valens stomped the last few strides to the others, fragile bodies crunching underfoot.

The locals rose from their huddle. The thick pelts they wore had, like Yasmi's fur, protected them from most of the scratching of the birds, though there were slashes across the backs of their necks and dark, sticky patches in their hair.

Lestavo spread his hands and gestured down at the space they'd surrounded.

Raul lay there, curled up into a ball, hands pressed to one side of his forehead. Blood was running through his fingers. He looked pale and his eyes flitted uncertainly from side to side.

"Hold still." Valens swung his pack down, opened it up, pulled out a strip of old cotton. Packing for a march was about priorities. Always keep food near the top, but keep bandages above that. "Hands away."

The lad did as he was told and immediately blood started to flow. Valens took a moment to see the wound, then pressed the bandage over it.

"Looks worse than it is," he said. "Shallow cut but lots of blood. I'll stitch it up and it'll soon heal. You won't even have a scar."

"I've seen your stitching," Prisca said. "He'll have a scar."

"Another birthmark." Raul's laughter was almost a giggle, but weak, uncertain. Valens glanced around, noting the reactions of Lestavo and his companions, hoping that they couldn't work out what that comment meant. Yasmi reappeared out of the trees and prowled over with a swaggering sway.

"How's your vision?" Valens asked as he helped Raul sit up.

"A bit blurry," Raul admitted, clutching the bandage. "Something big hit me in the head, then things got confusing."

A proper blow to the head. One of the bigger birds now lying on the ground had probably given its life for that. These things had been determined to get at Raul.

He really had riled up Jarrag.

"Poor creatures," Raul said, looking down sadly at one of the limp bodies.

"Poor creatures?" Valens snorted. "They tried to kill you, lad."

"Only because Jarrag made them do it. Now look at them."

Valens looked around. The ground was littered with feathered bodies, some still twitching or trying to hop away, others trampled beyond hope. He was used to the aftermath of battles, the dead and injured littering the ground, looters passing between them with knives and sacks and a vicious twinkle in their eyes. The groaning. The stench of blood. It hadn't brought a tear to his eyes in many years, but somehow, seeing this through Raul's eyes touched him.

"God's teeth," he muttered to himself. "We're going to have to bury them, aren't we?"

"Only those we don't eat." Lestavo held up a quail. "Good meat there, so."

There was an attitude Valens could cope with. There were practical problems to tackle, and hunger was one of them.

"Yasmi, go sniff out some water," he said. "Prisca, find firewood to heat it, I want to clean Raul's wound before I sew him up."

Or before he found someone with two dexterous hands who he could supervise in that sewing.

Prisca's eyes narrowed. He could see her on the edge of resisting. She'd never liked people telling her what to do, especially not people who she felt should be obeying her. But she knew as well as he did how much had shifted since Pavuno. They stared at each other and the habit of decades was reversed, Valens holding steady while Prisca turned to obey.

There was a flat, dry patch of ground under one of the trees, so Valens left Raul with the locals while he went there. Lestavo ambled after him, thumbs stuck through his belt, lively eyes staring with open curiosity.

"What's yon charm for?" he asked, pointing at the swift still dangling around Valens's arm. "Not for flying, I reckon."

"One of our allies gave it to me for luck." Valens opened his pack and started carefully unpacking onto the flat ground.

"Looks like it worked." Lestavo watched the items emerge. "What's that?"

"Whetstone for my blades."

"And that?"

"Spare shirt."

"And that?"

Valens focused on his task, trying not let the questions grate on him.

"That's what I was looking for," he said, holding up a roll of leather the size of his hand. "For fixing people, and sometimes things."

He unfastened the bundle and rolled it out for Lestavo to see. The little man squatted to peer into it more closely, examining the needles of different sizes, thin thread, slender tools for prying grit from wounds.

"What's that?" Lestavo asked, pointing at one of them.

Valens let out a slow breath. He shouldn't be bothered by this. Lestavo had protected his son.

"Thank you for what you did back there," he said. "For Raul."

Lestavo shrugged. "Just what you do."

"Not for most people." Valens thought about his own

reaction, the desire to lash out, fight back, take down as many of the birds as he could. To play the role of the slaying sword while these people formed a shield. "You lay there and took the hurt for him."

"It's what we do, when danger comes. Hold together. Protect who needs protecting."

Valens ran a hand across the fresh scratches on his scalp and the older scars underneath. Back in the day, he'd risked a lot for his closest comrades, but part of that had always been about showing his own prowess. You leapt to your comrade's defence, but you were still leaping, and it was for a warrior you knew, a comrade in arms. These people gathered in evershifting communities, moving from place to place, never knowing each other for long.

"Even if you die doing it?" Valens asked.

"Life comes, life goes, life comes again." Lestavo waved a hand from side to side.

"But your story lives on." Valens could understand that. Sure, it was better to live for a cause than to die for it, but at least if you died that way, then you might be remembered in song around campfires or in a story of old over a flagon in a tavern, one of those names that lasted into legend.

"I don't know for story," Lestavo said. "But we stand together or we fall together, whoever we are, and even if my life ends, when some life goes on, that's the thing."

"If you say so."

Yasmi emerged from the woods, human now and carrying a pan of water. Valens picked up the tool roll and headed back toward Raul.

This time, he tried to walk around the bodies of the birds instead of trampling them. Not just for Raul's sake, though the lad was still gazing at those fallen forms in a sad daze. Not for the sake of food either, though he didn't want to ruin anything that they could get meat from. It was for the sake of the birds themselves, to honour them.

Those birds had attacked together, just like Lestavo and his companions had defended together. There was heroism in that.

Even in the massed ranks of the Estian infantry, with their talk of holding the line and guarding the warrior next to you, it hadn't been like this. You fought to be the best, to be remembered. Valens's grief over losing Fabia had been tied up in the memory of how she'd gone out, that grim grin she'd worn facing a good death. Better to die like that than to grind on in anonymity. When he'd lost his hand, that was part of what he'd lost—the glorious finale. He hadn't won and he hadn't died memorably. He'd been weakened, robbed of his moment, of his story, and he'd been sunk since then.

But out here, heroism wasn't made alone. It was made together and in the long slog, these strange people enduring everything a broken land could throw at them. If they'd found another way, perhaps he could too.

"Are you all right, Da?" Raul asked, looking up at him from under the bandage, one eye closed beneath a crust of blood.

"Am I all right?" Valens asked, snapping out his trailing, tangled thoughts. "Yorl's eye, lad, have you taken a look at yourself?"

"Not many mirrors around here."

They both laughed, then Raul winced, and blood seeped from under the bandage. It hurt Valens inside to see his son like this, even though his best qualities had brought him here, his courage and selflessness. Would it have been easier if he hadn't raised the boy so well?

It didn't matter. Prisca was back with wood. They'd see to Raul's wound, then everyone else's. By the time that was done, night would be closing in, time to eat and sleep, ready to rise again and march on. The trees loomed over them, vast and dark, hiding whatever threats Jarrag offered next, vast bears or ferocious cats and frenzied birds. It didn't matter because together they would endure.

Chapter Twenty-Four
Tangled Up in Signs

By the time dawn broke, they were on the move already, Raul's pack resting a little heavier against his back thanks to the broken bodies of the birds that Lestavo had picked out for them to keep as food. There was no need to worry about preserving the meat; as long as it hung off their packs, the cold would do that for them. Even with his gloves on and a scarf pulled up across his chin, Raul felt its icy pins pricking at his extremities. He felt for the snowflake charm under his tunic, but that was to protect him with cold, not against it.

"It's not what I imagined from the stories," he said, staring up at trees as wide as houses, frost-hardened needles hanging from branches as stiff and sharp as spears.

"The real world never is," Prisca replied, her staff tapping at the frozen ground. "Stories exist to preserve important memories and to move people into action, both tasks more effectively accomplished by a clean, simple narrative. But if you are to rule a nation, then you must learn to grapple with clutter, compromise, and contradiction without letting them tangle others."

"This doesn't seem like clutter to me. It seems beautiful and intimidating, terrifying even, a place so much like what I know and yet so different. Trees too big to be trees. A mountain shaped like a nail. Birds that attack people instead of flying from them. Was that why Balbianus came here to die, instead of in the land he'd ruled?"

Prisca's laugh was as cold as the air.

"From what I've deduced, he came here out of desperation, one last throw of the dice to gain power and tip war back in his favour. And it worked, even if he didn't live to enjoy the results."

There was a thought that sent a shiver even through the parts of Raul that weren't already cold.

"He died to get the power from here?"

"You saw the play, what do you think?"

"I think that plays are stories, and I can't trust stories. Nothing in this matches up right."

"Clutter, compromise, and contradiction. We'll make a king out of you yet."

Raul touched his upper arm, where the brand that was meant to be his birthmark lay hidden beneath layers of warm wool. He hoped that she was right. The fate of his people depended on his ability to be that king.

The animal trail they'd been following stopped at a dense tangle of thorny growth, with tiny dark openings for the creatures of the forest floor to seek shelter. Raul hacked at it with his sword, but the strands just bent before his blows and then sprang back into place. Cutting through this would take a week.

"How do we get around this?" Raul asked, looking at Lestavo.

"Go back and find another way, so," the squat man said. "We'll get there in the end."

But getting there in the end wasn't enough. They needed to move fast, to stay ahead of Count Alder. He had horses and a hundred men, while they were four, with three travelling companions, trudging along on weary feet.

"Ma?" Raul looked at Prisca. Was that an expression of concentration on her face, or was it the blankness that said she was losing herself again? He didn't want to interrupt, and yet…

A sharp series of cracks made him look around, hand halfway to his sword, ready for trouble. Valens's and Yasmi's hands went to their belts as well, but the only thing moving was a vast, round leaf unfurling into a beam of sunlight that shone through the canopy. Around it were other leaves, rolled up tight as if against the cold. There was another crack as the frost sealing one of them broke and it unfurled into the light, a leaf as large as Raul's blanket, spread like the canvas of a tent above their heads.

He turned back to Prisca. To his relief, she was frowning as she crouched, clawing dirt from the track, and then she let it run through her fingers, looking for signs. He rubbed at the bandage over his forehead as he looked for those signs himself, but all he noticed was a lump of dirt, bound in roots like the creepers blocking their way, a sign of what they couldn't do. Had Jarrag made this grow to stop them, or had it always been here? Did that matter for anything other than his own understanding of the world?

"Which way?" he asked.

"I don't know, Raul," Prisca replied sharply. "Please let me think."

He took a few steps back. The others were settling at the base of one of the vast trees, backs against the rough bark, packs set aside. Valens rubbed at his stump. Yasmi straightened the line of masks on her belt, fingers lingering over the wolf. Lestavo and the other two travellers started playing a game with small blue stones and lines in the dirt.

Without taking off his pack, Raul sat down in a pool of sunlight near Yasmi and wrapped his arms around his knees, trying to hold in a little extra warmth.

"I'll give it a few minutes," he said quietly. "Until she's ready for help."

"Or you could let her do it herself," Yasmi said.

"What if I can help work out the signs?"

"And what if that destroys your mind?" She leaned forward and took his fingers in hers. He could feel her warmth even through their gloves, see the intensity burning in her eyes, shot through with the wolf's unsettling yellow. "It's destroying Prisca's mind already, I don't want it to ruin you."

"Maybe it's a price worth paying, for what we can achieve."

"And maybe it isn't. Maybe I'm not ready to pay that price."

She let go of his hand and leaned back against the tree, leaving his fingers cold and alone. With a pop, one of the vast leaves broke its frost and unfurled, blotting out the sunbeam that had warmed his cheeks.

Raul reached for his waterskin, wanting to dampen his dry throat, but then thought better of it. Better to save the water for later. This wasn't like the familiar hills back home; he didn't know when the next spring or stream would be.

He missed those hills that he'd never quite mastered, missed the locals who had never seen him as one of them. It had been familiar, a place he could understand, one where he could happily get on with what people told him to do. Now he was meant to tell others what to do, put on a confidence he didn't feel. That had been manageable at the rebel camp, where he knew the people and the rhythms of life, where the trees and animals were familiar. The further he got from that life, the more he felt his mask of confidence melting like the frost on the leaves, ready to crack open at any moment.

At least his da looked more relaxed than before, leaning in toward Lestavo like they were old friends, talking about the rebellion.

He shifted his pack and the dead weight of a bird flopped against his arm, its feathers broken, head hanging limp, eyes staring lifeless into the dirt. Some sort of magic had killed those birds, driven them to behave with suicidal destruction, to fling themselves into a fight that had nothing to do with them. Magic always seemed to come at a terrible price, from the cruelty of war to the unravelling of a sharp mind.

Over by the tangle blocking the path, Prisca was crouching, scratching at the dirt and scowling in frustration. Raul couldn't take away all the pain that magic brought, but he could help one person manage it. With his pack still on his back, he got up and walked over to his mother.

"How's it going?" he asked. There was no point lowering his voice as if that would somehow help; where Prisca was concerned, an intrusion was an intrusion was an intrusion.

"Signs everywhere, and none of them make any sense," she said, pointing to shapes in a tangle of roots. "A woman and a wall." She pointed to a flock of birds circling overhead. "Flight in the shape of a crown." She let dirt and debris fall through her gloved fingers, blowing across the path. "Soil falling one way, leaf fragments the other." She flung the last of the dirt down. "I don't know if my mind is failing me or Jarrag has stirred the wild against us, but I can't make sense of any of it."

"Can I help?"

Her shoulders stiffened and her finger tapped against her staff. After a moment, she nodded, just slightly.

"Why not? Perhaps you can find a connection I haven't."

Raul was glad of the acting lessons from Yasmi, which helped him to keep his expression still and serious. Prisca was trusting him again, and this time it was about the most serious challenge facing them. Who needed a kingdom when he had that?

"What sorts of things could those signs mean?" he asked.

"The crown is usually power, rulership, politics. Hardly relevant to where we are. Walls can be barriers and blockages, too obvious to be useful, perhaps protection or construction, but how does that help with any of this?" She spoke through clenched teeth, smacking the base of her staff against the ground for emphasis. "As for the dirt and the leaves, that should point at something useful, instead it's pointing two ways at once."

"Could you get your divining bowl out and see what it says?"

"Aren't you listening, Raul? We have no shortage of signs. What we lack is the coherence to read them."

"Can't the bowl help with that?"

"Have you listened to nothing I've—" She stopped herself abruptly, lips thin as she pressed them together before she spoke again. "I apologise. I lose track of what I have and have not taught you. Time has been limited, the circumstances difficult, and you excel in spite of how little guidance you have had."

"Thank you." He prodded at a root with his toe. Above them, vast leaves lay curled in the shadows cast by the canopy, still sealed in frost with half the morning gone. Time pressed in. "Could I suggest something?"

"By all means." She flung a hand in the air. "It's not as though I'm achieving anything."

"One of those books we stole in Pavuno—"

"Liberated."

"Right, yes, one of the books we liberated talked about personal relationships between a diviner and the signs."

"Osulwa's *Universe of the Heart*. I'm surprised you remember. It's not a text most people pay attention to."

"I liked the way he wrote, as though people mattered more than patterns."

"Ah, yes, Osulwa's infamous inability to achieve the requisite distance for objectivity. Honestly, it's a wonder anyone reads his work at all."

Raul hesitated. Had he chosen poorly, coming up with an idea that would expose his ignorance?

"Go on." Prisca's voice softened. "If it caught your attention, then perhaps it has value."

"I was thinking more about what Osulwa wrote, and about some of our conversations. Magic is so"—he looked for the word that set the right tone, that would impress his mother with his learning—"so contingent, so stuck in the variations of the moment, that it often can't be replicated. And divination's like that as well, something that emerges out of exactly what's happening here and now. But part of what's happening is the person doing the magic or reading the signs, what they bring to it." He took a deep breath. "So what do these things mean to you personally, not to the traditions of divination?"

Prisca shook her head, and he thought that she was dismissing the idea, but then she shrugged.

"What do we have to lose?" She pointed the flint tip of her staff at the birds. "A crown, to me, feels like something rising. My career ascending through the royal court, a kingdom becoming stronger under the right ruler."

"Something rising."

Taking the signs at their word, Raul looked up, saw a thorny tangle rising almost to the canopy and those vast, curled leaves frozen shut in the shadows.

"What about the wall and the woman?" he asked, then had another thought. "Is she on the outside or the inside?"

"The outside, I suppose." Prisca's staff tapped the ground. "That one I should have seen for myself."

"You were busy looking at the rest. What about the falling dirt?"

She snorted. "All I know is that it wasn't falling like it

should. The wind here isn't strong enough to separate the leaves from the other debris."

"Leaves." Raul blinked. Could a symbol be that direct? "The woman outside the wall feels like us outside this thicket. We can't get in, so we have to go around, not through."

"Hardly a great revelation."

"It's a start. And if rising comes into it, then maybe going around means going over, not left or right."

"You want to climb that?"

She pointed at the mass of thorny creepers that threatened to bend under any weight and tangle anyone falling into them.

But the leaves had separated from the rest.

Raul set his pack down and strode over to one of the vast trees, feeling lighter on his feet than he had in days. Reaching up, he grabbed a knot on its trunk, then set his foot in a crease of the bark and pushed himself up. The surface was rough under his hands, but its vast size made those creases and folds bigger, letting him climb without branches to cling to. It wasn't easy, sometimes hanging on by his fingertips while he pushed off a wrinkle with the tips of his toes, but he didn't stop even as the others gathered to shout up at him.

The first branch wasn't right for what he needed, nor was the one above that. His arms were aching and his knuckles scraped by the time he reached the third. Walking along it, arms wide for balance, felt so much easier than the climbing had done, and that feeling overcame the dizziness he felt any time he glanced down. When the branch started to thin, he stopped, drew his sword, and swung. He wobbled as the blade hit but managed to keep his balance for a couple of strokes, weakening the end of the branch enough so that when he sat down, straddling the side closer to the tree, he could snap the rest off. As it dropped, taking a mass of foliage with it, sunlight fell over a patch of the brambles it had obscured, and over the huge, furled leaves in between.

Frost gleamed as it melted. One of the leaves unfurled, then another and another, with a series of sharp snaps. Hanging down, they overlapped one another, running from the top of the tangled mass all the way to the ground.

"They're strong enough to take our weight," he shouted. "We can climb up them, use their veins like rungs on a ladder."

"Then what?" Prisca shouted back.

"Cut more of them off and lay them over the top. Walk across the thicket to the far side."

Everyone looked at Lestavo and his companions, people who knew these plants and this place.

"It's new." Lestavo smiled and clapped his hands. "Exciting. And aye, it could work."

Chapter Twenty-Five
Hunters

The skeletons of old undergrowth disintegrated beneath Yasmi's paws as she prowled beneath the trees, away from the tangle of thorns and the vast leaves that had carried the travellers over. In the time it had taken Valens to descend, climbing slowly and methodically with his one hand, she'd finally worked out how to fix her straps so that she could carry her pack on her back in wolf form. Now there was no need to keep shifting back and forth. She could stay as the beast, better suited to the woods and to the dangers they all faced. She could enjoy the satisfaction it brought: the smoother movements, the richer senses, the feeling of power. She could be ready for whatever came their way.

There was no need to rush through the forest now. She could relax and take her time, pick the path that left the least trail. Keeping pace with the others was so easy she had to slow herself down not to leave them all behind. It seemed strange to think that she used to put this body on and off so casually, treating it as nothing more than a costume for a play, a role to adopt for a scene at a time and then abandon for days on end. What a waste.

Off to her left, the others were tramping up another trail, following the scents of boar and deer. No, not following the scents, because they didn't know that those were there. Following the empty space, blundering on in the way humans did. This was why she needed distance from them, so that she wasn't surrounded by their noise and their smells, so that she could sense what else was happening in the world around them. The mountain lions that made their homes on these high slopes. The roosting bats. The tiny scurrying mice on the forest floor. A stream less than a mile ahead and a change in the plants beyond that, where the large trees struggled to set their roots and only the hardier undergrowth grew. Less fruit and flowers, more of the sharp smells of winter sap and evergreens.

There was another scent too, one she only caught when the wind blew from downhill, but that grew stronger each time that happened. A smell of mud and sweat with a faint, lingering trace of horse and hay.

The alarming smell of Alder and his warriors, far more of them than there were of the rebels. The smell of their pursuers closing in.

She growled at that smell, and something small darted away in fright. The temptation to chase it was there, an animal instinct growing louder with each day, but she ignored it. There wouldn't be much eating on that anyway. Better to press on. Better to wait for real prey.

Even through the trees, she could hear the others talking, Raul and Prisca discussing what they might use Balbianus's dagger for, speculating on how they could channel the power it held. Part of her wanted to go closer, to hear Raul's voice more clearly, to walk beside him and let him run his hand through her fur. Maybe even to be human for a few minutes, to tease the inn boy turned hero, to hear his voice join hers in laughter. But there had been less of that laughter lately, and though they curled up together for warmth at night, neither of them found much to say. They were too tired, too cold, too full of aches to play their parts in the new story they'd been writing for themselves, the tale of young love in hard times, and even Tenebrial would have struggled to write the words that would lift them up. When this was over, she could think about those things again, but not now. On this journey, Raul didn't need the woman—he needed the wolf, and she was happy to oblige.

She picked up her pace, moving swift and silent through the trees, out ahead of her people, her pack. Her pulse quickened and she grinned, feeling the edge of the excitement that came whenever she was on the hunt. Overhead, a vulture croaked. In the distance, another wolf howled.

Then came the other sound. Human footsteps. She slowed, sniffed the air, caught their scent. Faintly familiar but not enough to pin down beyond the earthy smell of humans, several of them moving through the trees on this side of the trail, taking a course that would let them head off Raul and the others.

Strangers.

Hunters.

Ambushers.

No growl this time. No sound that might give her away. She lowered her profile, legs bent, tail down, belly almost to the ground, and crept forward. Two could play at this game.

Like the plot lines of a play building toward its final act, the paths of the three groups came closer: Raul's party, tramping obliviously on; the strangers, quieter and more sure of their footing in the woods; Yasmi, a lone predator, slipping through the shadows of the forest floor, muscles tensed and ready to unfurl. All of them approaching an inevitable climax.

She caught sight of one of the strangers, a woman in furs and panels of woven reed with a bow in her hand and a pack strapped across her back, hair shaved short on one side, black streaks across her scalp. Beyond her was a man with a spear, then others Yasmi couldn't make out.

She bared her teeth, slid under a patch of ferns without even moving their leaves, curled her body to press close against the trunk of a tree. She was a part of the forest, and the forest was a part of her. She could lose herself in it, but she could save herself through it too, could bind herself to its shapes and shadows, seek its shelter, prepare the perfect attack.

The strangers approached slowly, hunters closing in, oblivious to who here was the real prey. Past them, Raul was laughing, a sound as delicious to Yasmi as fresh blood between her teeth, a sound she would gladly kill to protect.

Slowly forward, one paw at a time, around the tree and closer in, creeping up on the hunter with her bow, following the trail she had left through the undergrowth, sinking into her scent and the sight of her exposed back, the certainty of the kill. Mouth dry. Heart racing. Every inch of muscle quivering, tensed, holding her strength at the ready.

Closer. Closer. The hunters stalking Yasmi's pack and Yasmi stalking them. The vast expanse of the forest closed to a few strides. The woman approached the path, bow at the ready, the forest parting to give her a clear shot, but Yasmi wasn't going to let her take it at Raul.

Yasmi drew herself in, then leapt. She slammed into the woman's back, knocking her into the open trail. The two of them rolled across clumps of hardy grass, jutting rocks, and knotted roots. The woman's pack was between them, so Yasmi buried her claws in that, clinging on tight. She twisted her neck and snapped her teeth, trying to get at the hunter's throat. The woman shouted in alarm, dropped her bow as they rolled down the slope and slammed into the trunk of a tree.

Trapped between Yasmi and the tree, the woman thrust a hand under Yasmi's jaw, trying to force her head back, while with the other hand she scrabbled for something at her belt. Yasmi wasn't going to give her a chance to get a weapon. She brought one of her back paws up and raked her claws across the woman's arm, then down her thigh. Blood flowed, its rich, salty scent making Yasmi's heart beat faster. People were shouting, feet hammering the ground. She brought her rear paw up again, under the woman's pack and against her back, claws pushing through the fur tunic toward the flesh underneath, pressing harder as Yasmi's muscles tightened. She unhooked one of her forepaws from the pack and brought it around, claws extending, an inch from the woman's throat.

Hands grabbed Yasmi's shoulders, hauled her off. Her attacker fell and she fell with him, rolled over his body, twisted to her feet, tensed to pounce at...

Raul, lying in the dirt, staring at her with wide eyes and an outstretched hand.

"Yasmi, stop!"

She growled. The blood was on him, on her, on the ground, on the woman lying groaning against the tree. A red trail of hunger and exhilaration, of the kill to be completed. It was all she could do to hold herself steady, tail slapping against the ground, teeth bared, a fraction of a breath from the attack.

"Please." Raul crouched, empty hands held out, eyes locked with hers. His bandage had slipped and blood was trickling down his forehead, along the line of his eyebrow, and on down his cheek. "Stop. Look who it is."

Lestavo had reached the fallen hunter, was rolling her over, pressing a hand to a wound on her neck, holding back the flow.

Blood.

Pale flesh of the throat beneath.

Above that, a face, familiar now that she saw it out of shadows, ageing but not old, grey hair shaved on one side. Ferra, whose fire she had sat beside, whose food she had eaten. Ferra, who had helped them when the whole wild seemed like a threat.

Ferra, whose throat she had almost ripped open.

Yasmi whimpered, belly against the ground, anger and hunger warring with the guilt that rose like the jeers of a bitter audience. She'd been so sure that she needed to attack, to protect her pack, to keep Raul safe. The last gasp of a growl caught like nails in her throat as she watched the others watching her, felt the weight of Prisca's disapproval, Valens's disgust, and worst of all, Raul's disappointment.

"It's all right," Raul said, breath frosting in front of his face, a thin but merciful veil between them.

Still crouching, he crept toward Yasmi, while Lestavo frantically bound Ferra's wounds. The other people had emerged from the woods and stood with weapons pointing at them, their expressions a mix of grief and anger. Bows were raised, strings tense, arrows an inch away from aiming at her and Raul.

How could this be all right? She felt sick to the depths of her stomach, blood and hunger bitter in her mouth, bile burning her throat. The world through which she'd prowled so proudly closed in as flashes of the blood-soaked scene played encores in her mind. Flashes of tumbling in the dirt, thrashing and clawing, trying to kill a friend.

"It's all right," Raul said again, reaching for her. His hand hovered above her quivering paw, waiting for permission, and when she didn't withdraw he lowered it, brushed her fur with the worn leather of this glove. "It was an accident. You didn't mean it."

But she had. She had wanted to kill more than she had wanted to understand. She had been worse than a real wolf, which only attacked when it most needed to. She had been the theatrical wolf, the exaggerated monster, the beast prowling and howling through the forest. Worst of all, it had felt good.

Raul pulled off his glove and leaned forward, ran his fingers through her fur, stroked her cheek and the side of her neck. The warmth of his touch did nothing to soothe her trembling. If anything, she felt closer to being overwhelmed. She drew her paws back, curling into herself, and he wrapped his arms around her, ignoring the blood and the danger that she might snap.

She could feel the bulk of Ferra's body still, as real as if it lay beneath her paws. Strands of fur parting to let her claws through. Flesh parting. The stink of blood. When she swallowed, her throat ached.

Tentatively, worried that he might withdraw, she shifted her chin onto Raul's lap. His hand kept running through her fur and her skin prickled underneath, but she let him keep going, leaned into the movement, breathed the comforting aroma of his skin. The shaking lessened as her breath settled and the pounding of her heart with it. Now she felt another strand of guilt, smaller but more personal; his hand must be getting cold, and in this weather that could be dangerous.

Reluctantly, she slid her paw up her face, taking off the mask. Her body ravelled into its human form and she lay there, eyes closed, still resting in the warmth of his presence.

Footsteps approached. Yasmi forced her eyes open, looked up to see Ferra, bandaged and bloody but moving with steady determination despite a limp. An apology stuck in Yasmi's throat, caught in the tightness of her chest.

"Weren't smart," Ferra said, staring at Yasmi. "Was impressive, though."

"I'm so sorry," Yasmi whispered. "I saw you creeping up and I thought you were going to attack."

Ferra winced as she eased herself into a crouch. Under the trees, her companions were lowering their bows.

"Maybe you're not the only one wasn't acting smart." Ferra touched the bandage around her neck. "Still, think better about what you're fixing to do next time, so?"

"I will. I promise."

"Promise." Ferra snorted. "Word is word."

"Why were you creeping up on us?" Raul asked, somehow making the pointed question sound like open curiosity.

"Dangerous out here," Ferra replied. "Always so, but more now. You stirred up Jarrag, and he's stirred up the wild. Every creature with teeth and claws is on the hunt. Bats attacked us three nights back. *Bats.*" She shook her head. "Melt flood swept a lot away—tents, huts, caches stowed for another season, seeds we'd scattered for next year's food, creatures we'd have hunted through winter. The Withering's harder than before. Beasts that remain are hungry and fixing to feast."

"That's our fault," Raul said, hanging his head.

"Some, sure, and we all wish you'd thought more before sweeping through here, bringing your troubles in your wake. But Jarrag's made his choices too. Your ignorance we can perhaps fix, but his malice..." She made a sign with her hand, as if sweeping something from the air. "We live in the hills we're given, and seeing how they are, I reckoned it was best we find you."

"Why?"

"Because you've fought off everything Jarrag has thrown. Because he fears you enough to get right angry and ruin what he had." Her eyes glinted. "Because I need to keep my people safe, and I can use you for that."

Raul's hand had gone still, resting on Yasmi's hair. She moved it aside and sat up next to him. For all the ferocity in Ferra's last words, her tone was nervous, close to desperation. She'd been so steady when they met her before, but now she had real doubts for the future.

"Where are the rest of your people?" Yasmi asked, remembering the fifty or so that she'd seen before.

"Following along while we find the way. The young and what's left of our homes, they're slower to move."

"Then we'll slow down for them," Raul said.

"What about Alder?" Yasmi asked.

"One more reason to protect them. We've seen what he can do."

There it was again, Raul managing to be right in the worst way, making a decision she couldn't argue with but that could only bring them trouble. If they slowed down, then it wouldn't just increase the risk of Alder catching up; it would mean that Jarrag had more time to throw wild beasts and obstacles in their path. But what else were they going to do, ignore a plea for help from someone she herself had nearly killed?

A year ago, Yasmi could have walked away. Not now.

"There's a stream ahead," she said. "We can make camp near it so that we've got plenty of water and a chance to clean up." To clean up meant to wash off the blood. One of Tenebrial's scripts would have been specific, but she didn't want to linger on what the words evoked. "I smelled it out, I can find the way."

She lifted the wolf mask and her hand trembled as it came toward her face. Then Raul's fingers settled softly on her wrist, stalling her.

"Can you show us the way without that?" he asked. "Better for giving directions."

In spite of Ferra's bloodstained bandages, in spite of the tremble of dread that the thought brought, Yasmi wanted to sink back into the wolf, to escape into an easier life of instinct. Instead, she forced herself to hook the mask back onto her belt and rise onto two feet.

Together with Raul, she walked to the front of the group, a growing troupe of mismatched characters. The two of them set off up the hill, the others following behind, talking quietly to each other as they warily watched the wild woods to either side.

"You're right," she said, as much to convince herself as for any other reason. "We have to look after people who need us. Otherwise, what are we fighting for?"

"It's true," Raul said so quietly that only she would be able to hear him. "But it's more than that. I'm hoping that someday soon these new friends will help us win a war."

Chapter Twenty-Six
Under Control

By the time Raul woke in the morning, the stragglers of Ferra's group had reached them. There were more than fifty of them, some with wagons or sledge-like contraptions that they dragged along behind, others with animals carrying their possessions—a squat pony, two sturdy dogs, even a bear. He suspected that Jarrag always knew where the outsiders were in his domain, but if he hadn't before, then he certainly would now—the column advancing through the woods was unmistakable.

Accompanying so many people meant thinking about their needs, about keeping them together, about what sort of speed they could manage. He put himself at the front, rather than let Prisca's impatience or Valens's marching set a pace that the rest couldn't match. Valens was better used at the back, encouraging anyone who started to lag behind, just like he'd encouraged Raul when he was young. Prisca and Lestavo in the middle meant sharp eyes watching the mood of the group and watching for trouble in the wild to either side.

Raul had told Yasmi that he wanted her at the front to help him spot any trouble, and so that there was someone else who could put up a fight. Like too many things lately, though, it wasn't the whole truth. He wanted to be close enough to keep an eye on her if she became the wolf, for her sake and that of the people with them. He couldn't shake the worry that came with seeing how ferocious she'd been, almost out of control as she tore into Ferra, a sight that would have been shocking if he hadn't seen the signs of it stirring.

At least now they knew where they were going. Reading the omens in the smoke of last night's campfire, they'd found a wider trail than the animal tracks they'd been following. Generations of travellers had worn away the increasingly shallow dirt, leaving foot-smoothed stones outlined in thin patches of springy moss and wiry grass. Lestavo had smiled at it like he was meeting an old friend, but there was nothing friendly about what lay ahead. This was the pilgrim route Estian monarchs had walked to the hidden root of their power, the trail that locals had followed bringing gifts to appease a wrathful god. This was the road to Jarrag's Rest.

Crows circled in growing throngs overhead, and a cold, dry wind chaffed the travellers' faces as the trees thinned, their cover falling away. This was the wilderness, and in the absence of the forest, it should have been still, silent, empty. Instead, small shapes flitted between the rocks, too small and far away for him to properly see, while birds soared and cawed on the upper flows of a wind that shifted loose dirt as it swept lower over the ground, turning even the stillness of stone into a hint of movement that meant he could never relax, that his spine was stiff from walking on edge, shoulders braced, head swivelling from side to side, trying to find a danger he couldn't see, to prepare for the unknown. All around was the land that they had been promised, a place that was even more itself than they could have imagined, a place of vast trees and desolate mountainsides, of floods that came and went as if from nowhere, of bone-deep cold, shocking thaw, and scratching wind. A place that didn't feel quite real, but that Raul could see was more true than anything he'd imagined. Where the boundaries of the world grew thin, what remained wasn't emptiness. It was the bulging seams of the power behind their reality straining to pour through.

Far ahead, past a ridge and another valley beyond, a darkness lay on the rising slope of the mountain, an opening so deep and dark it could have been a hole in the day through which a starless night was seen.

"Ferra?" Raul called.

From further down the column, the grey-haired woman emerged, bow in hand, hurrying up the rocky trail. A slate-blue starling with an orange chest sat on her shoulder, pecking at a dried head of grain that had been tied into her furs.

"Aye?" she asked as she limped up to them.

Yasmi turned away, arms folded across her chest.

"Is that it?" Raul asked, pointing to the distant cave mouth. "Jarrag's Rest?"

"So's said."

"You mean you've heard that, or you know it?" All this time with these people, in their land, and he still didn't know their way of talking as well as he should. There was always more to learn.

"It's where you need to be."

"You're not coming with us?"

"We're with you for safety. That grows thinner the closer we get."

"Of course, I understand. After we get the dagger, we can join you again. You can come back with us, away from Jarrag and his influence."

"Back to your rebellion, so?" She tipped her head on one side and the starling on her shoulder did the same, the two of them staring the same challenge at him,

"That's part of it, yes. Together, we can drive out the Dunholmi, before they drive any deeper into the Withered Hills."

"And then we're all a happy part of Estis, aye?" She shook her head. "Lestavo, he'll follow you where you go just to see owt new. The rest, we don't want your country, so we don't want your rebellion."

How was he meant to respond to that? Get angry that they would take his protection now but not side with him later, try to pull on a sense of loyalty? That wasn't how the people of the Withered Hills worked, with their lives that flowed from one place to the next, homes and connections always changing. And it wasn't a way he was willing to behave. It didn't matter if the monarchs in stories demanded that people follow them. He might play that sort of leader, but he wouldn't become one. That was how you ended up with Dunholm.

"Thank you for being honest with me," he said.

"What else would I do?"

Figures appeared over the ridge ahead, people in wicker armour carrying bows and obsidian-tipped spears. The tension knotting Raul's shoulders grew deeper as he saw them, and particularly the towering woman in the centre.

"It's Ovida and her people," he said. "The ones who guarded the bridge against us."

"So Jarrag's sent them to stop us again?" Yasmi asked, hand moving to her masks.

"Not now," Ferra said. "When Jarrag's angry, he lashes out hardest at those who's close. They're here for safety in numbers."

"How do you know?"

"Words on the wind." Ferra stroked the starling's wing. "Withering ways, remember."

How many more were coming? Raul watched the skeletons of old leaves swept from the forest on a rising wind, ghosts of foliage dancing to the music of the wild, forming shapes out of the chaos. Surely it was worth reading those signs now, a small piece of divination that could prove crucial as they approached the final confrontation. The price was worth paying if it meant that he could help these people as well as those he'd left behind.

He opened his mind and watched the shapes, following instincts as much as conscious thought, letting the forms reveal themselves. A spinning circle of leaves like a wagon wheel, something in endless motion coming back around, above a knifelike spike of rock that spoke of violence and danger. Hardly a revelation that the conflict would keep coming, but the urgency of it indicated something more immediate than the cave mouth ahead or the rebellion they would return to after that.

Shifting his attention from those leaves, he watched the landscape, trying to find something more, something specific. That flock of birds, what shape were they forming? What about the patterns at the edge of the snowline on the peaks up ahead? Anything could be a sign if he could find a way to read it, so which ones mattered?

With a deep breath, he forced his attention back onto the path ahead. If he wore his mind out with too much of this, then he wouldn't be able to lead, and that was his role. People were counting on him.

"Raul," Yasmi said, and the yellow showed in her eyes. "Look."

Shapes were moving upslope, along the ridge, toward Ovida and her group. Low, prowling shapes, some large and some small. Shaggy wolves, fanged cats, a scurrying swarm of rats, more appearing with each moment. Raul looked around, saw that others were coming from the opposite direction. A bear loomed into view, teeth bared, the dark V on its flank visible from far away.

"They're surrounding them," he said, as rats emerged from holes in the ground. "Even above, look."

The birds he'd been watching flew lower. Ravens, crows, a pair of hawks, circling above the travellers.

As if sensing his scrutiny, the creatures moved faster, even the bear lumbering into a trot. Ovida looked around and shouted a command that Raul couldn't make out, drawing her people into a defensive ring.

Raul drew his sword and started to run toward them, Yasmi at his side. She pressed the mask to her face and shifted as she ran, going from two legs to four without missing a beat, bounding across the broken ground. She might just about reach Ovida before Jarrag's beasts did, but he stood no chance. Not unless…

He drew the swift charm from inside his tunic and clutched it so tight the edges ached against his palm. A swift for speed on their journey. It had worked for Valens fighting off the birds, perhaps it could work for him now. Not following the signs but using them, channelling and changing the shape of the world just a little, just enough for what he needed.

There was no hammer here for him to beat magic into the metal as he beat a shape into the world, like he'd done with Drusil at her forge. The only tool he had was his mind. He focused on the charm in the same way that he would focus on signs in the world, but pushing instead of pulling. Instead of hearing what the world had to say, he would make it hear him.

The bear roared. Wolves howled. Raul ran as fast as he could, heart thundering in his chest, but it wasn't fast enough. Yasmi was alone ahead of him, lashing out at rats as she ran through them toward Ovida, but the space ahead of Raul seemed vast and the beasts were almost there. A stone shot out from under his foot and he slammed into the ground, hands scraping, the edge of the charm cutting into the base of his thumb. He grabbed his sword, stumbled to his feet, squeezed the charm into the wound it had opened, screamed in frustration as he ran.

Suddenly, his legs were moving faster than ever, his feet more certain on the path. A thread of pain ran from his thumb all the way into his head, but he didn't need to make an effort to ignore it, he was so swept up in the moment, the rush of the wind past him, the sight of the animals closing in, and the certainty that now, as he passed Yasmi, he would be there in time. The world seemed to slow as he stretched out across the final few feet, sword swinging to catch a mountain lion at the front of the pack, to slice it out of the air as it leapt for Ovida. He slashed at a hawk as it swept down, hacked at a wolf, stamped on a rat, raised his sword and braced himself in the bear's path, riding a surge of energy like nothing he'd ever known. The bear slammed into him, bowling him over even as he carved a deep wound into its shoulder. He hit the ground, rolled, lost his grip on the charm, and though it still hung from his wrist as he got up, that rush of speed was gone.

No time now to worry about what had happened. As Ovida and two of her comrades thrust spears at the wounded bear, Raul covered their backs, fending off furred attackers. Everything was fur and blood and claws, swift movements and sharp blows, thrust and slice, block and dodge. Yasmi was at his side, the two of them tearing through Jarrag's horde alongside Ovida and her grimly steady companions. And past the swirling, messy melee others rushed up the ridge.

Then, as quickly as it had begun, the fighting was over. Animals and birds scattered into the wilderness, leaving Raul and his companions standing on a blood-slicked slope.

"Yasmi!" he snapped as she dashed after one of the mountain lions. "Don't run off alone!"

She turned and growled but took his warning, prowled back toward them with her tail swishing. Her teeth were bared and bloody as she approached Raul and lowered her head in front of him, let him run his hand through her fur.

Now the others were there, Valens fussing over Raul's wounds, Prisca peering at the brutal remains scattered across the ground, seeking signs in the guts they'd spilled. The thought of joining her made Raul's head ache even more than it already did. He found a rock to sit down on before he fell over, and Yasmi settled beside him, her wolf head in his lap and a satisfied rumble shaking her chest.

"That run," Valens said as he smeared something green and stinging into a wound on Raul's forearm. "How?"

Raul held up the charm between trembling thumb and finger. His pulse was still racing and the breath scratched in his throat. Where his blood had run across the charm, the metal was blackened and buckled like it had been warped by fire.

"I found a way to do more," he said.

Valens looked like his heart had been broken.

"Lad, if this does to you what it's done to Prisca..."

"I only used it for a few moments."

"Only a few moments and look what it's done."

"I can keep it under control."

Valens's grip tightened around Raul's wrist. He stared at Raul like he was reading a story written across his face.

"Be careful, lad. I believe in you, but I've heard those words before." He tucked the end of a bandage in, rolled the sleeve of Raul's tunic down over it, then straightened with a grunt. "I'd better help the others."

Most of the travelling column had reached them, and the people of the Withered Hills set to work butchering the bodies of the creatures they'd killed, taking furs and feathers, meat and bones. These were people who lived off the land, who didn't waste what it offered, even when that offer came trying to kill them. Amid the bustle, Valens helped Ovida tend to her people's wounds while Ferra and Prisca argued about how quickly they could move on.

Raul and Yasmi were left alone, a quiet space amid the chaos.

"How are you doing?" he asked, stroking her fur.

Yasmi growled.

"Are you going to shift back soon? I'd like to hear an answer in words."

Her chest rose and fell, then a paw touched her face. There was a movement in which the whole world seemed to bend as she became the young woman he knew, her head still resting on his lap, mask in her hand.

"I'm fine," she said flatly.

"Really?"

"What do you think?" She pulled away from him and sat cross-legged, staring down at the mask.

"I think that there's less of you than there used to be, and more of the wolf."

She scowled. "What do you expect? If I want to be effective, it's not enough to play the beast. I have to become it, again and again."

"Then don't do that."

"I have to." She looked at him. "You need this."

"I need *you* more."

"I . . ." She looked away, toward the wet sounds of Lestavo

slicing slabs of fat off the bear. "What we're doing here, it matters in a way my life never has before. I've made people laugh and cry, helped them to see the world through new eyes, but I've never made the world into something different. I've never lived the stories. I'm living them now, and the best way I can do that is as this thing." She held up the mask. "I know it's changing who I am. That scares me, but it thrills me too. For the most part, I've never felt more alive, but sometimes I stop and wonder if I've ever been more lost."

The strain in her voice was like the sound of a lamb lost in the hills, calling for the shepherd to bring it home, not knowing if it would ever be found. It made a different sort of ache inside Raul. He crouched in front of her and wrapped a hand around hers, careful not to touch the mask, not to seem as though he was trying to stand between her and the choices she had to make.

"I'm here for you," he said. "Whatever you need me to say or do."

"Thank you." Her eyes met his and the yellow in them receded, not vanishing but fading into familiar green. "That's what I need now, a friend I can lean on."

"A friend."

He nodded. Strange how a word like that could become bittersweet, but it was the word he needed to hear too. The world out here was too wild, too changing, he needed something else to stay what it had always been. He let go of her hand and sat back, looking up at the sky.

"Clouds are coming in from the north," he said. "We should get moving soon in case another storm comes in."

"I'll talk with Ferra and Prisca. Can you talk with Ovida and see how her people will fit in?"

"Sure. That sounds like something a leader should do."

She stood up, then held out a hand and helped him to his feet. His wounds tingled from Valens's ointment, but that was nothing next to the pounding in his head.

"Never mind me, are you all right?" Yasmi asked. "You look grey."

"Don't worry, I've got it under control."

Chapter Twenty-Seven
An End in Sight

Valens stood in the shadow of a lichen-speckled boulder, the ancient rock sheltering him from the wind as much as the sun. Ovida stood beside him, the only woman he'd ever had to look up to, and Ferra sat beyond her, back against the rock, feeding dried berries to a pigeon. They all looked in the same direction, back down the rocky trail they'd been ascending, to the distant edge of the woods from which a small column of warriors in blue was marching.

"Road's teeth, like I told you," Ovida said, her forthright tone reminding him of Fabia. "You know them?"

Valens squinted. When he was young, could he have made out faces at that distance? Probably not. Certainly not now.

"Dunholmi," he said. "Those white sashes mean officers or chosen guards, and I'd bet my boots they're led by Count Alder."

"They'll catch us soon, so?"

There were no horses. That was something. Dunholmi

chosen were hardy bastards, but they weren't used to marching on foot, which would help. Still, they were warriors, they wouldn't have got this far if they weren't fit to the task, and they weren't dragging the baggage the local people had, or the man from Ovida's group who'd had half his leg ripped out in the beast attack.

Valens eyed the distance between them, the angle of the slope, the state of the ground, thought back over long years of blistering marches.

"If we're lucky, they won't catch up before nightfall," he said.

"They'll see us, though," Ferra pointed out. "They'll know where we make camp."

"Which means a night attack." Valens looked around the boulder, across the valley that the rest of their group had started crossing, to the rocky slope with the cave in its side. Their destination. "You know this ground better than me. Can we get there today?"

"No," Ferra said.

"Maybe." Ovida scratched her chin. "Depends who you mean by 'we.'"

The wind blew harder, whipping up the blue surcoats of their pursuers. One of the Dunholmi stumbled, buffeted by the wind, but it wasn't enough to slow him.

"What will you do?" Ferra asked.

"Not my decision," Valens said with a sense of relief. "Let's ask."

Sticking to the shadow, he headed around the boulder and down the shallow slope beyond, picking up his pace into a steady jog. Ovida ran along beside him, her long strides matching his, and Ferra followed. They reached the column of travellers, which had swelled to over a hundred souls, and kept running past, heading for the front.

There was no missing Raul. Even wrapped in mud and bandages, he walked tall, striding confidently along the pilgrim trail, but never so confidently or so fast that he left anyone behind. Yasmi was walking on one side of him and Prisca on the other, the three of them leading the way across a narrow stream at the bottom of this last valley. Prisca was pointing at something on that final ascent to Jarrag's Rest, but she stopped as Valens and his companions joined them.

"What is it?" Prisca asked.

"Give them a moment to catch their breath," Raul said.

"Alder." Valens had caught all the breath he needed. "No horses but plenty of warriors, and he's less than a day behind."

"How much less?" It was good to see that Raul's hand went to his sword, ready for trouble.

"They'll get to us before we get to the dagger."

"Does it matter?" Ovida asked. "Aren't you going to fight them anyway?"

"Not yet, if we can avoid it," Raul said. "And I don't want to face them at the same time as Jarrag. If we get trapped between the two..."

Good, the lad was thinking strategically. They would need more of that once they got through this and launched the rebellion.

If they got through this.

Thick clouds had smothered the sky and now rain started

to fall, heavy drops that forced them to raise their hoods or accept a soaking.

"The important thing is the dagger, right?" Valens said.

"Correct," Prisca said. "There may be other opportunities rooted in the events associated with this place, but if there is any sort of power to be had, symbolic or metaphysical, then the dagger is the key. We will use it to tie Raul to Balbianus, and through that connection to tap into the strength of his heroic forebears, the essence of the kingdom."

Valens looked back along the column of people who had gathered behind them, looking for something like safety. The dagger might be key, but it wasn't the only thing that mattered here.

"We split," he said as the rain fell harder. "A small group heads fast for Jarrag's Rest, while the others go on down this valley, out of the way." He pointed along the path of the stream to where dark conifers marked the edge of another patch of forest. "It's an hour's walk to the trees, enough time to get out of sight before Alder catches up. That'll keep people safe from the fighting."

Ferra and Ovida exchanged a look through the water running from their hoods. Both nodded.

"Aye, it makes sense," Ferra said.

"What if Jarrag sends creatures after you again?" Raul asked.

"Got spears. Got bows."

"You've got children, the elderly, and the injured. We can't leave you undefended."

Not for the first time, the fall of Pavuno filled Valens's

mind. The crash of falling walls, the screams of panic as the population ran, his and Fabia's mad dash to hope and adventure. Their chance to be different from all these ordinary people with their ordinary deaths. Their chance to be heroes. They'd left everyone else behind, and in the end he'd left her too, all to become a failure and a washed-out drunk. So much for heroes and adventures. He didn't even have the ring to mourn her by anymore.

This time, he wasn't leaving anyone behind.

"I'll go with them," he said. "Watch for stragglers, defend the rear, swing a sword if Jarrag's beasts come hunting."

"We might need that sword." Raul looked up the mountain, then back the way they had come.

"You don't need me slowing you down when the mission's all about speed." Valens laid a hand on his son's shoulder. "You can do this."

Raul turned to Prisca.

"What about you, Ma? Maybe you should go with them too."

"I don't need your pity or your protection," she snapped.

"But if it goes wrong, people might need you to find a new way forward."

"I've heard you give excuses before, Raul. I didn't believe them then, and I don't believe them now."

"Fine, I don't want you to get hurt," he admitted, and his voice grew quieter. "Is that so bad?"

"Maybe you don't trust me to deal with whatever we face." She tapped the side of her head. "I told you, I will not be pitied."

"Ma, please…"

"This could be my last chance to make a mark on the world before my mind is stolen from me. A chance to face something unique and weave something powerful, something no one has done before, to rebind the power of the land and ensure its renewal. I will not risk that opportunity because I was not there, and I will not be robbed of my legacy."

"But…"

This time it was Yasmi who spoke up, the wolf flashing in her eyes.

"If we're running out of time, then we shouldn't waste it arguing. If Prisca can keep up, let her come."

Raul, the leader, sagged in resignation. Every argument that could be used had been used. All that remained was action.

"We go now," he said. "Da, get these folks out of here as fast as you can."

Valens held out his remaining hand, but instead of clasping it, Raul flung his arms around him. Valens clung to his son, the one good thing he had made in a life filled with death. Then he let him go, because the one thing he most owed Raul was to trust that he could see this through.

"Do right," Valens said, his throat tight around the words. "Like always."

Then Raul was striding across the stream and up the rocky slope on the far side, a wolf beside him and his mother following, the rain blurring Valens's view. Three of the four people who meant most to him in the world and this time he couldn't help.

"You heard." He turned to Ferra and Ovida. "Get your

people moving downhill. Someone tough at the front, just in case, and I'll take the rear."

Marching orders were meant to be clearer than that, more forceful and specific. But marching orders were meant for armies, not terrified nomads banding together to escape danger.

A murmur of confused questions rippled through the group, and then people started to turn, reorganising wagons, sledges, and pack animals to follow the new route. Usually, the Withered Hills folk were playful in their work, turning bags into improvised puppets, bouncing lines of poetry back and forth, laughing and chatting. Now there were only whispers and tense, huddled movements.

While they worked, Valens went down to the stream. He dipped a hand in its bracing water, wetted his parched throat, washed the dust and sweat from his face.

The water babbled as it broke across the shallow crossing point. Some folk said that fords were sacred to Laughing Loftus, because they could hear his voice in that sound. Valens had never really believed it, but he'd still made offerings to the god back in the day. It paid to have someone on your side, and jolly Loftus had felt like a better choice than the grim warrior gods his comrades preferred. War was around him all the time anyway, so why call for more of it? Better to bring laughter into his life.

Raul, Yasmi, and Prisca already seemed a long way off, ascending a switchback trail across the mountainside, off to face a god in his lair. Not a real god, maybe, but one powerful enough to turn this land and all its creatures against them.

Valens reached inside his tunic, past the wooden snowflake

from Issol's priests, and took out the charm that Drusil had given him. The gods knew, he still needed speed and luck, if they could be had, but what he needed more than that was to know that his son was safe, that someone was looking over Raul while Valens couldn't.

He hadn't prayed in years, hadn't made a proper offering since Pavuno fell and Loftus's temple with it, but the one prayer he remembered from the old days formed itself on his lips as he set the charm down.

"Laughing Loftus, I offer you this gift in joy, that joy may return to me when next we meet."

The charm slid off a stone into the babbling water, where it lay gleaming, its curved edge shining like a smile. Then Valens turned from his god and from his son and followed the people of the Withered Hills toward the shelter of the trees.

———————————————•———————————————

"There's someone watching us," Count Alder said as a bird fluttered away from the boulder on the ridgeline.

"Where, my lord?" Captain Brook asked.

"There."

A movement against the boulder, someone too large to fit in the shadow it cast, not quite agile enough to hide his movements. A vast, muscular figure that Alder recognised.

In that moment, he would have given up half his remaining warriors to have mounts for the rest, to press spurs to flanks and ride the rebels down. But the only beasts they had were the mules tethered beneath the trees.

He surveyed his forces. One warrior had been limping since a snake attacked them out of the floodwater, but the rest were fit, healthy, some of the best specimens Dunholm had to offer. They might have marched half the day, but they could still run.

"Time to pick up the pace," he said. "Our prey's almost in sight."

Chapter Twenty-Eight

Jarrag's Rest

The wind billowed around Raul, and icy cold rain ran from his cloak. The deeper winter that he'd called from the wild was making itself felt again. He shivered as he approached the looming entrance to Jarrag's Rest, a cave mouth five times as high as he was, bristling with chunks of broken rock like rows of ancient, uneven teeth. The wind whistled through those teeth, a shrill sound that made the hairs rise on his neck. As he drew close, there was a hiss and fire flared in the darkness, a tongue of flame rising to lick the ceiling.

Raul pushed back his hood as he stepped around the ragged rocks and into the cave, Prisca and Yasmi to either side of him. By the light of the fire, he could see a slab of stone worn smooth by centuries of use, its surface stained by things he didn't want to consider. Nooks in the walls held moss-spattered carvings, flaking pictures, tarnished jewellery, and objects that had rotten too far to be recognised, the remains of centuries of gifts to the so-called god. Between them, images decorated the stone, the simplified shapes of people and animals roaming through a forest of stylised trees, parading around a central image of a fire. From the altar to the offerings to the tableau with its message of the greatness of the divine flame, the whole place seemed like a version of other religious buildings he'd seen, no less powerful for its crudeness, the temple before temples were born.

The fire flared, making the shadows around the shrine sway and the images of ancient worshippers dance around their blazing god. Heat washed over Raul and his body tightened at the memory of the last fire, of an unbearable heat rushing across him to transform the world. His wounds itched under his bandages as he walked slowly toward the fire. Breath caught in his throat as the light winked off a ruby in one of the nooks, a reminder of the Red Eye shining over Pavuno, the star that had signalled the start of their failed revolt. Was he making a mistake, once again walking into the lair of an enemy far more powerful than he was?

It didn't matter. He had to do this. He'd told the rebels that he was going to get the dagger, to find a weapon that would help them throw off the Dunholmi. He couldn't let them down.

"Kneel." A voice roared out of the darkness at the back of the cave, a discordant chorus like the howling of the forest. Amid the flames, a face formed. "Offer me your obedience and I will not only grant you mercy, I will grant you power. As with Balbianus, I will give you the strength to drive your enemies before you."

Even after everything that he'd been through, the power of the presence shook Raul to his soul. But Yasmi had taught him well, made him into the performer he needed to be, someone who could sell the lie of confidence.

"What's the price for your power?" he asked.

"The only price is that you use it." The fiery face grinned. "Isn't that what you want? Make war on your enemies, drive my flame before you, carry my power into the world."

Raul stood facing the flames. He knew how reasonable the words sounded and how terrible their reality could be. He might lie to his followers and to the people of Estis, but he couldn't lie to himself. If he accepted what was on offer here, if he took the easy path, then the wheel of history would turn again, like that circle of violence he had read on the wind, and there would be nothing he could do to stop it while he lived.

"Perhaps we can negotiate alternative terms." Prisca approached the fire, watching the smoke swirl above it. "You tried to manipulate Valens through his loss, tried to shape our path by making the image of a quest. You clearly understand that different people have different motives, different deals to be struck. I'm confident that we can come to an arrangement."

"An arrangement?" Animals emerged from the darkness at the rear of the cave, their mouths moving in time as they spoke for Jarrag. There was a lizard with a head as long as Raul's body, a dagger-toothed black cat the size of a horse, a boar with tusks like sabres and bristles thick as quills. All of their eyes shone with fire. "What could you offer me except total obedience?"

Yasmi hunched over and growled, her own fur on end.

"Prisca..." Raul said in a warning tone.

"Trust me." She laid a hand on his arm. "I spent years twisted up in courtly intrigues, acted as ambassador to some of the most cunning neighbours we had. I can find a way through this. And as for you . . ." She turned her attention back to the fire. "After everything that you've seen of us, do you really think that we're going to be bullied into obedience?"

The flames leapt high, flinging shadows, and something gleamed in the darkness at the back of the cave, one last treasure hidden behind all the beasts. Raul could almost feel his hair curling, but he stood his ground as sweat soaked his clothes. While the flames rose and then fell, he set down his bag and removed his soaking cloak, felt a cool breeze against his back. He watched the fire, wondering how easy it would be to scatter. He watched the animals, trying to work out where their weaknesses would be, and resisted the urge to give his thoughts away by reaching for his sword.

Animals weren't meant to laugh, and the sound emerged all the more twisted from their throats.

"Very well," Jarrag said. "What would you like to offer?"

"Nothing," Raul replied, reaching into his tunic with his empty hand, wrapping his hand around a wooden charm.

"Raul." Prisca glared, but he replied with a small shake of his head.

"I'm not making deals with bullies and tyrants. We live free or die fighting."

———————————— • ————————————

As they approached the edge of the woods, Ferra just ahead, Valens looked back, up the trail Raul had followed. There was a glow from the inside of Jarrag's Rest, a light that should have signalled warmth and comfort in this cold and miserable place but that he could only see as danger.

He clenched fingers that weren't there anymore. The lad was as strong and smart and brave as anyone Valens had ever met. That was something he could trust his life to.

Then he saw them. Warriors—twenty, thirty, more—ascending the slope at a run. Rain had darkened their blue surcoats so that they barely stood out against the wet mountainside and the fall of dusk, but there was no mistaking them.

"Who's that?" Lestavo came trotting back from the column, head tipped on one side as he watched the movement.

"Alder," Valens growled.

"Thought you said he'd be slower?"

"I was wrong."

Lestavo whistled. "All those road's teeth, and Jarrag in the mix. Don't look good."

One of the warriors had spotted them and was pointing their way. While some kept running, others stopped to see what had got his attention.

Valens gritted his teeth, clenched his hand around the pommel of his sword.

"Keep moving," he said. "I'll stay, slow them down if they come for you."

"Come along," Ferra said. "They might not catch us yet."

"I said I'd protect you."

"We protect each other. It's the Withering way."

Valens swung his shield around and strapped it over his shortened arm. If he was going to do this, he was going to do it properly.

"Best we get moving." Ovida set down her pack and hefted her spear. "Go to them instead of letting them come to us, keep the fight from the young folk. Might give your boy a better chance, with us as a distraction."

"I thought that wasn't your fight."

She shrugged. "He kept peace on the bridge; I owe him a fight."

"Other folk looked out for me before." Ferra's pack thudded to the ground. "Now's time to pass on the good."

"I want to see these road's teeth up close." Lestavo pulled out two blades of black stone. "Seems this is the season for it."

A ripple of conversation was spreading through the column. Valens looked back to see others setting aside their burdens. Not all of them, not by a long way, that wasn't something you could expect; but enough that this didn't feel like one last doomed charge.

Die well, said a voice from the depths of memory, not a fake ghost whispering over his shoulder this time. But there were better things to do than die well. Perhaps, if he was willing to let others shoulder their share of courage, he could live well instead.

———————————•———————————

Fire flared with a brightness that half blinded Raul. A blast of heat seared him, but he tightly held on to the snowflake charm from Issol, his one ward against the flames.

From down the cave, the beasts roared and charged. Yasmi answered their cries with a ferocious howl. Prisca's bow twanged and an arrow hissed through the air.

Sometimes it seemed as though charms were only tokens, channels for wishful thinking. But Raul had made himself into a channel too, and in that blazing moment he opened himself to what the charm represented and everything that lay behind it: to the winter wrapped around the Withered Hills, to the snow on of the mountain above. Frost crackled across his skin. Clouded breath hit smoke.

He drew the charm from around his neck and stepped closer to the fire, to the heart of his opponent. Flames crackled as they drew back. Frost hissed and evaporated. The voice of Jarrag screamed, not through someone else's throat but directly into Raul's mind, a stabbing pain amid the throbbing ache that the magic brought. His heart hammered all the wilder as the bestial cries of battle echoed around the cave, as the heat closed in.

Then came another voice from behind, the forceful clarity of a Dunholmi aristocrat.

"Maybe I won't need to kill you after all."

Count Alder stood in the mouth of the cave, Raul's old sword in his hand.

Chapter Twenty-Nine
Blades in the Firelight

Raul forced himself not to focus on the fire or the beasts attacking his companions. He could only fight one threat at a time, and right now that threat stood six strides from him, pointing his own blade. The warriors standing in the dusk behind Alder looked distracted, glancing back down the mountainside, making them one more threat that could wait, but the count demanded attention at the point of a blade.

"You people," Alder hissed. "You have cost me good warriors and good horses, pain and indignity, for the sake of your pitiful, *impossible* revolt. But this ends here, now, with no one around to see your last stand, no one to tell your tale and rally rebels to a martyr's banner. Your cause dies in the cold and the dark, so far from civilisation that no one will even find your bones."

His left hand still clutched tight around the snowflake charm, Raul drew his sword with the right.

"Nice speech," he said. "How long have you been rehearsing it?"

Alder's lip curled, and the tip of the blade twitched. "Is that all you have to say in your final moments?"

"I'm sorry for the horses. They didn't deserve their deaths."

Raul lunged. Alder parried, knocking Raul's blade aside, and laughed as he made his own swing. That laughter died as Raul deftly dodged, then stabbed toward Alder's chest, forcing him to duck back. The ringing of blades joined the roaring of beasts and of the fire.

"I've done a lot more fighting since the last time we met," Raul said as he parried an attack, then launched into one of his. "I've learned."

"Not enough."

Alder drew another blade, a perfectly polished sabre, and went on the attack again.

Raul was good. He'd practised long and hard to get that way. But Alder was good too, and the best swordsman in the world would have a tough time fending off two swords with one. The flurry of attacks drove Raul back, away from the fire, toward the mouth of the cave. Rain blew in around them, and as it passed Raul it turned into snow.

"More North March magic?" Alder asked with a sneer. "These tricks won't save you now."

As a slash from his sabre forced Raul to parry right, the other sword lunged at his chest. He dodged, but not fast enough, and pain flared through his shoulder. A fresh wound, or an old one reopened? It didn't matter, the pain and blood were the same.

He stumbled back across the icy stone, out toward the winter and the wild.

Yasmi ripped a ragged wound down the side of the boar and snapped at the huge black cat, driving it back. She was strength and she was anger, she was the ferocity of the forest and the howl of the wild. Every breath tinged with blood made her heart beat harder and her claws strike stronger.

The giant lizard, bigger than any Yasmi had ever seen, was advancing on Prisca, jaws full of dagger teeth hinging wide, despite the arrows protruding from between its scales. It snapped those teeth as it advanced on the old woman, pressing her into a corner.

The boar barrelled into Yasmi, slamming her to the ground. She rolled from beneath its stamping hooves, howled and slashed, bared her teeth, readied to pounce.

The clang of swords drew her gaze, even through the blood and fury. She let out an agonised howl as she saw Alder there, driving Raul back, blood running from Raul's shoulder. The cat and the boar stalked toward her and the fire flared, but none of that raised the same sour dread she felt seeing Raul bleed.

He was too far away for Yasmi to help, with the beasts and the heart of the fire between them. But Prisca was closer, Prisca had glanced that way too, and Prisca had a bow.

Yasmi sprang over the boar, an arc of muscled grace through the air. The boar swung its head and a tusk gouged her hip, but she still hit the lizard, claws ripping away scales, and the two of them rolled across the rocks in a spray of blood. The lizard writhed beneath her, its long jaw pivoting around, while the boar and the cat closed in. Yasmi knew by the smells of blood and fury, by animal instinct, that she couldn't win. Not while she was just an actress playing at a wolf.

With a roar that shook the flames, she let herself go and let the mask take control. A distant voice in the back of her mind cried out in alarm as her last rational thoughts were scattered, flung to the four winds. The firelight and the fight, that was all she knew.

Blood and sweat.

Teeth and claws.

Kill or be killed.

The savagery of the lone wolf against the world.

———————————•———————————

The ruby in the pommel of Raul's old sword gleamed. The sword he'd lost, wielded by the man who had beaten him, who had taken Valens's hand, who still had Estis under his boot. A man sneering from behind that blade as he fended off Raul's attacks with one sword and prepared a fatal lunge with the other.

"Too bad no one will ever hear about this," Alder said. "But maybe it's not a story worth telling—after all, you're hardly a challenge."

Raul braced himself to dodge, even though he knew that it wouldn't help. He was out of space, pushed back against the wall of the cave mouth, out of options and out of chances, a fake hero about to die a real death.

Thud.

Alder twisted, knocked back by one of Prisca's arrows protruding from his shoulder. The elaborate, ruby-pommelled sword clattered to the ground. Raul flung himself from the wall and into Alder, driving his sword with the whole weight of his body.

Alder, his face an inch from Raul's, gasped, and blood flecked his pale lips. He staggered back, the sword protruding from his body, slipped on the ice-slicked stone, and tumbled out of the cave, down the steeply sloping mountainside.

Raul snatched up the ruby-pommelled sword, ready to face the Dunholmi troops. But instead of a force of chosen warriors ready to grab vengeance for their lord, he saw a sprawling melee, wild folk and warriors battling across the slope, Valens shouting orders at the heart of it all. The tide of war was turning against the Dunholmi.

As the dark of night closed in and the wind turned to snow around him, Raul clutched the snowflake charm tight and turned to face the flames.

Chapter Thirty
Perfection

Ice formed across Raul's skin as he clutched the charm tight. It melted and steamed as he strode into the cave, fending off the heat and the pain. The fire in the centre of the cavern burned brighter than ever, but smaller as well. It was diminished in size and in power, and though waves of heat rolled off it, they couldn't hold Raul back.

"Kneel!" Jarrag roared from the flames.

"No."

"Serve me."

"No."

"Then let me serve you." Jarrag's voice was shrill with alarm, words rushing out. "I can give you strength, dominion, an army of beasts. The power of the inferno. The chance to reap the world from your path."

"No." A small, simple word, hard to hold on to in the face of all the cajoling and all the danger, but it was all the anchor he needed as he approached the fire, steam swelling around him, and stepped into the flames.

The snowflake charm held the deep, wild winter now, in a way it could never have done at any other time, in any other place. Raul sank to his knees and plunged it into the fire.

———————•———————

The wolf that had been Yasmi flung itself at the boar, ripping claws down its side. The boar twisted, a mass of muscle, slammed her against the wall.

Before she could get back up, the cat was on her, hissing and gouging. The two of them tangled, rolled across the cave. Claws sank through fur. Teeth snapped. Blood flowed. She didn't know where one body ended and another began, only pain and desperation, panting breaths and hammering hearts.

She shook herself free, but there was no freedom from the dizzy pulsing of blood in her veins and in the air. Bodies flung themselves at her and there was no keeping track of what was where. Every movement was a threat, every body a target. She wasn't just the predator anymore, she was prey, and the only way not to panic was to let bestial fury win.

Howling, she flung herself at one beast, rending and tearing, ripping flesh and fur. Another slammed into her. She twisted, tore, soaked in blood that might have been hers or theirs or anyone's. Stumbled to her feet, held up by the red mist of the hunt.

The stench of blood.

The heat of fire.

Kill or be killed.

Something was moving still.

Raul expected a moment of climactic destruction as he plunged the charm into the fire; billowing steam and flying embers, a cloud of ashes as Jarrag's fiery strength scattered. Instead, the flames flickered, dwindled, collapsed, and the snowflake crumbled away. Raul was plunged into darkness and silence, nothing to distract him from the awful ache in his head.

There was a rustling, a click, and then a light. Prisca stood over him, holding their remaining lantern, one side of it dented in.

"I'm amazed this thing still works," she said, and held out her hand.

Something burst from the back of the cave, a wild storm of fur and blood that knocked Prisca flying and pounced on Raul. The light came and went as the lantern rolled across the floor, and in those fleeting moments Raul saw claws and teeth, a gaping maw, death closing in as the creature's weight pressed him down and a terrible growl filled his ears.

"Yasmi, please," he gasped.

She roared and tightened her claws on him. Blood dripped from between her teeth, running down his cheek.

"Yasmi, it's me."

Hot breath rancid with death. Teeth closing around his throat.

"Remember who you are."

She still growled, but the teeth stopped as they pressed against his skin, not tearing his throat out.

Not yet.

"Remember the things you love," he said. "Singing and dancing, fine wine and spiced cakes, delivering a perfect soliloquy. Your friends and family.

"Remember *me*."

Teeth drew back. The creature that was Yasmi stepped off him and backed away with a low rumbling growl. Even though she was limping, she looked larger and more ferocious than ever, blood dripping from her hip as well as her teeth and claws. A glimpse at the torn and broken bodies behind her made his stomach turn.

Raul rose from the ashes on the floor. Prisca approached, a knife in her hand, watching Yasmi warily, and picked up the lamp.

"Is she safe?" Prisca asked.

"Of course," Raul said. "It's Yasmi."

He meant it, even if he didn't entirely believe it, and he forced himself not to take a defensive stance as she approached, head lowered, tail down, ferocious confidence reduced to cautious steps. He made his hand steady and ran it across her head and down her back, trying not to pay attention to the stickiness of blood, to focus instead on soft fur and the heart beating beneath it, the warmth and solidity of his friend.

"Thank you," he said as the lantern beam swung across the heap of dead beasts. "Both of you, thank you for saving me."

Yasmi's growl was almost a purr.

"I believe that this is what heroes do on an adventure," Prisca said. "Now that we've slain the monster, shall we collect our reward?"

By the light of the lone lamp, the three of them walked

toward the back of the cave—Raul's comrades, his family, his pack, coming with him to the climax of their quest.

Prisca held the lantern high, illuminating a crude stone shelf at the very back. Light glinted off strands of tarnished gold wrapped around something darker, as long as Raul's forearm and tapering to a point. Carefully, barely able to keep his hand steady, Raul picked it up.

The scabbard must have been beautiful once, richly decorated with gold ornaments and a ruby at the top. The gold had been tarnished by the centuries, the gem had cracked, and the leather cover fell away in slimy lumps of rot across Raul's fingers. He set his sword aside, reminded himself that it wasn't what was on the outside that mattered, wrapped his fingers around a dust-caked handle, and drew the dagger.

Earth-brown flakes caught the light along the length of what had once been a blade but was now little more than rust.

Raul closed his eyes and focused on what this thing represented. Power and strength, royalty meeting the wild, the roots of the bloodline that built a nation. Try as he might, he found none of it. No connection, no sign, just a rusted remnant of broken glory.

"No," Prisca hissed. "It can't be…."

Yasmi whined.

A feeling swelled in Raul, surging up through his belly like the waters of an onrushing flood. It filled his chest until he was choking on the feeling, until it broke free despite all his determination.

Raul laughed so hard that the sound filled the cavern, so hard that his sides ached and he bent over gasping for breath.

He laughed until the ache in his head filled his skull and he thought that he might black out. All the strain, all the tension, all the feelings that had banked up inside him as he fought his way through the Withered Hills, all of it came ripping out.

At last, he caught his breath. The others were staring at him, Prisca's mouth hanging open. It was almost worth it to see her like that.

"Don't you see?" he said. "It's perfect. A pointless quest for a fake hero."

He tried to slide the rust blade back into the scabbard, but it broke on a warped edge at the mouth, fractured into pieces that fell to the floor. Still laughing, Raul set the empty scabbard and bladeless hilt down on the shelf.

"We can do something with them," Prisca said, reaching out but not quite touching the remains. "Have a new blade forged, use them as symbols of old stories, find a way to wind the old magic of the land through what remains."

"Forget it," Raul said. "Look around you. The only signs here are the symbols of Jarrag's power. This isn't the heart of Estis. It's one more piece of someone else's ground that we laid claim to in our so-called glory days. There's no essence of the kingdom to tap into, and if there really is a thinner place where magic comes through, then it comes through in the form of things like Jarrag, our enemies instead of our power."

"We've come all this way." Prisca scooped up a fistful of rust and tried to let it fall through her fingers, but it clung to her skin or fell in clumps, leaving no signs to be read. "There has to be something real."

"It was just a story, and we almost died for it." Raul ran his fingers through the soft fur around Yasmi's head. "But a story's not worth losing yourself for."

With a flicker like one last flame fading, Yasmi's eyes went from yellow to green. Her paw came up, her mask fell away, and she rose to her feet.

"I'm sorry," she said, and wrapped her arms around Raul.

"I'm not," he said, hugging her back. "We did our best."

Raul picked up his sword again, and they headed for the cave mouth. Against the slate grey of a winter night stood Valens, holding up a burning torch. Beyond him, locals were sorting through bodies, those of their friends and those of the Dunholmi. Snow fell gently across the hills, fat flakes spinning as they floated down, not a terrible storm like Jarrag had summoned but natural winter weather.

"Where's Alder?" Raul asked.

"Haven't seen him," Valens said. "Might be in one of the heaps."

"Everyone knows that the villain isn't dead until you see the body," Yasmi said. "Tenebrial says that audiences need the catharsis."

"Are we an audience?"

"Aren't we?"

Raul sat on one of the rocks at the cave mouth and sagged. His hands shook like he hadn't eaten in a week. Words, images, and ideas jumbled against each other in his mind, pieces of a broken statue rattling painfully against the insides of his skull.

"Did you see?" he said. "What I did in there. The magic, channelling the...the..." What was the word he needed?

"The essence of winter, putting out Jarrag's flame. You saw, right?"

His da and ma exchanged a look, one he hadn't seen since their conspiracy was revealed, perhaps not even since they'd left behind their tavern in the hills.

"It was impressive," Prisca said. "But also foolhardy. Grappling with powers like that on your own could easily have gone wrong."

"But..."

"You beat Count Alder in a fight," Valens said. "That's more than I managed. That's a story they'll be telling around campfires for years to come."

"I..."

Instead of lifting him up, their words were emptying him out, but through his jumbled thoughts he couldn't even begin to work out why. All he had was his own sense of disappointment, knowing that his grand magical achievement hadn't been what his parents wanted. Hadn't he left this feeling behind?

Yasmi crouched in front of Raul.

"Hey," she said, lifting his chin so that he looked her in the eye. "You didn't just beat Alder, you got your sword back, the symbol of the rebellion all those prophecies are wrapped around. That's something we've got out of this, right? And all thanks to you."

Her smile drew a smile out of him, and he flexed his fingers around the sword's hilt. It wasn't everything he'd hoped for, but it was a start.

"Aye," he replied. "So's said."

Chapter Thirty-One
What We Can Weave
in the World

As they made their weary way back through the Withered Hills, Raul expected the locals to leave them. But as they marched through days of tumbling snow and of crisp blue skies, over rocky ground, through forests, over rivers, and across the heights that split the hills, the caravan grew. There were young people and old people, ones with rolling homes and ones with all their possessions heaped on their backs. Some had dogs that yapped along behind them, birds in cages or fluttering above their heads, a lone lumbering bear. There was even a train of Dunholmi mules that they'd found at the edge of the forest, which bore hefty burdens with plodding solidity, seemingly indifferent to the change in their human companions.

"Why are so many people following us?" Raul asked Lestavo around the fire one night.

"Because you stopped Jarrag," Lestavo replied with a grin. "They're all fixing to see what the man who did that looks like."

"Not all," Ovida said sternly, firelight dancing in her eyes like a ghost of the power she used to serve. "Some are scared. You drove out something powerful, and they don't know what comes next. That makes you the safest place to be."

"But most are here out of gratitude." Ferra looked up from an arrow she was fletching. "You made the Withering safer, and they're fixing to pass that good along."

"How does following me help with that?"

"Haven't you heard them talk about you, seen the way they look? You freed them from a dangerous power, and there's nowt better for passing that on than helping you free your own."

"They're coming to join the rebellion?"

Ferra looked at Lestavo, who was grinning from ear to ear.

"Go on," she said.

Lestavo pulled a bag out from behind him and tipped a heap of sticks, vines, and old fur out.

"Tomorrow night, we play puppets," he said, holding out some of the pieces. "Share remembrance of all we've seen, fix on what's to be done next. We'll weave one of you in."

"Yasmi," Raul said. "She knows how to perform."

"Not too daft for a prince, so?" Lestavo winked. "Nowt's set in the stars, but I don't see us turning back now."

Raul leaned forward, enjoying the calm of the evening despite its cold, the stars shining like a thousand points of hope amid a dark expanse.

"That's amazing," he said. "Thank you."

"Don't go thinking we'll join yon kingdom," Ovida said, waving forcefully in the direction of Estis. "We fight for you, and you don't try to rule us after, so?"

"So." Raul nodded, then placed his hand over his heart. "I swear by everything I hold dear, the Withered Hills will be our friends, nothing more or less, free and wild."

"Nowt you do could make us any different," Lestavo said with a chuckle. "Some beasts can't be tamed."

Yasmi built her puppet, a baby bear with wide eyes and claws made of thorns. Raul didn't go to watch when she joined in their play, not wanting to remind them that he was an outsider, but the next day, the folk of the Withered Hills were still with them, marching on more determined than ever.

Conversations around campfires became the way markers for Raul's journey, each one a sign of how far he'd come, not just in crossing the wilds but in getting to know the people travelling with him. He told jokes and swapped stories, joined in singing local songs, put on a three-hander play with Yasmi and Valens that drew laughter as his da kept forgetting lines. The days of travel were tiring and the nights were the bitter cold of deep winter, but warmth and energy were renewed in companionship.

Still, something was missing. Even after his weeklong headache had faded, his limbs felt heavy in the long hours of walking and his chest felt empty. They'd gone so far only to miss out on what they were after, and though he worked hard to keep up the confident mask of leadership, his thoughts were faltering.

They were nearly out of the Withered Hills by the time

he managed to gather Yasmi, Valens, and Prisca for an evening without anyone else to listen or interrupt. A spirited wind snapped at the canvas of the tent that Ferra had found for them, and out in the night the Withered people were singing in rounds. Raul and his companions sat in a circle in the light of Drusil's lamp.

"You saw the ruined tower up ahead?" he asked.

"We could hardly miss it," Prisca replied.

"That means we're at the pass out of the Withered Hills. Tomorrow we'll be back in Estis."

"The Withered Hills are part of Estis."

"That's not what these people think," Valens said softly.

"It's also not the point." Raul took a deep breath. "The day we leave the hills is the day we return to our work, to gathering the rebellion and preparing for war. We were meant to come home with a powerful symbol of Estis, maybe even with magic drawn from the land. That was the thing we could rally people around, and we don't have it."

"We have you." Yasmi reached across the gap between the two of them, a few inches that felt like a thousand leagues, and squeezed his shoulder. "When people hear you talk, when they see how you act, they'll join up."

"And when they hear the stories and prophecies," Prisca said. "Certainty is a powerful thing."

"Perhaps," Raul said. "But I don't feel certain anymore. We failed, and I think we need to try doing things differently."

"Differently how?"

"I'm not sure, but..."

"But you've got an idea." Valens smiled. "Out with it."

Raul took a deep breath. It was true what he'd said, he wasn't certain about this, but…

"What if I focus on magic, using divination and channelling power like I did at Jarrag's Rest? I walked into that fire and I drove Jarrag out. Maybe I could do that to the Dunholmi somehow; be a wizard king instead of a warrior one."

Yasmi's fingers dug into his shoulder as she looked at him with alarm.

"Think about how you've been since then," she said. "Drained, pained, who knows what else. That was just using it once. If you keep doing this, you'll destroy yourself."

"Sometimes we have to make sacrifices, right, Da?"

The lamplight shone bright and steady on the leather-wrapped stump of Valens's wrist as he stared at the space where his hand should have been. When he looked up, his expression was grim.

"Not sure I believe in sacrifices anymore. Even if I did, I'd never let you be the sacrifice." His voice dropped to a whisper. "Not again."

Raul, his stomach fluttering, tapped a crooked finger against his lips. He'd spent days thinking this over, finding the courage it would take to commit to the course. He needed something to give him a sense of purpose, to show that they were bringing strength out of the wild. In spite of their reactions at Jarrag's Rest, he'd hoped that his family would back him up, would hold him steady.

At least Prisca was bound to agree. She was the one who'd built a cause around prophecy and the magic that empowered it.

"Ma?" he asked, looking to her for support.

"It's a bad idea," she said, trailing a finger through the dirt and studying what remained. "For two reasons. The first is that we've spun our prophetic web around the concept of a warrior king, a bold young man with a sword. Changing course now risks unravelling that. We don't want people to have any doubt, or to start examining the prophecies more closely before we're done. If I had years to plant the seeds of a more esoteric vision, it might work, but we don't have that luxury. The Dunholmi are after us already, and if we lose momentum, then we lose everything.

"The second reason is the risk to you. I don't mean that personally, though I do share Valens's affection, however poorly I might display it. I mean it pragmatically. I don't know whether a precedent exists for what you did at Jarrag's Rest, channelling such monumental raw power through a single person. In years to come, once the kingdom is free, I look forward to seeing scholars spend years studying it and working out how it might be replicated, as well as the wider implications for what we can weave in the world. But right now, all we know is that it was an awesome and…"

She paused, her face stiffened, and her fingers curled in with frustration. Though he desperately wanted to hear all she had to say, Raul refrained from trying to suggest a word. His ma deserved her pride.

"It was potentially devastating," she said at last. "For all we know, it will destroy your mind the next time you do it. I very much doubt that you can sustain such efforts over the course of a long military and political campaign, which is what we face. And if our leader, in whom so much is invested, keels over dead in the middle of the war, then we could lose everything." She shook her head. "I admire your ambition, Raul, and your willingness to risk yourself for Estis, but this is not an appropriate solution."

Raul sagged. When he'd taken on the task of raising a rebellion, these were the people who had given him the strength he needed. Now, there was none of that.

"Fine," he said, head hanging as he looked down at the dirt. "I'll think about what you've said."

"That's all we want," Yasmi said. "Remember, we believe in you."

At that, he managed a half-hearted smile. Sitting up straighter, he gathered his thoughts.

"There's something else," he said. "Prisca, when we get back, I want you to leave again."

Her face hardened and her voice become cold.

"I feel that I have more than proved myself. After everything we've just done, that you would consider me a...a..." Those fingers curled in again. "That is utterly unfair."

"This isn't a rejection. It's the opposite. I need you to go out into the world as our ambassador, to find Estian exiles and negotiate with them, to rally them for the fight."

"Wait." Valens scowled. "How can we trust her?"

"We have to." Yasmi sighed. "She knows the people, and she knows how to travel quickly. Raul's right, there's no one better."

Raul locked eyes with Prisca. Her expression was never soft, but it was no longer dark and brittle as flint.

"My mind," she whispered. "It's not what it was. Do you really want to trust delicate diplomacy to a grey-haired diviner who's starting to lose her words? What if I misjudge a situation or say the wrong thing?"

"Your mind might be a little blunted, but it's still the sharpest one we have. I won't waste that."

"Are you sure?"

"I'm sure. You were right, we need to act now, while Alder's out of the picture and no one's replaced him yet. That leaves the occupiers weaker, and it gives us an opportunity. If we're going to seize it, we need all the help we can get."

As he said that, he felt some of his old strength returning, a sense of purpose swelling in his chest that he'd not known since the night they stormed the palace, back when the world was so different. After everything they'd been through, the people of Estis still needed him, and he needed to live up to their faith.

"Tomorrow evening, once we're through the pass, don't wait for anyone," he said. "Get out into the world and get to work."

"What about the rest of us?" Yasmi asked.

"We'll be spreading out too, but slower, finding the people who were with us before, the ones they've spoken with since, even some who've never considered rebellion. We've journeyed into the wild and we've beaten Count Alder, so we have a story to tell. More than that, we've brought back what we need to win."

"But the dagger…"

"This isn't about the dagger anymore. It's not even about

magic." Raul smiled. At last, here was something he felt comfortable with. "It's about something even better."

———————●———————

Count Alder's home city burned. Butchers, tanneries, and storehouses blazed like beacons. Whinnying roars of terror ripped through the night as stable blocks collapsed in smoke and flame. People ran screaming, burning clothes flaring behind them, skin charring, eyes melting, hair flaring into dust and smoke. Everything that mattered to him was turning to ash, and he walked through it untouched. Sweat ran from his brow and soaked his shirt, but it wasn't drawn out by the inferno. The heat eating him came with the pain that throbbed through his body. He burned from inside.

As he reached the square in front of the palace, a scorching wind seared his cheeks. The flames across the building pirouetted into a new form, a face twisted by fury.

"The North Marchers," Alder growled. "They did this, didn't they?"

Who else could it be?

"They will do this," the flames replied, "unless you stop them."

"I will. I swear it."

"I can help."

The lips of the face contorted, forming an ash-black V. Alder realised that he had seen that sign as he crossed the Withered Hills. It had been in the fur of beasts, the bark of trees, drawn on the faces of backward locals. After travelling so far, the sign only revealed its meaning to him now.

But how was he here? He had been in the hills. There was fire then too, and a face, and a cave, and that brat of a Marcher boy, their fake king, their upstart, their mockery of nobility. Alder had fought him, and then . . .

"I'm dead, aren't I?" No muttering, no evasion. A hard truth had to be faced.

"Not quite," the fire replied.

"But I'm dying." And if he died, he would never be able to fulfil that oath. The House of Alder would fail, and from that failure Dunholm would fall.

"I can save you," the voice replied.

"Then do it." His chest ached, and he didn't think it was from the smoke. Somewhere far beyond this, his body was twitching and sweating, racked with fever pains. Somewhere far from this vision of disaster, in a reality almost as grim, his end was close.

"Aren't you going to ask what my price is?"

"No." What was the point? He could accept death—not just his own but that of his house and his kingdom—or he could grasp at survival. He would grapple with the conse-quences later, for now he had to seize the chance before his last breath slipped away. "I accept. Give me power. Give me life." He reached out his hand and a flame stretched to meet it. He closed his fist around that flame, held steady through the searing heat. "Give me vengeance."

The fire which had consumed his city flared hotter, brighter, its light driving back the night. It washed over and through him, consuming his body, consuming his world. His mind was heat and pain. He screamed as he bent back on himself and then . . .

He flopped onto hard stone in the cold of a cave. Not the grand cave where he had fought the boy, but a small, cramped cave lit by washed-out winter light. A few feet from him, Captain Brook and Captain Thorn sat with their backs against the wall, Brook scraping a knife across a stone, striking sparks as she tried to light a fire.

Alder pushed himself onto his elbows. A horse blanket fell away, revealing stained and crusted bandages wrapped around his chest.

"Thank Harl," Brook said.

"Didn't think you'd live." Thorn spat out of the cave mouth into the falling sleet.

"I had help."

Alder sat up, his body shaken by a fevered shivering that felt as much like cold as heat. The flesh beneath the bandages was agony, and a broader throbbing of pain swelled from there, but he wasn't going to die.

Not now.

He held out his hand. Fire flowed from his palm and ignited the pathetic pile of sticks his officers had assembled. Their eyes went wide.

"Magic," Brook whispered, knife and stone hanging limp in her hands.

"Fuck," Thorn mumbled.

"We will turn these people's weapons against them," Alder said.

Both of them looked at him in shock.

"No." Thorn shook his head. "It's not worth it. This is wrong."

"It's necessary."

"I'm having no part of it."

Thorn leapt up, bumped his head off the ceiling, turned toward the mouth of the cave. He screamed as Brook buried her knife in his calf and twisted. By the time he fell to the ground, she'd yanked the knife free. A swift stab to the throat ended his protests, blood steaming as it spurted into the fire.

Alder gazed indifferent at the fallen body. He'd held some hopes for the captain, but the house of Thorn had been brought low by its dissent before, so it was hardly surprising to see its heir meet the same fate. Someone else would have to redeem that family's honour.

Brook wiped her blade and bowed her head to Alder, who allowed himself a half smile.

"What now, my lord?"

Chapter Thirty-Two
The Prince in Waiting

Anleri wouldn't even have been a village if not for the mining camps in the hills above, whose traffic had created roads and a junction, the need for a weekly market with its own mud square, two storage barns, eventually an inn serving ale to miners and providing cramped rooms for the merchants who came to negotiate with them. Once it was there, peasant farmers started using the space, bringing in their surplus to sell, carving more fields out of the forests. Anleri had swelled to a mighty sixty-three inhabitants including children, a big place by the standards of the region.

As Raul hiked up the road in the sunshine of a dwindling winter at the head of a long, slow caravan from the Withered Hills, there were at least a thousand tents in the fields around Anleri, and he felt like every single person they passed was staring at him.

Valens was standing by the side of the road, a notched measuring staff in his hand, shouting at the people putting up tents. His words became white clouds in the air, but his face was turning red.

"I said three strides between them, and ten clear around the latrines! You're warriors now, act like it!"

He shook his head and set the work aside for long enough to wrap Raul in a crushing hug.

"This is…" Raul looked around, wide-eyed. "This is a lot."

"Efron's been all around the Granite Shires and the Riddleroot Holdings while we were gone, performing your story. Others went through the small towns and the borderlands. Then there's Appia's dockers in Pavuno, talking to boat crews, spreading news along the rivers." Valens grinned. "Now word's spreading fast that you beat Alder. There's a lot of folk who want what comes next."

"Still…" Raul was used to organising a few score of rebels, maybe speaking to a hundred at once on a good day. Seeing and hearing and smelling this throng of people, like a city without the shelter of its walls, and knowing that they were all here for him, it was dizzying. He'd been able to wrap his mind around the hundreds of wild people following him out of the Withered Hills, because they turned up a few at a time, a slow growth he could get used to. And sure, he'd heard that more were coming, but he'd avoided the thought of what that might look like. This was unavoidable.

"You'll be good." Valens slapped him on the shoulder. "Yasmi's got you a place to stay and to hold meetings. Look for the players' wagon out front."

"Our new friends will need space." Raul gestured at the long trail of wagons, walkers, and rolling houses behind him.

"I've got it." Valens held up his measuring staff. "You go rest."

The old warrior started shouting commands before Raul was even two strides past him. The thought of rest was appealing, but Raul had other work to do, conversations to have, things to arrange. For now, he would have to accept the weariness and sore feet.

The theatre wagon had its stage out, and half a dozen members of the troupe sawing wood for shelters in front of it. Efron, supervising from the stage, waved enthusiastically at Raul, then directed him through the door of the nearest house, a two-storey building made with care from local pine logs and neatly split planks. The downstairs room, with its stone fireplace and kitchen implements at the back, was surprisingly well lit, and in the middle of the room was a round table, around which Yasmi was assembling chairs.

She smiled as Raul walked in.

"This was Tenebrial's idea," she said, tapping the table. "It's more egalitarian as council tables go, a nice symbol. I thought you'd like it."

"Thank you." Raul smiled back uncertainly. They'd not seen each other since leaving the Withered Hills and had no chance to talk alone between Jarrag's Rest and then. He felt as though a string was drawn tight through him, making his belly ache.

"There are smaller rooms upstairs," Yasmi continued, straightening the coloured scarf that hung across her masks. "Space by yourself to get some quiet and some sleep. I think you'll need a way to escape the crowds, once word gets around of who you are."

"I'm not sure about this." Raul bit his lip. "What about the people who live here?"

"A merchant and her family. They only come here in the summer, spend their winters in one of the big towns." Her expression darkened. "She trades iron ore to the Dunholmi weapons foundries."

Raul laughed. "Even when we steal people's houses, we do it in a righteous way."

"Not steal. Borrow."

"Is there enough space upstairs for us to rehearse?"

"Of course." She headed for the stairs in the corner. "And a costume chest for you."

"I'm not sure I need costumes."

He followed her up the stairs, heart hammering as he watched the way the masks shifted on her hip, how the sunlight shone through her strawberry-blond hair.

"Of course you need costume changes, even if you don't want to call them that. You can't dress the same way for a wagon raid and a siege, never mind talk local leaders into joining us. And then there will be the international diplomacy…"

"The what?" He steadied himself against the wall at the top of the stairs.

"Prisca's out talking to exiles. Do you really think that she won't talk to mercenaries and foreign princes too? Or that you can avoid them once you're king?"

King.

There was another thought he'd been avoiding. Not a position he deserved, but one he would need to hold at the end of all of this. That thought was more terrifying than all the battles that lay ahead. He swallowed and followed her through a doorway.

"This is your room," Yasmi said. "We can rehearse in here when we don't need much space, to make sure no one sees."

As if to make her point clear, she closed the door, revealing brightly coloured clothes hanging from pegs.

"These are your more formal outfits, stage clothes neatened up so that they'll withstand a close encounter. We'll need better later, but they're good enough for now. Shirts, tunics, trousers, those are all in the chest at the foot of the bed. Armour's in the other trunk, which means you also have a spare seat. I know there's not much space for you to pace about, but it's all yours."

"All mine." The room was as small as the one he'd had back at the inn, and more cramped thanks to its contents, but space of his own was a rare and precious thing, and his shoulders were unknotting already.

He unfastened his sword belt, hung it from a hook on the wall, and started unlacing his mud-encrusted boots.

"I need another acting lesson," he said. "To get the right tone before I talk to all those people out there."

"What sort of lesson?" Yasmi sat on the armour chest, legs crossed beneath her, and ran her fingers across her coloured scarf.

"One to help me motivate people, to convince them it's worth the fight. You saw what I was like before, I couldn't even hold a few dozen rebels together, now there are hundreds, even more, and it's all hanging on me."

The steadiness of her gaze calmed him, soothing the panicked beat of his heart.

"I saw you before," she said. "But I saw you in the With-ered Hills as well. All those people you brought together to resist a monster. If you did that for them, you can do it for all of Estis."

"You really think so?"

"I know it. Believe in yourself, like I believe in you."

His heart was racing again, but not with fear anymore.

"I need to play the warrior hero." He set one boot aside, then got to work on the other. "Prisca was right. I can't inspire people through magic, the charms are too uncertain and there's nothing dramatic about taking twenty minutes discussing what a shape in the tea leaves means. They've been fed stories of heroes wrenching freedom from the hands of tyrants. I need to be the perfect version of that." He wrestled the other boot off and pushed them under the bed. "Or at least, that's how I need to appear."

Yasmi, her head tilted on one side, looked him up and down.

"All right," she said. "I've taught you this already, so I know you can do it. Neck straight, head high, shoulders back, chest out." She got up and laid a hand on his chest. "Too far. You're meant to be a real hero, not a storyteller playing the part."

With soft touches, she fixed his stance, fingers running across his ribs, up his back, down his shoulders. Every adjust-ment was marked unforgettably in his memory.

"Next, costume." She turned to the wall, hands on hips. "These are too grand for real fighting, but for a speech to your followers..."

Followers. There was a word that jarred, even after all these months. He was just an orphan from an inn in the hills, it was ridiculous that anyone was following him. If they realised the truth…

"Hey." Yasmi snapped her fingers in front of his face, bringing him back into the moment. "Take your shirt off."

"My shirt?"

"To try these on." She held up a silk shirt and a black tunic with red trim.

"Oh…yes."

He started lifting his shirt, hit her with his elbow, mumbled an apology as she took a step back. When he finally got the wretched, sweat-stained item off, he found that she was staring at him.

"What?" he asked.

Yasmi's smile started a fluttering in his belly like leaves in a spring wind.

"You don't need me to dress you up as the perfect hero," she said. "You're him already."

Raul swallowed. He felt light yet heady, the moment demanding something from him that he couldn't quite grasp. But Yasmi knew better, and Yasmi always guided him right. He took a step closer, leaving barely a hand's breadth between them.

"We should talk about before…" She looked away and crumpled the fine theatrical tunic in her hands. "In the hills."

"Which part?" he asked. "The conversations? Sleeping wrapped up together for warmth? You almost ripping my throat out?"

Gently, he lifted her chin and her eyes met his again.

"All of it," she whispered.

He hesitated. Did he dare do this, now that they were back in their real lives, where changing one thing meant changing everything?

"There's only one part I care about."

He wasn't sure which one of them moved, but their lips met, and suddenly his arms were wrapped around Yasmi, while her hands ran across the skin of his back and up through his hair. His heart raced at her touch, and she let out a happy gasp as his fingers caressed her neck.

Yasmi kicked off her shoes, dropped her mask belt, pushed him back toward the bed.

"I don't really know what I'm doing," he admitted, old worries bubbling up from below.

"Don't worry," she said as she reached for his belt. "It's another entertainment, and I already taught you how to act…"

———————————— • ————————————

Valens was glad that they waited until dusk for the speech. Efron talked about lighting and contrast, about the drama of the moment, but what mattered to Valens was having time to prepare a place where thousands of people could hear Raul speak. In the end, they set up the theatre wagon at the top of a pasture outside the camping grounds, then spread word through the leaders of the different bands to tell people when and where to come.

By the time the fires were lit either side of the stage, there was a rumble of excitement through the growing crowd, despite the cold and the fresh rising wind that promised rain during the night. Some of them were travellers from the Withered Hills or rebels who had fought alongside Raul before, but many more had never seen him. They knew the stories, they knew the cause, they knew why all of this mattered, but they'd never seen the figure around which the threads were wound. So here they were, waiting to see him for the first time. The heir to Balbianus, vanquisher of Count Alder, prince in waiting and wanderer in the wild.

Their king.

Valens stood at the back of the crowd. He wouldn't hear the words so well, but he didn't need to, and this way he could watch for trouble. There was no reason to think that they'd been infiltrated by the Dunholmi, but overconfidence got you killed.

"I'm rather pleased with the new backdrop," Efron said, gesturing toward the stage. "Painting the pierced moon in that particular red makes it stand out better by firelight, don't you think?"

"It's good," Valens replied, carefully surveying the crowd, memorising more faces, watching for anything out of place.

"And the stage is far sturdier than it was last winter, so it shouldn't creak as he's speaking."

"That's good."

"I believe that the acoustics here will also work well. The curve of the hill behind, the open space to reduce any other echoes, and a clear night to carry his voice."

"That's good."

"But ultimately, the success of a performance depends on—"

"You've really helped." Valens squeezed Efron's hand. "Happy now?"

"My sweet, I am absolutely terrified. We are about to plunge into something that I've never faced, but whose horrors I've imagined in the telling of a thousand tales. This should be the most ghastly moment of my entire life. But I have you back, the real, strong you, and that makes up for everything."

Valens looked down at Efron, and then, though he felt awkward and embarrassed with all these strangers around, he leaned over to kiss him.

"For me too."

With their arms around each other's waists, they turned to face the stage.

Cheers ran through the crowd as a lone figure walked steadily up the steps at the side of the stage. Firelight illuminated the red edges of Raul's tunic like streaks of blood and flame; shone off the broach on his breast, a brass blade through a silver moon; gleamed in the ruby pommel of the princely sword at his waist. They'd discussed giving him a crown but decided that it was too presumptuous. Besides, the lad didn't need it. Everything about him, from his clothes to his posture to his smile, screamed nobility.

Valens squeezed Efron tight. His life wasn't death and failure. He had done good things.

Raul held up his hands and waved for quiet. The smile he shone on the crowd was grateful, amused, indulgent, even encouraging. It took a while for silence to fall.

At last, Raul spoke.

"Friends, neighbours, people of Estis and beyond, thank you from the bottom of my heart. Thank you for your time and attention. Thank you for coming to this place. Thank you for caring enough about our land that you are willing to risk your lives for each other and for the brighter days ahead."

They'd had a long argument about that line and whether to remind people that they were risking their lives. In the end, Raul's honesty and Valens's desire to reinforce a commitment had won out, and Tenebrial had reluctantly rewritten the part.

"When I left for the Withered Hills, I went in search of a relic from the past, old magic to give us strength. But in the end, I found something more powerful than that. I found people with hearts full of courage, with a will to resist the oppressors, with a strength to set themselves free. I found a bond beyond my imagining, in the comradeship we forged fighting against the Dunholmi. I found the one thing that could carry me on in the face of all the threats their empire can throw at us.

"I found you."

He spread his arms wide as if to embrace the crowd, and though the words themselves were simple, even obvious, he made them sound like a heart swelling with pride and joy. The crowd went wild, and this time it took far longer for the cheering to subside.

Valens made a mental note to keep on planting actors in the crowd. A few people in the right places really got the cheers going.

With an effort, Raul asserted order again.

"Every day, more people come to us as word spreads

through the land. From the peaks above Pavuno to the border plains; from the crafting halls of Deladale and Rianti to the farms of the Winding Vales.

"But that word has spread even beyond us, and this rebellion isn't just about Estis anymore. It's about our friends from the Withered Hills, about anyone the Dunholmi have conquered who wants to rise up. It's about choosing our own path, living our own ways, being the people we were born to be, free and true."

This time, he couldn't stop the cheering, but acting lessons and careful staging let him shout across it, and that added to the passion of the performance, the conviction he radiated with every word.

"We've shown that Count Alder can be beaten, that the riders of Dunholm can be defeated, that we can win. We have found a weapon greater than any spear, any bow, any sword. We have found hope!"

This time, Raul didn't even try to quiet them. He stepped back, arms held high, and beamed out at the crowd. Valens had never seen the lad smile so wide in all his life. He really was a leader.

Valens wished that Fabia could have been there—she'd secretly enjoyed a good speech, even though she always mocked them. This was her success as much as anybody's, what the two of them had committed themselves to, body and soul, as the walls had fallen. Fabia should have lived for it, but at least her death hadn't been in vain. He'd spent years mourning her loss, but now he could celebrate her achievement.

"A new moon rises!" Raul shouted.

"A new moon rises!" the crowd roared back.

Valens glanced around. The players had slipped out of the crowd and gathered at another set of wagons downhill, where casks were waiting to be broached and sheep were roasting over open fires. Tonight, there would mutton and ale, stories and songs, a celebration to mark their victory and tie these people closer together.

Tomorrow, the hard work began.

Chapter Thirty-Three
Burning the Past

A blackbird fluttered out of the trees, past the wooden keep on its artificial hill, over the walled compound at its base, to the drainage ditches cut through riverside pasture where Raul and his companions lay in wait. It fluttered down, guided by Withering Hills gifts that Raul still didn't understand, and landed on the palm of his outstretched hand. He tugged the thread binding a scrap of cloth around its leg, unravelled the scrap, and noted the symbols drawn on it.

"They're ready," he murmured.

Word spread along the ditch, whispered from lip to ear. At the ends of the line, some of the smallest and most stealthy rebels slithered from their hiding places and across the dew-dappled ground to the other ditches. Raul let the bird go and it flew off again, over the river and the rooftops of Rianti, a black shape against the predawn grey of the sky.

Someone else came crawling across the ground, from the direction of the fortress gates. Raul braced for trouble, just in case, but as expected it was Lestavo, a grin on his face and two lengths of sturdy rope stretching out behind him.

"Strange place," the little man said as he took his place beside Raul.

"But you've done what was needed?"

"Of course." Lestavo made a clicking sound and a quiet growl floated their way.

Raul took the end of one of the ropes. Beside him, Yasmi slipped on a broad mask. Her shoulders hunched and her back stretched as her grey shifter costume turned to shaggy brown fur. By the time she turned around to let Biallo and Ferra fasten harness across her shoulders and tie the rope tight, she had fully transformed into a hulking grizzly bear.

The ditch couldn't hide Yasmi any longer, but that wouldn't matter. The other bear, the real one, which had come with one of the groups from the Withered Hills, was lumbering up from its riverside hiding place, led by its handler. If anyone in the fortress looked this way, they couldn't help seeing that something was amiss.

Fortunately, they were going to be busy with other things. Smoke had started to rise from the far edge of the walled compound, and hints of flame flickered above the walls. Cries of alarm were going up.

"Blood for luck," Raul said, and made a pointing gesture.

"Blood for luck," the others quietly chorused, several of them touching charms before they reached for their weapons.

Then it was time.

The bears lumbered away from the ditch and the fortress beyond, and the ropes strapped to their harnesses tightened, straining against the fortress gates. The bears grunted, the ropes creaked. Raul ran out of the ditch and hundreds of warriors followed him, racing toward the walls.

No battle cries. No words of encouragement. Instead, silence bought them time, while the fire on the far side kept the enemy distracted. Raul ran as hard and as fast as he could, shield on his arm and sword in his hand. Along the line were Ovida and Ferra, Valens and Biallo, dozens of other familiar faces, people he trusted, people he had helped train. They ran as if their lives depended upon it, and with good reason.

The ropes strained. One of the log gates creaked and bulged around its hinge.

Still they ran, halfway across the open ground, halfway to the enemy and the building they used to show their control, the place from which taxes were raised in Rianti and the surrounding countryside, from which harsh laws were enforced, from which riders galloped out to punish any resistance. While the commotion grew on the far side, the rebels ran in silence, unseen.

It couldn't last, not with one of the hinges snapping and a gate about to break loose. A cry of alarm went up. Arrows flew, just one first, then two, then a small volley, alarm and low light making most of the shots fly wide, though someone screamed and fell.

"A new moon rises!" Raul bellowed, and the others joined in, even the warriors of the Withered Hills. Despite the arrows hurtling toward them, they rushed toward the walls.

Hinges broke with a crack and the gates burst open. One slammed to the ground while the other smacked back against the wall, its force flinging defenders off the parapet. Raul raced through the gap and his warriors came with him, shouting and screaming.

Spearmen were gathered on the far side, in the plain blue of the Dunholmi infantry levy. Half dressed, half awake, still rushing to form a line, they stood against the rebels. The two sides collided with cries of fury and agony, with the clang of clashing metal and the sickly wet thud of spear heads through flesh. Raul tilted his shield as a spear struck, pushed it up past his head, and lunged in to run the wielder through. For a moment, his sword lodged in armour and muscle. Another infantryman dropped her spear and drew a sword to fight up close, but Valens was in and hacking her down before she could even swing at Raul.

Arrows rained down from the walls, inescapable as hundreds of warriors jammed together in the gate. Valens bellowed commands and the front rank formed a shield wall while those behind raised their shields as protection above each other's heads.

A monkey scrambled up the wall, swept a paw across its face as it leapt over the parapet, was the real Yasmi for only a second before another mask fell into place. A leopard ripped one of the archers open, slammed a second off the wall, ran roaring after the others as they fled.

The enemy line wavered. They'd inflicted as much hurt on the rebels as they'd received, but now the battle hung in the balance. Raul spotted a captain in his white sash straightening formations, rushing warriors to fill gaps, sending archers to the roofs of stables, barracks, and storerooms that filled the compound.

"That way," Raul said, pointing with his blade.

Without hesitation, Valens and Ovida advanced on the warriors between Raul and the officer, and the whole shield line moved with them. Ovida lunged and stabbed with her spear, Valens swung and hacked, the two of them carving an opening in the Dunholmi formation, driving their opponents back. The ferocity of their advance left them both exposed, a position they couldn't hold, but they didn't need to. Raul charged through the gap, straight at the officer.

The captain couldn't miss what was coming. He brought his shield up, raised his sword, and braced for the attack. Yelling for all he was worth, Raul swung his sword in an overhand blow.

The captain must have thought that he'd got lucky, facing such a crude and obvious attack. He caught it on his shield and slashed at the gap Raul had left. But that gap was deliberate. Raul brought his own shield up and almost knocked the sword from the captain's hand, almost won the fight in that moment.

First dramatic strikes became the swift, steady flow of combat, the two of them testing each other's defences, trying to exploit weaknesses, working out which of their own tricks the other already knew. Like many of the Dunholmi elite, the captain had clearly been raised for war. His movements were swift and fluid, his footwork sure and graceful. But he had learned to fight on horse as well as foot, while Raul had committed his whole martial education to fighting this way, in the steady grind of foot soldiering that Estis considered noble and that his father knew. That, along with determination and readiness for the fight, gave him an edge. He let his opponent attack more, even drew him into it, enduring the battering against his defences while the battle raged around them. He let the captain think he was winning, let him grow confident, and then, just as the rhythm of the fight seemed fixed, Raul stepped forward instead of back. His shield slammed into the captain's face, a sabre lunge faltered, and Raul hacked the man's arm off at the elbow. The officer fell screaming, blood spraying from the stump.

The defenders' last hope of leadership was down and their line collapsing. They fled through the compound, past fallen bodies and the flames engulfing one side of the palisade, to the second set of gates that guarded the steps up to the keep. But those gates were barred, and the rebels came after the defenders pressing up against them, hacking down anyone who wasn't fast enough to surrender.

Arrows kept falling into the enclosure, fired from the roof and archery loops of the keep. Valens and Ovida slammed their shoulders against the gates, but they were firmly barred from inside.

Yasmi ran over in leopard form, claws bloody and fur spattered. At a nod from Raul, she became the monkey again and went scrambling up the gate while the rebels fired their own bows at the keep, hoping to keep a few of the defenders' heads down. The volleys from the other side faltered a little as Yasmi went over, changing shapes even as she dropped from the gate, and landed with a heavy thud. Something creaked, then the gates swung open, and she stood as a bear on the far side, waving a tree-trunk-thick bar above her head.

Rebels rushed through the gate and up the slope, shields raised against the arrows that fell with redoubled force. Yasmi stomped up with them, swung the bar back, and slammed it into the door at the base of the keep like she was swinging a battering ram. Once, twice, three times, then the door burst open and the rebels rushed in.

Raul waited at the bottom of the slope, catching his breath. The enemy were broken, he wouldn't be needed now, and besides, he'd told Biallo to lead this part of the attack. It was a chance for the actor to prove his worth as a commander, and Valens would report back on how he did. As Valens had pointed out, they were going to need more leaders than just Raul if this was going to work, if a mess of desperate rebels was going to become an army.

Ferra, a quiver empty on her back and bow hanging idle in her hand, emerged from between the buildings.

"You've frayed the road's teeth right good, Warborn," she said.

"So's said," Raul replied with a grim smile.

"You mocking my talk?" She raised an eyebrow.

"I'm trying to show that I've listened, and that I'll act on it."

"Careful, you don't want to play the adder with me."

"Honestly, I meant to be respectful, but I can stop if you want."

She wrinkled her nose, then shook her head. "Nowt wrong with it, I suppose, least not so long as we're following you."

At the top of the keep, a furred figure with a tail raced hand over hand up the flagpole. The royal banner of Dunholm fell, blown away on a changing wind, and a few heartbeats later a new flag flew, a moon pierced by a dagger all in red against a black background. At that moment, the sun emerged above the hills beyond Rianti, and the bright light of dawn fell over the land.

Valens trudged down the slope from the keep. He stopped two strides from Raul and bowed his head.

"Your Highness," he said.

It felt strange, and not only because it came from Raul's own da, but he understood that they needed this now. The rebellion was held together by his story, and they needed to act like that story was real. He was His Highness now, the uncrowned prince, and later His Majesty, with a coronation to mark their victory and consolidate all they'd achieved. Assuming they won, but right now, it felt like they couldn't lose.

"The place is ours," Valens said. "Our first real victory."

"The first of many."

"We should pick a garrison."

"No." Raul shook his head. He'd been rethinking this while he crouched in the ditch, waiting for their moment. "Empty the place out and burn it to the ground. I don't want to leave even the stumps of what they built."

"Are you sure, lad?" Valens pressed his thumb and finger to his forehead. "Place like this takes a lot of work to build."

"Places like this are how they fight, and we can't beat them their way."

There was also the part he couldn't say out loud, not with so many of their people around. Sure, some were celebrating, and others had started looting, but a lot were waiting to hear what he had to say.

A place like this could be useful, that was true, but it was most useful as a symbol. If they kept it, they might start to look like the oppressors they were supposed to be overthrowing. They might even start to act a little like that, with walls between them and the ordinary Estians whose town they'd just freed. But if they burned the fortress down, they showed their own people that the age they'd suffered through really was being swept away, and they showed the enemy how far they were willing to go to win.

Signs and stories. Almost as much as swords and spears, they would win the war. This was a big win, and they needed to mark it hard, before anyone else asked the question he was asking himself: could they have achieved more?

"I told you all when we first left Pavuno, the age of empires is over. A new moon is rising, and a new world in its light."

———————•———————

Yasmi stood as close as she could bear to the burning fortress, letting the heat from the blaze wash over her. In some ways, it was a pleasant change from the winter cold she would return to when she stepped away. In others, it was an uncomfortable reminder of what they'd faced in the wild, and she wished that Issol's snowflake charms could still hold back some of that heat. But this wasn't the Withered Hills, and as Prisca had explained, these things were fickle, dependent on the contingencies of circumstance. Those once potent charms were now just carefully carved pieces of wood.

Darkness was falling again and most of the rebels were

on the move, their commanders leading them away from the town to make sure that there wasn't any trouble tonight. Ordinary people had reasons to fear armies no matter which side they were on.

The wolf mask felt heavier than ever in Yasmi's hands, not just the weight of its magical wood but of memories. The thrill of the hunt and the fight. The way the world had lit up to the wolf's senses. The feeling that this life, this body, this way of being was so much more real than what she'd been before.

The taste of Ferra's blood. The sound of Raul pleading with her not to kill him.

Raul walked up and laid a hand on her shoulder.

"I need to go," he said. "Are you ready?"

"I'll catch up."

"I can leave Valens, so there's someone here just in case."

"You need Valens to organise people."

"Someone else, then. Biallo, or maybe Ovida?"

"I have these." She patted the masks on her belt. "'I need no guard while I hold this weapon and the strength of my hate.' *Earl Trannet's Revenge*, act four, scene three." She put on a smile. "Besides, I'll catch up soon."

"All right." He looked at the mask she was holding. "You didn't use that today."

"Thought I'd try some of the others."

"That's good. They were really useful for getting us in. You should use them more."

And avoid turning into a ferocious monster that rips our friends' throats out, he didn't say, but if she was thinking it, then he had to be too. Here he was, the weight of the whole kingdom on his shoulders, still trying to be considerate to her.

Why couldn't she have found an ordinary, self-centred boy she could use and throw away, someone she could tell to clear off when she needed time to herself?

She leaned up to kiss him, then patted him on the behind. It was a good behind.

"Go play the prince. I'll be there soon."

He grinned, then hurried away. So easy to keep him happy. Her mother had been right about those things.

Her mother had also given her most of the masks, one last gift on top of years of training. After a lifetime of shifting through these shapes, she had passed them on to her daughter, the promise of a life most people could never even imagine. These faces she had worn were all that remained of her, and just thinking of how they shared that connection made Yasmi's heart ache.

She looked around, but no one was coming, and if there was trouble, then she could run off in a dozen different ways. So she took her time, watched flickering shadows bring the mask to life, ran her fingers across its delicately carved surface, relished the beauty of every nuance of shape and shade.

If she started wearing it again, soon she wouldn't stop. It was too easy to sink into its raw, aggressive power, to cast aside the complexities of her life and become the wolf. It felt real, and maybe it was, but if that was what she wanted, then she could carve out a different sort of real. The mask wasn't the answer, it just felt like it was. Even now, when she hadn't worn it in weeks and there was no need for the wolf's strength, the urge to put it on was almost irresistible.

If she kept it, sooner or later she would give in.

Unlike Raul, no one had written a destiny for Yasmi. She could choose to become a strolling player, a royal minister, maybe even the wife of a king. What mattered was that she chose her own fate, not let it be dictated by someone else's script.

"I'm sorry," she said—to the mask, to herself, to her mother's memory.

Then she threw the mask into the fire.

For a long time, Yasmi stood there, watching the weirdwood burn with blue-green flames and fighting the urge to snatch it out. And as she watched, she wept, for herself, for her mother, and for what could have been.

Chapter Thirty-Four
A Message

When he joined the infantry levy, Cuff had hated the boredom of guard duty. His mama had told him that soldiering would be exciting, a chance to see the world and prove his mettle like Auntie Brun did. The hours of standing around with nothing to do hadn't lived up to that dream, and at first he'd resented it. A skirmish with bandits, two blisteringly long marches, and more time digging over latrine pits than he could bear to count had made him see things differently. Boredom was a blessing, if you let yourself enjoy it, and right now he missed proper boredom, the sort you could really sink into, when the gates didn't open all day and no one even came with a delivery between shift changes, the sort of day when the palace gates of Pavuno had represented a haven of peace.

He groaned as a rider in royal livery came galloping up the street, scattering locals as they came. It looked like he was going to have to open the gates again.

"Bet you two beers it's another urgent message for the

count," Somm said, shifting her spear from the crook of her arm to her hand so they could put on a show of declaring that none should pass.

Cuff eyed the rider.

"Nah, look at the mud on him. This one's from the hills, come to warn Master Tur and the garrison about another rebel attack."

The rider hauled on their reins, bringing the horse to a stop so close it flung dirt in their faces.

"I have an urgent message for the count," they declared.

"Count's not here," Cuff said. It was an unwritten rule that whoever lost the bet also had to deal with the new arrival. "Been in the far north since before midwinter. We've told all the other couriers the same thing."

"Are you seriously telling me that the governor of this province has been absent from his duties for over three months?" The messenger glared at Cuff like it was his fault.

"He's been dealing with duties in the north," Somm said. She was always sticking up for the count, even though he'd have no idea who guarded his gates. Cuff reckoned it was that thick, wavy hair of his that did it. "Rebels and that."

The truth was, the count had been gone long enough for confusion to set in at the palace, confusion that turned into panic when the rebels went from raiding the supply wagons to seizing towns and burning down forts. That was when the delicious boredom of guard duty had turned into actual work, as messengers, troop commanders, and local loyalists hurried back and forth in an ever-growing stream of desperate, unfocused activity.

"I need to the see the count," the messenger insisted. "I have an urgent missive from the king."

"No count around," Cuff said. "You can talk to the chamberlain or the captain of the day, depending on what it's about, but we'll need to see your seal first."

"I am a servant of the crown!"

"Anyone could say that, and we don't let just anyone in, especially not after what happened last year." Cuff smiled his most stubbornly uncooperative smile, the one he saved for officers and wealthy merchants. "Orders of the count."

The messenger, fuming, started rifling through their satchel.

"You might want to get out of the road," Somm said.

"I told you already, I am a royal messenger and I expect to be treated with dignity."

"Sure, but I reckon that's a royal governor riding up the road now."

Cuff peered past the messenger, down the road. A buzz of uncertain excitement was rising from the people on either side of the street as a group of riders headed toward them. Sure enough, the riders were led by the count himself, his surcoat stained and bulging, his regular horse limping along behind. Beside him rode Captain Brook, under whose command Cuff had first marched to Estis, and behind them some of the count's chosen, though not half as many as had ridden north with him in the autumn.

The messenger might have been a servant of the king, but they clearly weren't smart when it came to the moods of powerful people, because they stayed in the middle of the road, holding out a scroll.

"Count Alder, I come with orders from His Royal Majesty,

who insists that you report most urgently upon the state of your province."

Forced by the oncoming riders, the messenger twitched their horse aside at the last moment, but kept the scroll held out. Without even looking at it, Alder took the parchment, which burst into flames in his hand, then crumbled away in ash.

"Tell my royal cousin that the North March has risen," he said, still heading for the gate. "Tell him that I will be preparing my forces, but that the full weight of Dunholm will be needed to crush this menace once more." His dark eyes flared brightly and he turned to stare at the messenger. "Tell His Majesty that we can no longer indulge in mercy, and I look forward to serving him in the field."

Cuff and Somm snapped out of their slack-jawed staring and rushed to open the palace gates. The messenger, their expression colder, stared at the ashes drifting from Count Alder's hand.

"As you wish, my lord," they said, then set their spurs to their mud-spattered horse and galloped away.

The count and his column of cavalry rode on into the palace. Once the gates were closed, Cuff and Somm stood staring at each other, their spears in the crooks of their arms.

"Did you see his eyes?" Somm asked, grinning. "That's a lord I'd happily march after."

"Just because you want to get inside his tunic," Cuff said, failing to suppress a shudder of unease at what he'd seen.

"And you don't?"

Cuff hesitated. There was something about those eyes.

"Who cares about that?" he asked. "Didn't you hear what they said? We're going to war."

The story continues in...

FORGED FOR ROYALTY

Book THREE of Forged for Destiny

ACKNOWLEDGMENTS

Thanks to the team at Orbit, in particular Stephanie Lippitt Clark, for helping me continue with this particular quest. And huge thanks to Milena for the support, encouragement, and inspiration.

MEET THE AUTHOR

ANDREW KNIGHTON is a full-time freelance writer and has published short stories, novellas, and comics in a range of venues. His fantasy novel *The Executioner's Blade* was described by Adrian Tchaikovsky as "a perfect balance of action and character wrapped about a delightfully twisted mystery" and by Anna Smith Spark as "a very enjoyable, fast-paced read." You can learn more about Andrew by visiting andrewknighton.com.

Find out more about Andrew Knighton and other Orbit authors by registering for the free monthly newsletter at orbitbooks.net.